IT
SHOULD
HAVE
BEEN
US

IT SHOULD HAVE BEEN US

ANNA B. DOE

USA TODAY BESTSELLING AUTHOR

It Should Have Been Us by Anna B. Doe
Publisher: Wild Heart Publishing d.o.o.
Lukarišće, Croatia, 2023
Print on demand

Copyediting and Proofreading by Once Upon A Typo
Cover Design by Qamber Designs

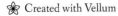 Created with Vellum

Sometimes two people have to fall apart to realize how much they need to fall back together.

BLURB

My high school sweetheart, the boy who shattered my heart, is back in our small town, and there will be no avoiding him for the next two weeks...

Only there is nothing boyish about Miguel Fernandez. The NFL's best rookie defensive end is even more wickedly handsome than he was four years ago—tall, with abs for days, all that unruly hair, and eyes so dark they swallow you whole.

And that's exactly what he's doing every time our paths cross.

I shouldn't let it affect me. After all, there was a good reason why we broke up in the first place. But no matter how much I try to put some distance between us, it's impossible to stay away when our childhood friends are getting married.

Not only is he attending the wedding. He is *in* the wedding— the best man to my maid of honor. There will be no escaping the boy who destroyed me completely with his betrayal or stopping the secrets I kept from coming out...

PROLOGUE

MIGUEL

Four years ago

"You can't do this, Miguel!" my father yells, his brows pulling in that familiar scowl that he wears only for me.

The family disappointment.

The black sheep.

"I'm not going to pay for you to go off to college and play some stupid game."

His words shouldn't hurt.

After all, this isn't the first time he's thrown them at me. I've stopped hoping that things would change and he'd finally see me for who I am. That he'll at least try to understand what football means to me. What it could mean for our family, but no. My father only ever thought of football as a silly kid's game.

"I'm serious, Miguel," Dad continues, clearly on a roll. "You have to stop playing games and do what's right. Get a degree and find a real job so you can take care of your family. I've supported this nonsense up until now..."

"You've supported what exactly?" I scoff, pulling the zipper on my duffle bag and throwing it over my shoulder. "You haven't supported anything, Dad! We've been having the same ol' fight for as long as I can remember." I shake my head, done with this conversation. "Besides, I don't need your money. I'm going to Michigan State on a *full football scholarship.* That's right. That little game, as you call it, is paying my way for the next four years, and I'll do my best to go all the way." I give him a pointed look. "With or without your approval."

No matter what I do, say, or accomplish, my dad will only see football as a stupid game played by his immature son who isn't ready to grow up and be a man.

I don't want to care what he thinks. God knows it would make things so much easier if I didn't, but I couldn't help myself. That little boy inside of me still craved his father's approval. I've tried to turn off this part of me, but it's not as easy as flipping a switch.

Grabbing the second duffle, I go toward the door where my dad's standing, his tall frame filling the doorway, arms crossed over his chest.

He always seemed larger than life, with his wide shoulders and grim face tanned from all the hours spent out in the sun, working in the fields. But somewhere in the last couple of years, I've outgrown him, and now we're standing eye-to-eye. He's become older, too. There's more gray in his hair, and the lines around his eyes and mouth are deeper.

"You do that, and you're on your own. I mean it, Miguel. I will not support this foolishness."

"I don't need you to support anything, Dad!" I yell right back, running my hand over my face in frustration. "Didn't you hear a word of what I've been telling you for the last few months? I got a *scholarship.* And not just any scholarship. A full ride at the Michigan State University. All because of this silly game, as you like to call it. I'll come out of college debt-free, and if I'm lucky enough with an offer to play pro just like I've always wanted."

"But what if you don't?"

I grit my teeth, my stomach clenching with unease. I didn't allow myself to think about the what-ifs. About what will happen if things don't go as planned. I'm going to college. I'm going to graduate. I'm going to play football professionally. Not succeeding wasn't an option.

"But what if I do?" I challenge.

Dad shakes his head. "Be realistic, Miguel! You're living in a fantasy world. One day, that bubble will burst, and you'll be left with nothing."

My fingers clench and unclench around the strap of my duffle as I try to keep my cool. I needed to get out of there before saying something that I'd regret. "At least I'll know that I tried."

Pushing past him, I start toward the stairs.

"If you leave because of *that*, don't bother coming back."

My steps falter as his harsh words echo in the hallway around us, the soft hair at the nape of my neck rising.

I expected the fight. I expected him not to agree with my decision or support it. But I hadn't expected... this.

For a while, neither of us says anything. It's like time has stopped altogether.

If you leave because of that, *don't bother coming back.*

My fingers tighten around the handles of the duffle bag. "Then I guess I won't be coming back," I say softly, surprising even myself.

I don't allow myself to turn around and look at my father. Instead, I take two steps at a time, my eyes focused on the path in front of me.

I need to get to the door.

I need to get out of here.

I need...

"Miguel?" Mom's soft voice stops me in my tracks. "Are you all packed? Do you need anything else?"

I turn toward her, giving myself a moment to take her in. Her dark hair is pulled in a bun, so it's out of her makeup-free face. An apron is tied around her waist, the scent of spices spreading through the air from the kitchen.

"Yeah," I croak the words out. Closing the distance, I pull her in a hug, pressing my mouth against the top of her head. "All packed."

She pulls back, a wary look in her eyes as she watches me. "Are you sure?"

"Yeah." I clear my throat and force a smile out. "I'll be fine, Mom."

Just then, the stairs creak, and my whole body tenses because I know Dad's standing at the top, watching us.

"I know you'll be okay, but I'm your mother, and I worry. This is the first time one of my babies is going away," she murmurs into my shoulder. "Please make sure to take care of yourself and eat, okay?"

Her words have me chuckling softly because, of course, she'd be worried about me not eating enough. As if that was possible. But if you asked Margaret Fernandez, we never ate enough. That's one thing my southern mother always had in common with Abuela Maria, my father's late mother.

My chest rumbles, and I feel that grip around my lungs tightening. "Don't worry about me, Mom," I force the words out. With one final hug, I take a step back. "I'll be just fine."

I don't bother saying goodbye as I turn toward the door and exit the house. Throwing my duffle bags in the back of my truck, along with a few other boxes I packed, I turn the key, the ignition coming to life. I had to work my ass off for a year straight, saving every penny I earned by helping around the

IT SHOULD HAVE BEEN US

farm so I could get this rusty old truck, but it was one of the rare things that was all mine.

With one last look in the rearview mirror, I press my foot against the gas and leave behind the place that's been my home for the past eighteen years.

The need to get the hell out of this godforsaken town is overwhelming, but before I can leave, there is one more pit stop I have to make.

Not bothering with the blinker, I turn down the familiar gravel road until an old farmhouse comes into view. The two-story house has been my home almost as much as my own has.

Just like the girl sitting on the front porch with a book clasped in her hands.

Rebecca lifts her head when she hears the car nearing, a smile forming on her lips the moment she spots me.

Pulling to a stop, I get out of the car and go to her, taking a seat on the porch swing next to her.

"Hey, Red," I whisper, brushing my lips against the top of her red hair. It wasn't one of those artificial bright colors. No, Rebecca's hair was a rich, dark brown hue that, at times, seemed red. She described it as mahogany. I loved watching it under the sunlight and seeing all the different shades playing in her long strands.

"Hey." She slips a bookmark between the pages, putting it on the side and turning all her attention on me. "How did it go?"

I run my hand through my wild locks, pushing them away from my face. "He told me if I leave to play football, I shouldn't bother coming back."

Rebecca's mouth falls open. "What? Miguel, I'm so sorry." Her hand covers mine, giving it a firm squeeze. "I'm sure he'll think better of it and change—"

I shake my head. "I don't think that'll happen, Becs. He

hasn't changed his mind in the last eighteen years. He won't start now."

Rebecca pushes me back and climbs into my lap, her palms cupping my cheeks. "You don't know that."

I love that she's optimistic, but she doesn't know my dad. None of my friends know him, not like I do.

"I'm not keeping my hopes up. If he wants to do this, he can do it."

"Miguel..."

I cover her hands with mine, intertwining our fingers. "Come with me, Rebecca."

She's the only good thing that has come from this town. The only person, besides our mutual friend Emmett, who understood where I was coming from.

"Finish the semester here." I squeeze her hand tightly, the words coming out in a rush now that I have finally voiced them out loud. "Then you can transfer to Michigan State. We can forget about this fucking town and be together."

I wanted to ask her to come with me ever since she told me she was accepted to a local college, but I didn't want to be an asshole or make her feel bad for not getting into any other colleges she applied to.

Tears glisten in Rebecca's eyes as she just stares at me, not saying anything.

I cup her face, running my thumb over her cheek. "Rebecca? What's wrong?"

"I can't." She shakes her head. "I can't leave with you."

"I know, baby. But it's just a few months, and then you can look into transfers and..."

"You're not listening, Miguel," she whispers. "I *can't* leave. Not now, not ever. My family needs me."

I pull back; her words are like a blow.

My family needs me.

6

"I thought I was your family too," I say, the accusation clear in my voice.

We had plans, dammit.

We've been talking about a life, a *future* for the last couple of years, ever since we started dating.

Rebecca and Emmett have been a constant in my life since we were born. The town called us the Three Musketeers for a reason. But somewhere along the way, she's become so much more than a friend. At first, I was scared. Scared of destroying the only good thing in my life and chasing away the person I loved so much. But Rebecca convinced me it wouldn't happen. That it'll be the two of us against the world.

"You are. You're my family too. But Matthew needs me. Mom needs me. I can't just up and leave."

"Matthew has your mom, Becs. He'll be fine. They'll be fine."

But I didn't have anybody.

My father all but disowned me. Emmett and Kate were going together to Blairwood and Rebecca...

Rebecca's lips press in a tight line. "I can't, Miguel," she whispers once again, her voice soft and apologetic. "I'm so sorry. But I just..." One lone tear slips down, and she brushes it away with a quick swipe of her hand. "I wish things were different, I really do, but..."

"But you don't want to come with me. I get it," I nod my head, trying to keep my emotions under wrap as I get to my feet and place Rebecca on the ground.

"It's not like that, Miguel." She grabs my hand. "I want to come, but..."

"You can't," I repeat her earlier words. Sliding my fingers in my hair, I give the strands a firm tug as I turn my back on her. "Dammit!"

"Michigan isn't at the end of the world," Becky continues in a hurry. She wraps her fingers around my forearm and tugs me back. "We'll make do. We'll visit every chance we get. It'll work out. *We'll* work out. I love you, Miguel."

Cupping her cheeks, I lean down and press my mouth against hers. The kiss is hard, unyielding. I tilt her head back, my tongue demanding entrance into her mouth. And she lets me in. With a quiet moan, her lips part, her soft tongue meeting mine, and we kiss desperately, my hands roaming her body as I try to memorize every inch, every soft sound she makes, every hitch of her breath as I touch her.

Breaking the kiss, Rebecca wraps her arms around my neck, pressing her cheek against my shoulder.

"It's going to be fine," she repeats. "We're going to be fine. We'll find a way to make this work."

That knot in my stomach that was there the whole summer grew larger as I sat in my truck that day and drove away, unease creeping up my spine no matter how many times I repeated Becky's words to myself.

We'll be fine. We'll make it work. I love her, and she loves me, and it's going to be enough.

But no matter what I told myself, that uneasy feeling didn't go away.

And I was right.

Because not even a year later, we broke up.

CHAPTER

I

MIGUEL

Welcome to Bluebonnet Creek, Texas.

Population: 11,209

"11,210 starting now, I guess," I mutter to myself as I pass by the sign and enter the place that used to be my home, the uneasy feeling making the bile rise in my throat.

"Temporary."

It's just temporary.

But no matter how much I try to reassure myself of it, the panic builds inside the pit of my stomach. My hands grip the steering wheel tighter as I continue driving down the empty road. The bright oranges and reds had given away to the darkness some thirty minutes ago, the black sky matching my mood perfectly.

Never, not in a million years, have I imagined myself returning to Bluebonnet Creek.

The last time I was here—four fucking years ago—was the day I left for college. After an epic fight with my dad, I ran out of the house, the echo of our heated words still ringing in my head, along with the sharp *bang* as the truck door shut with finality before I drove away.

I swore I'd never look back.

And I haven't.

I went to Michigan State, had an amazing college career, and got drafted into the NFL my junior year. Although people tried to tell me I should wait and finish college and get more experience, I decided to quit and join the pros.

I could always finish college, but I only had so many years I could play professionally, so I decided to use every single one. Yes, there was always a risk of riding the bench for a while, but as it turns out, there were a few teams that needed a new defensive end and badly. One of them was the Austin Lonestars, and they picked me as a third-round draft pick. Not too shabby if I do say so myself.

So I quit college and spent the last year playing for the Lonestars. I won't lie; the shift was hard, the pace of a professional team brutal, but somehow, I've found my place in Austin. I kept my head down and worked my ass off. The team had a good season but lost in the second game of the playoffs. The loss sucked, but what sucked even more was the injury I received in the second quarter. I was trying to tackle one of their receivers when I was bulldozed by their tight end, which resulted in a dislocated shoulder and a broken clavicle. As far as injuries go, this wasn't the worst thing that could have happened to me. What it was was annoying as hell, but I was determined to focus on physical therapy and getting better by the time summer camp rolled around to reclaim my spot.

Then the invitation came.

I knew it would happen. It was just a matter of time.

As if he can read my thoughts, my phone beeps with an incoming call. I glance at the screen before pressing the answer button on my steering wheel, the call connecting through the speakers.

"You here yet?" a deep voice with a familiar Texas drawl asks.

"Hello to you, too, man," I say dryly.

"By the sound of your voice, I'd imagine so," my best friend continues, not caring the least bit for my animosity. Then again, why would he? His life was playing out just as he planned it. Soon enough, Emmett would have everything that he's ever wanted, just like I have everything that I have ever wanted.

Do you really?

Ignoring the annoying voice, I push it to the back of my mind just like I do any other shit I don't want to deal with.

Instead of answering, I shift in my seat and grunt in agreement.

"I really hope you brought better manners for my wedding, Fernandez. You know you'll have to make a toast as my best man, right? Kate will not appreciate your grumpy-ass grunts. Nor will my mother, for that matter."

"Well, then you should have picked a different best man, Santiago."

Emmett snorts. "As if that was ever an option."

"No, I guess it wasn't," I agree, rubbing my hand over my jaw.

Emmett and my family have lived next door to each other since we were kids. Well, as next door as two families who own ranches can live. We've spent most of our childhood together. From playing in the fields to helping our families run the businesses and playing football side by side, all the way from pee wee football through high school when our lives took us in separate directions. We've stayed in touch; our college teams even played one another on a few occasions, but things were different now.

We were different now, and yet...

"Want to meet up tonight?"

I contemplate the idea for a moment. It would be good to catch up with my best friend. But then there was the question of that other thing. The one that we've been avoiding for the last three years.

You'll not go there. You'll not think about her. Not just yet.

The headlights illuminate the familiar sign for my family's ranch, and that vice grip around my throat tightens even more. No, I wasn't ready to go back home and see my parents for the first time in four years, but I also wasn't ready to have a one-on-one with my best friend.

Selfish?

Maybe, but at this moment, I didn't have it in me to care.

"Nah," I shake my head, although I know he can't see me. "I'm tired from the drive. Rain check?"

There is a beat of silence as he weighs my words. For a second, I think he'll insist, but in the end, he lets out a sigh. "Fine. Breakfast tomorrow? I have to take care of some things on the ranch, but I can meet you at the diner around ten."

I look at the clock on the console. Thirteen hours. He was giving me thirteen hours. It's not much, but I guess I can't push this off much longer. Not now that I was back in Bluebonnet.

"I'll meet you there in case they don't run me out of the town the moment I get out of the truck."

Emmett's laughter booms from the other side of the line. "You can only wish you'd get off the hook that easy. Better chances are they surround you and torture you. There is no fun in letting you walk away."

"That's what I'm afraid of."

"Don't do something stupid, Fernandez. I'm not in the mood to look for a new best man just a couple of weeks before the wedding."

"I'm not making any promises." I slow down as I near the crossroad, debating my options. "I've gotta go," I mutter absentmindedly. "See you tomorrow."

"Tomorrow."

I hang up, my gaze fixed on the sign. I could make a turn and go home to face my parents. The original plan was for me to come here, do the wedding, and get the fuck out before anybody even realized I'd stepped foot in Bluebonnet. I don't know who I was trying to fool because the chances of me coming here unnoticed were equal to the possibility of the Giants winning the Superbowl. But that illusion was shattered when Mom found out that I agreed to be Emmett's best man. She called me immediately and insisted I promise her I'd get my ass home for a visit, something she's been trying to get me to do ever since I left. Unsuccessfully until now, that is.

I could go home, face the demons I ran away from, or I could go into town and prolong the inevitable for a few more hours.

It's not even a choice, not really.

My foot presses against the gas pedal, and the car starts accelerating once again, that knot in my throat loosening as soon as I pass the familiar gravel road.

It doesn't take long for the first signs of life to start appearing. Houses lining up by the side of the road, lamps illuminating the streets, signs—some old and rusty, some new and shiny—pointing you this way and that.

I'm driving almost on autopilot. You'd think I'd forgotten. After all, it's been years since I was last here, but it's like no time has passed.

Before I know it, I'm driving down the main street. Slowing, I let myself take in the little town where I grew up. New shops have found a way to appear between the ones that have been here probably since the town's conception. What looks like a new boutique opened across the street from the local diner, just in between Mrs. Smith's bakery and Mrs. Timothy's flower shop. Scoop, the best damn ice cream shop in the county, is still sitting on the corner of Main and Dawson Road, and just across from it is Mr. Jamison's hardware store.

I continue driving down the main road, watching a few people walk by on the street, their probing gaze not missing anything as I pass by. Tomorrow morning, I know I'll be the talk of the town as soon as the shops open. I spot a few new places, something that looks a lot like a gym, and even a bookstore and a coffee shop with a big sign hanging over the door, Reading Nook.

So many little changes have happened since I was last here, and I wasn't really sure what to make of it.

I'm about to take a turn to go to my high school when my eyes fall on the rusty sign for the local bar, The Hut. The last time I was here, they wouldn't even let me inside. But by the number of cars parked in front of it, the place is packed.

It's not really strange, considering it's after nine p.m. on a Friday night.

Just then, the door opens, and a few people get out, chatting and laughing.

I debate stopping for a moment. Somebody will most likely recognize me, but it's either that or reverse and drive home to face my parents.

The bar it is, then.

Making a U-turn in the parking lot, I drive around until I find an open space and park my SUV, killing the engine. Letting out a sigh, I lean back in my seat, slowly unclenching my fingers from around the steering wheel before letting them drop into my lap.

My body feels stiff from the hours of driving, but I push the door open, get out of the truck, and walk toward the bar, mentally bracing myself for the inevitable.

A few unfamiliar people standing outside give me curious looks as I walk past them and push the door open, only to immediately be assaulted by the noises coming from the inside.

The loud country music mixes with the sound of laughter and people talking.

I scan the packed space as I make my way through the crowd. It's mostly ranch hands and town's people. I recognize a few of the faces, nodding in acknowledgment as I make my way to the bar on the other side of the room.

Mick, the owner, is standing behind the bar, wiping a glass. He raises his brow at me as recognition flashes on his face, "What can I get'cha, Fernandez?"

Sliding onto the barstool, I look over the selection of bottles behind him. "Jack on the rocks. Make it a double."

He nods silently as he makes my drink, placing it in front of me.

Just when I think I might get through this day without talking to anybody, somebody drawls out slowly, "Well, I'll be damned. If it ain't Miguel Fernandez!"

The hairs at the back of my neck prickle as I turn around slowly and come face to face with Lucas Johnson. We went to high school together and played on the football team.

"Hey, man." I move closer, taking his offered hand. "What's up?"

"Same old, same old. I didn't know you were back home."

Back home.

The words make my stomach roll uncomfortably. Saying *back home* sounded so final, so... permanent. I was most definitely not back home.

"I'm just visiting for a while."

Lucas nods. "You're here for Emmett's wedding, right? That one's been the talk of the town."

It didn't surprise me at all. Santiago's have always been a well-loved family in our little community, and Emmett was the perfect golden boy: A great student, football player, and son all in one. He helped bring the championship home and went to college on a football scholarship, where he kicked ass and was so good he could have played professionally. But instead, he decided to return to his hometown and help on his family's ranch and marry his high-school sweetheart.

He's everything that you've never been and never will *be.*

"Yeah," I rasp out, pushing the dark thoughts back. "I'm here for the wedding."

"Sweet. Although I'm not surprised. You and Santiago have always been glued together."

"That's right." I take a sip of my drink, savoring the burn of the whiskey as I contemplate how to get out of here.

If Lucas notices my reluctance, he chooses to ignore it and simply continues, "I never thought I'd see you here, though. How long has it been since you've been home?"

Years.

"A while." I shrug. "I've been busy."

"Playing professional football." He slaps me on the shoulder, and I must make a face because he turns serious instantly. "Shit, is that the shoulder you injured?"

I force out a smile. "It's fine. The shoulder has healed."

I was still going to PT, and there was some lingering pain when I went overboard, but for the most part, I didn't lie when I said I was fine.

"That's good, dude. I can't wait to see you back on that field. You had an amazing year. I even think the Lonestars could go all the way this time around."

"We'll see about that," I say non-committedly and rush to change the subject. "What have you been up to?"

"Oh, nothing much." He lifts his hand, signaling Mick for a refill. "Been running my pop's construction business for the last couple of years since he retired. What can I get'cha to drink?"

I shake my head. "I'm good, thanks."

"You sure?"

"Yeah, I have to drive to my parent's place."

The last thing I needed was to go home smelling of alcohol.

"So what's new around here?" I ask, spinning around in my seat. "You married?"

"Nah, but there is a girl over in Merrywill. We've been seeing each other for a few months."

"That's good, man."

My eyes scan the space, taking everybody in. I vaguely remember some guys that worked on the ranch, and I'm pretty sure that's old Mr. Lopez sitting there in the corner.

"Not as good as the dating pool is in Austin, I'm sure."

"It's—"

The words die on my lips when my eyes connect to a familiar pair of hazel eyes, and it's like I've been run down by a train.

All the air is sucked out of my lungs, the noises turning into a dull murmur.

I'm not sure why I'm so surprised.

I knew she was still here. It was the main reason why we could never work out. I had to leave, and she insisted she had to stay.

I knew I'd have to see her sooner rather than later, but I never imagined it'd be this soon.

But with my luck, is it really surprising?

I just stare at her, completely transfixed.

Three years.

It's been three years since I've laid my eyes on her.

It was the day she walked away from me. The day she didn't give me a chance to explain. No, she condemned me, like every other person in my life has.

It hurt.

It hurt so fucking much.

She was supposed to be different.

She was supposed to be mine.

And in the end, she was just like everybody else.

My throat works as I swallow the bitter taste left on my tongue and allow myself to take her in.

She looks the same but, at the same time, different. More mature.

All that gorgeous auburn hair is falling down her back in loose waves. I watch it sway as she tilts her head to the side and tells something to an unfamiliar blonde woman sitting opposite her before she turns to the guy next to her and smiles at the dude.

Jealousy, hot and heavy, fills my chest. I tighten my fingers into a fist, feeling my nails dig into my palms.

The guy is sitting in a dark corner, so I can't see his face. Who's he to her? A boyfriend? Lover? Husband?

Just thinking about it makes my stomach twist in knots.

It doesn't matter. She's not yours; I try to reason with myself. *Hasn't been for a while.*

Three years to be exact.

"Miguel?" In the distance, I can hear Lucas demand my attention, but I can't force myself to look away.

Before I get a chance to decide what to do, she turns her head, scanning the space as if she can feel me watching her.

I hold my breath as her gaze moves over me, like I don't exist, but not even a second later, she whips her head back, doing a double-take.

Those hazel eyes widen, and a dozen different emotions flash on her face in quick succession. Surprise, panic, hurt, longing, anger, love...

One moment, they're there, out in the open; the other one, they're gone, an unfamiliar mask shielding her face.

"Rebecca."

CHAPTER

2

REBECCA

"I know, I know, I'm sorry I'm late," I say as I slide onto the bar stool across from my friend Savannah. "I totally lost track of time."

"And that's new, how?" Savannah raises her perfectly shaped brow at me, a smile playing on her red lips.

I narrow my eyes at her, which only makes her laugh harder. Her head falls back, her blonde mane swaying with the movement as amusement twinkles in her sky-blue eyes. Savannah and I met last year, just after she moved to Bluebonnet, where she's working as a first-grade teacher. One day, she entered my bookish café, Reading Nook, and we started chatting, and just like true book lovers, the rest is history.

She's right, though. These days, I was rarely ever on time. Then again, between all the fires that needed putting out, both at work and home, I was surprised I was still alive.

I mockingly laugh. "You're so funny."

"I know, thanks. But lucky you because I took the liberty and ordered you a margarita." Savannah picks up her own glass and takes a long sip, draining the rest of it.

My brows quirk up. Savannah wasn't a big drinker, so when

she drank, it was because she was upset about something. "What happened?"

"Oh, I just had a fight with Mark." She gives me a pointed look as if daring me to say something. "Yes, *again*."

I lift my hands in the air defensively. "I didn't say a word."

This time.

I tried telling her a dozen times before that her boyfriend is a douche who's treating her like shit. She deserves so much better, but she won't listen because the asshat has the tendency to sweet-talk her into forgiving him every time after a fight. He'd make promises and act like a decent human being. For a while, at least. But sooner rather than later, they'd get into it all over again.

"You didn't have to," Savannah lets out a sigh. "Your face says it all."

"I think you need this more than I do." I slide my drink across the table toward her before looking around until I spot a server and flag her for another round. "What did he do this time?"

"He was supposed to come this weekend, but in the end, he decided he'd go on a boy's trip instead."

"Didn't he say that last weekend?"

Savannah grabs my glass and takes a long pull. "Sure did."

"What an asshole!" I place my hand over hers, giving it a firm squeeze. "I'm so sorry, Sav."

"It's fine."

"It's absolutely *not* fine."

She deserved better, so much better than a stupid, immature boy who's constantly putting everything else above her.

"Well, it's not, but he's right. It was my choice to leave Houston and move here."

"He did *not* say that."

Savannah laughs bitterly. "Oh, he did. He kept telling me I

should just move back with him, and we could see each other any time I wanted. As if it was that easy."

Savannah was a year older than me. After finishing college, she got a job in Houston, where she met the asshole, but last year she decided to move back to Bluebonnet because Mrs. Parker, her grandmother, had some health issues. Savannah wanted to be there to help the woman who raised her. As it just played out, one of the first-grade teachers was retiring, which worked perfectly for her, but the asshat didn't want to move with her and leave his big corporate job. Hell, I don't even know if he came to town more than once.

"What an arrogant piece of shit. I swear to you, if he was here right now, I would have kicked him in the balls."

"Umm, should I come another time?"

We both turn around to find Nico standing next to our table. A beer is in his hand, and with the other, he's rubbing at the nape of his neck as he gives us a wary glance.

"Are you an arrogant, self-centered bastard?" I ask, just as the waitress comes with our drinks. She gives me a nasty look, but I ignore her, shifting my attention to the man in front of me.

The corner of Nico's mouth lifts upward, revealing a dimple in his cheek. "Well, I most certainly try not to be." He glances from me to Savannah and back. "Do you want me to leave?"

"Nah, it's fine." Savannah waves her hand. "It's not like it's anything new. Mark always has something better to do than come here to visit. By now, I shouldn't be surprised."

"Screw him," I turn toward her, placing my hand over hers and giving it a squeeze. "He's the one at a loss here. And we'll have an amazing night, drinking margaritas, and who knows, maybe you find a nice guy to dance with that'll make you forget about that piece of shit."

"Yes to the drinks, no to the guys. I think I've had enough of them for the moment." Savannah's gaze darts toward Nico. "No offense."

"None taken." Nico shakes his head, sliding into the open seat next to me.

"Besides, didn't you say that you can't stay long?"

I bite the inside of my cheek, feeling that familiar prickle of guilt rising inside my chest anytime I was away from home. The weight of responsibility I've been carrying on my shoulders for the last four years feels heavy.

She's fine, and she's not alone, I remind myself. *Nothing will happen if I have a few drinks with friends.*

"It's okay. I can stay and make sure you get home if that's what you need."

"Good, because I feel like drinking tonight." With that, she downs her drink, making a face when the alcohol burns down her throat, and lifts her arm to flag the server for another round. "Okay, so enough about my annoying boyfriend. What's up with you two?"

"I just came from the station. It's been crazy this past week," Nico says as he takes a pull from his beer bottle.

"What happened?" I ask, glancing at him. Nico decided to forgo college and went to the police academy instead, and last year, he'd been transferred to work in Bluebonnet. "Did Mr. Brown think somebody is trying to break into his house again?"

"On the clock," Nico sighs. "And then old Mrs. Willow called earlier today because her cat climbed the tree and wouldn't get down, and since the fire department was busy with a call of their own, I was the lucky guy who had to deal with that mess." He looks down at his naked forearms. "The damn cat scratched me when I finally managed to get to her. Vicious beast, that one."

I can't help myself. I start laughing as Nico visibly shudders.

"Poor little thing," I coo, patting him on the hand. "Now you get a chance to show off your scars to the ladies."

"You just laugh, but that's not even the worst part. After I was done, she tried to set me up with her granddaughter!"

"She did not," Savannah gasps. "What is she, forty or something?"

"Most likely," I agree. Mrs. Willow was in her late eighties if I wasn't mistaken, and she was still holding strong. I swear that woman will outlive us all. "Not into older women, Nico?" I wiggle my brows, unable to stop teasing him. This is just too good.

"Not that much older!" Nico protests when I lift my eyebrow in challenge. "Not that there is anything *wrong* with older women, it's just... You know what? I think I'll just shut up now."

His cheeks turn pink in embarrassment, which only makes me laugh harder. I didn't realize how much I needed a relaxing night with friends until this very moment. Hearing about Nico's misadventures was a nice bonus, too.

"You're the worst, Becky!" Sav protests, taking a sip of her drink.

"Hey, I wasn't the only one laughing!" I nudge a still-blushing Nico with my elbow. "C'mon, I'll get you a new beer as an apology." I turn around, looking for the server, but The Hut is *packed*. It might just be easier to go to the bar. It was pretty full, mostly guys nursing their drinks. "What about you, Sav?" I start to turn to her when a tall figure with dark, curly hair catches my attention and makes me do a double-take. "Want another o—"

The words die on my lips, my mouth falling open as my gaze sets on a familiar face. A face I never thought I'd see again.

I suck in a sharp breath, but it's like my throat is closed, and the air can't reach my lungs. All noise falls into the background as I stare at him from across the room. My hands shake, palms clammy with nerves.

It can't be. My fingers tighten around the stem of the glass in my hand as I just stare, completely in shock. *This can't be possible.*

Time seems to slow down as we just watch one another, neither of us breaking the contact as the air fills with tension. I blink and then blink once again, but he's still here. Standing just mere feet away from me.

Three years.

It's been three years since I last saw Miguel Fernandez.

Three years since he broke my heart, and I haven't seen or talked about him since. I couldn't. It just hurt too much.

But even the time and distance didn't make this ache dull in the slightest. All those feelings that I've been shoving to the back of my mind, locking them in a box, hoping they'll disappear, are back, front and center, with just one glance at him. As is the pain. That twisted, searing pain seems to be tearing me in two.

"Becky?" A hand lands on my shoulder, startling me. "Are you okay?"

From the corner of my eye, I can see Nico watching me with a worried gaze.

I shake my head silently.

No, I wasn't okay.

Whatever he must see on my face has him looking around, trying to find the cause of my distress, and I know the exact moment when he sees him.

"Shit, is that Fernandez?" Nico asks as my gaze moves back to the man in question.

And he's still there.

Shit indeed.

"Who's that?" Savannah asks, the curiosity evident in her voice.

One of the biggest advantages of hanging out with Savannah, except of how amazing she is, is that she didn't know me in high school. She didn't know the Becky from before. She didn't give me wary looks. She didn't watch me like I was broken. To her, I was just Becky. And I liked it that way, but I guess that is gone now.

Savannah's probing gaze lands on me. "Are you okay, Becs? You look like you've seen a ghost."

More like a living nightmare.

"That's Miguel," Nico explains. "He and Becky used to date in high school."

Savannah's brows shoot up in surprise. "Really?"

Just then, Miguel slides from his stool and starts to walk toward us.

Fuck.

I grab my bag and jump to my feet. "I'm sorry, Sav, but I have to go. I can't stay here right now. I'll call you later."

Not waiting for her answer, I go straight toward the door. She calls my name, but I don't look back. I can't.

Pushing through the crowd, my eyes are firmly set on the door—my escape.

The warm air hits me in the face the moment I shove through the door and stumble outside.

My heart is beating a mile a minute, my breaths coming out in harsh pants as I all but run toward my car, grateful that I have on my chucks. I'm just unlocking my trusty old truck when I hear the door bang open, laughter spilling from the bar out into the quiet night.

"Rebecca!"

The hairs at the back of my neck rise at the sound of my name coming from his mouth.

Rebecca.

He always used my full name when we were alone.

Some nights, I could still hear him whisper it into my ear.

Swallowing the lump in my throat, I climb into my truck. The door slams loudly as I close it and slide the key in place, starting the car.

In the distance, I can hear the heavy footsteps getting near. "Rebecca, wait!"

Unable to resist it, I lift my gaze to the rearview mirror, catching sight of Miguel running after me. I allow myself a few seconds. That's all. I look at him for just a few seconds before I pull out of my parking space, press my foot against the gas, and speed out of the parking lot.

My mind is an onslaught of emotions and memories as I drive away. The sound of my heartbeat is echoing in my eardrums so loudly that I can barely hear the roar of the engine. My fingers grip the steering wheel so tightly that my knuckles turn white.

I drive on autopilot through the empty town streets; the only good thing about living in this godforsaken town for so long. The street lamps give away to the darkness as I move out of the town and toward my house.

Miguel is here.

Miguel is here.

Miguel is here.

How is this even possible?

When did he get back?

For how long is he staying?

Why?

Why is he...

Before the question can even form completely in my mind, my heart sinks as the realization slams into me.

"N-No." My soft whisper echoes in the cabin of the truck as my stomach tightens.

A crossroad appears in front of me. I stare at it before

quickly shifting right. Thankfully, nobody is driving down this road at this time of the night, so there isn't a risk of killing anybody as I make my way down the familiar gravel path.

He wouldn't do this to me. He would have at least told me. He knew what happened. Parts of it, at least. He would have told me and let me prepare for it. This is all just one big mess. This—

A house appears in front of me, the dim lights illuminating the living room.

Good, they're still awake.

My truck barely comes to a stop before I jump out of it. I stomp up the stairs, pressing the doorbell a couple of times impatiently, my whole body shaking with suppressed anger.

There is a beat of silence as the sound of the doorbell echoes inside before I can hear footsteps coming closer. Muffled laughter comes from the other side before the key turns, and the door is pulled open, revealing the tall frame of one of my best friends.

As if in slow motion, Emmett turns toward me, and I watch as his smile falls the moment his eyes land on me, concern shining in his dark eyes.

"Becky, wha—"

"Did you know?" I ask, not giving him a chance to finish. The words come out in a rush as I glare at Emmett, my fingers clenching and unclenching by my side as I try to keep myself in check while I wait for his answer.

We've been best friends our whole lives.

Hell, at this point, I considered him my brother.

He was there for every major event in my life, good or bad. I knew he'd be there. I knew he'd have my back.

And right now, I feel the pit of my stomach open. My accusation rings in the night while something that looks a lot like guilt flashes on his face.

"You've seen him."

I blink at his words, his *admission*, coming like a kick to my gut. Yes, I came here to confront him about it, but a part of me, a teeny-tiny part of me, hoped that I was wrong. That my best friend wouldn't betray me like this.

"'You've seen him?'" I spit out, my fingers clenched so tight I could feel my nails biting into my skin. That anger that's been brewing inside me ever since I saw Miguel coming back to the surface. "You knew?! You knew, and you didn't think to tell me?"

Emmett takes a step forward, extending his hand toward me. "Becky..."

I move out of his reach, not wanting his hands on me.

Not wanting anything to do with him.

He's my best friend. My brother.

How could he have done something like this to me?

"You knew," I whisper softly, shaking my head as the tears burn my eyes. *He knew, and he didn't tell me.* I still couldn't wrap my head around it. "How could you do that to me? Why?"

He opens his mouth, but before he can say anything, Kate appears in the doorway. "What is going o—" Her smile falls when her gaze shifts to me. "Becky? What's wrong? Why are you crying?"

I glare at Emmett, wiping the tears off my face. "Why don't you ask your fiancé?"

With that, I turn my back to them and get the hell out of there.

CHAPTER

3

MIGUEL

My breathing is heavy as I bend forward. I press my palms against my knees, trying to catch my breath as I watch the bright taillights of that old, rusty, cherry-red truck disappear down the road, taking away the only woman who has ever been able to bring me down to my knees, leaving dust and memories in its wake.

Six years ago

"You're good with Becs. She drives like an old lady anyway," I tell Kate, unable to stop myself from teasing her. There was just something about seeing the fire burn brightly in those hazel eyes when she got angry at me. And just as predicted, Rebecca doesn't disappoint.

"Hey now!" Her palms find their way to my chest and shove me away. "I don't drive like an old lady."

"Oh please, you forgot who taught you how to drive."

Her eyes narrow as she places her hands on her hips. "Well, if my driving sucks, then we know who's responsible for it, now, don't we?"

Well, shit, I fell right into the hole I dug myself.

"C'mon now," I let out a groan. "That's totally unnecessary."

I'm a damn good driver. The problem was her. The old cherry-red Ford was her dad's, and she insisted on driving the thing, even though she sucked at driving stick. She tried to shift too quickly, and the engine would roar in protest.

"What is unnecessary is that you think you can talk to me like that, Miguel Luis Fernandez."

Well, shit.

Rebecca pulling out my middle name never ended well for me.

"Becky," I take a step forward, the anxiety rising inside of my chest as I see the hurt flash in her eyes.

I didn't mind bickering with her, but I hated when we fought. Rebecca was my best friend, maybe even more than Emmett was. More than that, she was my person. She knew my family situation. She was the person I went to when I felt like shit and needed to vent. She was the one who understood me and stood by me no matter what.

She shakes her head, taking a step away from me. I watch her stiff back as she lifts her chin in defiance like the fucking queen she is before she turns on the balls of her feet and walks away.

Now

Somebody laughs loudly, bringing me back to the present from the trip down memory lane. Squeezing my knees, I straighten, my hand lifting to rub at the ache spreading inside my chest.

I did my best not to think about Becky or Bluebonnet since we broke up, and so far, I've succeeded, but one look at her, just one fucking look, and all that effort is crashing down.

I run my fingers through my hair. "Fuck!"

Fuck, fuck, fuck.

I'm not sure why I'm this surprised. I knew she was still here. After all, Bluebonnet was in her blood. That was always our biggest problem. While I couldn't wait to get the hell out of here, Becky just wouldn't leave.

Not to go to college, and certainly not for me.

Heart still racing, I push upright and focus on that disappearing dot until she's long gone, and the only thing left is darkness.

What the hell was I thinking? Going after her like that?

I wasn't. That's the whole problem. If I just stopped and thought about it, I would have realized how stupid of an idea that was. But I was never good at stopping to think when Rebecca Williams was in question. That girl had me wrapped around her finger so tightly I couldn't think clearly any time that she was in my vicinity.

"What the hell are you doing here, Fernandez?"

My back goes still at the question thrown at me. Willing my muscles to relax, I turn slowly and face my old teammate. Just like me, he's gotten a few more inches on him since I left. Although he stopped playing football after high school, he's still keeping in shape. His wide shoulders fill the dark blue shirt, and there's a dusting of stubble covering his clenched jaw, and his fingers are fisted by his sides.

I lift my gaze to his. Something about his stance made me defensive. "I don't see how that's any of your business, Nico."

I always had a suspicion that Nico had a thing for Rebecca, and seeing him tonight with her only confirmed it. It made my blood boil, but I had to remind myself that she wasn't mine. Not any longer. There was nothing that I could do. Nothing that I should do. But knowing that didn't take away the bitter taste from my mouth.

"It is when you're chasing after a woman who's clearly trying to get away from you."

I narrow my eyes on him. "What are you? A cop?"

Nico takes me in slowly, assessing me. I make sure to keep still, my glare firmly in place as his eyes meet mine. "As a matter of fact, I am."

Great, just fucking great. Talk about bad luck.

"You know I wouldn't do anything to her. We're..." My words trail off as I try to find the right label.

Childhood best friends?

High school sweethearts?

Ex-lovers?

None of those felt right. Not when it came to that woman. Even after three years of separation, the hurt and heartbreak couldn't break this bond that was between us since we were kids.

"Broken up," Nico finishes for me. "And she clearly doesn't want anything to do with you. Don't do something stupid to make me have to arrest you."

Arrest me?

Is he for real?

"Is this a threat, officer?" I ask, my voice dropping lower as I glare at him.

"It's just a warning, Fernandez. You've hurt her enough as it is. Stay the fuck away from her."

With that, he turns his back to me and walks toward the bar.

Was he telling the truth? Is he just worried about her? Like a friend would be? Or was there something more? Was there something going on between those two? Were they together?

Just thinking about it had the bile rising in my throat.

"What is going on between you two? Are you guys together?"

The question is out of my mouth before I can stop it, one feeling seeping out of every gritted word.

Jealousy.

Nico stops in his tracks as I silently curse myself, his eyes meeting mine over his shoulder. "I don't see how that's any of your business."

My fingers clench so tightly that my nails are digging into my palms. Without another word, Nico walks away, and I just stare at him until he's inside the bar.

"Fucking hell." I turn around and go to my car. Sliding into the leather seat, I tilt my head back and pinch the bridge of my nose.

So much for avoiding any drama, I should have just gone straight home.

But then you wouldn't have seen her.

The soft lines of her face. That vivid glow of auburn shining in her dark hair. The look of utter surprise and later heartbreak when she recognized me.

It's like Rebecca's image is burned into my mind.

Curling my fingers into a fist, I pound it against the steering wheel, hating every second of this.

None of this would have happened if she just would've given you a chance to explain.

But she didn't.

She condemned me and turned her back on me without a backward glance.

Clenching my jaw, I slide the key in place and start the car. My mind is still reeling from everything that had happened at the bar as I drive through the dark streets.

The old house is enclosed in darkness as I pull in front of it some fifteen minutes later, killing the engine. My stomach is twisted in a tight knot as I just sit in the car and stare at my childhood home. Four years and an NFL career behind me, and still... And *still,* being here makes me feel like a selfish, petulant boy who walked away from everything he knew so he could pursue a dream nobody thought he was capable of accomplishing.

A loud *creak* snaps me out of my thoughts. I look out the window, my eyes going to the barn that's a few yards away, just in time to see the door close behind a tall figure. I suck in a breath as I watch the man lift his hand, rubbing it over his face. His hand drops, and he looks up, only to stop in his tracks when he spots me.

The light on the barn illuminates his face, and I feel a part of the tension seep out of my body.

It's not him.

At least I got a little bit of a reprieve until tomorrow, that is.

I guess it's now or never.

Uncurling my fingers, I open the door of my SUV and slide out of the car.

"Well, well, well... look at who the cat dragged in," my brother says as he slowly takes me in.

His arms are crossed over his chest. He's filled out since the last time I saw him. His shoulders are wider, the muscles more prominent. But while my body was honed by professionals in a top-notch sports facility, his has been defined by nature and the hard work that is ranching. Although only six years separate us on paper, he looks much older than twenty eight in real life. His skin is already tanned from all the work he puts in, and deep wrinkles line his face as he scowls at me from a distance.

Nobody can accuse Fernandez men of a warm welcome.

"It's good to see you too, Aaron."

"It would have been better to see you here at the dinner Mom made in anticipation of you coming back home, but just like always, the only person you ever think about is yourself."

His words were a blow I should have expected, but it didn't lessen the bite they had to them.

Shit. I should have known Mom would try to make a fuss about me coming, although I tried to tell her she shouldn't bother. She was never good at listening. And one thing she hated the most of all was when her boys were fighting, which was more often than not.

"I told her I'd probably come in late."

"You didn't have a problem stopping at the bar, from what I've heard."

Dammit. I knew this would come back to bite me in the ass. I just didn't realize how soon that'd happen.

Aaron shakes his head disapprovingly. "News travels fast in our small town, or did you forget that now that you moved to the big city, brother?"

My fingers clench by my side at his jab. "I didn't come here to fight."

"What I'm surprised about is that you came at all. The last time I saw you, you said something along the lines of..." He tilts his head to the side, tapping his finger over his chin as if he's thinking. "Oh, right, I'll never step foot in this godforsaken town ever again."

"Trust me, I wouldn't have disrupted your little family if Emmett didn't threaten to have my ass kicked if I didn't show up. And then, *Mom* insisted I should come here. If it were up to me, I'd be out of here before the wedding was done."

Aaron scoffs. "Why am I not surprised? You were always good at walking away."

"You know why I walked away," I grit, trying to keep my cool. "Hell, you should be happy. This is always what you wanted for your life, and now you don't have to share it."

Aaron's eyes narrow at me. "Don't you dare tell me what I wanted."

My jaw clenches as I just stare at my brother. I know he's pissed, but hell, so am I. Then again, it wasn't anything strange. All our lives, we've been at each other's throats to the point some days, being on opposite sides of the ranch didn't help us keep our cool.

"Just go inside," Aaron sighs, and suddenly he looks so damn tired. His hands fall by his sides. "Mom left the door unlocked and made your old room."

With that, Aaron turns around and starts walking in the opposite direction, to where his house is.

"Aaron," I call out after him, loud enough so he can hear me but not loud enough to wake the whole house. "The last thing I wanted was to disrupt your lives."

Never in my wildest dreams did I think I'd be back here. Having to deal with the fallout of what happened four years ago. All the harsh words that were spoken.

Aaron comes to a stop and looks over his shoulder. There is a beat of silence, and just when I think he'll leave me hanging, he shakes his head. "What's done is done."

CHAPTER

4

REBECCA·

Putting the last of the chocolate batter in the pan, I wipe my cheek with the back of my hand, pushing an unruly strand out of my face. I'm not sure why I try because the next thing I know, the stubborn lock falls back in my eye.

Cursing silently, I place the mixing bowl into the sink and grab the coffee cup off the counter. It was my third one today, and considering it's not even seven a.m., I think that's saying something. But screw it. I barely slept last night. Every time I'd close my eyes, I'd remember what happened, and I was wide awake all over again. I dare anybody to judge me.

Even thinking about it now has a shiver of unease going down my spine.

Miguel is back home.

It was one possibility I never allowed myself to think of because I knew his stance on this town. The issues he had with his father and everything that played out on his last day in Bluebonnet.

A loud knock comes from the back door. My whole body freezes for a split second. Then my heart starts beating wildly inside my chest. Swallowing the knot in my throat, I slowly look up, only to find Emmett's face peeking from behind the glass.

Chill, it's just Emmett.

It's not like *he*'d come here looking for me.

Or that I wanted him to.

No, I most definitely did *not* want him to.

Emmett smiles sheepishly at me and lifts his hand in a small wave.

It's one of his I'm-your-best-friend-and-I-need-you-to-remember-how-cute-I-am-although-I'm-a-man-and-I-messed-up smiles.

Good thing I've known him for the better part of my life, and that smile doesn't work on me.

My fingers flex around the cup before I put it on the counter and march to open the door.

"What?" I bite out, crossing my arms over my chest. I was still irritated with him for what happened yesterday, and I wanted him to know it.

Emmett lifts a little bag in the air. "Peace offering?"

I narrow my eyes at the bag. "You mean a bribe?"

The corner of my best friend's mouth twitches upward. "Mom's chocolate chip cookies."

Damn, he knows me so well.

Not that I'd let him know he has me. "I can make my own damn cookies."

Emmett's smile widens. "I can see that."

He points at my cheek. "You have a little something right there."

Pushing his hand away, I wipe at my cheek. "What do you want, Emmett?"

Ignoring my question, his gaze moves over my shoulder, taking in the mess that's my kitchen. "What are you making?"

The better question was, what I *wasn't* making.

"Muffins. With blueberries." I quirk my brow at him. "And extra chocolate."

His favorite.

"Damn, Becs, you're not playing fair."

Serves you right.

"I never said I was." I tilt my chin in his direction. "What do you want, Santiago? I've got work to do."

"Cookies. Here." He hands me the bag, which I reluctantly take as he slips past me. "I'm not even going to make you work for it."

I roll my eyes at his retreating back. "So generous of you."

"It is. Those are the best, and you know it."

I did know it. God knows I've tried to replicate Mrs. Santiago's recipe on more than one occasion, but they never tasted quite the same, and Emmett's mom didn't want to tell me what her secret was.

"Fine, now that you delivered your bribe, you can go." I shoo him away, but he doesn't move a muscle.

"You're so lucky that sass doesn't work on me, Becs."

"Oh, yeah? You haven't seen real sass yet, mister" — I jab my finger into his chest, done with playing this game — "What were you *thinking*?"

Emmett lifts his hands in surrender. "I wasn't, okay?"

"Clearly!" That damn strand falls into my face, so I flick it back. "If you were thinking, none of this would have happened."

Just saying it out loud brought back the thoughts of last night.

The shock of seeing Miguel standing in The Hut.

He was always tall, but he gained a few more inches in the last few years. His shoulders were broader, the lines of his face harder, more mature, but then there was his hair. The ends of those dark locks were still curling when he let it grow out too long. Something he was still doing, apparently.

Gorgeous, he was so fucking gorgeous it was hard to watch.

I press my lips together as I push the images back, trying to dull the ache that I've been fighting ever since I laid my eyes on him.

I couldn't deal with this. Not now that I was running on coffee, sugar, and sheer determination.

I turn on the balls of my feet, going back into the kitchen. Work. I needed to immerse myself in work and forget that the last twenty-four hours had ever happened.

Not that Emmett gets the memo; that man's relentless. "You don't want to talk about him. At all."

His words have me pausing for a second. I glance over my shoulder and glare at him. "So it's *my* fault?"

"Shit." Emmett raises his hand and runs it over his face. "I didn't say that."

"It sure sounded like you did."

For a moment, an uncomfortable silence settles over us, and I hate it with every fiber of my being. Emmett and I have been best friends since diapers, and I couldn't take fighting with him, but damn it, his words hurt.

My throat bobs as I swallow. I'm not sure if Emmett can see the emotions battling on my face. He curses softly, and the next thing I know, his strong arms are wrapped around me. "I'm so sorry, Becky," he whispers gently, and some of that resolve I've been holding onto cracks.

I hug him back, burrowing my nose into his flannel shirt. The scent of sandalwood, horses, and hay clings to him like a second skin. The smell of home.

"I should have told you he was coming back. I thought I had time to figure out how to broach the subject. Time to prepare you, but... I just didn't know *how*. Every time I even try to say his name, you close off, and I don't know what to do. I don't know what happened with you two or how to fix it, Becs. I just... I don't know. And if that makes me an asshole, so be it."

I take a step back. "He's your best friend."

"So are you."

"Exactly. I'd never take that away from you. *Either* of you. You shouldn't have to choose between the two of us, Emmett. *That's* why I don't talk about him. Because whatever happens between us, you'll always be friends, and I don't blame you for it. But I had the right to know he was coming back."

Maybe if I did, it wouldn't have hurt so much.

Seeing him like that.

Maybe if I knew, it would have been easier.

Or maybe I'd just hide in my house until he left to prevent myself from running into him.

"I really am sorry, Becky."

"I know." I let out a sigh. "I just need... time."

To figure this out. To deal with this. To find a way so I don't hurt so much every time I see him.

Because let's face it, there will be no avoiding Miguel Fernandez, not in a town the size of Bluebonnet.

"How long is he staying?"

"A couple weeks. Until the wedding."

Shit, the wedding.

"Right, the wedding."

Because our joint friends are getting married. So I'll have to sit with him through the bachelor and bachelorette party. And the wedding itself. Easy peasy.

"I'll just try my best to avoid him until then." I nod, more for my benefit than Emmett's, as I grab my coffee cup. "Shouldn't be too hard."

"He's not just coming to the wedding, Becs." The gentle tone of Emmett's voice has the fine hairs at the back of my neck rising. It's like he's tiptoeing around the ticking time bomb, and the time bomb is me. My fingers tighten around the cup, the lines of my vision turning blurry as I hold my breath, waiting for him to finish. "He's *in* the wedding. He's my best man."

Of course he is.

Of-fucking-course he is.

CHAPTER

5

MIGUEL

Coming back home is like I've walked back through time. My room is still the same as it was the day I left, and even though I didn't set up my alarm, hoping to avoid the confrontation with my father for as long as possible, it's like my body didn't have any problem catching up. No, I was awake at the crack of dawn.

I lay on my back, staring at the ceiling and listening to the clatter of pans and dishes coming from downstairs, along with the soft voices of ranch hands passing through the kitchen as they prepare to start the day's work.

My fingers curl and uncurl by my sides as my body urges me to move.

Because contrary to my father's low opinion of football players, we weren't used to slacking around and doing nothing. No, most days, I was up as early as I was when I lived here, going out for a run before I got my ass to the training facilities, where I'd have my conditioning and prep for our upcoming game: watching film, team meetings, checkups with the doctors and PTs, and whatever social media thing our PR wanted us to do at the moment, just to name a few. My days were packed, which worked just fine for me. It left me with less time to think about things I shouldn't.

Rubbing my hand over my face, I let out a sigh and push upright. The bed creaks as that familiar twinge of pain shoots through my shoulder. I roll it back, trying to loosen the stiff muscles. The surgery and PT had definitely helped, but I had an inkling my shoulder would never be quite the same as it was.

Grabbing a clean pair of shorts and a tee, I pull them on before making my way across the hallway to the bathroom. Once there is nothing else left for me to do, I reluctantly go downstairs.

Animated chatter and laughter come from the kitchen as I slowly make my way there. I stop in the doorway, taking in the scene that was an essential part of my childhood. Most families consisted of parents and children, but ours... Ours was all that and so much more. My parents have embraced every ranch hand that passed through these fields with open arms, and they've turned into our makeshift family.

"I'm telling you, Margie, that husband of yours is getting crankier and crankier in his old age," Dylan says. The gray-haired man is around my father's age and has been on the ranch as far back as I can remember. So far, he felt like an honorary uncle to me when I was a kid.

My mom snorts, her whole attention on the scrambled eggs she's preparing. "My husband has always been cranky. Old age has nothing to do with it. Some days I don't even know how I put up with his shit."

Her answer, the one I've heard so many times in the past, makes the people sitting at the table laugh.

"You know, if you ever decided to ditch him, I'm looking for a wife."

Just as he's finishing, the back door opens, and my father's tall frame fills the doorway.

"Are you hitting on my wife again, Dylan?" Dad asks. That deep scowl I'm familiar with is etched between his brows.

Dylan's grin widens. "She's one hell of a woman and a cook."

"And she's mine. You go and find your own woman," Dad grumbles.

He turns around, and I suck in a breath as his eyes connect with mine. All the air is kicked out of my lungs as we just stare at one another, neither of us saying anything. Time ticks by slowly, the eerie quiet settling over the room. Or maybe it's just all in my head.

That frown between his brows grows deeper, like it always does, the disapproval clearly written on his face. "Miguel," Dad mutters, his lips pressing in a tight line as he just stares at me from across the room. "I see that you're back."

This was such a bad idea. I should have never come here.

Mom's head snaps up at the sound of my name, her eyes widening in surprise when they land on mine. The shock lasts all of five seconds before she puts the pan to the side and launches at me, all of her five-foot-nothing frame slamming into me with a force worthy of a lineman three times her size.

"Miguel!" Mom's hands wrap around me as she pulls me in a hug. "I didn't realize you were up. Why didn't you say anything?" She takes a step back, her hands sliding to my shoulders, as she takes me in, a beaming smile on her face growing wider as her eyes mist with unshed tears. "Just look at you! God, how I missed you."

"Hey, Mom," I rasp, my voice tight with guilt at making her cry.

Guilt at ignoring her for the past few years, although she didn't deserve it in the slightest.

Just... guilt.

She wipes her tears before squeezing me tightly once again. Margaret Fernandez might be a whole foot shorter than me, but she was a force to be reckoned with. My body relaxes in her

45

arms as her familiar scent surrounds me. Fresh air, hay, and wildflowers mixed with a dash of sugar that I always associated with my mother.

"It's so good to have you back home," she whispers softly, holding on for a second longer before pulling back. "C'mon, c'mon, sit down." She pushes me toward the open seat at the table. "Breakfast is ready."

I catch sight of my father, his eyes still glued on me. My stomach clenches with unease. He has yet to say anything, although what is there to say? We said our piece four years ago, and after that, I was surprised he let me stay here in the first place.

"You didn't have to bother for my sake."

"Oh, shush!" Mom pats me over the shoulder and pushes me toward the table. Only when I'm in my seat does she go back to the stove. She grabs the pan with scrambled eggs, putting it on the table along with the bacon. "We all have to eat something."

"And everybody knows Margie is the best cook in a hundred-mile radius, ain't that right?" I turn to Dylan to find him watching me with his dark eyes, his mouth curved upward. "Well, I'll be damned, Miguel Fernandez decided to come back home and visit his family? I thought you were too good for us regular folk now that you're an NFL superstar."

I rub the back of my neck, suddenly feeling self-conscious about his compliment. "I'm hardly a superstar."

"Oh please," he slaps me over my injured shoulder, and I have to hold back a wince. "You helped your team go all the way to the playoffs last season. I'm pretty sure everybody in this town thinks you're a superstar."

The chair screeches loudly against the floor as my dad takes a seat at the head of the table, doing his best to avoid looking at me. Did I expect something different? Maybe he'd throw me out. Then again, if Mom insisted on me coming here, there was no way he'd do that. So I guess we were playing the ignoring game, which was more than fine by me.

I shift my attention back to the man next to me. "Well, the team is pretty amazing, and I'm excited to get back on the field."

"How's that shoulder of yours doing?"

I roll it instinctively, feeling that twinge in the joint. "Not too bad. I'm still doing my PT, and I hope I'll be back to one hundred percent by the start of summer camp."

"That's amazing to hear. We're all loo—"

"Will you stop chit-chatting and get to your breakfast?" Dad asks as he stabs his fork into a piece of bacon, his eyes narrowing on me. "Some of us have real work to do."

My whole body stiffens at Dad's harsh words.

Of course he'd think that. It was one of our main fights, even when I was playing in high school. For him, football was just a game, and he didn't think it was worth all the attention I gave it.

I guess some things never change.

"See what I told you? A freaking grumpy asshole." Dylan shakes his head, not in the least bit worried about the hard glare pointed his way. "He's been insufferable the last few days. You'd have thought he'd be happy to have his son back home."

Dad's eyes meet mine for a split second before he pushes back from the table. "I'm done. I'll see you out in the fields."

A heavy silence falls over the room saying more than any words could.

I watch my father's retreating back as he marches out of the house and toward the barn. Aaron meets him halfway, a little boy by his side. Aaron's son. I haven't seen my nephew since he was just a baby. I watch as dad leans down and ruffle's the boy's hair, before the three of them make their way to the barn together. I can feel a jab in the middle of my chest—jealousy.

A hand lands on my shoulder, and I look up to find Mom giving me a soft smile. "He'll come around."

No, he wouldn't. He didn't come around for all these years, so I didn't see that changing anytime soon.

That annoyance Dylan was talking about? It was because of me. Because the last thing my father wanted was to have me back under his roof, albeit temporarily.

My phone rings through the Bluetooth connection the moment I enter the city limits. After the tense breakfast, I helped Mom clean up and did my PT, which left me with barely enough time for a shower before I had to leave to meet Emmett in town.

Checking my screen, the corner of my mouth lifts as I press the answer button, and the call connects.

"Miss me already, old man?"

There is a beat of silence, and, for a moment, I think he might have hung up on me, but then the surly voice of my teammate spreads through the cabin. "Who you calling old, Rookie?"

"Rookie, my ass. Don't you think it's time for you to stop calling me that? I think I deserve the upgrade after last year."

"What you deserve is to have your ass handed to you so you learn your place. Do you kiss your mother with that mouth, Fernandez?"

"Sure do, and I didn't hear any complaints. Besides, you really have to face the truth. You're an old man by league's standards, Walker. Just accept it already."

Blake Walker is one of the linebackers on the Austin Lonestars' team, defense-team captain, and, at thirty-four, one of the senior players on the team. He took me under his wing the moment I stepped into the facilities, and we've been on the same page from the very first day. I'm not sure if there was something he saw in me, a potential of sorts, or if he just appreciated the fact that there was one guy on the team he didn't have to worry about getting his ass in trouble outside of the field. Whatever the reason, we just clicked on and off the field, and it showed.

"The fuck I am, I can still outrun you any day of the week, Rookie."

"You can always *try*," I point out, unable to hide my smirk.

For all his trash-talking, we were pretty evenly matched. I might have been a tad faster, but all the years in the league taught Blake a thing or two about being calculated, which put us on an even playing field.

"Oh, trust me, the moment you're back, I'll show you just how wrong you are." There's a beat of silence. "How is being back home?"

This morning's interaction flashes in my mind. "It's... home."

I didn't like talking about my family, but Blake was with me when Emmett invited me to the wedding. He didn't understand my reluctance, which, in hindsight, he's right about. My best friend is getting married, and I should be thrilled about it. So I told him how and why I left. It was hard to explain our dynamic to people. While most parents would be delighted to find out their son was playing professionally, my dad thinks I'm wasting my time playing a game and acting like an immature kid, which couldn't be further from the truth.

"That good, huh?"

"Yeah," I mutter, my fingers tightening around the steering wheel as more houses appear in my line of sight.

"When's the wedding again?"

"Two weeks. After that's done, I'm out of here."

I had PT to finish so I could get cleared to join my teammates for the next season. Oh, hell, maybe I'll even go on vacation. After this, God knows I deserve it.

49

"You never know. A lot can change in two weeks."

I shake my head, although I know he can't see me. "Nothing that will make me stay."

I loved my life back in Austin. I was happy there doing what I was meant to do, but more than that, I wasn't planning on staying somewhere I wasn't wanted.

By more than one person.

Because even if by some miracle my dad changes his mind, there is still *her*.

And she most definitely doesn't want to see me here.

Her running away yesterday like the devil's at her heels is a testament to that.

"If you say so..."

"Trust me, the last thing people here want is for me to stay. I'm here for the wedding, and that's it."

Turning onto the main street, the diner comes into view, the faded old sign illuminated by the bright late-morning sun.

"And on that note, I'm outta here. I'm meeting the groom as we speak."

"Good luck, man. Talk soon."

With a goodbye, I hang up the call and pull into the parking lot. The place is filled with trucks, so I look around for an open space when I spot a dusty white pickup. My best friend's leaning against it, his arms crossed over his chest. He replaced his once trusty ball cap for a Stetson, the brim throwing shade over his face and keeping it hidden from view.

Pulling the truck into the open spot next to him, I kill the engine and slide out.

Emmett pushes from the truck and comes to meet me.

"Hey, man, long time n—"

The words die on my tongue as his fist connects to my gut, making me double over.

"Fuck," I hiss, my hands covering my middle as the pain

spreads through me. Looking up, I glare at him. "What the hell was that for?"

"I promised I'd make you pay if you made her cry, or did you forget that?"

I don't bother asking him to explain. We both know who the *her* he's talking about is. The warning he gave me all those years ago.

To me, Becky was a friend before she turned into my everything, but to Emmett, she was the sister he never had, and to say he was protective of her would be an understatement.

"You should feel lucky I didn't break your nose instead, but Kate made me promise not to do it. Something about the wedding photos, apparently."

"How lucky," I mutter dryly as I straighten to my full height. "Besides, how is this *my* fault? I wouldn't even be here if *you*" — I jab my finger into his chest — "hadn't invited me to come."

"Well, you said you were going home!" Emmett protests. "I figured I'd stop by her place this morning and tell her. Although, seriously, why did I believe you? I have no idea."

"Sorry to disappoint," I say dryly. "Besides, you knew for the last few weeks that I was coming."

Emmett lifts his hat off his head and runs his fingers through his hair. "Yeah, well, we both know how stubborn Becky can get. You can't just come and talk to her about something if she sets her mind on not doing it. And trust me when I tell you, she does *not* want to talk about you. I tried it."

His words shouldn't hurt, but they do.

I lift my hand, rubbing at the center of my chest. "I'm not surprised at all."

At first, I kind of expected it. Waited for it even. Waited for Emmett to call me and rip me a new one from miles away for hurting his best friend. But the call never came, and even when we talked, he didn't mention it. Not until I told him we broke up.

"It's good to see you, man," Emmett says, snapping me out of my thoughts as he pulls me into a one-armed hug.

I slap him over the shoulder. "Same."

For all the bullshit that's going on with Rebecca and my dad, I am glad to see my best friend. Our paths crossed barely a handful of times in the last couple of years, mainly when football brought us together.

"C'mon, let's get to Letty's. I'm sure you miss some good ol' Letty's special."

My stomach growls loudly in confirmation.

Emmett chuckles. "I thought so, c'mon."

The moment we step into Letty's diner, all heads turn toward us, which, thankfully, isn't that much since it's the middle of the morning, and most people are out in the fields working.

"Well, look who decided to stop by," Letty drawls out slowly, her accent thick as one of her eyebrows rises. "We all thought you forgot about us."

Emmett nudges me with his elbow, and I glare at him before turning my attention to the older lady. Mrs. Letty has to be at least seventy at this point. Why she isn't retired, only she knows; then again, she always seemed like the kind of woman they'd have to drag to the grave straight from here. This diner was her whole life and always has been.

"As if there is a chance I'd ever be able to forget about you, Mrs. Letty," I say, flashing her my most charming smile. The one that earned me more than one extra muffin in my younger age, but this time, Mrs. Letty isn't budging. She crosses her arms over her chest.

"So, there is a good reason why you haven't visited your family in the last four years?"

Of course, she'd think it's my fault; hell, they all thought I was the one to blame, that I wanted to stay away and did it out of spite or whatever. Nobody ever thought twice about why I might not want to come back.

"Things have just been busy." I shrug, not wanting to go at it with her.

"Busy," she repeats, the skepticism clear in her voice. "Well, boys, take a seat, and I'll come grab your order in a jiff. Or, you know, four years."

"Damn, maybe this wasn't the best idea after all," Emmett whispers as we turn around to find a place to sit. "I don't think I've ever seen Letty hold a grudge against somebody."

"Why am I not surprised I might be the first?"

Spotting an empty booth in the back, I slide into the leather seat and let my gaze scan over the space. The place has hardly changed since I left four years ago. Same dark hardwood tables, the same red and white checkered tablecloths, and the same plastic menus.

"Did she get anything new?" I ask as I pull one menu and start looking at the selection.

Emmett scoffs. "Have you met Letty?"

"Stupid question."

Nothing much changes around here. If it ain't broken, why fix it?

"What can I get'cha, boys?" Mrs. Letty asks, appearing out of nowhere, a coffee pot in her hand.

"My usual, Mrs. Letty." Emmett smiles at the older woman.

"Of course. How is that gorgeous girl of yours?" Mrs. Letty asks, a beaming smile spreading over her mouth. "Any updates on the wedding?"

"She's doing okay. Been busy with the wedding stuff and setting up the business."

Mrs. Letty nods. "I've heard! She's opening a rehabilitation center up on the ranch?"

"That's right, ma'am."

"She's always been a good one. You lucked out."

Emmett's grin widens. "Don't I know it."

"Glad at least one of you appreciates the good women in their lives." Those sharp eyes turn to me, giving me a pointed look. So much for subtlety. "And what can I get you, Mr. Fernandez?"

"Mr. Fernandez? Seriously, Mrs. Letty? Mr. Fernandez is my dad."

"No, your dad is Luis. You, Mr. Hot-Shot-Football-Player, are Mr. Fernandez," she says as she fills our mugs with coffee.

"*Ouch*," Emmett mutters quietly so Letty won't hear him.

I glare at him. So much for best friends sticking up for one another.

"So what can I get'cha?"

Letting out a sigh, I place my order—what used to be my usual at the diner—which earns me a huff before she turns on the balls of her feet and marches back to the counter.

"Talk about making a man feel welcomed," I comment dryly, shaking my head.

"It's all your damn fault. Not only did you walk away, but you also broke Becky's heart in the process, and you know how much people around here love her."

But what about my heart?

Nobody asked about that. Nobody asked me what exactly happened that day. They just assumed that I did something wrong. When, in reality, she was the one who walked away without even giving me a chance to explain.

"So, how are the wedding preparations going?" I ask, pointedly changing the subject to the reason why I came here in the first place.

Emmett lets out a groan. "They're... going. Mom and Mabel have all these ideas they keep throwing at us, even though Kate was pretty specific that she wants a *small* wedding."

"Yeah, good luck with that, dude."

There was no such thing as a small wedding here in Bluebonnet. It was an all-town affair, and considering how loved and respected the Santiago's are in the community, they'll be lucky if they manage to keep it contained at all.

"I just want it done and over with so I can enjoy my wife."

"I can hardly believe you're not enjoying her as it is." I quirk my brow at him, but he just hums non-committedly. Not that I expected anything different. Kate was always off-limits to anybody. "Didn't you guys move in together?"

I remember Emmett mentioning he officially asked his dad to buy a part of the Santiago land a couple of years ago, just around the time he proposed to Kate. Since then, he's been working his ass off to build their house, which was finished just recently.

A smile flashes on my friend's face. "We did, but I'm ready to call her my wife. I've been ready for years now, you know that."

I did. Emmett would have married her straight out of high school. That's how crazy he was about her. Hell, he would have married her that first day he met her. Period. A part of me thought he was bonkers, but he knew they'd end up together.

Kate didn't mind going with him to college, a bitter voice reminds me. *It's hard to work on a relationship when one party isn't invested in it one hundred percent.*

"Just a few more weeks."

"*Two* weeks," Emmett corrects, letting out an exaggerated sigh. "Two weeks too long if you ask me, but I guess it'll have to do."

"C'mon, you waited this long. What is two more weeks?" Lifting my cup, I take a sip of my coffee.

Fucking shit.

I'm about to spit the coffee back into the cup when Mrs. Letty appears, our food in tow. One of her sharp brows lifts as she watches me.

"Is everything okay?"

I force myself to swallow down the coffee. There isn't a chance I'll let that woman see me squirm.

"Perfect."

Those watchful eyes stay on me for a moment longer before she places the food in front of us. "You boys enjoy."

Highly unlikely.

The muscle in my cheek twitches from the forced smile, but I don't let it fall until she turns her back and returns to her other customers, making sure they're all set and refilling the coffees.

With a different pot.

Motherfucker.

"What was that about?" Emmett asks me as he digs into his food.

"Is your coffee okay?"

"Yeah." Emmett's brows pull together. "Why?"

"Because mine is like somebody dropped a whole-ass bag of sugar in it, that's why."

Fucking small-town noisy Nellies.

"Oh, shit," Emmett bursts into laughter, the sound drawing a few curious glances our way. "This is just too good. Way to go, Mrs. Letty."

I kick him under the table. "Whose side are you on?"

"When it comes to this particular topic? Mrs. Letty's."

"Of-fucking-course." I jab my fork into the sausage and lift it so I can give it a tentative sniff, which only makes Emmett laugh harder. "You just keep laughing at my expense, Santiago."

"You can't deny it's funny."

"Oh, *sure*. Nothing screams funny like getting diabetes because an old lady has a vendetta against you. Why do I have a feeling that she might have spit in my food?" I ask, looking distrustfully after the woman who stops by another table, all smiles. "Letty loves me."

"If I were you, I'd be worried if she put some kind of laxative inside the food." Emmett grabs ketchup and puts some over his fries.

I place my fork back on the plate. My appetite is suddenly gone. "Thanks, man."

"Hey, she might have loved you once, but things change, dude." Putting the bottle away, his eyes meet mine, and any amusement that was there is now gone. "It might not seem that way at first, but things have changed, even around here."

A shiver of unease runs down my spine.

For some reason, I don't think he's only talking about Letty's weird behavior.

"Then why invite me to come back?"

Emmett simply watches me from across the table for a moment, not saying a word. Just when I think he'll ignore my question, he says, "Because no matter what happened over the last few years, you're my best friend, and I want you by my side on the happiest day of my life. I might not know what happened because both of you are too stubborn to say anything, so I'm not even going to try, and after this conversation, I'm going to stop pestering you about this whole topic altogether, but tell me one thing."

My fingers itch to curl, but I force myself to sit still. "What?"

"Was it worth it?"

I didn't have to ask him to explain what he meant. I knew it. I knew him. Emmett would never put his career in front of his family, in front of the person he loves, but I wasn't my best friend. My family hated me for the path I took. The woman I loved walked away from me without giving me a shot, so was it worth it? It had to be. Because my dream was the only thing I had left.

I run my hand through my hair, letting out a humorless chuckle. "I'm playing in the freaking NFL, what do you think?"

I expect Emmett to laugh with me, but he's quiet, his face completely serious. "I think that's not the answer."

"Well, it's the truth." I let my hand drop on the table. "I'm living my dream."

All alone. In a place that's not my home. Away from the people that were once my family.

"I'm playing the game I love at the highest level possible and earning a shit ton of money while doing so. All the things you could have had too, if you wanted them."

"Maybe I could have, but that was never my road to take." He shakes his head. "Don't get me wrong, I want you to be happy, Miguel..."

"I am happy, dammit."

"Okay. I'm glad to hear that. I just worry about you, that's all."

"No need for any of you to worry. I'm fine." I roll my shoulders back, feeling that familiar twitch.

Emmett notices it, too, because he tips his chin in my direction as he extends his fork and grabs the piece of sausage I cut. "How's that arm doing?"

I watch as he chews slowly, willing myself to relax. "Still working on it, but it'll be like new by the beginning of summer camp."

"It better be. You guys were so close to winning that damn trophy, and your first season, no less. I'm proud of you, man."

"Thanks. It was a hard year."

"People giving you trouble?"

"No, nothing like that. The team is okay, and we've been working well. I think they have a good mix of newbies and senior players, which definitely helped."

"Makes sense," Emmett nods his head. "Having a good team is always the key. By the way, the food tastes okay. I think you're safe from any laxatives."

I look skeptically at my plate. "Only time will tell."

"I guess you're right about that."

Still, I pick up my fork and dig into the scrambled eggs. Emmett was right; they tasted good. Better than good, really. And since I barely touched my food this morning after the interaction with Dad, I was starving.

It's just a couple of weeks. You can do it.

"Anything you need me to help with for the wedding? We doing a bachelor's party? I'm pretty sure I could book us a trip to Vegas and..."

"No Vegas." Emmett shakes his head. "I figured we'll just throw a party at the lake. Like in the good old days, only this time, some of my college friends will also be joining us. But you can bring out the booze if you really want to help. Apart from that, everything is pretty much settled. Dad and I are still working on the arch for the ceremony, but that should be done this week, too."

"Arch?"

"Yeah, Kate saw this wooden arch on Pinterest or some shit, and she thought it looked nice." He shrugs. "So I talked to Dad and Bradley, and we decided to build it."

Of course he did.

"Well, if you need any help, let me know. I feel like I'll go out of my mind here if I keep sitting still."

"If you need work, there's always something that needs to be done around here. Or are you too big of a star now to work on a ranch?"

"Your jokes are getting old, Santiago."

"I'm still laughing."

Just then, his phone rings. He pulls it out, checking the screen and letting out a long sigh. "Duty calls."

He gets up, pulling his wallet out of his pocket, but I wave him off. "It's on me."

"You sure?"

"Just go already. Put out the fires."

"Okay, talk soon? We can go and grab drinks at The Hut one night."

"Sounds like a plan."

With a lift of his hand, he answers his phone as he goes for the door. I sit there for a moment longer, finishing my meal. Pulling out a few bills, I place them on the table as I, too, get up.

Mrs. Letty glares at me all the way to the door, so I make sure my smile is extra wide as I push the door open and slide into the hot Texan afternoon.

I know I should probably go back to the ranch, but I wasn't ready for another round with my dad. Not just yet.

Maybe I could find a place to sit and get some work done.

Stopping by my car, I grab my backpack from the passenger seat before I walk down the street. A few people who are brave enough to step outside under the now scorching heat nod their heads in recognition. I return the gesture but don't stop to chat with them. Instead, I take in the mix of old and new shops on Main Street until my gaze falls on the newly opened coffee shop.

Reading Nook.

Perfect.

I swear I can still feel the sugar Letty put in my coffee on my tongue. I wouldn't mind changing that. Crossing the street, I push open the door. The AC blasts in my face the moment I step inside, a soft *chime* spreading through the space as the woman behind the counter turns her head toward me.

"Hell—"

The words die on her lips as she blinks, surprise, and a flicker of pain flashes in those familiar hazel eyes as they settle on mine.

The eyes that used to stare at me with so much love.

"Rebecca."

CHAPTER

6

"Hey, I'm done for today." Jessica's dark head peeks into the kitchen, and she looks around, taking in the mess. "Will you be okay on your own? I can stay if yo—"

"Don't worry, I'll be fine." I dust my hands off. "Just give me five to finish here?"

"I can do that." She tips her chin toward the freshly baked peanut butter cookies. "You will want to bring those with you. Maybe even the muffins. We're running low on everything."

Why was I not surprised?

"Will do."

With a nod, Jessica lets the door close as she returns to the front of the café. The place has been buzzing with customers since the moment I opened it. It feels like half of Bluebonnet needed either coffee or treats today, and I had an inkling suspicion it had less to do with their desire for sweets and more to do with the latest gossip.

God bless little Jessica Richards for stepping up like a pro after I called her and for allowing me to hide in the kitchen and focus my frustration on baking.

Jessica was a year younger than Matthew, and while my younger brother chose to go to college on the other side of the country, Jessica stayed in Bluebonnet and attended the same community college I did.

Earlier this spring, the café was extremely busy, so she offered to jump in. And while I wasn't one to give up control easily, the café has grown recently. Add to it all the wedding craziness that I knew was coming my way, and I had to admit to myself that I couldn't do it all on my own. But with everything going on right now, I was more grateful than ever for her help.

Tucking a strand of hair behind my ear, I go to the sink and wash my hands before grabbing two trays of fresh goodies and going up front.

Jessica wasn't lying. Quite a few tables were occupied, and there was a line of customers waiting to be served.

"Are you sure you'll be fine?" Jessica asks again as I finish putting the cookies in place.

If the situation were different, I might have asked her to stay, but I overheard her the other day talking with one of her friends about going shopping.

"Yup, you go. Have fun."

Jessica nods, taking off her apron before ducking from behind the counter. I turn toward my next customer, only to realize it's Nico. He's dressed in his police uniform, his fingers looped through the belt hoops on his pants.

He takes me in for a moment before a small smile slowly appears on his face. "Busy day?"

"Apparently, everybody's craving coffee today."

Nico looks around the café, spotting a few people giving us curious looks. "Mhmm... I'm not sure coffee's the only thing they're interested in."

"Well, the coffee is the only thing they're gonna get. What can I get'cha, officer?"

"Two black coffees and..." He glances at the display, his face lighting up. "Are those peanut butter cookies?"

"Sure are. I just baked them, too."

Nico groans softly. "Damn, Becs. You're killing me here. Okay, gimmie a dozen of those, too."

"A dozen?" I grab a box and tongs and start packing his order. "Please tell me you're not planning to eat them all on your own."

"I wish. The last time I brought them to the station, I had to fight with everybody in order to have *one*, so I figured I'd better be safe than sorry this time around."

"That's so nice of you." Closing the lid on the box, I place it next to the register before starting on the coffees. "You done for today?"

Nico snorts. "In some eight more hours or so. I figured some good coffee couldn't hurt."

The corner of my mouth curls upward at the compliment. I worked my ass off to build this café from nothing, and I was happy and proud people of Bluebonnet wanted to support it. "Thanks." I put the two coffees on the counter next to the box with the cookies. "That will be..."

Before I can turn to the register, Nico's hand covers mine, his voice dropping lower so only I can hear him. "How are you doing?"

Blinking, I look up from our joined hands into his brown eyes, some of the happiness I felt only a moment ago fading. "I'm fine."

"You ran out of The Hut so quickly yesterday. I was worried about you."

"Don't you start too. There is nothing to—"

The bell above the door chimes just in time to save me.

"Hell—" I turn toward the door, but it's like I've been hit by a semi-truck.

This can't be happening.

But it is.

Because that's just my luck.

My palms turn clammy, my heartbeat thundering inside my chest so loudly I can hear it echo in my eardrums, dulling out all the other sounds.

Because he's here.

Miguel Luis Fernandez.

Out of all the places in this town he could have gone to, he's here.

"Rebecca."

My name is a rasped croak that sends a shudder down my spine. We haven't talked or seen each other in three years, and my body still reacts to him like it always did.

Three damn years.

It's been three years since anybody has called me by my full name.

I've always been Becky or Becs to most of my friends and family.

But not to Miguel.

Not when it was just the two of us.

Only this time, it wasn't just two of us.

A lump forms in my throat, making it hard to breathe.

There were half a dozen of Bluebonnet's residents that were currently sitting on the edge of their seats as they watched this unfold.

Shit.

I open my mouth, to say what, I'm not sure, but Nico is faster. He turns around, and I can see his whole body bracing for an attack.

"What do you think you're doing here, Fernandez?"

Miguel's gaze lingers on me for a moment longer before it shifts to Nico.

"I'd assume the same thing as you, trying to get some coffee."

Nico opens his mouth, but I wrap my fingers around his

arm. "Don't," I whisper, although it's pointless. The only sound filling the space is the radio softly playing in the background. Everybody else has quieted down, their eyes on us, waiting to see what'll happen.

But it wasn't their gazes that burned the most.

It was Miguel's eyes that were locked on where my hand was resting on Nico's forearm.

I pull my hand back, clasping my fingers together.

Nico turns to me, his brows pulled together. "You don't have to do this, Becs."

He was wrong, though.

I had to do this. We were making a scene as it was; kicking Miguel out of Reading Nook would be the talk of the town, and that's the last thing I wanted.

"We broke up ages ago. It's going to be fine," I mutter softly, turning to the register. It takes me a couple of tries, but I finally get the right total. Nico just shakes his head before giving me the money.

"If he gives you any issues, you call me?"

I nod my head but stay silent. Nico finally gives up and grabs his things, shoulder checking into Miguel's on his way out. I can see Nico's lips move, but I can't decipher the words from the buzzing in my ears.

Miguel's jaw clenches, but he doesn't take the bait. Those dark eyes meet mine, and slowly, he closes the distance between us.

"W-what..." My voice comes out hoarse, so I clear my throat. "What are you doing here?"

"This is a coffee shop, right?" He looks around as if he's trying to figure out if he's in the right place.

Smartass.

"Yes, this is *my* coffee shop. What do you want?"

He watches me for a moment, those dark eyes glued to my

face as if he's drinking me in, trying to memorize every line of my face.

"Can we talk?"

Talk? He wants to talk? Here and now? With half of Bluebonnet watching?

"We don't have anything to discuss." I start to take a step back, but his fingers wrap around my wrist. While Nico's hand on mine felt nice, Miguel's touch was like I'd been burned. A zap of electricity shoots through my arm at the point of contact, my whole body shuddering at the touch.

The memories of the past flash in my mind, overwhelming me in its intensity.

Don't go there.

I chant those words like a mantra. My eyes fall shut for a moment as I try to compose myself.

"That's bullshit, and you know it," Miguel says, a note of irritation in his voice.

Bullshit?

My eyes snap open. I tug my hand out of his grasp, my fingers wrap around my wrist, rubbing at the sensitive flesh as I shoot him a death glare. "No, I don't think it's bullshit," I whisper softly, leaning in so only he can hear me. "We said everything that needed to be said. Now you can either order what you came for, or you can leave."

Miguel's jaw works as he watches me. For a moment, I'm not sure if he wants to strangle me or turn around and leave. But in the end, he surprises me by choosing neither.

"Black coffee. And two of those peanut butter cookies."

"Okay, I'll pack—"

"Oh, no." He flashes me a smile, but there is nothing warm or loving in it. "I'm staying here."

CHAPTER

7

MIGUEL

I can feel Rebecca's gaze bore into the side of my face from her spot on the other side of the counter. She's been hiding there ever since I got here, only leaving her little sanctuary when it was absolutely necessary, which wasn't that often. Granted, this place was busy, and apparently, she was the only person working.

I watched her move behind the counter, making coffees, packing treats, and talking to people for the last two hours while I sat here and pretended that I'm busy. The idea of getting any work done fell through the moment I saw her in Reading Nook. With no one other than Nico. What was he, her guard dog?

Just thinking about it had my teeth grinding together, which was crazy. We weren't together. She could do whatever she wanted, date whoever she wanted. Hell, maybe she did date the tool.

And now I was seeing red.

Fuck.

Rebecca's laughter spreads through the room, making my head snap up. She's talking to a woman around our age who's holding a little boy on her hip. A genuine smile spreads over

Rebecca's mouth as she extends her hand to ruffle the boy's messy hair.

Beautiful.

She was so fucking beautiful when she laughed. It hurt to watch her, and yet I couldn't look away.

That was always the main problem when it came to Rebecca. It was hard to be close to her and impossible to walk away.

As if she can feel my gaze on her, she looks up, and that smile is gone almost immediately.

Her teeth graze over her lower lip as she stares at me, her expression completely void of emotion. I'm unsure how long we stay that way until the woman finally draws her attention.

Shaking my head, I return to my laptop, but the empty screen is mocking me. So much for that.

The bell chimes, and I catch sight of the woman as she passes in front of the glass window. I turn, facing the shop, but the place is relatively quiet. Another man sits a few tables away from mine, but his whole focus is on his laptop. And then a group of girls are chatting and giggling in the back.

With nothing else to do, Rebecca slips from behind the counter and starts cleaning off a few tables. I watch her work, doing her best to avoid me.

Deciding to call it quits, I turn off my laptop and put it into my backpack. Throwing it over my shoulder, I get to my feet just as she's passing by my table.

"Can we talk?" I ask, running my fingers through my hair.

She pretends like she doesn't hear me, but this time around, there is almost no audience to see us clashing heads together, so I wasn't about to let it go that easily.

"You know I'm Emmett's best man," I say as I chase after her. "You can't avoid me forever."

"I can damn sure try my best," she mutters under her breath.

"I heard that."

She glares over her shoulder. "I wasn't trying to be quiet."

"Seriously? Is this how it's going to be?"

Like, how stubborn can one person be?

"I already told you we've said everything that needed to be said. I don't s—"

"Did we say it before or after you turned your back on me and walked away?" I grit between clenched teeth. I grab her hand, tugging her to me. She collides into my chest, her lips parting as she sucks in a breath, those hazel eyes widening in surprise as a jolt of electricity goes through me.

Six years ago

"Rebecca!" I yell as I run after her, pushing the tree branches out of my way. I can feel one dig into my skin, and I know it'll leave a gash, but I couldn't care less about it.

The only thing that mattered was the painful look in Rebecca's eyes and that I was the one who put it there. Now she was running away, and my heart was beating so fast I could swear it would jump out of my chest.

"Fuck! Rebecca, just wait."

"Leave me alone, Miguel," she shouts back but doesn't bother to slow down.

"I'm not leaving you here."

I finally catch a flash of red in the moonlight.

There.

Pushing myself harder, I start catching up to her until my

fingers wrap around her wrist, and I tug her to me. Rebecca collides into my chest, and I wrap my arms around her.

"Let me go, Miguel," she protests, trying to struggle out of my hold.

She's wiggling in my arms, her body rubbing against mine as she turns around, her palms pressing against my chest. Where earlier there was sadness, now there is anger, and I can feel that grip around my heart loosen slightly. Angry Rebecca, I could deal with.

"I'm not letting you run away."

She jabs her finger into my chest. "Let me go, or I'm going to scream."

I grab her hands in mine to stop her from poking me. "As if anybody will hear you so far out in the woods."

Her nostrils flare as she inhales deeply, tugging her hands back.

"I'm not joking, Miguel."

I shrug my shoulders, knowing it'll only piss her off further. "Go ahead, I dare you."

I don't even get to finish before she starts to open her mouth, but before she can utter a word, I pull her closer to me, my mouth crashing against hers.

Now

"Me?" she lets out a strangled laugh, snapping me out of the fall down memory lane. She tugs her hand out of my grasp, and this time, I let her. "You're putting this on *me*?"

All the color has drained from her cheeks, making that dusting of freckles that always appeared in the summer months on the bridge of her nose stand out even more. Rebecca always hated those freckles. She thought they made her look like a little girl. I, on the other hand, loved every single one of them. I remember staring at them, tracing them with the tip of my finger, and later on with my mouth as I peppered kisses over every inch of her body.

Every. Single. One. Of. Them.

How is it possible that somebody looks so different and yet exactly the same three years later?

It feels like a lifetime, but also like not enough time has passed.

I raise my hand, pressing it against that aching spot in the middle of my chest. It's the exact same spot in which a hole opened the day she walked away from me, not even wanting to listen to what I had to tell her.

I think that part was the one that hurt the most.

"Did you or did you not walk away?"

She, the only person who claimed to love me unconditionally, the only one I allowed myself to trust, turned her back on me and walked the fuck away.

Nails dig into my skin, a bite of pain shooting up my arm.

"What the hell was I supposed to do? Huh? Stay there and wa—"

Just then, the doorbell rings, cutting off anything she wanted to say. She presses her lips in a tight line before turning toward the door.

But I still can't seem to move my gaze from her.

I'm drinking her in like a thirsty man in the desert, trying to memorize everything that is Rebecca Williams.

The way the red in her hair seems darker. The way the plain black tank top clings to her chest. The way the cutoff jeans show off her long, tanned legs and the curve of her ass.

Get a grip, dude. I shake my head, snapping myself out of my thoughts and shifting my attention toward the door to find two of the biggest gossips standing in the doorway, gaping at the two of us with interest.

"Miguel Fernandez, I've heard the stories, but I couldn't believe that you'd come home after all this time," Mrs. Miller says as she moves further into the café, her bony hand clutching the handle of her wooden walking stick, and Mrs. Tyson at her heels. "What brings you here?"

I open my mouth, but before I can say a word, Mrs. Tyson scoffs. "What do you think he's doing here? The boy finally got his head out of his ass, so he came home to make things right, Trish."

"I know that, Milly." The other woman shakes her head exasperatedly. "I just want *him* to realize it, too."

"He's a *man*. You know how they are. If it ain't biting him in the ass, he ain't seeing it. My late George was just like that. God rest his soul."

"You mean the devil? That man was insufferable on a good day."

"But I think Miguel still has hope. He's back, after all."

"What Miguel is is *leaving*," Rebecca grits through clenched teeth, a fake smile plastered on her face. "I just heard Mrs. Fernandez called him to bring home some flour so she can finish preparing dinner."

I blink, unsure if I heard her correctly.

"Oh my, you can't keep your mother waiting." Mrs. Tyson nods decisively.

Still glaring at Rebecca, I force out a smile. "I wouldn't dream of it."

Mrs. Miller taps me on the shoulder. "After all, you have more than one woman in your life you have to make up to. C'mon, Milly, let's see what Becky baked for us today."

The women loop their hands together and go toward the glass display, but I didn't doubt it in the slightest that they were listening intently to everything we said.

I move closer, leaning down so my lips practically brush against the shell of Becky's ear. This close, her sweet scent fills all of my senses. Roses, jasmine, and sugar mixed with something that's uniquely Rebecca.

My gaze meets hers, observing those long eyelashes as they fan over the line of her cheekbones. The way the color drains from that pretty pink mouth—a mouth I've kissed a thousand times before—because of how hard she's pressing her lips together.

Seeing her this close stirs something inside of me.

Something I haven't felt in so long I almost forgot what it was.

Lust.

"This isn't done yet," I rasp out, my fingers wrapping around the strap of my backpack to stop myself from reaching for her.

Not bothering to say anything else, I turn on the balls of my feet and go toward the door.

That damn bell jingles loudly as I step into the scorching afternoon heat, beads of sweat forming on my face instantly. Still, I force myself to breathe in the fresh air, hoping it'll help me clear my mind.

Your friends. You're here for your friends, so you can stand by them as they get their happily ever after. That's it.

But no matter how many times I repeat it, I can't erase her scent from my head, nor can I forget the way her hand felt in mine.

A perfect match.

A missing piece.

Fitting, considering she broke my heart and didn't even bother to look back.

CHAPTER

8

REBECCA

"Rebecca!"

Miguel's rushed footsteps pound against the ground as he chases after me, but I don't dare turn around.

I keep my head low as I run through the woods, hot tears burning my eyelids as I try to navigate the dark space around me.

I was so sick of all of this.

Of him.

Why did it have to be him, of all people?

Whoever thought falling for your best friend is sweet and perfect never had to deal with Miguel Luis Fernandez and his bullshit.

A tear slides down my cheek. Huffing in irritation, I wipe it away with the back of my hand.

I'll not be crying over that stupid man, not any lo—

Miguel's hand wraps around my wrist as he tugs me back to him.

"This isn't done yet," he growls, those chocolate eyes burning brightly even under the dim moonlight. They're the last thing I see before my back connects to the hard surface of the nearby tree, and his mouth crashes on mine.

I suck in a sharp breath as I startle awake. My heart is beating wildly inside my ribcage as I look around, trying to orientate myself.

My room.

I'm in my room, and everything that happened was just a dream.

I let my body relax into the pillow as I run my hand over my face, feeling the sweat clinging to my skin.

Well, I guess not everything.

Miguel being back in Bluebonnet was very real, and I didn't know what to do about it.

I wanted to ignore him, but I knew what he said was true. Two people can avoid each other for only so long in a town the size of Bluebonnet Creek, and if the last couple of days were any indication, we were all out of luck.

Groaning, I turn around and bury my head into the pillow, letting it swallow my scream in frustration.

Why?

Just why did he have to come back?

Seeing him brought back all the memories that I thought were long forgotten. All the feelings that I safely stored away: the betrayal, the frustration, the pain, the...

And why did he want to *talk*?

After all this time, he thought now was the time to do a recap of what happened all those years ago?

Screw this.

Screw *him*.

Pushing the covers back, I roll out of my bed and slip into my flip-flops as I grab the scrunchie off the nightstand. Quickly,

I pile my hair in a messy knot on top of my head before I stop in the bathroom and splash some cold water over my face.

Looking up, I face my reflection in the mirror. My skin is pale, with dark circles visible underneath my eyes. The combination makes the freckles over the bridge of my nose stand out more than usual.

Grabbing the towel, I wipe my face before descending the stairs. The downstairs is eerily quiet as I make my way to the back of the house.

Coffee.

I need coffee if I want to get anything done today.

The floorboard creaks as I step inside the kitchen, reminding me for the hundredth time that I should have somebody take a look at it.

It's just one of the gazillion things on my to-do list.

One thing at a time.

The tall frame next to the stove catches my attention.

"Goo—" I look up just as my brother turns around abruptly, wide green eyes meeting mine as he lifts the spatula as if it were a weapon.

My heart skips as I come to a standstill and raise my palms in the air so he can see them clearly. "Hey, it's just me, Becky," I say softly, hoping to reassure him.

There is a split second when Chase stands completely still. I hold my breath as I observe him silently. His chest rises and falls rapidly, and I can see the beads of sweat covering his forehead. His fingers are wrapped so tightly around the spatula that I'm surprised he hasn't broken it in two.

The whole interaction lasts just a few seconds, but it feels like a lifetime before Chase blinks his eyes, his gaze coming into focus and giving me back my big brother.

Or what was left of him anyway.

"Becky." He lets out a shaky breath. I watch as he wills his fingers to relax, and he gently lowers his hand, his free one rising to run over his face and through his messy hair. "You shouldn't sneak up on people like that."

I don't bother pointing out that I didn't sneak up on him.

I knew better than that.

Chase entered the army the moment he turned eighteen. Our family was struggling financially, and Mom was still dealing with depression, even though it had been years since Dad died.

A heartbeat, that's all it took, one rash decision and our family was wrecked. Dad was gone, and a part of Mom left with him. Chase, as the oldest of the three of us, felt responsible. Like he had to be the head of the family. I tried to convince him we'd find a different way, but he just kissed me on the forehead and told me everything would be alright as he walked away.

He lied.

Nothing was okay.

A few months ago, Chase got injured during his last tour. Most of his physical injuries were slowly healing. The broken bones, scrapes, and burns were mending, and he had just recently started physical therapy for his leg. His hearing, on the other hand, was injured beyond repair. The blast from the bomb was so strong it damaged his eardrum. He wasn't completely deaf, but his hearing will never be what it used to be. I tried convincing him that he should go and learn some ASL so we could communicate more easily, but he insisted that he was fine, so I decided to let it be for now. What worried me was that his heart would never recover. Nor would his mind. Although he tried his best to hide it, some nights I would wake up to the sound of him crying for help, tossing and turning in the sweaty sheets, but whenever I tried breaching the subject of his nightmares, he would just turn his back and walk away.

Still, I didn't miss the fact that the dark scruff covering his jaw has become thicker in the last few weeks, and the bags under his eyes are so dark they seem like twin bruises.

I spot Shadow, Chase's German Shepard, brush against the side of his leg, her sharp, dark eyes meeting mine. The two of them have been partners for the past two years. She was with him when the explosion happened; one of her legs was injured in the blast, and she was still limping on that paw, but that didn't stop her from being there for Chase. It's like the dog could sense when his PTSD was intensifying, so she was always there to offer him support.

"I'm sorry," I apologize as I move inside the room. "How are you feeling? Did you sleep at all?"

"Like usual," Chase grumbles. "Fuck."

He turns around to the stove, but it's already too late. The scent of burnt scrambled eggs reaches my nostrils. I open my mouth to warn him, but before I can utter a word, he grabs the metal handle of the pan and starts to lift it. He gets to the sink before he curses and drops it.

"Here." I move quickly, opening the faucet and gently pushing his hand under the lukewarm spray as I inspect the red mark on his palm. "I don't think it's too serious."

Chase chuckles humorlessly. "What's one more scar?"

I bite the inside of my cheek to stop myself from saying something I shouldn't. But it's hard. So damn hard when all I want is to shake him and remind him that he's still here, *alive*. It's not like it will make any difference. What happened out east haunted him, and I know he wondered why he was still here when so many of his friends died that day, but I would never stop being grateful for getting my brother back—broken and bruised, but weren't we all in some ways?

Turning off the faucet, I grab the towel and wrap his hand in it. "How about I make us some breakfast? We both know I'm the better cook."

A flash of light shines in my brother's eyes, but it's gone almost as quickly as it appeared. Still, I count it as a win. "Be my guest."

"Sit down."

Tossing the remnants of his burned eggs into the trash, I pull out a new pan. Then, I turn on the coffee machine before grabbing all the ingredients while waiting for my coffee to brew.

I look over my shoulder, meeting Chase's eyes. "You want some, too?"

Chase silently shakes his head as he slowly makes his way to the table. He was still limping on his right leg, and I doubted that the doctor cleared him to walk without crutches, but I knew better than to probe.

These last few months, I've learned how to pick my battles regarding my older brother, and this one wasn't worth it.

Adding some sugar and creamer, I take a long pull of the black gold, enjoying that first hit of caffeine in my system. God knows I'll need it to survive today.

Less than five minutes later, I've already finished half my cup, and the bacon is sizzling on the stove. I'm adding eggs when I hear footsteps in the hallway. I turn around just as Mom appears in the doorway, her dark purple flower nightgown still on as she looks around the room, disoriented.

"Good morning. Did you sleep well?"

"Morning. Yeah, I..." A frown appears between her brows. "What time is it?"

"Just after seven," I flash her a reassuring smile. "I'm making breakfast. Do you want some?"

There is a heartbeat of silence as Mom glances from me to the pan and then back, in which I hold my breath. "Did you burn something?"

A chuckle breaks out of me as relief spreads through my body. "Chase was cooking. Needless to say, it didn't end well."

"Chase?" Her head goes to the table where Chase sat down, Shadow's head resting on his knee. She rushes toward him, her arms wrapping around his shoulders as she squeezes him tightly.

I see my brother flinch at the contact, but then, after a moment, he relaxes, his arms slowly curling around her slender waist.

"Hey, Ma."

She pulls back, her hands cupping his cheeks as she looks at him. "When did you get home?"

"A while ago."

Turning around, I finish preparing breakfast as I listen to the two of them talk. Chase has been a silent grump ever since he returned home, but even he couldn't say no to Mom.

"And the first thing you decide is to cook?" Mom tsks loudly.

Chuckling softly, I turn off the stove and plate the food.

"What can I say? I like living on the edge."

She slaps him on the shoulder. "That's not funny, young man. Let me just go and..."

"Sit down." I slide the plate in front of my brother and the open space next to it.

"Oh, I could have helped you."

"I don't mind doing it."

"Well, at least one of my children knows how to cook, so I guess I did one thing right." Mom flashes me a smile, and a bitter-sweet ache spreads inside my chest, but I choose to ignore it and focus on the happiness hidden beneath it instead.

I turn around, going back to the counter to refill my coffee, when my phone rings on the counter.

"Hey, Becky, I—"

"Hey, I know why you're calling. You don't have to worry. I talked to Emmett and—"

"Shit, I—" her words are cut off, a gagging sound coming from the background.

My brows pull together as I listen intently. No, not gagging, more like retching.

What the hell?

"Are you okay? You don't sound that good. Do you need me to come over?"

Chase's eyes narrow as he watches me closely, but I wave him off as I wait for Kate to stop throwing up.

"Kate, seriously, I'm co—"

"I'm fine," she says finally, after what feels like forever. "Just a stomach bug."

"A stomach bug?" I repeat skeptically.

"Or maybe I ate something bad." She lets out a long sigh, and I can hear the tiredness in her voice. "I've been throwing up since last night."

"Shit."

"Shit sums it up perfectly."

"How can I help? Do you need me to bring you anything?" My head is already spinning with all the options and schedule rearrangements, so I can stop by her house and bring her whatever she might need. "I can go in town and bu—"

"I'm good. Emmett already stocked me up, and his mom brought soup last night."

Of course they did. Emmett carried Kate like a drop of water in the middle of his palm, and his family wasn't any different. Kate was the daughter they always wanted. It wouldn't surprise me if his mom stopped by their place later to make sure Kate was alright and to see if she needed any help around the house.

"But I have a big favor to ask of you."

"Yeah, sure. Anything, you know that."

"I have a cake tasting scheduled for today at two, but there is no way I can do it. Just the thought of it has my stomach rolling."

"Cake tasting?"

"Yes, I know you're super busy with your café, and I hate even asking, but..."

"No, it's fine. Jessica is opening this morning, so I'll double-check if she can stay until I get back, and I can do the tasting."

"You sure?"

"Yeah, I'll figure something out."

Kate lets out a long breath. "Thank you. I owe you."

"Oh, please. Don't you dare mention it. I'll pick something out. Is there a particular flavor you guys don't want?"

"I don't care. I don't want anything right now. Just thinking about food makes me want to puke. But pick something tasty?"

"Tasty, gotcha. You try to rest, okay? And call if you need anything."

"Mhmm..." Kate murmurs, clearly out of it.

I let out a small chuckle. "Go to bed, Kate."

"Will do."

Shaking my head, I hang up and open my messages. First, I texted Jessica to see if she could hold the fort until I got back. Her confirmation is instant. Then, I opened the thread with Emmett.

ME:

> I'm pretty sure your fiancé fell asleep in the bathroom, it might be good if you went home and put her to bed.

EMMETT:

> Shit.

> I thought she'd feel better by now.

> I'll go check in on her. Thanks for letting me know.

ME:

> No worries. You take care of her. I'll go for the cake tasting later.

EMMETT:

Double shit. I completely forgot about that.

ME:

Why am I not surprised?

You take care of Kate. I'll figure the whole cake thing out.

EMMETT:

You're the best.

ME:

Remember that before you piss me off next time.

Placing the phone on the counter, I grab my plate and join Mom and Chase.

"What was that all about?" Chase asks.

"Kate isn't feeling well, so she asked me to go and pick out their wedding cake." I dig my fork into my food. "Thankfully, Jessica can stay at the shop until I get back."

Since Jessica started working, I've decided to take two days a week where I'll get to sleep in—and by sleep in, I mean not wake up at the crack of dawn to be in the café baking before the shop opens. So, usually, I'd prepare everything for her the night before, and she'd come in and simply pop it into the oven. Although I've seen her playing around with decorating cupcakes lately, and she was actually pretty good at it.

My gaze darts toward Mom before shifting back to Chase. "Will you guys be okay here?"

"Yeah. Besides, Linda will be here soon. Go. Do what you need to do."

CHAPTER

9

MIGUEL

The downstairs is eerily quiet when I descend the steps the next morning. Some of the tension leaves my body, so for the first time since I came home, I allow myself to take in the small details that have changed since I've last been here. The new comforter, photos of my family that were taken in the time I've been gone, the new lamp standing in the corner of the living room next to Dad's ugly old armchair. I still remember Mom begging Dad to throw it out before I left, but apparently, there was a line of what he would do for his wife, and tossing that old thing out would be crossing it. Still, the majority of it was the same.

Bypassing the kitchen, I enter the mud room and slip on my running shoes before heading out. It was still relatively early, just after seven, but the sun was already burning brightly in the sky, making me squint the moment I stepped outside.

A loud rumble of an engine catches my attention. The old pickup truck is still running in front of the garage. The truck was probably my dad's age, if not older. What used to be a bright red color was now rusted, making the pickup seem maroon instead.

Just then, a man steps out of the barn, carrying a bunch of

wooden boards over his shoulder. I see the planks start to wobble, so before I can overthink it, I rush toward the person, grabbing them at the last second.

"Here, let me—"

Dad's dark scowl meets mine over the edge of the boards. His breathing is ragged, cheeks bright red from exertion, and a droplet of sweat slides down his forehead. Neither of us says anything as I help him place the boards into the bed.

I've barely seen him since after breakfast yesterday. He'd been working out in the fields the whole day until it was time for dinner. The meal was tense, with Mom carrying the majority of the conversation until Dad finally got up and left the table, claiming he was tired.

Letting my arms drop, I wipe my hands against my basketball shorts. "Are you guys fixing fences? I could he—"

"We didn't need your help the last four years while you were off playing games, and we sure as hell don't need it now," Dad bites out sternly. He shoots me a death glare before he turns on the balls of his feet and marches back into the barn.

My fingers curl into fists by my sides as I try to keep my temper in check. "Just a couple of weeks. Just a couple of weeks," I repeat the words like a mantra.

I don't know what I expected. For things to be different? Yeah, fat chances of that happening. Dad wasn't one for change. And just because Mom wanted me to come back home didn't mean he shared the sentiment.

Then, why let me come at all?

It made no sense.

Hearing the footsteps coming from the barn, I turn around and start jogging in the opposite direction. The last thing I wanted was to go for round two with Dad right now.

I'm not running even for a couple of minutes when the sweat starts forming on my skin, plastering my shirt to my back.

I keep the pace even as my feet pound against the gravelly road. The only road that leads into Bluebonnet. It takes me a good mile before I get to the crossroads, but instead of going toward town, I make a turn toward the Santiago ranch.

I'm panting by the time the big two-story white house comes into view. A newer model Range Rover is parked in front of it, but there is nobody in sight. Slowing down, I make my way around the house.

"Well, well, well... Who do we have here? And here I thought you forgot about us."

I turn toward the sound of the familiar southern drawl to find a small, red-haired woman standing on the back porch, her arms propped on her hips as she quirks her brow at me.

"Forgot about you?" A smile slowly spreads over my lips. "I don't think that's possible."

Mrs. Santiago shakes her head and opens her arms. "Come here so I can give you a hug."

Even though she's standing on the porch, with three steps on me, I have to lean down so I can wrap my arms around her.

"It's so good to see you, Miguel," Mrs. Santiago whispers, her hands rubbing my back. "How have you been doing? When did you get back?"

Some of that tension that's been left after my interaction with my dad seeps out of my body. Mrs. Santiago was like a second mother to me growing up, and I didn't realize until this moment how much I've missed her in the years I've been gone.

"It's good to see you too, Mrs. S." I take a step back, letting my arms drop to my sides. "I'm doing fine. I just got into Bluebonnet a couple of days ago."

"A *couple* of days ago?" She slaps me over the shoulder. "And I'm seeing you just now? I swear to you, young man, we'll have a few choice words." She shakes her head and scoffs. "He's been here for days and didn't even bother saying hi!"

"It's not like that, Mrs. S. I was just busy…"

"Oh, I see where this is going."

I chuckle softly. "Will you forgive me if I help you carry that bucket into the house?" I tip my chin in the direction of her feet, where a bucket almost as big as her is sitting on the floor.

"I guess that wouldn't hurt."

Still laughing, I grab the bucket in one hand and start toward the house. I'm pretty sure I heard her mutter something about men and their big hands as she followed after me.

"Where is Mr. Santiago?" I ask as I gently place the bucket on the kitchen counter.

"Oh, he's somewhere around here doing God knows what." She waves her hand as she starts sorting through the veggies. "I think he and Emmett talked about going to check on the cattle. You want to drink something?"

"No, I think I'll just go look for Emmett if that's okay with you."

"Sure thing. I have to get this soup going anyway." She looks up, her eyes meeting mine. "I know you're busy and probably want to see your friends now that you're in town, but make sure to stop by for dinner one day, okay?"

"Will do, Mrs. S."

With a wave, I slip out through the back door. There are a few ranch hands mingling around. One of them spots me, so I start walking toward him. "Hey, have you seen Emmett?"

The guy, probably around my age, if not younger, lifts his cowboy hat, running his fingers through his hair before placing it back on. "Yeah, he just— Oh, he's coming."

I turn around, and sure enough, Emmett's truck is pulling behind the Range Rover, and he gets out, shielding his eyes as he watches me.

"Fernandez? What brings you here?"

I lift my shoulders in a shrug. "You said you needed help?"

"Not enough work over at your place?"

"Not for me," I mutter dryly, still pissed at my dad for brushing me off so easily.

Emmett must notice my irritation because he slaps me over the shoulders. "C'mon, we'll find you something to work on, but first, you need some proper clothes. Not this rich city boy bullshit."

"Oh, fuck off, Santiago." I jab him with my elbow in the ribs. "What are you doing here anyway? I thought you'd be out in the fields."

"I was, but then I heard Kate wasn't feeling well, so I checked in on her."

He starts walking toward the barn, so I follow after him.

Kate? Sick? My brows shoot up. "What's wrong with her?"

"A stomach bug. She's been throwing up since last night. Although I don't know why, we ate the same damn thing, and I'm feeling fine."

"Maybe it's that stomach of yours that's used to all kinds of bullshit."

"I just hate seeing her sick and not being able to do anything about it." Emmett shoots me a death glare as he slips into an office and goes straight for the duffle sitting in the corner. He rummages through it for a moment before he tosses me a pair of jeans and a shirt.

"Seriously?"

"Yes, seriously. Let's see if you still got what it takes, cowboy. Or did the city pamper your ass for too long, and you forgot what it's like to work with animals?"

I toss the clothes on the chair and strip my shirt off. "I'll show you whose ass got pampered these past four years."

Emmett chuckles. "I don't want to see your skinny ass, Fernandez. Some of us have fiancé's waiting for them at home."

"Hey, you were the one who brought it up."

Sliding the shirt on, I slip the buttons in place before changing into jeans and a pair of boots. Thankfully, Emmett and I are roughly the same size, so his clothes are a good fit because he's right. Most of my work clothes were left behind when I left for college, and there was no way I'd be fitting in any of them now. Not that I wanted to go back home right this minute.

"Okay, boss, whatcha got for me?"

Emmett looks up from his phone, a smirk forming on his lips. "Look at that. He dresses like a cowboy. Let's see if he still remembers how to get his ass on the horse."

I give him a dull look. "You want my help or not, asshole?"

"C'mon, you know I do." Sliding his phone into his pocket, he opens the door, and we step outside.

"You're acting like you were home the last four years when, if I remember correctly, you were up north, hanging out with the Yankees."

"Studying how to lead a ranch. What did you study again?"

I roll my eyes. "Business."

"Right, and the last I checked, you still didn't get that degree." He quirks his brow in a challenge.

He had me there. I had a really good football year my sophomore and junior years of college, so after talking to my coach, I decided to enter the draft early. He wasn't too happy about it, insisting I should finish my degree, but I wanted it. I wanted to play professionally so badly I decided to go against his advice. However, I did promise him and myself I'd get that degree. "I'm actually taking online classes. I have one this summer. It'll be slow, but I'll get that degree finished."

Emmett nods his head as we continue toward the barn. "That's good, man. Football is great, but we both know how quickly things can change."

That was true. I've seen it happen a few times this season.

Fatal career-ending injuries. Not making the final cut. Your luck could turn in a matter of minutes, and then you'd be left with nothing and no backup plan.

"You've got a good agent?"

"Yes, Andrew Hill. He seems like a solid guy, and his agency is one of the best right now. My buddy, Blake, is working with him, too, and he seems happy."

"That's good. You need somebody to look out for your best interests."

"That's the idea." I look around the barn, the intense smell of horses and hay filling my lungs. "You plan on using me to shovel horse shit? Is that your idea of revenge?"

"Nah, I'll leave that for the other people. We're going out riding. Still remember how to saddle the horse?"

That fucker.

I move past him, making sure to check his shoulder on my way. "Of course I fucking remember how to saddle a horse."

Emmett's laughter echoes in the room as he joins me, and together, we saddle our horses and get them out of the barn.

Hopping back on the horse feels like riding a bike. My body was so used to the movement I slipped back into the saddle like no time had passed. Emmett nods at the few ranch hands as we pass by.

"I wanted to go out and check the pastures. Make sure everything is in place, and see if any herds need to be moved."

"Sounds good. Lead the way."

The moment we're far enough from the barn area, we shift into a trot.

My heart rate rises as I lean closer to the horse's neck, my body adjusting to the familiar rhythm as we run over the ground.

Fuck, I missed this.

I missed this a lot.

Contrary to my father's low opinion of me, I didn't hate this lifestyle. I didn't hate the hard work. I didn't hate the animals. I didn't hate being out in the open. There was no way I could ever hate the land that was an intrinsic part of me for the better part of my life.

I just loved football more.

We don't talk as we ride across the Santiago property. I let Emmett take the lead, and I followed him as we went from pasture to pasture. In some parts, Emmett even gets down from his horse to check a fence here or there or talk to the people working the ranch.

It takes us three hours before we finally get back. My legs feel wobbly underneath me as I hop off the horse, every muscle in my body feeling the workout.

I'll be feeling the consequences of riding after so long tomorrow, and I'll be feeling it *good*.

Shifting the reins into one hand, I turn around to find Emmett scowling at his phone.

"What's wrong?"

"Kate hadn't texted me," he mutters, his fingers typing over his screen.

"Maybe she's sleeping," I point out. "You said she wasn't feeling well."

"Maybe." He looks up, his gaze going toward the lake and a slightly smaller house with a dark rooftop built next to it. His place. A home he built for Kate and himself.

My stomach clenches, something bitter making it roll. It takes me a moment to realize what.

Jealousy.

I'm jealous of my best friend. Of what he has.

"Go and check in on her," I tell him softly.

Emmett's head whips toward me. "What? No, I have to cool down Thunder and..."

I take the reins from him. "I'll take care of Thunder; you go and check in on your girl. I know you're dying to."

"She'll hate it. Tell me I'm being too nosy."

"Probably," I agree with a chuckle. "But it'll give you a peace of mind to know she's well enough to grumble about it. So go."

Emmett weighs his options for less than a minute before nodding. "Yeah, I think I'll do it. You sure you're good here?"

"I think we've just established I still have it in me, old man."

"Yeah, yeah, you just think that. The jury is still out. You can't get your cowboy hat back that easily."

"Screw off, Santiago."

"Gladly." Emmett slaps me over the shoulder. "Thanks for doing this, man."

"Anytime." He's already walking away when I yell after him. "You need me to take care of something else while I'm here?"

Suddenly, he turns around. "Actually, there is something that you can do..."

CHAPTER

10

REBECCA

"Thanks, Becky." Mrs. Johnson smiles at me as she pats me on the shoulder on her way out of the café. I place the plate and cup on my tray before wiping the table clean. Since I needed to do the tasting later, I decided to stop by the Reading Nook to make sure everything was running smoothly before I left.

Just as I turn around, I see a woman holding the door for Mrs. Johnson before entering the store.

"Mrs. Santiago!" A big smile spreads over my face as I rush to hug the older woman. Her hands wrap around me tightly as I inhale the scent of wildflowers and sugar that's all her. I take a step back, taking her in. She's wearing a maxi dress that flows around her. Her ginger hair is styled in perfect locks curling around her face. "What are you doing here? I didn't expect you today. Did you get a new haircut?"

Mrs. Santiago lets go of me and places her hand on her hip as she raises her brow in a challenge. "I didn't realize I had to announce myself when I was coming over, young lady."

"Of course you don't, but you are a creature of habit."

Mrs. Santiago left the ranch exactly twice a week. Usually, mid-week to do some grocery shopping, which is when she'd stop for a coffee and chat, and then on Sundays to attend church, after which she'd invite us to come over for dinner.

"You have me there." She slides her hand around my waist. "And yes, I'm actually coming from the salon. I had to get a little refresher and tame all the grays in my hair before the wedding."

"Well, it turned out pretty great. And with that sage green dress, you'll look stunning at the wedding."

"Oh, please." She waves her hand. "I'm just an old lady. No need for me to look stunning. That's for you young ladies."

"Nonsense. Everybody gets to feel stunning regardless of our age. And you, Mrs. S., are one beautiful woman inside and out."

"Thank you, honey. How have things been here? How's your mom? How are *you*?"

The way she asks that final question has me stopping in my tracks as the hair at my nape prickles to attention.

I slowly turn toward her, my eyes meeting hers. "You saw him."

I don't need to tell her who I'm referring to. She already knows.

Mrs. Santiago has been a mother figure to me my whole life, but especially in the last few years. She stepped in when my life was falling around me and helped me pick up the pieces. She was there at my darkest and loneliest time, and our bond only strengthened further. I wasn't sure I would have been able to survive the last few years if it weren't for her.

"I did." She gives me a soft smile.

Nodding, I step away from her. Needing to busy myself, I slip behind the counter and start preparing her order. Just like her schedule, her coffee order is predictable.

"He came to our house this morning looking for Emmett," she continues, not fazed in the slightest, as she takes the seat at the counter. "He seems to be doing well."

"That he does."

"What happened when you saw him?"

My hand stills on the coffee machine as I glance at her over my shoulder. "How do you know I saw him?"

That stubborn brow is up once again. "The return of Miguel Fernandez and everything he's been up to since he came here was the main topic at the salon today."

I close my eyes for a second, inhaling deeply to calm myself.

I love this town. I love the people in it. But damn, they can be nosy.

Letting out a breath, I blink my eyes open to find Mrs. Santiago still watching me intently, only now there is worry hiding in her gaze.

"How are you, really?"

"I'm fine."

"Don't you dare lie to me, Rebecca Allison Williams. I know you better than that."

The machine beeps, so I remove the cup and place a lid on top of it before joining her at the counter.

"What do you want me to tell you?"

"The truth. Always the truth. You know I love Miguel like a son, but what he did to you..." she shakes her head, her lips pressing in a tight line.

"It's been ages. I got over it. I'm—"

"Bullshit," Mrs. Santiago interrupts me, my eyes bulging at her harsh tone. "If you got over it, you'd have a boyfriend right now, maybe even be married."

I feel my cheeks heat under her watchful gaze.

"I've just been busy." I tuck a strand of my hair behind my ear.

Mrs. Santiago scoffs. "That's an excuse, and you know it. You've been guarding your heart ever since that day you came home from Michigan crying, and I had to take you to the hospital."

The ache that I've been suppressing these past few years rises to the surface at her words, the memories of that day as alive as ever.

I look away, forcing them down, down, down.

A warm hand touches mine, making me realize I've been gripping the counter for dear life.

"I hate seeing you hurt, sweet girl."

"I'll be fine." I don't miss the skepticism on her face. "I will," I insist. "He's here for the wedding, and then he'll be gone, and everything will be like it was before."

She raises her hand, her raspy palm cupping my cheek. "I really hope so. Because if he breaks your heart again, he'll hear from me."

"That won't happen."

I wouldn't let it happen.

Not again.

Miguel and I were over.

"Okay."

Letting her hand fall, she swings her purse to the front of her chest. "There was actually a reason I came to see you. I was checking in on Kate, and she asked me to give you this."

Mrs. Santiago pulls out a familiar light-yellow notebook from her bag. Kate's wedding planner.

"How is she doing?"

"Slightly better. She was sleeping when I left her. That stomach bug sure did a number on her. The poor girl looked so pale."

"That sucks. Hopefully, she'll feel better soon. The last thing she needs is to be sick on her wedding day."

"Let's hope that's the case. If nothing changes, I'll make sure she goes to her doctor."

"I don't doubt it for a moment," I let out a soft chuckle. Mrs. Santiago loved pampering her son's friends, embracing Kate and her sister, Penelope, into her fold felt natural for the woman.

I flip through the pages until I find the notes about the cake, along with a few images from Pinterest that Kate found as inspiration.

"Do you need help with any of it?"

I shake my head. "I think I'm good, but thank you."

"That's good. I can't believe the wedding is just around the corner."

Neither could I. It felt like this last year passed in a blur of organization. Since Kate was at Blairwood, she relied on Mrs. Santiago, her Aunt Mabel, and me to help her organize some things, and we spent most of the winter break making decorations for the wedding.

"There is just so much that has to be done. I'm actually on my way to make sure the tent, tables, and chairs will be delivered on time, and they're like we agreed."

We chat for a bit longer about the wedding plans before Mrs. Santiago kisses me goodbye, leaving me with enough time to clean around the café and refill the display between customers before I have to go.

"I shouldn't be too long," I tell Jessica as I take off my apron. "But if you need anything, I have my phone."

"I'll be fine. Go, do your thing."

I glance at the clock. "Shit, I'm already late."

Grabbing my bag from the back room, I dash for the door. "I'll be back soon."

Beads of sweat appear on my forehead as I get out in the hot afternoon. I quickly check the street before crossing to the other side and power-walking all the way to the shop a few streets down.

The bell chimes as I push the door open and enter the shop.

The cool blast of AC hits me and makes goosebumps appear on my skin. Small Treats is the only bakery in town that specializes in cakes, and Kate, being the person that she is, insisted on getting as much of the wedding stuff done locally as possible. The place has been run by the Wilson family since it opened in the early 80s.

"Hey, Becky! How are you doing?" Lisa, one of the Wilson children, asks.

Although a few years younger than me, I've seen her around town. Her older sister, who was my age, left town to go off to college, where she met her husband and moved away.

"Hey, Lisa. I'm doing good. You? Done with school?"

"Yup, I was so ready for it to be over."

I let out a small chuckle. "I can imagine."

Once upon a time, I felt like her. Ready to be done with school and start my life until I realized that with age came responsibilities you never thought you'd need to face. Not at such a young age, and the future I thought I'd have could never exist.

"I'm so ready for my culinary school to start, though. What can I do for you?"

"That's amazing. Congrats! I actually need to talk to your mom. Kate was supposed to come to sample the cakes for her wedding, but she's not feeling well, so she sent me to do it for her."

"Oh, that sucks. At least it's not too close to her wedding day."

"True that." It would have sucked if she was sick on her wedding day after all the preparations and everything. "Hopefully, it's just a bug, and she'll be back to her old self soon."

"Fingers crossed! Mom's in the back. I'll let her know you're here."

"Thanks."

Lisa slips through the door into the back room, and I move closer to the counter, checking out the different options they have in the shop. My mouth waters at the sight of the strawberry cake in the display, reminding me I haven't eaten anything since breakfast.

The doorbell chimes once again, and I instinctively turn around, but the smile on my face drops when I see the person standing in the doorway.

"Miguel."

CHAPTER

II

MIGUEL

"Miguel."

My steps falter, a shiver going down my spine at the sound of my name in that low, husky voice that some nights I could still hear in my dreams.

What the hell is she doing here?

At least, I'm not the only one surprised by our encounter. Becky's mouth falls open for a second before she can school her features. That mask of indifference slipping into place as her eyes narrowed at me.

"Rebecca." I nod in greeting.

Her eyes twitch at the use of her full name, and I have to force myself to keep my face straight.

God, I missed messing with her.

It was so easy to rile her up; it always has been. I loved watching that fire blaze in her hazel eyes, loved seeing her fierce temper come to life. Fighting with her was always the best because I knew once we made up, it would be just as good as the fight was, better even.

My stomach clenches at the anticipation, and I must remind myself that this wasn't why I was here.

She grits her teeth, her fingers curling into fists by her sides. "What are you doing here?"

"I'm here to taste some cake."

"What?"

"I'm here for the cake tasting," I repeat, rolling my shoulders. I could feel that twitch of pain stabbing through my shoulder. Or maybe it was the tension building inside of me. "Emmett asked me to come. He and Kate were supposed to do it, but she's not feeling well."

"Emmett..." She lets out a long breath, and I can see her nostrils flaring slightly. It takes me all of two seconds to connect the dots. "But you knew that."

"Of course I know that. Because Kate called me this morning and asked *me* to come and take care of the cake stuff! Something Emmett is well aware of."

That mother fucker.

I should have known he had something up his sleeve when he asked me to do this. There was just something about the way he asked the question. I didn't think too much about it at the time because I was looking for an excuse to stay out of my parent's place, but thinking back now...

"Huh," I say slowly, feeling the corner of my lips tilting upward. "So, I guess we're both here for the cake tasting."

"Both..." Those big eyes widen even further, color slowly making its way up her neck.

I know I should probably be as pissed at Emmett as she was. The asshole did this on purpose. He was playing with fire by pushing us together, and he knew it. But I couldn't deny a part of me was glad for it. If for nothing else, it was worth it for the look of complete outrage on her face.

I raise my brows at her. "Yes?"

"That's not ne—"

Before she can finish, Mrs. Wilson comes into the room.

"Hey, Becky, it's so nice to see you." The older woman wipes her hands on the towel as she glances from Becky to me and back, curiosity clearly written on her face. "Miguel, well, what a surprise."

"More like a nuisance," Becky mutters to herself, but nobody misses her quiet jab.

Deciding to ignore it, I turn to Mrs. Wilson and give her my most charming smile as I extend my hand. "Mrs. Wilson, it's so nice to see you again. You look just like you did before I left."

Becky makes a gagging sound as Mrs. Wilson blushes, waving me off.

"Oh, please! I guess some things never change. You're still the same charmer you were four years ago."

I let out a small chuckle, rubbing the back of my neck. "I'd love to think I grew up a little in the last few years."

The woman gives me a once-over. "Well, you certainly did that."

Becky lets out an irritated sound. "I'm sorry to interrupt, but can we focus on the task at hand? Some of us have to get back to work."

Mrs. Wilson turns her attention to Becky. "Of course, honey. I'm sure you're really busy. C'mon, let's sit down, and we can get to tasting." She turns around and goes to the table in the corner, glancing over her shoulder as she walks. "Lisa told me about Kate. I have every—"

Turning on her heels, Becky marches after Mrs. Wilson. I tune them out as my eyes scan her from head to toe. The swing of dark red hair falling down her back, the seductive sway of her hips with every step she takes, the way those cutoff shorts hug her ass like they were made for her.

Get a grip, dude, I chastise, running my hand over my scruffy jaw.

Swallowing the lump in my throat, I follow after the

women. My hand falls on the back of the chair, only to collide with hers. Rebecca looks up, those big, round eyes meeting mine. Up close like this, I could see the mix of different colors in her irises. The moss green, mixing with brown, and a few specks of gold sprinkled in between. The dark, long lashes surrounding them.

"What are you doing?"

"Tasting cake?"

Her teeth grind together. "I told you already. I don't need you here. I can do this myself."

Oh, I didn't doubt it for a second. Nobody could accuse Rebecca Williams of being incompetent. But this wasn't about that.

It was about her wanting to establish control.

Her wanting to chase me away.

But she should know me better than that.

I pull the chair out for her. "I don't mind. I like cake."

"I'll go and grab the samples," Mrs. Wilson says, leaving the two of us alone in a staring match.

Becky narrows her eyes, clearly exasperated with me.

Well, that makes two of us, Red.

"Shouldn't you be avoiding sweets?" She takes a seat, making a point of sliding her own chair closer to the table. "You know, so you can stay in shape?"

Stubborn woman.

I wait for her to glance back at me before quirking my brow at her. "Worried about me, Red?"

Those hazel eyes flash angrily, and I know I hit a nerve. "Don't call me that."

Two can play this game, sweetheart.

"It's off-season." I shrug nonchalantly, sliding into the chair next to hers. "Besides, it's not like a little bit of cake will hurt anybody."

I lean back in my chair, sliding my hand over my flat stomach. My finger slips under the hem of my shirt, tugging it upward and revealing my abs.

Rebecca's gaze zeroes in on my movements, her eyes trailing my arm and locking on the patch of revealed skin. My stomach tightens as the warmth spreads through me, her fixation almost like a physical touch.

Almost, but not quite.

"See something you like?" I ask, my voice coming out rougher than intended.

The color spreading over her cheeks turns brighter at being caught staring.

"As if," she scoffs, looking away.

"Mhmm, totally imagining things."

Her lips press in a tight line, and I swear I can hear her grind her teeth, which only makes my smile widen.

"Besides, I'm the best man. It feels like it's my duty to give my opinion on the cake if the bride and groom can't be here. It seems only fair."

Just then, Mrs. Wilson joins us, a tray with plates filled with different kinds of cakes in her hands. I flash her my most charming smile. "Wouldn't you say so, Mrs. Wilson?"

The older woman blushes visibly. "Of course! More opinions are definitely welcome."

I turn to Becky, who's throwing daggers at me. "See?"

"Whatever." She rolls her eyes at me. "Let's get this over with."

Mrs. Wilson puts the tray on the table in front of us. There are half a dozen plates, all with a single slice of cake on top of them, a couple of forks, and glasses of water. "Okay, here are some of the flavors I discussed with Kate and Emmett when they were here last time. Take your time trying them out, and I'll be back in a bit."

Rebecca opens her mouth as if she wants to protest, but just then, the door chimes as another customer walks in. Pressing her lips together, she glances at me, and we just stare at one another for a moment.

Blinking, she ducks her head, breaking the contact. Her hair falls in her face, shielding it from my gaze, and my hand itches to reach out and tuck it behind her ear. To feel that silkiness between my fingers once again, wrap it around my wrist as I...

Do not go there.

I clench my fist, my nails biting into my palms.

"I guess we should get to tasting," Becky murmurs, utterly ignorant of the thoughts swirling inside my head. Maybe it's better that way. I was pretty sure she wouldn't like them one bit.

I shouldn't like them either. Shouldn't be thinking about them. Shouldn't be thinking about *her*.

We were done.

Because of her.

She was the one who left, after all. The one who didn't have a problem with walking away without a backward glance, without giving me a chance to explain.

Rebecca picks one of the forks and jabs it into the first piece of cake, a dark biscuit with light brown frosting. She brings it to her mouth, wrapping those pretty pink lips around the fork.

My dick twitches as I watch her chew, a low moan coming from deep in her throat.

Fuck me.

Why did I think this would be a good idea again?

Becky nods her head absentmindedly as she digs into the second cake, this one with strawberries, and once again, that little moan comes out slightly louder this time.

I shift in my seat, moving toward the table so that she doesn't notice the bulge growing in my lap.

Although I know I should look away, my eyes stay locked on

her mouth, on that trace of frosting clinging to the corner of her lips.

She must feel my eyes on her because she looks up, her tongue darting out and sliding over her lips, only to miss that bit of frosting.

She eyes me suspiciously. "Didn't you say you want to taste the cake?"

There are so many things I want to taste, cake being the last thing on my mind.

"Yeah," I mutter, my voice coming out rough. I clear my throat, shifting my attention to the plate.

Just focus on the freaking cake, Fernandez.

That's all.

Cake.

Blindly, I reach for the fork, stabbing it into the piece closest to me and bringing it to my mouth. The sweet taste of chocolate touches my tongue. My eyes fall shut, and I let out a loud groan.

"Fuck, that's good."

It's been ages since I ate cake. Probably the last time I was in Bluebonnet, and I forgot how good it tasted. Considering going pro has been my whole focus these past four years, I've been keeping up with a rigorous nutritionist and workout schedule. And that meant cutting some things out of my life. I could already see my team doctor giving me dirty looks, but this might just be worth it after all.

The silence is the only thing that greets me. Blinking my eyes open, I find Rebecca staring at me. Her eyes are focused on my mouth, a soft flush spreading over her cheeks as her teeth sink into her bottom lip.

The corner of my mouth twitches, but I do my best to keep my composure.

So, I'm not the only one affected by this. Good.

Taking a piece of cake, I extend the fork toward her. "C'mon, try it."

Her mouth falls open, a look of panic flashing over her face for a split second before she narrows those hazel eyes on me once again.

"I'm doing no such thing," she mutters, her cheeks turning an even brighter shade of red.

"Aren't we here to sample cake? You can't not try all of them. How will you know which ones are the best?"

"Oh, I know all about your *sampling*." She shakes her head, an unamused smirk twisting her mouth. Her voice is cold, but I don't miss the angry bite hiding behind her words.

"Rebecca..." I try, but she ignores me. Her fingers grip the fork in her hand so tightly her knuckles have turned white.

"Fine. I'll taste the damn cake," she utters, changing the subject. Ignoring my fork, she goes for the cake herself. She takes a piece and brings it to her mouth, all the while pretending as if I'm not there at all. Little wench. My fingers twitch with the need to put them on her shoulders and give her a firm shake, but I hold back the urge.

Instead, I watch her chew slowly, mindful of every line of her face; as if I stare long enough, I'll be able to understand the woman sitting next to me. Back in the day, I knew her face like I knew my own. I could read her like a book. No matter how hard she tried to hide her emotions, she couldn't hide them from me, but right now, I wasn't sure what was going through her head. And I hated it. Because maybe if I could, I'd understand where things went wrong and why we fell apart.

Finally, she places the fork on her plate, still not uttering a word.

My chest tightens with unease like a heavy weight has fallen on me.

"Re—"

"How are we doing over here? Did you find something you like?" Mrs. Wilson asks as she joins us once again.

Rebecca swallows, nodding. "Good. I think we should go with the peanut butter and chocolate one." She points at the first cake. "Everybody loves chocolate, so I don't think we can go wrong with something *reliable*." She gives me a pointed look before shifting her attention to Mrs. Wilson and flashing her a smile. "And then maybe two different types of cupcakes. One with fruit and another chocolate option?"

"Great choice. Hopefully, the bride and groom will like them."

I didn't think either Kate or Emmett cared one bit for the cake or the other details. They just wanted to finally get married and be together.

"Well, let's hope so. I like them, so I might just be tempted to eat them myself otherwise," Becky chuckles.

"So glad to hear it, honey. I'll write that down for ya."

"Great. Thanks, Mrs. Wilson. Now, if you'll excuse me, I really need to get back to Reading Nook."

Before I can react, she gets to her feet and slides her bag over her shoulder, dashing for the door like the room is on fire.

I push back, the chair scraping against the floor. "Rebecca, wa—" The bell above the door chimes as she exits the bakery, yelling a loud goodbye. "Fuck!"

I run my hand over my face, letting it drop by my side, when a hand pats my shoulder, reminding me I'm not alone.

"Sorry, Mrs. Wilson."

"It's fine. Just give her time. She's been hurting for a very long time."

Her words make my stomach tie in a knot as the trepidation sinks in.

"She isn't the only one," I mumble, that familiar irritation at what had happened growing inside of me. All the things that could have happened differently if only...

If only.

Shaking my head, I give the woman a small smile. "Thanks for the cake, Mrs. Wilson. It's as amazing as always."

"Of course. Maybe you should try that charm of yours on her. It worked the first time."

I shake my head. "I don't know about that. We're too broken for that."

"Oh, please. There is no such thing as too broken. Even the smallest pieces can be put together if one wants to." She gives me a pointed look. "The question is, do you want to?"

CHAPTER

12

REBECCA

"Hey, I'm home."

Stepping inside the house, I make sure the door is locked, and the key is safely stored in my bag before slipping off my shoes. My feet ache from standing all day at the café. It was another long day with countless customers, most of whom wanted to talk about *him*. Apparently, somebody saw us sitting together at Small Treats the other day, and now everybody thought we were back together. It was annoying as hell, and Jessica couldn't come fast enough so I could disappear inside the kitchen once again. Seriously, by the time he gets out of Bluebonnet, I'll have to give that girl a raise.

Silence greets me as I turn around and walk down the hallway. I peek into the living room to find it empty, so I continue to the kitchen, where Linda is cleaning.

"Hey, Linda, where is everybody?"

The older woman turns around, a smile on her lips. "Becky, I didn't hear you come in. Chase got a call from the shelter about a stray dog roaming around, so he went to check it out. And your mom is up in her room. She had a tough day, so I put her to bed early."

"Shit." I run my hand over my face.

Mom having a rough day was never a good thing. And after today, this was the last thing I needed to hear.

I glance up the stairs. "I'll go check in on her."

Linda offers me a sad smile and a nod. Turning my back on her, I take two steps at a time as I climb up. The door at the end of the hallway is left slightly ajar. Bypassing my room, I go straight for Mom's, pushing it gently open all the way.

Just like Linda said, she's sleeping in her bed. Her chest rising and falling evenly under the sheet. I slip inside and walk closer to the bed, my heart aching at the sight of her.

She looked so peaceful when she slept. Like the woman she used to be. Before.

Lifting my hand, I tuck a strand of her silvery hair that slipped onto her face back as I watch her for a moment longer, soaking in this rare moment as the ache makes my heart tighten.

With one last caress, I pull back, exiting the room as quietly as I entered and leaving the door slightly open. Dropping my things into my room, my sight falls on Kate's wedding planner. I was hoping to drop it off after the tasting, but things at the café got crazy, and then Mom had one of her episodes...

There weren't enough hours in any given day for me to do everything.

Glancing longingly toward the open door of my bathroom and the bathtub that's calling my name, I let out a sigh.

Later tonight, I promise myself.

My reflection in the mirror catches my attention as I start to turn around. My ponytail is a mess, and I'm pretty sure there is a chocolate stain on my shirt.

Grabbing the hem, I pull the shirt over my head and toss it into the bin before slipping into a fresh one. I rub the stain on my face off and run a brush through my hair, calling it good.

On my way out of the room, I pick up the binder, my phone,

and keys before gently descending the stairs so I don't wake Mom up.

"Linda, I have to go over to Kate's for a moment. It shouldn't take too long. Will you be okay?"

I hated leaving her alone now that I was actually off work, but I knew that if I didn't go to Kate's now, I wasn't sure when I would be able to do it. Besides, I wanted to check in on her because she hadn't texted me today when I asked her how she was doing.

"Of course. You go on ahead. We're good here."

"You're a lifesaver, Linda. I'll be back shortly."

I quickly make my way to the truck. The old thing coughs in protest, but on the third try, I manage to start it.

Go to the mechanic. Just another thing to add to my never-ending to-do list.

The soft country music fills the cabin as I drive to Kate and Emmett's place. Their house is lit up when I park in front of it some ten minutes later behind an unfamiliar black SUV.

Did their college friends arrive already? I was pretty sure Kate said they were coming a couple of days before the ceremony.

Unbuckling my seatbelt, I go toward the door and ring the bell. It echoes inside the house for a moment, but soon enough, I can hear the footsteps moving closer.

"You look like crap," I say the moment the door opens, and I'm met with Kate's pale face. Her blue eyes look tired, and the dark bags underneath are even more prominent against her ivory skin.

Kate tucks a strand of her dark hair that fell out of the messy bun behind her ear. "Don't you start with this too."

"Start with what?" I walk past her and down the hallway. "Why aren't you resting?"

"Start nagging. Emmett's been coming home to check on me five times a day, and if he's not here, he keeps texting. And then there is Mrs. Santiago and even Aunt Mabel was here, and then Dad stopped by earlier today also. My house is starting to feel like an airport."

"Because you have people who care and are worried about you."

"I know, and I feel guilty even saying it." Kate lets out a sigh. "But if one more person comes and brings something to eat, I'll have nowhere to put it."

"So I shouldn't have brought my new cherry and dark chocolate muffins I baked for you to try?" I ask, lifting the bag in the air.

Kate's attention turns to the bag, and I can see interest peak behind her eyes. "Dark chocolate, you said?"

"Mhmm... I guess, if you *really* don't want it, I can take it home..."

I don't get to finish before Kate snatches the bag from me. "Gimmie."

Laughing, I watch as she opens it, pulls a carton out of the bag, and grabs one muffin, biting into it.

"Damn, this is so good."

"Is it? I wanted to make something that's not too sweet." I shrug, the edge of the notebook digging into my arm. "Oh, and I brought you this too. I'm sorry I didn't get it back to you the other day. I was planning to, but Mom wasn't feeling well, and by the time I helped her to bed, it was already late."

"It's fine. We're almost done anyway. How was the cake tasting?"

"It was..."

I look around, trying to come up with an appropriate answer, but Miguel's face is the only thing that comes to mind.

Frustrating? Infuriating? Overwhelming?

There were so many feelings swirling inside of me at that

moment, all tangled up together to the point I didn't know where one begins and the other ends.

It was all too much.

Miguel's scent was impossible to ignore since we were sitting so close together, his knee bumping into mine under the table. That little boy's smile that spreads over his face when he tastes something he likes was like a kick to my gut because it threw me back to the past when I would bake something new, and he'd try it for the first time. It was like I was sixteen again and just wanted to see the boy I loved smile.

"Let's go out," I croak out, my voice tight. Not waiting for an answer, I start toward the sliding door. "We can sit on the back porch and..."

"Becky, don—"

I come to a stop when I see the two figures working under the setting sun right before the dock that leads out onto the lake stretching out behind Emmett and Kate's house. The golds, oranges, and reds illuminate the golden skin that's on display, his muscles flexing as he holds the arch while Emmett works on pinning it in place.

"I'm so sorry." Kate's hand falls on my shoulder, snapping me out of my thoughts.

My throat bobs as I swallow. "He's here."

Of course it was him.

I should have known the moment I saw the car parked out front, and I should have run.

"I tried to tell you." Kate nibbles at her lower lip. "Are you angry?"

I force out a smile. "Why would I be angry? He's your friend and Emmett's best man. Of course he'd be here."

I just wish I knew so I could stay the hell away.

"He's been helping Emmett at the ranch since he got back. I

think he's just looking for an excuse to stay away from his parent's place."

I could see how that would be the case, knowing how things turned out the last time Miguel and his dad were in the same room.

"You don't have to give me any explanations, Kate. I just stopped by to return your planner and let you know the cake is taken care of, or maybe you know that already, considering Emmett sent Miguel to join me."

Kate lifts her hands in surrender. "That was his brilliant idea."

"Oh, I know, and he'll get his soon," I mumble, my attention once again straying to the men.

"And you have my full support." Kate's hand slides around my waist. "How did it really go, though?"

"Fine."

"Bullshit. You don't look fine."

No, I didn't feel fine at all. I felt unsettled. I knew it would be hard to avoid Miguel because this damn town was too small as it was, but I couldn't imagine that he'd be jumping out at me from every nook and corner.

"You don't look fine either." I glance at her, changing the subject. "Have you gone to the doctor yet?"

Kate's eyes narrow. "We were not talking about me."

"Well, tough luck, isn't it?"

"You can't avoid this forever, you know?"

My lips press in a tight line. "I can damn sure try."

Kate's face softens. "What happened between you two, Becky?"

The sound of Miguel's laughter has me looking up and watching him.

I could still see the expression on his face the last time I saw him. It was etched into my memory, as vivid as it was the day it happened.

The shock on his face at seeing me.

The desperation as the realization of what was going on set in.

The anger when I walked away.

My stomach tightens, and my hand presses against it.

The pain as the last string holding onto the world I knew shattered into pieces all around me.

I shake my head, pushing the memories back. "It doesn't matter, Kate. He's here. He's your friend, not that I'd ask anything different of you. What happened happened. It's behind us and has been for years. He's going to leave after the wedding, and I'll go back to my life, and everything will be like it used to be."

"I'm just worried about you. You've been different since we got back. Quieter. More reserved."

"I just have a lot on my mind, that's all."

A hand slips around my shoulder, pulling me into a firm body. "And look who finally showed up."

MIGUEL

Becky's elbow connects with Emmett's gut, pushing him away. "Get your sweaty ass away from me, Santiago."

I couldn't believe she was here, but it was her alright. There was no mistaking that particular shade of red hair for any other person than Rebecca. She and Kate were standing on the front porch, leaning against the railing and talking, which gave me a minute to compose myself.

"If I remember correctly, you didn't mind our sweaty asses when you jumped all over us after winning a football game back in the day."

"Then you were in my good graces, which I can't say is the case right now." She gives him a pointed look, crossing her arms over her chest.

The corner of Emmett's mouth tips upward, but he schools his features quickly. "I don't know what you're talking about."

"Oh, you know perfectly well what I'm referring to."

Her gaze moves over Emmett's shoulder, those hazel eyes settling on mine. For a second, she just stares at me, and I can feel goosebumps rise on my skin under her watchful eyes.

"Miguel," she tilts her chin in greeting, that mask of complete indifference on her face before turning back to our friends, and I know what's coming even before she opens her mouth. "My job here's done. I think I'll leave you—"

Running away once again.

At this point, I wasn't even surprised.

"Nonsense!" Kate protests. "You should stay for dinner. I put the lasagna Mrs. Santiago brought over in the oven a little while ago. I think it should be done by now."

"Kate," Rebecca sighs. "I don't..."

"C'mon, Becs. We have yet to talk about the party next week."

I open my mouth to say I'll just go when Kate turns to me, a stern expression on her face. "None of you are leaving. I have all this food in the fridge that people brought over that I don't know what to do with. So you'll sit your asses down, eat the food, and we'll talk about everything that has to be done for the party once our friends from Blairwood come. Was I clear?"

"Yes, ma'am," I say, just as Rebecca mutters, "Fine."

"Great. Now I'm going to..."

Emmett gently pushes Kate toward the loveseat. "Sit your butt down while I go check the dinner."

Kate looks over her shoulder. "I can do it."

"But you don't have to." He presses a kiss to the top of her head. "Be back in a bit."

Kate is shaking her head, but she doesn't try to protest.

I could see why Emmett was worried, though. When I first got to their house earlier, she was white like a wall. Apparently, she's been throwing up again. Since then, some of the color has returned to her cheeks.

"I swear this man drives me crazy."

"He's just worried about you." Rebecca slips into the chair next to Kate. "So, what did you want to discuss about the party?"

I listen with half an ear as the two of them talk about the party and all the stuff that needs to be taken care of by then. Banners, and bows, and balloons, and a dozen other shit like that. At one point, Rebecca pulls out her phone and starts making a list. Like seriously, it's just a party.

It doesn't take long for Emmett to come back to the porch, plates and cutlery in one hand, two beer bottles in another.

"Can you bring the booze?" he asks me as he sets the table.

"You know it. Anything else?"

"Nah, I think we have everything else under control."

He dips back into the house for the drinks and the food before finally joining us.

I grab a piece of lasagna and dive into it. Emmett and I've been working all afternoon, and I am starving. Besides, Mrs. Santiago's food was always delicious, and this wasn't an exception.

"Here you go." Emmett hands Kate a plate, but she eyes the

plate carefully, that little bit of the color that had returned to her cheeks draining from her face.

"Umm... you just eat."

Emmett's eyes narrow as he takes her in. "Again?" He lifts the plate to his nose and smells the food. "It seems good." His attention shifts to me. "Does it taste funky?"

"No, it's perfect as usual."

"It really is good," Rebecca agrees, wiping her mouth with a napkin. "Are you sure you're okay?"

"Yeah, fine. Maybe my stomach is still recovering from earlier."

"How about I go and make you some soup?" Emmett starts to lower his plate on the table, but Kate places her hand on his thigh, giving it a squeeze.

"Eat, you've been working all day. I'll just take one of these muffins. But please don't tell your mother I didn't eat it. She'll think I hate her cooking, which is not the case."

"That's not true. Mom loves you and is worried. She would try to bring something else, though."

"That's what I keep telling her!" Kate sighs. "I just feel so bad for not eating, but I'm really apprehensive it'll all come back out if I do."

Emmett cups her cheek. "It's fine, baby. Just eat those muffins. I don't think I saw you eat anything all day."

"I had breakfast, and we know how that turned out," she sighs. "I just hope it passes before people start coming over."

"When is that happening?"

"The Blairwood crew will be coming on Friday morning, and Mom in the afternoon."

My brows shoot up. "Your mom is coming?"

Kate and her sister moved to Bluebonnet when we were seventeen, but then her mom suddenly showed up and tried to take the Adams sisters back to LA. In the end, they managed to convince her to let them stay here, but I didn't realize she would be coming to the ceremony.

"Yeah, we sent her the invite, but I never imagined she'd want to come back. Not after staying away for so long."

"Huh, interesting."

"I guess something's in the air since everybody seems to be returning home these days."

I turn to Rebecca, not missing the silent jab from her. My lips press into a tight line as the irritation spreads inside of me. And here I thought tonight was going well.

"If the person's worth coming back for, I don't see why it would be surprising." The words are out of my mouth before I can think them through.

Rebecca flinches like I slapped her, and I feel a foot connect with mine under the table.

"Yeah, I guess you're right. *Some* people are worth coming for, and others will show you their true colors when you catch them unprepared."

She pushes her chair back, gets to her feet, and starts picking up plates. "I'll take care of dishes."

Without another look in my direction, or any of us really, she slips back into the house.

"Seriously, dude?" Emmett hisses the moment she's out of earshot.

"What?" I ask defensively, my gaze zeroing in on Rebecca's form as she moves in the kitchen, her mouth moving as if she's muttering to herself. Knowing her, she's probably cursing me. It wouldn't be the first time. "She started it first."

I know I probably sound like a petulant child, but seriously, did she have to bring this whole thing up? She knew why I couldn't come home back then. Even if the entire situation with my dad hadn't happened, between my class schedule and practice, games, and traveling, I barely had enough time to sleep, much less drive twenty-plus hours to get back to Texas to see her. I hated it, but she refused to move with me, and she knew what was at stake—my future. *Our* future.

Phone calls and texts were our best bet and primary form of communication. If she answered them, that is.

Four years ago

My fingers clench around the strap of my backpack as I listen to the phone ring, and ring, and ring.

Where the hell is she?

"Hey, babe," Rebecca says when she finally picks up the phone.

"Hey..." There is a loud rumbling filling the background. My brows pull together. "Where are you?"

"Driving back home," Rebecca sighs. "I had a class, and then I stayed in the library to work on a project. I turned off my phone so I could concentrate, but time just flew by."

"Oh, I tried calling you, but you never picked up."

Or answered any of my messages, but I bite my tongue to stop the words from coming. I knew she was busy too, but damn, I missed her. We've been inseparable our whole lives, to suddenly be away from the person that was your everything... I didn't know how to deal with that.

"I'm sorry. It's just been a crazy day, and I really needed to finish this assignment because it's due tonight."

And now I feel like a whiny asshole.

"Don't worry about it. I'm acting stupid. I was anxious because you always text me on game day, but..."

"Shit, I completely spaced out. How did the game go?"

"We won." The corner of my mouth twitches upward. "Wiped the floor with them, actually. Forty-two to zero."

"That's amazing. Did you get to play?"

"Yes."

The post-game excitement is still coursing through me, and now that I've managed to talk to Rebecca, I finally feel at peace. I get into describing the final touchdown when she suddenly interrupts me.

"Shit, I have to go, Miguel."

"What?" *Go? Where was she going? Didn't she just say she was driving home?* "But we just started talking."

"I know, and I'm sorry. I'll call you later, okay? I really need to go."

"Is everything okay?"

"Yeah, I just... I'll call you later."

"Yeah, fi—" The call disconnects. "—ne."

Now

The sliding door opens, snapping me out of my thoughts. Rebecca steps out, her eyes landing on mine. The cold indifference shining in her irises shakes me to my very core. I was used to Rebecca's anger, hell, I expected it, but this... This was something different.

Before either of us can say anything, a phone buzzes on the table. Something flashes on her face, but it's gone so quickly I don't get a chance to process it before she grabs the device. "I need to take this."

ANNA B. DOE

Without another word, she gets up and slips into the house.

"What is that all about?" I exchanged a look with Emmett, who just shrugged his shoulders, but from the worried expression on his face, he knew what was going on. He just didn't want to tell me.

"I really need to go," Rebecca says to Kate as she exits. "But if you need anything else for the party, let me know, okay?"

"Sounds good. And we have the final dress fitting next week."

"Right, pick me up for that one?"

"You know it."

"Call the damn doctor, Kate." With a quick hug, Rebecca grabs the rest of her things and leaves without another glance my way.

Running my hand over my face, I let out a sigh. "I hope she didn't leave because of the comment."

Kate shifts her attention to me. "Not that you weren't a jackass, but Becky just has a lot on her plate right now."

"What does that mean?" I ask, feeling the irritation sizzle under my skin at the vague comment.

What the hell was going on with Rebecca that they felt like they needed to keep it hidden from me?

"It's Becky's story to tell."

There it was again, evading the answer.

Was it just because of me and the history we shared, or would the answer be the same regardless of who was asking?

And more important than that, why couldn't I just let it go?

I grab one of the muffins from the box and pop it into my mouth. The rich taste of dark chocolate mixed with cherries hits my tongue, and I groan loudly.

"Fuck, that's good. Did you make it?"

"No, Becky brought those."

I guess I should have figured that out. Rebecca was always

the one who was doing something in the kitchen. Usually, I was the one who she'd bring the first batch of whatever new treat she came up with. She always joked that it was because I had a strong stomach, but the reality was that I didn't need a strong stomach. Everything that she prepared was just that good.

My thoughts run a hundred miles an hour as I polish off the rest of the muffin and dust off my palms.

"I guess I should let you guys rest."

I push to my feet, but Kate's soft question stops me in my tracks.

"Miguel?"

"Kitty," Emmett tries to take her hand, but she brushes him off.

"No, Emmett, I have to say this."

I look at her, my brow rising. "Say whatever you want to say."

"I love you, but you hurt Becky one more time, and you'll have to deal with me."

"I wouldn't expect anything different."

CHAPTER

13

REBECCA

"Hey, can you keep an eye on the café?" The door to the kitchen closes behind me as I glance at Jessica, who's making an order for a customer. "I want to drop these off at school for Savannah. She was supposed to pick them up, but she forgot. I shouldn't be too long."

Since Savannah coached peewee football for the summer, she brought her team muffins every Friday so they could wrap the week up on a high note. It was really sweet, and I had so much fun decorating them differently each time, but today, she was nowhere to be found.

Jessica glances up as the machine buzzes, the smell of caffeine spreading through the room. "Yeah, sure."

"Thanks." Untying the apron around my waist, I eye the coffee pot. "But before that..."

I quickly make Sav's favorite order, placing the lid on the to-go cup so it doesn't spill. Coffee in one hand, the bag with goodies in the other, I jump into my truck that's parked in the alley next to the café. It takes me a few tries, but the dumb thing finally comes to life.

I wave at a few people as I pull out of my parking spot and drive toward the school. Since there aren't many students in

Bluebonnet, all grades are on the same campus, only in different buildings, with the athletic fields situated by the parking lot. My gaze falls on the high school football field. It's a natural reaction. I'd spent countless hours of my childhood sitting on those bleachers as I watched Emmett and Miguel practice and play football. It didn't matter if it was sunny or raining. If they were on the field, I was usually right there with them, a book in hand, cheering them on.

I expect the field to be empty, but just as I'm about to look away, my gaze zeros in on the lone figure jogging around the track. Almost on instinct, my foot lets off the gas, and the truck slows down. My fingers tighten around the steering wheel as the figure moves closer, the anticipation making my heart beat wildly in my chest.

Of course, it's him.

Miguel.

Who else would it be?

I was seriously starting to question what the hell I did to deserve this much bad luck when it came to this man.

It shouldn't be this hard to avoid him. Yes, Bluebonnet was small, but still. It felt like I was being punished for something.

He's wearing a pair of basketball shorts and sneakers. A ball cap is propped on his head, but even so, I can see his hair curling around the brim, headphones covering his ears as he jogs under the bright morning sun. His skin glistens with sweat, making me wonder how long he's been at it.

I sink my teeth into my lower lip. I know I should drive off, but I couldn't force myself to look away.

It had been years since I last saw him work out or play. The day we broke up, I made a promise to myself to not seek him out. I blocked him on social media. I didn't watch sports on television, not that I had time to do it anyway. I wouldn't even have known he made it to the pros if I hadn't heard it from the people in town, especially after his team made it to the playoffs last season.

He made it.

He got his dream after all.

A part of me was happy for him. I knew better than most how hard he worked, but the other part... The other part couldn't help but wonder, was it worth it? Him leaving, his betrayal, my heartbreak... was it all worth it?

Forcing myself to look away from the figure on the field, I press my foot against the gas and drive to the smaller field on the side.

Parking my car in the first open space, I grab the bag and coffee cup and jump out. Almost immediately, I'm greeted by the loud yelling coming from the sidelines.

Following the sounds, I find Savannah standing by the field. A ball cap is placed on top of her head, a whistle hanging around her neck as she cheers loudly at a girl who's probably five or six that's rushing toward the end zone. Some of her friends, standing by Savannah on the sidelines, jump around as the girl all but falls into the end zone.

A smile curls my lips as I watch Savannah fist pump in victory, just as the kids rush toward their friend on the field, pulling her in a group hug.

"Good game, Coach," I say as I come to a stop next to her.

"Hey, Becs." Sav turns around, a beaming smile on her lips. "Thanks. It's good to see the kids happy."

"I brought you coffee and muffins."

Her eyes fall on the package in my hands. "Shi— Shoot. Grams was being difficult, so I was running late and completely spaced out."

"No worries. I figured, so I decided to drive here and bring you your order. Which seems to be right on time for a celebratory snack."

When nobody applied to coach peewee football, Savannah decided to step up and do it herself. Although she doesn't know much about the game, she felt terrible when she heard about it and saw how some of her kids were disappointed.

"You're a Godsend. How much do I owe you?"

"Coach!" kids start yelling, demanding Savannah's attention.

I wave her off. "We'll settle it later. Go and have fun."

Savannah points her finger at me. "Don't think I'll forget." She takes a step back. "Drinks this week?"

I nibble at the inside of my cheek. "I don't know, Sav. I've been so absent with all the wedding stuff going on. I don't..."

"C'mon, it's just one drink. An hour tops. I need somebody to complain about Mark."

"Ugh, what did he do now?"

I swear I don't know why she couldn't just dump the guy and be done with him already. She deserved so much better than the guy who always put himself first.

"I'll tell you over the drinks at The Hut. It'll even be my treat since I know you won't let me pay for the muffins."

I guess she had me there.

"Fine." I lift my finger. "*One* drink, and I get to choose the day."

"Perfect!" She flashes me a grin as the kids pull her away. Shaking my head, I turn around and start walking back to my car. As I leave the kid's field, my gaze instantly goes to the larger football field.

Biting the inside of my cheek, I look at it momentarily. I should go to my vehicle and get back to the café. I had barely enough time to breathe these days, but it was like an invisible string was pulling me toward it.

I slowly move closer until my fingers touch the metal fence surrounding it. I curl my finger through the metal loops as I

ANNA B. DOE

inhale deeply, the scent of freshly cut grass invading my senses.

How many times had I sat out there on the bleachers?

Too many to count.

It didn't matter if it was practice or a game; if Emmett and Miguel were out on the field, you could find me sitting on the bleachers watching them. It was like seeing magic happen. They were that good.

Memories from high school, the ones that I locked into a box after Miguel and I broke up, rush back to the surface, making it hard to breathe.

Cheering them on from the bleachers.

Running to the field after the game and jumping into their awaiting arms.

The first time Miguel slipped his jersey over my head.

The heated look in his eyes as he took me in.

His hands cupping my cheeks.

The feel of his rugged fingertips as they caressed my face.

I close my eyes, that familiar ache squeezes my lungs, making it hard to breathe.

Go. My throat bobs as I swallow the lump that has formed there. *I need to go.*

I shouldn't have come here in the first place.

There was a reason why I avoided it this whole time.

And now that he was back, it was even more important that I stay away and protect myself. Protect my heart.

My ears are buzzing as I unlock my fingers from the fence and turn around, but all the air is kicked out of my lungs as a hard body connects with mine.

I suck in a sharp breath as I stumble back from the force of the collision, my gaze locking on a pair of familiar brown eyes.

Strong fingers curl around my biceps, and a jolt of electricity courses through me at the contact as I'm yanked forward. I extend my hand, bracing myself for impact; only my hand touches his chest. His very firm, very naked chest. His hot skin burns my palm, but he's holding me so close I can't pull away.

"What the hell are you doing?" I ask, letting out a shaky breath.

"What am I doing?" His eyes narrow as he stares at me. "You bumped into me."

"I was turning around to go to my car, and you were doing what exactly?"

I let my eyes lower as I take him in—a mistake because he's wearing a pair of dark basketball shorts and nothing else. His perfectly sculpted chest is glistening with sweat under the late afternoon sun, and *damn*, he looks fine. Better than fine, really. Miguel was always muscled, even when we were in high school. I guess it was a mix of conditioning from playing football and helping his dad on the ranch. Back then, he was a man compared to the other guys our age, but seeing him like this shows me just how much of a boy he used to be. But there is nothing boyish about the hunk standing in front of me right now. At six-foot-three inches of pure muscle, he's towering over me by a good foot. His shoulders are broader, his muscles harder, every line defined to perfection, a machine built to tackle down his opponents, and he doesn't seem to have a problem showing his body off.

A finger slides under my chin, and he lifts my face up, a cocky smile flashing on his mouth.

"My eyes are up here, Red," Miguel rasps. His warm touch, in combination with the low and husky voice, makes my stomach tighten and shivers run down my spine. So much so that it takes me a moment to process his words.

Fuck.

I was totally caught staring.

And the asshole knew it.

131

Color rises up my cheeks, and I curse my redheaded ancestors for making it so easy for people to know how uncomfortable I am.

I shove his hand away, taking a step back, which only makes it easier to stare at his form. His chest is still rising and falling rapidly from running around the field. His shirt is hanging from the back pocket, completely forgotten. A Lonestars ball cap is sitting on top of his head, a pair of headphones covering his ears. As if he can read my mind, he slides them around his neck.

"So, what was exactly the reason you ran into me?" I ask, ignoring his comment.

That smirk grows even bigger because he knows exactly what I'm doing. "I didn't see you until you were already in my way."

"Yeah, right. Whatever." Shaking my head, I spin on my heels, but before I can take a step, his fingers wrap around my hand.

"Wait."

I clench my teeth together. "Can you not do that?"

"What?"

I lift our linked hands. "This. As a matter of fact, can you just stay away from me?"

My phone starts buzzing in my back pocket. I try to reach for it, but he doesn't let go of my hand.

Miguel pulls his brows together. "I don't think that's possible, considering the wedding is just around the corner."

"Well, I don't see a reason for us to interact before that. Or during the wedding, for that matter."

"So, what should I do? Just ignore that you're standing right there across from me?"

"Yes, you should do exactly that." I tug harder, my hand finally slipping out of his grasp. "It's not that hard. You didn't have a problem ignoring me for the past three years, so now shouldn't be any different."

He takes a step closer, his whole body towering over me. "Are you serious right now?"

I lift my chin higher. "What do you think?"

I haven't cowered in front of him before, and I sure as hell won't start now. No matter how much the voice at the back of my head screams for me to run while I still have a chance.

Miguel just stares at me, the tension building between the two of us. I swear it's like a living, breathing thing. The air sizzles, making it hard to breathe.

"What happened to us, Rebecca?" he whispers softly after what feels like forever.

The way he says my name makes me shudder.

It's like a caress, like the way he used to say it when we were just two crazy kids in love, and nothing mattered. When we still believed in fairytales. When we thought we could surpass everything if we were together.

But we weren't together.

Not for a long time.

I swallow the knot in my throat as I force the words out. "You."

I have to get out of here.

Taking a step back, I'm ready to bolt, but his hand is on mine once again, holding me hostage.

"Me? You're blaming me when *you* were the one who left. *You* were the one who didn't give me a chance to explain. *You* were the one who told me you'd stand by my side no matter what and then turned your back on me. You, Rebecca. Not me. *You.*"

Each softly spoken word is like a slice to my heart, tearing down the patched-up pieces I worked so hard to put back together after he shot through my life like a wrecking ball.

My phone stops buzzing, but almost as soon as it's done, it starts again.

Shit.

Nobody calls me, especially not twice in a row, not if it's not urgent.

"We're not doing this, Miguel. Not here. Not now. Not *ever.*"

I yank my hand out of his grasp and turn to walk away, my hand slipping into my back pocket to pull out my phone. My gaze falls down, and my heart sinks when I see the name on the screen. The knot is back in my throat, tighter than ever. I press the answer button and lift the device to my ear.

"B-Becky?"

The sound of my name uttered in a stuttered mess makes my heart stop in my chest.

"Linda?" My grip tightens around my phone. "What's going on? What happened?"

"I'm s-so s-sorry, Becky," she hiccups softly. "So sorry."

All the air is sucked out of my lungs as Linda cries on the other side of the line.

No, no, no.

"What happened, Linda?" I ask, the pit in my stomach growing larger by the second.

"She was here. I swear she was here a minute ago, but I just turned around and..." Linda's quiet sobs make understanding her hard.

"Linda, I need you to take a deep breath for me and tell me what happened."

More soft sniffles come from the other side of the line. I try to keep my cool as she sucks in long gulps of air. My yelling at her won't accomplish anything, I knew that, but damn.

What is going on?

Not knowing was going to drive me crazy.

From the corner of my eye, I can see Miguel move closer, but I do my best to ignore him. There was only so much I could deal with at the same time, and the whole situation with my mom would always take precedence.

"What happened?" I repeat softly once Linda's breathing returns to normal.

"We were in the living room. She was knitting and watching her TV show like she always does, and I was sitting there with her, but then I had to go to the bathroom. I was gone for a minute. Maybe even less, and the next thing I know, she's gone."

Shit.

My eyes fall shut for a moment as my brain goes into overdrive, trying to come up with all the possible scenarios.

"Did you look around the house? Maybe she went up to her room."

Mom could get moody sometimes, and she wanted to be left alone. Usually, she'd close herself in her room.

"I checked the whole house, b-but..."

Another hiccup comes through the line, and I want to scream at her to spill it out already, but I bite my tongue.

"But the front door was left open."

Double shit.

I bite the inside of my cheek, and my heart starts to race faster as my brain comes up with all the possible scenarios. Where could she have gone? So many places. So many possibilities. When she was like this, it was hard to tell what she might do. Where she might be. What if she was lost? What if she got hurt? What if—

"Becky?" Large hands fall on my shoulders, startling me out of my thoughts.

I blink to find Miguel's worried eyes locked on mine. "What's going on?"

I shake my head as Linda continues explaining what happened on the other side of the line.

"I went out, tried to call her and look for her. I hoped she just went out, but she was nowhere to be found. Not in the backyard, not on the road that leads into town. I called Chase, but he went into the city for his doctor's appointment and..."

And he wouldn't be back for at least a couple of hours, if not more.

Not that he could help.

Not when she got like this.

"Becky?" Miguel urges, his grip on my shoulders tightening, but I turn my back to him.

I couldn't focus on him. Not now. There were more important things to deal with at this moment. Miguel and I? We were at the bottom of that list.

"I didn't know what to do, and you always told me to call so..."

I did tell her that. Of course, I did. She was my mom, after all, and I had years of experience dealing with this.

"This is what we're going to do... I'll get into my car and drive around and try to find if she made her way into town. You stay at our place in case she comes back. Maybe she just went out for a walk. And call Mrs. Santiago, tell her what happened. Maybe she went over to their place. I'll have my phone on me, so call me the second you find something out, okay?"

"O-okay. I'll call her right now."

"Good. I'll talk to you soon."

Hanging up, my hand tightens around my phone.

A plan.

That's what I need. I need to come up with a plan and fast.

God, what if something happened to her?

I shake my head, cursing silently at myself. I couldn't think that way. I couldn't spiral. There was no time to lose. She was fine. She had to be.

I just had to find her.

I did it in the past, so I'll do it again.

She will *be fine.*

Determined, I start walking toward my truck, or I would if a hand didn't yank me back. "What the hell is going on, Rebecca?"

"Will you stop this?" I jerk my hand out of his hold. "I don't have time for this."

"Well, I'm not letting you go until you tell me what the fuck is wrong." Miguel's eyes glance over my face, and I can see the worry dancing under the anger. "Who's Linda?"

Shit, I didn't want to do this, not now. "Miguel, I really…"

"Something is wrong. I can see it on your face." His fingers on me tighten, giving me a little shake. "And no, I don't fucking care what the hell is going on between us now. You're clearly upset, so I'm not letting you deal with this alone."

No, he wouldn't. Miguel always used to take care of the people he loved. He was caring and protective.

Not that I believe he was still in love with me.

Too much time has passed. We were too broken.

His hand raises to my face, his thumb skimming over my cheek gently. "What's going on, Red?"

A shudder runs through me at the touch, a swarm of feelings I couldn't identify—didn't want to recognize—slamming into me.

"Mom is missing." I swallow the lump in my throat, pushing the feelings back. "I don't have time to deal with all of this."

I catch the flash of surprise in Miguel's eyes, but I don't wait for him to say anything. Using this opportunity, I slip from his grasp and jog across the parking lot to my ride. Unlocking my truck, I slide into the driver's seat and pray to all the gods as I slide the key in place and turn it. The engine protests for a heartbeat, but then it starts.

"Thank God."

I'm about to reverse out of my parking spot when the passenger side door opens, and Miguel jumps inside.

I stomp on the break, my fingers gripping the steering wheel. "What the hell do you think you're doing?"

"I'm going to help you."

"You..." The words die on my lips as we just stare at one another. I want to fight him on it, but then I remember that Mom is out there, lost, confused, and all alone. "Whatever."

Checking my review mirror to confirm there isn't another lunatic willing to jump in front of my bumper, I pull out on the road and start driving back to my house.

If it was just a few minutes like Linda had said, she couldn't have gone that far, could she? Driving back home made the most sense.

"Who is Linda? And what did you mean when you said your mom is missing?" Miguel asks, breaking me out of my thoughts.

"Exactly what I said," I mutter quietly, my eyes scanning the road in front of me. "She's missing. As in, she was home, and now she's gone."

Miguel shifts in his seat. "How long has she been missing? Maybe she just left to go to town to grab something?"

"And how would she do that if I have the truck with me?"

"Okay, so maybe she went to Santiago's? Or hell, maybe she even went to my place? Both of those are just a short walk away."

"Maybe," I whisper, my fingers curling around the steering wheel tighter.

The same thought crossed my mind. They were both just some

twenty minutes away on foot. She could have gone to either of those places, but I knew better than that. Today was a bad day. She was on the edge from the time she woke up and didn't want to listen to anything I told her. And when she's completely lost like that from the morning, there would be no getting out of it anytime soon.

My phone chimes, making me jump in my seat. I quickly grab it from the bag, hoping it's Linda with some news, but no such luck. Still, I answer the phone, putting it on speaker so I can continue driving.

"Becky, what the hell's going on?" Emmett's deep voice comes from the other side of the line. "Mom just called me and told me your mom's missing?"

"Yeah, she left the house a little while ago. I'm just driving back toward the house and hope I spot her somewhere along the way."

"Dammit," Emmett curses. "Okay, I'll tell the guys to be on the lookout in case somebody sees her wandering around."

"Thanks, Emmett," I whisper softly, my teeth sinking into my lower lip to stop it from wobbling. "Just... call me if you see her? I don't know in what state she'll be when we find her. This morning was hard."

"I'm so sorry, Becs." His gentle voice only makes my heart ache more.

You and I both. You and I—

"What do you mean, this morning was hard?" Miguel asks suddenly, interrupting the quiet. "What am I missing?"

Well, shit.

I close my eyes for a second. A heavy silence settles over the cab of the truck, like a ticking time bomb has just exploded in the small confines.

This is exactly what I didn't need.

When my eyes flutter open, I notice the knuckles of my

fingers have turned white from the force with which I'm holding the steering wheel.

"Miguel?" Emmett asks slowly, the curiosity evident in his tone.

Why wouldn't he be curious? The last he knew, Miguel and I weren't on speaking terms.

"Yes, who else would it be?"

Oh, I don't know, just about anybody else.

Emmett ignores his question and asks one of his own instead. "What the hell are you doing there?"

"He jumped into my car like the idiot that he is," I say quickly. I need to cut this off at the root before they really get into it. "I need to go, Emmett. I don't want to get in an accident on top of everything else, and I need my phone in case somebody calls me with news about my mom."

"Yeah, of course. I'll keep an eye out. Let me know if you find her."

"Will do," I promise.

"But just so you know, *both* of you, this isn't done."

No, I didn't think it was.

"Talk soon."

With a quick goodbye, I disconnect the call. Just then, I spot a flash of silver. My heart speeds up, only to plummet to the bottom of my stomach when I do a double-take and realize it's not Mom.

She's going to be okay. She has to.

Miguel's hand lands on my thigh, snapping me out of my thoughts. His touch is like a fire, burning through my layers and imprinting into my skin. "Tell me what's going on, Rebecca. Why are you so worried about her?"

I let out a long breath. I might as well go and say it. It's not like he won't see it soon for himself. "She isn't the woman you remember. She... She's losing herself."

"Losing..." He pulls his brows together, a confused look on his face.

"She was diagnosed with early on-set Alzheimer's," I explain, my gaze focused on the road.

The words feel heavy. It's like all the air is sucked out of the small space, making it hard to breathe. It always felt that way when I said those words out loud. Like I was writing our death sentence. Although, in reality, it's been written way before now, and nothing I did or said would ever change that. Because Alzheimer's was precisely that—the worst kind of all death sentences.

Losing Dad was painful, sure, but at least it was quick. One day he was here, the next he was gone. This was different. Mom was as healthy as a woman in her fifties can be, but her mind was betraying her. It was a slow and painful death where you have to watch the person you love lose themselves bit by agonizing bit. Watch their blank stare as they forget you ever existed.

"Alzh— Fuck, Rebecca, why didn't you say something?"

Why didn't I—

My fingers sink into the leather of the steering wheel as I hold onto it for dear life. The anger boiling inside of me, mixing with the fear, so I just let it out. "You weren't here, so I don't see how this has anything to do with you," I bite out.

Hurt flashes on Miguel's face at my outburst, and I instantly feel shitty for saying those words out loud.

There were a lot of things to be angry at when it came to Miguel and me, but Mom's disease didn't have anything to do with him. On the contrary, really. He was a part of the reason why I hid it in the first place. Miguel had big dreams, and I wanted them to come true. I really did.

At first, I didn't even know what was happening. I thought Mom was distracted or that her depression was acting up again.

But as more little "accidents" started to happen, like Mom forgetting to pick up my brother from school, not remembering simple things and recent appointments, and even almost setting the kitchen on fire, I knew something was up. I just didn't realize how hard it would be to get her to a doctor and get her the help she needed. Maybe if I was faster...

Don't think that way, I chastise myself.

I knew better than to do it. There was no stopping this disease once it struck. No cure. Just waiting.

I knew I couldn't leave my brother alone with her. So I did the only thing I could. I kept quiet and stayed home to take care of my family. If one of us had to give up our dreams, that person was me. What I didn't count on was that giving up my dream would mean I'd lose Miguel in the process.

"You're right. I wasn't here." Miguel just nods, turning his attention back to the road.

My throat tightens at the empty tone in his voice.

I knew that voice well because I used to be the one pulling him out of that state after his fight with his father.

Stupid, stupid, stupid.

Swallowing the lump, I force the words out, "Miguel, I..."

"Do you remember what she was wearing this morning?" He doesn't allow me to finish before changing the subject, his voice completely cold and business-like.

Letting out a shaky breath, I weigh my options. I could try and apologize, but I knew it'd fall on empty ears.

So, instead, I decided to focus on what matters—finding Mom. Everything else could wait.

"Dark blue summer dress. Her hair is more gray than red these days, too."

"Okay, any places where you think she might have gone to? Did she do something like this in the past?"

The suffocating fear I felt when she disappeared the first

time flashes in my mind. It was my senior year of high school, and I just got home from school to find the door to our house wide open. The water was running in the sink. I was already annoyed because my brother's teacher called me since she couldn't get a hold of my mother, and nobody came to pick up Matthew, so I had to do it instead.

I was so angry at Mom because this wasn't the first time that she'd been forgetful in the last few months. I didn't know what was happening with her. Was it the anniversary of Dad's death? It was nearing, but it had been a while since it affected her that much. But then I realized the house was empty, and the guilt slammed into me all at once. However, when my mind started to come up with all the different scenarios of what could have happened, the fear took root.

What if somebody took her? Or did she walk away? But why? It hadn't made any sense. So after searching the house and the yard from top to bottom and calling all our neighbors to get the same answer—Mom hadn't been there in days—I left Matthew home to wait in case Mom came back while I searched for her. It took hours. Hours of driving down the streets of our little hometown until I finally found her.

Blinking, I get back to the present and clear my throat. "A few times, but it's been a while. There are a few places where she usually goes to, but since Linda told me she's been gone only a little while, I want to drive home to make sure she isn't still around there somewhere."

"Who's Linda?"

"Mom's caregiver," I admit softly.

This topic was another hard pill to swallow. Linda is amazing. She really is. And Mom seemed to like her for the most part, but there was always this shame I felt when I had to leave her. I knew there was nothing that could be done to stop it. I had to work so I could help support my family. I couldn't stay with my mom twenty-four-seven and give her the care she needed. But none of it made any of this easier.

Miguel doesn't say anything, so I stay quiet.

What is there to really say?

I didn't want or need his apologies; I just wanted to find Mom and make sure she was alright.

For the next half an hour, we sit in the cab of the car in complete silence and just drive. At one point, I thought I might have spotted her, only to realize that it was not her but Mrs. Willow.

Linda meets us when we get back to the house, but a small shake of her head tells me all I need to know, so we head back into town.

First, I drive past the spot where Dad died. My hands are squeezing the steering wheel so tightly I can feel my nails digging into my palms, the physical pain the only thing grounding me and helping me to not think about worst-case scenarios. But the spot is empty, so I continue past it and toward the outskirts of town, where the cemetery is located. I park in front of the metal door and leave the ignition running as I jump out of the car. "I'll be back in a few."

I don't wait for his response as I enter the silent space, my eyes scanning for any sign of living as I walk toward where Dad's buried. Only his grave is empty. The flowers that I left there a few weeks ago, now completely dried out, are the only thing waiting for me.

I stare at the stone headpiece for a second, wishing my dad was here. Expecting him to know how to deal with this. Hoping he could take off some of the weight sitting on my shoulders, but as soon as those thoughts pop into my mind, I push them back. Nobody deserves to watch their loved one go through this. Nobody.

"I'll find her, Dad," I promise, my hand skimming over his tombstone before I turn around and get back to the car.

"Nothing?" Miguel asks, worry dancing in those brown eyes.

Silently, I shake my head as I pull out of the parking space, and we're back on the road.

"Should you maybe call the police? Somebody?"

"Not yet." I shake my head before he can even finish his question. "People who need to know are looking for her."

"Are you sure? The more people there are, the more likely—"

"There she is," I whisper, stomping on the break so hard the truck jerks forward.

Miguel's hand presses against my chest, holding me back from connecting to the steering wheel.

"Rebe—" Miguel doesn't get to finish because I'm already putting the truck in park and jumping out. I can hear him cursing quietly behind me, but I don't bother slowing down.

I'm breathless by the time I come to a stop in front of the gazebo. Mom is sitting on the grass under a tree next to it, that faraway look on her face.

I'm about to take a step forward when a hand touches my shoulder, startling me.

"I was just about to call you," Mr. Maverick says softly. "She's been there for a while, just staring into nothing. I tried talking to her, but she kept asking about your Dad."

"Thanks, Mr. Maverick." My throat bobs. "I'll go talk to her."

The old man nods, his eyes darting toward my mother, a sad, understanding look on his face. "Such a shame."

Swallowing the lump in my throat, I slowly close the distance between us. I knew better than to startle her, and the last thing I wanted was to make a scene. There were a few more people standing on the sidewalk, watching us with interest. Mom deserved better than to be the topic of the town's next gossip.

"Mom?" I call out gently once I'm in hearing distance.

For a moment, there is no reaction from her whatsoever, but then she blinks and turns those hazy brown eyes toward me.

"He didn't come," she whispers softly.

Her eyes are on me, but it's like she's looking through me instead.

"I'm so sorry, Mom."

"He promised me." She blinks, one lone tear falling down her face as her voice grows louder, more frantic. "He promised me he'd be here, but he's not! Why, Gigi? Why? Did I do something wrong? He said he loved me, but if he did, he'd be here, he'd..."

Shit.

I knew exactly how bad things were when she thought I was her younger sister. It was strange to me that she confused me with a woman who lived on the other side of the country and whom we barely saw, but I guess Mom and Aunt Georgiana used to be closer when they were younger.

"Hey," I crouch down so we're on the same level, my hands falling on her shoulders to stop her from thrashing. "Hey, it's okay. He's just late. You didn't do anything wrong. He's just late."

"How can you know?"

"Because I saw him, okay?" The lie slips easily from my tongue. It took me a while before I realized that was the only thing that would calm Mom enough and get her to go home with me.

"You saw Jackson?" she asks, the skepticism clear in her voice.

"I'm here, aren't I? How would I know where to find you

otherwise?" I give her a moment to think it through before continuing. "I saw Jackson, and he asked me to tell you he'd got caught up at work, and he won't make it today, but he wanted me to give you a ride back home."

I watch her process my words and pray to God that she believes me. Usually, she did, but some days...

"That man, always working so hard." Mom shakes her head, wiping away her tears.

"That he is," I agree, letting my palms slide to her upper arms. "How about I help you up, and we go home, huh? It'll be the two of us. Girl's night. We haven't had one of those in forever. What do you say?"

"Okay," she finally agrees.

I help her up to her feet. When she walked away, she forgot her shoes, so her feet were bare and dirty from the mud and grass, and God only knows what else. I want to look at them, but I know it'll only make her more upset, so I bite my tongue and let it be. Her feet can wait. She didn't seem to be hurt in any other way, which was the only thing that mattered.

From the corner of my eyes, I spot Miguel walking toward us, but I give my head a small shake, hoping he'll get the memo and stay away as I gently lead Mom toward the truck that's still left standing in the middle of the street.

I pull open the passenger door and usher her inside, making sure she's buckled in before closing the door behind her. Only now that she's safe do I close my eyes and let out a shaky breath, the relief slamming into me like a wrecking ball.

She's fine. She's fine. She's fine.

"Are you okay?"

My eyes snap open at the sound of that familiar husky baritone, and I come face to face with Miguel's dark eyes. Worry and something that looks too much like sympathy dance in his eyes, so I glance away, not wanting to face it.

The last thing I need or want is his pity.

"Yeah, I need to get her home. She's had a hard day." I run my hand over my face. "I'd give you a ride back, but... she gets really upset around people she doesn't know when she's like this."

"It's fine. I parked my car at school. I'll just jog there."

"School, right."

I completely forgot what happened there. It felt like the whole interaction was ages ago and not less than a few hours.

"Okay, then." I look around, my teeth grazing over my lower lip, as I finally meet his gaze. "I... thanks."

Different emotions swirl inside of me, tying my stomach in knots. I couldn't forget what happened between the two of us, but at the same time, I felt grateful for having him with me today. I hated his pity, but at that moment, all I wanted to do was curl in his arms and ask him to make it all go away.

It was that last thought that made me take a step back. Not waiting for an answer, I walk around the truck. Miguel doesn't say anything, and he doesn't stop me. Sliding into the driver's seat, I take a quick glance at the rearview mirror, the hair at my nape rising to attention.

He's still standing there. Still watching.

For a moment, it feels like we fell back through time, and I'm that seventeen-year-old girl again.

"Who was that?" Mom asks, breaking me out of my thoughts.

That knot in my throat becomes more prominent, but I force my hand to put the car in drive and slowly pull away. "Nobody."

CHAPTER

14

MIGUEL

"We found her," I say in the way of greeting as soon as the call connects.

"Fucking finally," Emmett lets out a long breath in relief. I'm glad that he could breathe because my chest still felt too small for my lungs to fully expand so I could inhale. "Is she okay?"

"Define okay," I murmur, my vision still set on the small dot that's Rebecca's truck driving away from me.

Silence falls on the other side of the line, that irritation I've been pushing back since the moment she told me what was going on coming out in full force.

My fingers clench around the phone. "How long did you know?"

"I found out when we got back. It was totally random. I was stopping by her house one day to bring her something. We were chatting in the foyer for a minute when her mom came to look for her, but when I greeted her and asked how she was doing, she just stared at me blankly as if she didn't know me at all. I didn't know what to make of it. Her mom started to get upset, so Becky ushered her toward the living room, and later on, she finally admitted that she had Alzheimer's. Apparently, the whole thing has been going on for a while."

A few weeks. He's only known for a few weeks.

I know hearing this shouldn't make me feel relieved, but it did. I wasn't the only one Rebecca excluded. She did it to both of us.

"A while?"

"Yeah, not that I was surprised that she kept it quiet," Emmett sighs. "You know how stubborn she can be. I tried getting more info from her, but her lips were sealed shut. At least she hired some help, and Chase is back."

"Chase is back?" I haven't seen Rebecca's older brother in years. Since he joined the military back when we were just freshmen in high school. He rarely got home, and Rebecca barely mentioned him. I remember how devastated, heartbroken, and scared she was when he left Bluebonnet. Those first few days after he left, she was like a ghost. Almost like she was when she lost her dad. Just a shell of the girl I knew. But now he was back. "Like on leave?"

"No, Chase is back for good. He was injured during his last deployment and..."

Somebody yells his name in the background.

"Coming!" Emmett shouts back, his voice slightly muffled like he removed the phone from his ear. "Listen, they need me. Thanks for letting me know you guys found her."

"Yeah, sure. Talk soon?"

We say our goodbyes, and I hang up the phone, running my free hand over my face. I let it drop by my side as I start jogging toward the high school, where I left my car earlier, my thoughts still on Rebecca.

Her mom has Alzheimer's, and now her brother is back from the war because he's been injured.

And I had no clue about any of it.

Guilt starts gnawing at me from the inside out. I should have been there. I should have held her hand when she found out and reassured her everything would be okay. I should have—

Nothing. You should have done nothing. She's not yours to have.

My gaze darts toward the football field. The last of the sun's rays are slowly disappearing behind the horizon. How many days have I spent out here? Too many to count. The football field was my safe space, my home. And Rebecca? She was a part of my home, too.

Five years ago

"I knew I'd find you here."

My head snaps up at the sound of the soft voice, my eyes landing on the only woman who's ever been able to make my heart stop beating, and this time is no exception.

I lift my hand to shield my gaze from the setting sun. Rebecca is standing on the field, her auburn hair shining more red than brown. A summer dress teases her knees, her arms curled around the letterman jacket.

My letterman jacket.

Something swells inside me, my hand rising to rub at the middle of my chest. "Hey, you. What are you doing here? I thought you headed home."

Recently, Rebecca had started to drive her younger brother around. That meant that she only caught the beginning of the practice before she had to go pick him up at his school.

"I did, but I had to go buy something in town, and since you

151

didn't answer any of my text messages, I figured I'd pass by the field on my way home."

"Practice ran late."

One dark brow quirks upward in a challenge.

"It did," I defend.

"I don't see any other players hanging around."

"Okay, I might have stayed a bit longer."

Not only did I use every spare minute to practice so I could get the best chance at attracting any prospective college scouts coming to our games this season, but staying late here meant spending less time at home with my dad. I'd take it; however, I'd pay for it tomorrow by waking up at the crack of dawn so I can do my share of work before I go to school, but it's all worth it.

"How are things at home?" Rebecca asks, breaking me out of my thoughts.

"Fine."

She moves closer. Even though I have a good foot on her on a typical day, she looks even tinier when I'm in my full football gear. Her hand lifts, rubbing at my cheek.

"You know I'm here for you. I'll always be here for you."

Closing the last of the distance, I slide my hand to the back of her neck. She sucks in a breath, her lips parting as my fingers slide between those gorgeous, silky strands, tightening as I pull her toward me.

"And I'll always be there for you, too, Red," I whisper as I crush my mouth against hers in a hard kiss until neither of us can breathe. Only then do I let go, my eyes blinking open to find an almost starstruck look in her eyes. "You're my ride or die, Rebecca Williams. My forever."

Now

I blink the memory away, but it's harder to push back the conflicting feelings that that broken promise awoke inside me.

Before we were a couple, she was my best friend.

I should have been there for her, just like she was there for me when I needed her.

For the better part, anyway.

Running my hand through my hair in frustration, I turn my back to the football field and go to my truck. My movements are automatic, which is good because my mind is still stuck on what I saw.

The faraway look that appeared on her face before she started toward her mom. Like she was shutting down all of her emotions and bracing herself for what was to come.

The careful way Rebecca handled her mother like she might break at any time.

The stiffness of her shoulders.

The way her lips pressed together almost imperceptibly.

Today clearly wasn't her first rodeo with a situation like this.

How many?

How many times has something like this happened? How many times had she had to take care of her mom? How many times did her mom go away without telling anybody? How many times did Rebecca look for her all alone because she was too stubborn to ask for help?

Because I knew her.

She wouldn't have asked for help.

Not from me, not from Emmett, and certainly not from the people in this town.

Stubborn woman.

Muttering quietly, I make the turn, and it takes me a moment to realize where I'm going.

My fingers clench around the steering wheel as my heart starts to beat faster.

It was instinctual. Honed from many, many times, I'd done exactly the same thing over the years.

To seek her out. Made sure that she was okay. Because she so rarely opened up. To everybody else, she was a badass. Nothing could faze Rebecca Williams, but I knew her. I knew her tender heart and how it could bleed without anybody noticing.

Just a quick stop.

I won't even get out of the car.

Just pass by her place to make sure they made it home safely.

Yes, just a...

All the thoughts that were swirling inside my head were gone as I slowed down my car when I came to the two-story farmhouse in front of me. The bright yellow color is slightly faded, but the place still looks tidy. The grass is neatly cut, and there are pots with flowers decorating the front porch. A light is on in the kitchen on the first floor. But that's not what draws my attention.

No.

It's the woman sitting in the darkness on the swing on the front porch. She's hunched forward, her elbows digging into her knees, her face buried into her palms.

She must hear my car because she looks up, and I can see traces of tears clinging to her cheeks.

A pain I haven't felt in years slams into me, and everything I had told myself mere seconds ago goes up in the air.

Fuck this.

Putting the car in park, I jump out and jog toward her.

There is a split-second moment in which she looks around,

her fight or flight response kicking in, only there is nowhere to go.

"What happened?" I ask as I climb the steps, the need to do something, anything, to stop her from crying, like a vice grip squeezing around my throat.

I could never take her tears. There was just something about seeing this strong, resilient woman break that shattered me. It didn't matter what I had to do. I'd do it just to erase that look from her face.

"Is it your mom? Did something happen?"

"No," Rebecca whispers, her voice hoarse from crying. "Mom's fine. I just put her to bed."

Embarrassment flashes on her face, and she looks away, wiping away at her cheek with the back of her hand.

I move closer, crouching down in front of her. My finger slips under her chin as I slowly turn her to face me.

Her hazel eyes are filled with so much sorrow, and my heart breaks for her.

"How long?" I ask softly.

I'm not sure why it was so important for me to know this, but it was.

There is a beat of silence as her teeth worry her lower lip, guilt flashing on her face as she says softly, so softly it takes my brain a moment to register her words.

"Since high school."

Since high—

"What?"

High school? She's been hiding this for more than four years? Not just that, but during the time we were together? How did I not notice?

I've been to her house countless of times, first as her friend, then as her boyfriend. I think back, trying to figure out how I might have missed it, but I come up empty. Looking at Mrs.

Williams today, it was so obvious that something was wrong with her, but back then...

"You've known for that long, and you didn't tell anybody?"

You've known for so long, and you didn't tell *me*.

Pink spreads over her cheeks at the accusation, the guilt in her eyes shining like a beacon in the night.

Knowing this hurt more than I could even put in words.

Back then, we were inseparable. Not just because we were dating. Rebecca was my best friend. More than that, she was *my* person.

Somebody who knew me so well that I didn't have to open my mouth, and she'd already be there. She could read me without any issue, and I was the same. I knew her tells. I could read her moods. We were connected in a way I could never truly explain. That's why it hurt so much when she walked away. It was like I lost a part of my very soul, and I didn't know how to move on.

Except, maybe I didn't know her as well as I thought in the first place.

"It wasn't like that. In the beginning..." She lets out a long sigh and lifts her hand to rub at her temples. "In the beginning, things weren't so bad. It started small. Mom would lose her keys, misplace groceries, forget where she put something... It was little things like that. I never gave it much thought. People are forgetful. Hell, I was forgetful more often than not. So what if each thing had a place in our kitchen? Maybe she decided to reorganize and forgot, you know?"

"What happened then?"

Her throat bobs as she swallows, her gaze falling down. "Then little things became big things."

"Like?"

"She would forget to pick up Matthew from school or one of

his activities. She said she was going out shopping, only to return hours later with no groceries."

"Shit, Rebecca..."

Her shoulders lift in a half-hearted shrug. But I knew better. I could see how much it pained her to tell me this story.

"By the time I noticed something was wrong and I took her to the doctor, it was already too late."

My fingers tighten around her chin, turning her toward me. "This isn't your fault."

"I know that. I know it wouldn't have made any difference if they discovered it earlier. Alzheimer's is a progressive disease, and it only gets more aggressive with time. But if I knew... maybe I would have been kinder to her. Some days, I was just so frustrated and angry at her. I needed her to be my mom. What I didn't realize was that it's not that she didn't want to be what I needed. She just couldn't. She was fighting an invisible enemy, and they were winning."

"I'm sure she wouldn't blame you."

"It doesn't matter. I blame myself enough for the both of us."

"Does she remember anything at all?"

"Some days she does. Some days, she's just my mom, and everything is like it always was. Other days, *most days* if I'm being completely honest, she's gone."

Rebecca gets up, and I let her. She walks toward the railing, her palms pressing against the wood as she glances out at the dark sky. Stars are scattered around like twinkling lights illuminating the path, the crescent moon shining brightly.

This was my favorite part of Bluebonnet.

You just couldn't see something like this in the city.

Winter or summer, when things got hard, I'd go out and look up at the sky, and let the familiarity of it help me settle down.

My gaze zeroes in on Rebecca's back. On the taut line of her shoulders. The goosebumps spread over her skin. The way the moonlight makes the red in her hair seem brighter and more vibrant making me want to bury my head in the crook of her neck.

Would she still smell the same?

Like roses and sugar and home?

Because that's what she always was for me.

Home.

Not this town, or my family, or even football.

Her.

As if she could feel my eyes on her, she turned around, those hazel eyes meeting mine. "I'm just so tired," she whispers softly, tears shining in her eyes. "So damn tired. Watching her like this is chipping away at the pieces of my soul, and I'm not sure how much more I can take. How many more people do I have to lose before it'll be enough?"

The raw pain in her voice is killing me.

I hate this for her. I knew how much she cherished her family. It destroyed her when her dad died, and then her brother joined the army, and now this.

What about you? A little voice at the back of my head taunts me. *You left her too.*

Only I didn't. If it was up to me, I would have never let her walk away. But she made the call. She was the one who walked away.

Yet, you didn't try to stop her.

One tear slides down her cheek.

"Rebecca," I rasp, taking a step closer.

Her name, a whisper, and a plea.

I cup her cheek, brushing away the tear, her gaze holding mine hostage. Tonight, her eyes seem more green than brown. Her lips part, her tongue darting out to slide over her lower lip.

For a while, neither of us says anything. We just look at one another. It's so familiar, all of this, and yet so different.

Something flashes in her irises. I suck in a breath as my thumb rubs over her cheek, brushing the last of the tears away. My fingers slide to her nape, twining between the silky strands of her hair.

I'm not sure who's the one who makes the first move. The only thing I know is that her body is brushing against mine. Her hand on my chest. My head bends down. Her warm breath touches my skin. And then her mouth is on mine. Or mine is on hers.

I don't even care.

All I know is that we're kissing. My lips slip over hers, refamiliarizing myself with the shape of her mouth, even though there is no need for it.

She fits against me perfectly, just like she did when we were seventeen. My grip on her hair tightens as I tilt her head. Her lips part on a soft moan as my tongue slips into her mouth.

And *fuck*. She tastes the same, too. Like the sweetest of addictions and the addict I am, I can't get enough of her.

"Red..." Groaning, my free hand lands on her hip, fingers digging into her skin as I pull her closer to me.

All those luscious curves press against my chest, her body molding to mine as her hands wrap around my neck, and we deepen the kiss. The last few years have been erased with a swipe of our tongues.

She nips at my lower lip, her hand sliding up and down my back, sending shivers through my spine and rock my core. My dick is painfully hard as it nestles against her lower belly, my knee slipping between her thighs as I press her against the railing. I take control, deepening the kiss.

Her fingers slip under the hem of my shirt, dancing over the muscles of my back. I can feel her heat against my knee as she rubs against it, seeking friction...

The sound of the engine pulls me out of the haze that's

159

Rebecca Williams. My eyes snap open just as the truck comes into view, the bright headlights blinding me.

"Fuck," I mutter, squeezing my eyes shut as I pull Rebecca closer to me, making sure she's covered from the view of whoever just came here.

The engine turns off, and the blazing lights are gone. I blink a few times, my vision coming into focus just as the car door slams shut, and a tall frame moves closer, coming to a stop at the porch.

It's been years since I saw Chase Williams. The guy has always been built. Hell, he even used to play defense on the football team. But it seems like he somehow got bigger in the time he's been gone. He has at least a couple of inches on me. His muscled arms are crossed over his chest as he frowns at me, a disapproving look on his face. And he's not the only one. What looks like a German Shepherd is standing by his side. The dog's dark black and brown fur makes him blend with the night, except for his eyes. Those dark eyes watch me carefully, and I have a feeling that if I make one wrong move, the animal won't have a problem jumping at me and ripping my throat out.

Still, I lift my chin a bit higher. He might be Rebecca's big brother and have some kind of wolf mix next to him, but I wouldn't cower in front of him.

"Chase," Rebecca pushes past me, her voice slightly breathy from our kiss. "You're back."

That icy gaze stays on mine for a heartbeat longer before it shifts to his sister. "I came as soon as I could. Did you find her?" he asks in a low tone.

"Yes." Becky pushes a strand of her hair behind her ear. "She's in bed. She got all the way to town, looking for Dad."

That frown between Chase's brows grows deeper, but he just nods, a contemplative expression on his face.

Rebecca places her hand on his forearm. "She's fine."

Chase visibly flinches, but he doesn't pull back. Instead, he meets her gaze. "And you?"

"I will be."

Another nod as he clears his throat. "I'll be inside."

With one final glare in my direction, he turns on the balls of his feet and walks away. I watch his stiff back, and for the first time, I notice something else.

A limp.

It's barely discernible, but it's definitely there.

"Is he okay?" I ask once he's out of earshot.

Rebecca turns to me, a surprised look on her face. Almost like she forgot I was there for a second.

"Yeah, he..." She lets out a sigh. "He was injured, but he's been doing better."

"I'm so sorry, Rebecca."

"He's home and in one piece, that's the only thing I could have ever asked for."

The words are even; like she repeated them enough times, they've become a mantra. Then again, when you go off to war, there are no guarantees. Hell, there are no guarantees anywhere.

"Re—" I start, reaching for her, but she takes a step back, glancing away.

"I should go. Check in on Mom." Another step back. "I... Thanks for helping today."

Her fingers curl around the doorknob.

"Yeah, sure."

"Goodnight, Miguel." With one final glance at me, she steps into the house.

"Ni—" The door closes before I can even finish. "—ght."

I run my hand over my face, my thumb skimming over my lips. I swear I could still feel Rebecca's mouth pressed against mine. Feel her taste on my tongue.

Fuck.

What the hell have I done?

REBECCA

"I didn't realize Miguel was back in town."

Chase's gruff voice makes me jump in surprise. "Dammit, Chase!" I chastise, turning around to face my brother. The hairs at my nape stand at attention from the scare he just gave me. Not that he cares. No, he just lifts his brow in a silent question as he keeps staring at me.

I thought he was already in bed, considering the house was empty when I came inside, but I guess I was wrong. Or maybe he simply couldn't fall asleep, just like me. Although the demons haunting us were vastly different.

Letting out a shaky breath, I turn my attention to the water slowly heating on the stove because, yes, I'd rather watch water boil than face my brother. Not that it helped much. I could feel his probing gaze on the side of my face. A lot of things have changed about my big brother since he got back home, but he was still as intuitive as they came and could read people like an open book.

I tilt my head in his direction so he can easily read my lips. "You'd know it if you bothered to go into town and talk to people every once in a while. It's the only thing people have been talking about for the past week."

Chase scoffs. "Hard pass."

I look up so he can see me roll my eyes at him. "Why did I think otherwise?"

Chase was always on the grumpy side, but he's become a downright recluse since he got back home. If it didn't have something to do with his doctor's appointments or the rescue dogs, he didn't want any part in it. I tried to understand him and give him the time he needed to heal, but some days, I just wanted to shake him and knock some sense into him.

Chase shrugs as he goes for the coffee machine, pouring a healthy dose of black gold into a mug.

"That won't help you fall asleep, you know," I point out, but he chooses to ignore me, taking a sip from his mug.

"What did he want?"

Why couldn't he just let this go?

The kettle starts whistling, so I turn off the stove. My teeth sink into my lower lip as I pour the water over the bag of lavender and chamomile tea. The intense scent of herbs reaches my nostrils almost immediately. The tea was done locally, and it was one of the only things that helped me when my anxiety became too much. God knows I needed it today.

I swear I could still feel Miguel's mouth on mine. The firm press of his lips against my own burning my skin with their touch. Those calloused fingers roamed my skin as his hands slid under the hem of my shirt. The spicy scent of his cologne, sweat, and something else. Something masculine and all Miguel.

Stop it!

I shouldn't be thinking about the kiss. Hell, I shouldn't have kissed him in the first place. What was I thinking?

I wasn't. That's the problem. I was too wound up and vulnerable after everything that had happened. Mom disappearing, looking for her, having to deal with her questions about Dad... Every time she got like that, it was like she was scratching at the barely healed wound, ripping it open once again.

And then he came, and it was like I was thrown back in

time. It was so easy to forget everything that had happened between us. I could lean on him like I've done so many times in the past. Miguel was the only person who I allowed to see me like this. The only person who knew how to put my pieces back together.

If he wasn't the one dealing the final blow.

I should have never let things get that far.

"Becky?"

Giving my head a shake, I push those thoughts back. Curling my fingers around the mug, I lift it to my face, inhaling the sweet scent.

"He heard about Mom, so he came to help. That's all."

Not a complete truth, but Chase didn't have to know that.

"Oh, is that why he was mauling you on our front porch? My bad."

My head whips in my brother's direction at the snarky comment. His face is completely impassive as he watches me intently.

"I..." My lips part, tongue sliding out and darting over my dry lips.

Chase's brows raise. "You what? Didn't think I saw it?"

No, I knew better than that. Did I think he'd bring it up? Not really. More than talking in general, Chase hated discussing mushy stuff, and this definitely fell under that category.

I glare at him. "Being a nosy busybody doesn't look good on you, big brother. Maybe this town is affecting you more than you'd like to admit."

Chase scoffs. "Hardly."

"Mhmm... Keep telling yourself that."

The silence settles over us once again as I lift the mug and take a tentative sip of my tea. Shadow appears from the hallway, and with one look at her, Chase walks toward the back door. His limp was always more noticeable late at night after he'd been up and about the whole day. Shadow slips outside, and Chase turns to face me.

"I think we should talk about Mom."

My stomach sinks at the firm tone in his voice, and I can feel the bile rise in my throat. "What about Mom?"

"I think we should look into a more permanent solution."

I'm shaking my head before he can even finish the sentence. "That's not..."

"Becky." Chase places his hand on mine, my brother's green eyes staring into me. "I know this is hard for you, but Mom's not well, and she's not..."

"You don't know anything!" It takes everything in me to keep my voice level as I pull my hand out of his grasp. If the situation was different, I'd celebrate the fact that my brother willingly reached out to me, but I hate the direction in which this conversation was going. "You weren't here, Chase. I was." My fingers clench around the cup so tightly my knuckles turn white. "You didn't have to deal with any of it. *I* did. The mood swings, the tantrums, the confusion, the uncertainty... I was here for all of it. I covered for her, I forced her to go to the doctor, and I was the one who didn't give up until we had an answer. So don't you dare come back and try to boss me around and tell me what's best for us. Don't you..." A hiccup breaks out of me, so I bite the inside of my cheek, trying to stop a new one from coming.

Chase just sits there and watches me, completely calm.

"I know that. I know that me leaving put a bigger burden on your shoulders, and you had to deal with all of it on your own. But you're not alone any longer. Let me help."

I let out a shaky breath. I knew he was right, but I'd been dealing with everything on my own for so long I didn't know how to let go. I didn't know if I *could*. Because what would happen if he left again? No, if the last few years have taught me anything, it's that there is only one person I can rely on —myself.

"The work isn't an issue, it's just… I don't think I can put her in an institution. It would feel like I'm giving up on her. I—" I shake my head, unsure of how to explain this.

Yes, taking care of Mom was hard. There was no denying it. It wasn't even the fact that most days she didn't remember me, although I couldn't deny that it hurt every time it happened. It was other things. How even the smallest of things would get her annoyed and frustrated. How stubborn she'd become when she set her mind on something. Like getting out of the house and going in search of Dad.

"We're not giving up on her." Chase shifts in his seat, the loud screeching of the chair snapping me out of my thoughts. "I've mentioned it to my doctor, and she suggested putting her in a facility that deals with people with Alzheimer's and how that might be the best thing for her. She'll be surrounded by specialists, receiving the best care, and being monitored twenty-four-seven, but more than that, she'll be surrounded by people just like her."

"I get that. I really do, but they don't know her like we do."

"But do we really know her?" Chase challenges. "We know our Mom, but we don't really know the woman she becomes when she forgets the last twenty-plus years."

"I…" I run my hand over my face. "Let me think about it, okay?"

"Do that." Those serious eyes meet mine. "You deserve to be happy, Becs."

"I'm not the only one."

CHAPTER

15

MIGUEL

It doesn't matter. I blame myself enough for both of us.

Becky's words still ring in my head long after I'm lying in bed. I keep tossing and turning, the events of the previous day playing in my head on repeat.

I still couldn't believe that she suspected something was wrong, even back when we were together, but she didn't tell me a word of it. Not even a hint that something might be going on with her mom or that she was worried.

Just the thought made me irritated.

There I was, sharing everything with her—confessing my deepest, darkest secrets, telling her about my problems and fights with my family. I gave her my all, only to realize she never did the same. Not really.

Letting out a frustrated groan, I turn to the other side, punching my pillow with my hand as if a more comfortable pillow would help me sleep better. But I knew better than that. My gaze darts to the curtains, and I can see the first trace of light peeking through them. It was still early, before five, and the house was quiet, but I knew I wouldn't be falling asleep anytime soon.

Turning to my back, I run my hand over my face before I toss the cover and get up.

If I'm not going to sleep, I might at least do something useful.

Slipping on a tee and a pair of basketball shorts, I slide out of my room and carefully make my way down the stairs. From my previous experience, I skip the third one from the bottom, not wanting to wake up my parents.

Stopping in the kitchen to grab some water, I make my way to the mud room, where I put on my running shoes and start out. The sky is still relatively dark, with only a few rays of sunshine peeking through the clouds. I take a few minutes to warm up and stretch my muscles, and just as I'm planning to start running, a figure coming toward me catches my attention.

A flash of surprise passes over my brother's face when he finds me standing in front of the house. His eyes take in my attire, and he tips his chin toward me. "Going for a run?"

There is no missing the judgement in his tone. My fingers clench at his question, the irritation spiking inside of me. "Just because I left the ranch doesn't mean I don't get up early and don't work hard."

I can see the muscle in Aaron's jaw twitch at my comment, and a part of me feels bad for lashing out at him but raising my walls came naturally when the topic of football and my family were brought together.

"Look, I'm sorry for snapping like that." I run my hand over my face. "It's been a crappy night, and I'm irritated."

"Is there a time when you're not irritated?" my brother challenges.

So much for trying to make peace.

"Well, you haven't been the most welcoming, either, now, have you?" I shake my head. There is just no sense in this conversation. The only thing that'll come out of it is us getting into a brawl. It wouldn't be the first nor the last time. "I'm out of here."

Getting into a jog, I run past him and down the driveway. My feet pound against the gravel. It takes everything in me to hold back and keep a steady pace when all I want to do is run. Get the hell out of this town and never look back.

Rebecca's tear-stained face flashes in my mind, mocking me.

I grip my fingers into fists as I push harder.

Fuck steady pace.

I keep my gaze on the ground as I push harder. I need to get out this restless energy that's been brewing inside of me for the past week. Gritting my teeth, I look up. I'm so amped up it takes me a moment to realize where I am.

The treehouse.

I glance at the wooden structure that I've been to a countless of times in the past. Rebecca's dad built it for her when she was a little girl, but over the years we've hidden here. It was our place more than any other in Bluebonnet. Hell, even Emmett didn't know about it.

No matter how much I tried to forget her, my body somehow found a way to get to her.

A part of me isn't even surprised. I've done it so many times in the past I've lost count. She was my safe harbor. The one person that always had her door open for me. The one person who listened without judging.

She was my person.

But you weren't her person.

The thought sobers me up quickly. Cursing loudly, I turn around and change my direction abruptly.

I push as hard as I can; my muscles protest the movements, but I don't slow down. I run around our property limits, focusing on the steady pounding of my feet against the ground.

But no matter how hard or how fast I run, I can't get the image of Rebecca's face out of my head.

"You were up early today," the sound of Mom's voice snaps me out of my thoughts. I look up from my laptop to find her standing in the doorway, giving me a curious look.

"I couldn't sleep, so I went for a run."

The house was quiet when, about an hour ago, I returned home, and after a quick shower and a coffee, I decided I should probably sit down and get some work done.

"I can see that. I knocked on your door to see if you wanted breakfast, but you were already out." She glances at my laptop. "Are you busy?"

"I'm just finishing something. What's up?"

She enters the kitchen and walks toward me. "I was thinking you'd maybe want to go to the store with me?"

My brows shoot up. "To the store?"

"Yes, to the store. Why is that so strange?"

"Because you never asked me to go to the store with you. If I remember correctly, the last time you took me, you told me I was a hooligan and you'd never bring me ever again."

Mom places her hands on her hips and gives me that stern look I was very familiar with. "Last time I took you to the store, you were ten, and you and your brother got into a fight and took out a whole shelf."

I wince softly as the memory flashes in my mind. As always, she's right.

"I'd assumed you'd grown up since then and learned how to behave in public. Besides, I barely get to see you, so excuse me if I want to spend a little time with my son before he scurries off once again and doesn't return home for another four years."

There is no anger in her voice, but I can't help the guilt that slams into me; her words are like a punch to my gut.

"I'm sorry, Mom."

"It's fine." She waves me off. "Kids are supposed to grow up and live their lives, form their families. You're here now, and that's what matters." Her gaze goes to my laptop, her eyes narrowing as she reads over my shoulder. "Is that... an essay?"

Fuck.

"It's nothing important." I turn around and quickly check if the file is saved before I close it. "C'mon, let's go—"

"Why would you write an essay?"

I let out a sigh, knowing there was no way she'd let this go now that she saw it.

I run my hand over my jaw, feeling a few days old stubble scratching at my fingers. "It's for class, okay?"

"Class? But didn't you..."

Her voice trails off, and it doesn't take a genius to figure out how that was supposed to end.

"Drop out of college to enter the draft?" I finish for her. "No, I put it on pause. I'll be taking summer online classes until I can finish. I'll probably need that degree eventually."

"You're..."

A beaming smile spreads over her lips, her hand cupping my cheek. "I'm sorry. I shouldn't have assumed."

"It's fine."

She wouldn't be the first nor the last person who judged me before getting the full story. Closing the laptop, I push to my feet. "So, are we going to the store or what?"

"Yeah, of course. Just let me grab my bag."

Ten minutes later, we're in my SUV, driving into town. Mom chatters all the way there, telling me all the things that I've missed since I've been away. I listen with half an ear, making appropriate noises every now and then, so she knows I'm listening, although barely.

One thing I most definitely didn't miss about Bluebonnet was all the gossip mingling around.

Once at the store, I grab the cart and trail after Mom as she pulls out a list—a physical one—and starts tossing things inside like her life depends on it.

I spot the hygiene aisle, the empty shampoo bottle in my bathroom flashing in my mind. "Hey, I'll just go and grab something."

Mom waves me away without lifting an eye as she compares two bottles of God knows what, so I push the cart toward the shampoo section. It takes me a moment to find the right one, and when I return to where I left Mom, she's nowhere to be found.

I glance left and right.

Where is sh—

"Miguel Fernandez, what a pleasant surprise!"

I turn around to find two women standing together at the end of the aisle. They're almost like twins, dressed in matching summer dresses and heels, their long hair falling in curls down their back, bright red lips curling in a smile as their eyes take me in from head to toe.

I stare at them, and it takes a moment until it finally clicks from where I know them.

"Mary Sue?" The brunette's smile grows bigger as I switch my attention from her to the blonde. "And Lauren?"

"And he remembers us! Oh my. And here I thought you've forgotten us now that you're a star," Mary Sue giggles, her hand brushing against my bicep.

"Hardly." I force a smile out. "How are you two doing?"

"Oh, same ol' same ol'. Nothing much changes around these

parts. Not like it does in a big city. The better question is, what brings you here?"

"Emmett's wedding," I comment, glancing over her shoulder. *Where the hell did Mom disappear to?*

"Right, he and Karmen are finally tying the knot?"

"Kate," I correct, although I'm pretty sure she knows it. We all went to high school together, after all. It's not like they got along well with Kate or Rebecca. Mary Sue and Lauren were on the cheerleading team, and there was always this weird animosity between the girls on the cheer team and everybody else. Most of them thought they had some kind of claim on the football guys, but that kind of thing never mattered to Emmett, or me for that matter.

"Silly me, I totally forgot. I can't believe they're still together."

"Still going strong. No—"

Before I can finish, Lauren interrupts me. "What about you?" Those unnaturally long eyelashes bat in my direction. "Are you dating somebody right now?"

"I..." *Shit, they're not wasting any time, are they?* "No, I'm focusing on football right now."

Seriously, where is...

But it's not my mother who catches my attention. It's the woman standing with her.

Rebecca.

I watch a beaming smile appear on my mother's lips when she notices her. Mom pulls Rebecca into a hug that she returns, her lips move, but I can't decipher the words from this far back.

I come to a stop and just stare at the two of them. Over the years, I've seen Mom and Rebecca interact a hundred times, both in my house and outside of it, and yet, something about this whole situation didn't sit well with me.

The two of them are still friends?

I don't know why, but I hadn't expected that to be the case, but apparently, I couldn't be more wrong.

Rebecca must feel my gaze on her because she slowly looks over Mom's shoulder, her lips parting as her eyes settle on mine, the surprise evident on her face. But then, her gaze moves to the side, and I can see her expression close off, her lips pressing in a tight line a second before fingers that are still holding onto me wrap around my arm.

"Miguel?"

Reluctantly, I shift my attention to the women next to me. "Sorry, what were you saying?"

"I was wondering how long you're staying here. Maybe we could catch up sometime. Hang out."

"And how'd your husband feel about that, Lauren?"

The hair on my nape rises at the saccharine-sweet voice coming from behind me. I turn around to find Rebecca and Mom have joined us. Rebecca's full attention is on Lauren, and I can't help but notice the amused look on Mom's face.

Seriously?

"Well, I-I..." Lauren tucks a strand of hair behind her ear. Her cheeks turned a beet red.

"They're not together any longer, although I don't see how that's any of your business," Mary Sue chimes in, glaring at Becky.

"Oh, I'm so sorry to hear that, Lauren," Mom joins in. "That must be hard for you. Second marriage in the last few years."

If possible, her cheeks turn even brighter. "Well, it is what it is. C'mon, Mary Sue. I just remembered what I forgot to buy."

She grabs her friend's hand and pulls her in the opposite direction.

Mary Sue looks over her shoulder at me. "I hope we get to catch up while you're in town, Miguel."

Yeah, I think not.

I had enough problems without adding the two of them to the mix.

Rebecca mutters quietly something that sounds a lot like, "I bet you would."

Her back is stiff, and her fingers are wrapped around the basket she's carrying.

"What did you say?" I ask, leaning closer.

Her whole body jerks at my question. "Nothing," she says quickly, taking a step back.

"That poor girl, just jumping from one man to another." Mom shakes her head. "Bless her heart."

I let out a snort. I couldn't say I was surprised. Both Mary Sue and Lauren had been jumping from one available guy to the next. It didn't matter who he was as long as he was an athlete, preferably on the football team.

Mom turns to me, eyebrows raised. "I thought you got lost, and I'd have to send out a search party."

"I'm not five." I push the cart closer, my attention still on Rebecca, but she's avoiding my gaze.

Today, her long hair is in a braid that's sliding over her shoulder. Her face is bare of makeup, accentuating the dark circles under her eyes.

Did she also have a hard time falling asleep after everything that had happened last night? Or did something happen with her mom? Is that why she stayed up late? Did she have another episode and try to run away? Did—

"Considering you were twelve the last time I had to do just that, I don't know if that's encouraging."

I force myself to turn my sights on my mother. "And that was totally Aaron's fault. He was the one who suggested we play hide and seek."

Mom tsks, shaking her head. "I'm not even going to

comment on that." She turns back to Rebecca. "Things those boys put me through."

"I can imagine." Rebecca's lips curl into a smile, but it doesn't reach her eyes. "It was nice seeing you, Mrs. Fernandez. You should stop by the Reading Nook when you're in town."

"I'll do that, honey." Mom pats her shoulder affectionately. "Say hi to your mom for me."

"Will do." With one last smile in my mom's direction—all while pointedly ignoring me at the same time—Rebecca walks away.

My eyes are glued to her retreating back until she ducks behind the corner.

And I'm not the only one.

"That poor girl," Mom sighs. "Always carrying too much weight on those slender shoulders."

That much was true. Rebecca hated being a burden to anybody. After her father's death, she was forced to grow up too quickly, as all of the Williams' children were, but I guess even back then, as the only girl in the family, she carried the heaviest load while her Mom was grieving the death of her husband.

"You and Becky seem cozy."

"Is that a problem?" she asks, and I don't miss the note of defensiveness in her tone.

Turning my attention back to my mother, I find her eyes narrowed on me, one of her brows arched.

"No, of course not." I lift my hand, running my fingers through my wild curls. "It's just an observation. That's all."

"I've known Becky since she was a little girl. I don't know what happened between the two of you, but I don't see why it should change anything between—"

"Wait, what?" My brows pull together at her comment. She doesn't know what happened? How is that possible? It seemed like everybody in this town knew what had happened, and they didn't have an issue showing me exactly how they felt. Just look at Mrs. Letty.

"I've watched Rebecca transform from a young girl into the amazing woman that she is today, running her own business, all while taking care of her family, and I can only be proud of all the things she's accomplished."

"Not that. I meant the other part."

A frown appears between Mom's brows. "What other part?"

"What do you mean you don't know what happened?"

"How would I know?" Mom shrugs, placing her stuff in the cart. "You barely answered my calls back then, claiming you were too busy with school and football."

She gives me her who-do-you-think-you-are-fooling look as she turns around and starts walking again.

Cursing silently, I follow after her. "I told you we broke up."

Everything after Rebecca and I broke up was kind of a blur. I was pissed at her for doing what she did, so I decided to drown my sorrows in drinking and partying. God knows how long I'd have kept up with it, too, if my Coach hadn't sat me down one day and threatened to bench my ass if I didn't get my life in order.

"*Weeks* after the event. Looking back, I remember seeing Becky around town. She was like a walking, talking ghost. There, but completely empty and lifeless. Sad. I tried talking to her, but she'd just brushed me off, saying she was busy. She didn't even bring it up until you told me, and I asked what happened, and even then, she just avoided answering. Said things didn't work out. Not once did that girl say anything mean about you or what had happened. I'm not even the only one who had asked, I'm sure. You know how nosy people in this town can be. If people had asked me when you'd be back, I'm sure they did the same with her, knowing you guys were dating, but I haven't heard a peep of what caused the rift between you two."

177

I lift my hand, rubbing at the middle of my chest, where I can feel an unfamiliar tightening.

I didn't know what to do with this whole situation. I thought Rebecca had told them what happened, and that was the reason why I was getting the side eye from the people of Bluebonnet. And now that I knew that wasn't the case, I didn't know what to do about it.

Nothing, there is nothing that you should do.

A flash of red in my peripheral vision catches my attention. Almost on instinct, my gaze follows until it lands on her.

Rebecca is standing in the checkout line, pulling out the things from her basket, and that damn jab inside my chest only grows stronger, more insistent.

"You didn't seem surprised to see her," Mom's comment brings me out of my thoughts, so I force myself to look away. I didn't have to give her any more ammunition than she already had. Or, based on the glint in her irises, any ideas.

"I saw her already."

"At The Hut?"

Of course, she would have heard I went to the bar. There was no way that little tidbit wouldn't find its way to my family.

"Yes, at The Hut."

Among other places.

Because she was everywhere, and there was no escaping her. Not as long as I was in this town.

Mom harrumphs. "Well, you better be careful of what you're doing."

"Me?"

"Yes, *you.*" Mom jabs me in the chest. "She might have kept quiet about what had happened between you two, but it doesn't take a genius to figure it out. I saw that girl in the aftermath of your breakup, and she was devastated."

Seriously? My mom too?

My fingers curl around the bar of the cart so hard my knuckles have drained of color. "So it's immediately my fault?"

"I'm not saying it's your fault or hers. I know better than that. Relationships take two people, and so does the breakup."

I open my mouth to protest, but she jabs me once again. "You might be all grown up, Miguel Fernandez, but some things never change. Whatever you do, don't go breaking that girl's heart once again."

Great, even my own mother was against me.

"Shouldn't you be worried about my heart?"

Just when I think she'll jab me once again, her palm flattens against my chest, her expression softening. "I am. Why do you think I'm saying it? I can see the way you look at her."

"I don't look at her in any way."

She lets out a soft chuckle. Her hand cups my cheek, and she gives me a small pat. "Wouldn't you like to think that?"

CHAPTER

16

What the hell was I thinking?

I wasn't. That was the whole problem, wasn't it? I let my impulse take over.

No, not impulse.

Jealousy.

Just thinking about it has the color rising up my cheeks.

I wasn't jealous of the women Miguel was talking to. I had no right to be. Miguel wasn't mine. Not any longer. But all rational thought left my brain when I saw no one other than Lauren and Mary Sue fawning over his every word, their claws sinking into his arm possessively, all while staring at him like they wanted to devour him.

Seriously, what was wrong with them?

But then again, was it really surprising? Mary Sue's been jumping from one guy to the next even before we finished high school, trying to find somebody she could drag to the altar. Lauren, on the other hand, did exactly that. *Twice* so far. And both times ended up terribly, but apparently, she still hasn't learned her lesson.

"What's with that frown between your brows?"

I jump in surprise at the question to find Savannah standing in front of me, a contemplative look on her face.

"Geez, give a girl a little warning, would ya?"

"That's why you have the bell."

Well, that was the idea, but I guess I was too stuck in my own head to hear it. Not that I would tell her that.

I check the time on my wrist. "You're here early."

"I finally got a few extra minutes, so I figured I'd get here and check in on you. Plus, I need that double espresso of yours like yesterday."

My brow quirks up as I make my way to the coffee machine and start making her drink. "Bad day?"

"More like a bad week. Grams is being stubborn, per usual. And then I had a fight with Mark."

"What did he do this time?" I look over my shoulder just in time to catch her rolling her eyes.

"He has another work weekend." Savannah slips into the chair at the counter, crossing her arms in front of her.

"Wasn't that his excuse last week? Like seriously, how many work weekends can one person have?"

"And when I asked him exactly that, he had the audacity to say that not everybody was as lucky as teachers to have the whole summer off. Can you imagine that?"

"Lucky?" my mouth falls open. "That is the stupidest thing I've ever heard. Did you punch him? Please tell me you punched him."

Savannah chuckles, but the amusement doesn't reach her eyes. "If he were in front of me, I would have been so tempted. I swear."

"And nobody could blame you for it." I place the coffee cup in front of her. "Here you go."

Savannah takes a long sip from the cup, her eyes closing for a second as she savors the taste of the black liquid. "This is exactly what I needed," she sighs happily. Those blue eyes open and turn their focus on me. "Anyway, we don't have long before people start coming, so forget about my stupid boyfriend. What's going on with *you*?"

There is no missing the curiosity in her irises, and by the tone of her voice, I know precisely what she's asking. *Who* she's asking about.

"Me? Nothing, just busy with..." I shrug, pick up a rag, and start to clean the already spotless working surface. Anything to avoid Sav's intense gaze. Not that it helps. I can feel it probing into me on the side of my face. "Well, everything."

"Mhmm... Does that everything include your ex-boyfriend?"

My hand bumps into the glass that's sitting on the counter, and it falls on the floor, shattering loudly and drawing attention from the few patrons sitting in the café.

"*Shit.*"

Savannah laughs. "If you've decided to smash things, it must be bad."

"It fell."

Not that the idea of smashing something into Lauren and Mary Sue didn't cross my mind, but...

I look around until I spot the broom in the corner. I carefully jump over the glass to grab it and start cleaning up the mess I made.

Looking at the million shattered pieces on the ground makes me unsettled. It almost feels like an ominous premonition of sorts.

"Yeah, yeah, so what's going on with the football hottie? I still can't believe you dated a professional football player and hadn't mentioned him once in all the time we've hung out!"

And I wanted it to stay that way, but apparently, my wish wouldn't come true thanks to all the gossip going around this town.

"He wasn't a professional football player when we were together. And I didn't mention him because there was nothing to say. Miguel and I broke up ages ago," I mutter, hoping that if I brush it off as something insignificant, she'll drop the subject, but I should've known better.

Savannah gives me a pointed look. "That's not how it looked to me the other day in The Hut," she sing-songs, leaning closer to me. "The guy ran after you like the prince after Cinderella. That hardly screams done to me. So? What gives?"

"Are you already getting in the role for when the kids come?"

Savannah runs a monthly book club for kids here at the Reading Nook. We had three groups, and the youngest ones were supposed to come today.

Can't they hurry up already?

As if she can read my mind, Sav shoots me a knowing glare.

"Your evasive skills suck, Rebecca. Now spill. I don't want to find out everything from the gossip rags."

"I was just surprised to see him there, that's all."

"How long has it been since you guys saw each other?"

Three years, five months, and thirteen days.

Not like I was counting or anything.

"A few years."

"So?" She nudges me with her hand.

"So what?"

"How does it feel to see your ex back in town?"

Annoying. Overwhelming. Unsettling.

It was like no matter where I went, he was there, and I couldn't escape him no matter how hard I tried. And then there was yesterday and that damn kiss.

I bite the inside of my cheek.

I swear I could still feel his mouth on mine. The way his body enveloped mine completely, pulling me in the cocoon of his warmth. It was funny because although I've been in Bluebonnet my whole life, feeling Miguel's arms wrapped around me felt like I was finally, *finally* home once again. He made me feel safe and secure, like no matter what happened, I'd be able to survive it. We'd be able to survive it.

"What are you thinking about?" Savannah's hand grips mine, bringing me out of my thoughts.

But there is no we. There hasn't been for a while.

I shake my head. "Nothing."

"Your face says otherwise." Savannah's expression turns serious. "Did he do something? Because if he did, just say the word, and we'll go and wreck his car or something. I read this one book in which a girl put an open tuna can into her ex's car, and he couldn't find it, so the smell got so bad he had to tow it."

"She did what?" I let out a strangled laugh.

"I'm telling you, the girl was vicious." She wiggles her brows. "Wanna try it?"

"No, silly. I just..." My smile falls down. I didn't know what to tell her or how to explain this thing between Miguel and me. It was too damn complicated, our lives too intertwined together. "He's everywhere, you know? No matter what I do or where I go, he's around, and it's messing with my head. He wasn't supposed to come back."

He wasn't supposed to turn my life upside down with his demanding presence and reckless kisses that made me feel alive for the first time in the last three years.

"Becky..."

Before she can finish, the bell jingles once again. Grateful for the disruption, I look up, a smile forming on my lips, but it falters a little when I see the woman standing in the doorway.

"Rose?"

What is this? A freaking high school reunion?

"Becky?" Those blue eyes widen, lips parting in surprise as she stares at me across the room.

Rose Hathaway or I guess now it's O'Neil, if it's to be believed by the town gossip, looks exactly like she did four years ago when she left for college. Her long dark hair is pulled into a high ponytail, not a strand out of place, and her makeup is impeccable, a pretty summer dress hugging her curves.

Rose looks around the space, uncertainty written on her face. "Is this the place where the reading club happens?"

"That's the one, but this one is..."

A high-pitched screech interrupts me, and a little boy rushes past Rose and toward the glass window.

My heart does a little flip inside my chest, and I can feel a jab of pain shoot through my heart at the sight of him as he places his little hands on the glass and stares at the cupcakes with big blue eyes.

"I'm so sorry," Rose mutters as she finally catches up to him. Her hand falls on his shoulder, and she pulls him away from the glass. She crouches down so she's at his level and starts moving her hands.

I blink, and it takes me a moment to realize what's happening.

Signing.

She's using sign language with the boy.

Her son.

The first time I heard about it was around the Christmas holidays. I was in the store when I overheard two old ladies talking about the shotgun wedding between Rose and her high school boyfriend, John O'Neil, because she got knocked up.

And even though we weren't friends any longer, hadn't been for years at that point, a part of me felt bad for her.

It couldn't have been easy to go off to college only to end up pregnant barely a few months into the semester and have to quit before you even had a chance to start enjoying it.

Not that Rose seems to mind it.

Rose smiles at the boy, her hand cupping his cheek gently as she leans in and presses a kiss on top of his dark curls. Smoothing her hand over the back of her dress, she gets to her feet, her piercing blue eyes meeting mine. "I really am sorry about that. Cupcakes are Kyle's favorite, and he gets excited when he sees them."

"No worries." I look down at the boy. He's so adorable; I can't help but smile. He's a mini version of Rose. He's probably three or so, and some of that baby fat still clings to his face, making his cheeks round and pink. His brown hair is a mess of mussed locks, and a twinkle of mischief shines in his blue eyes. I lift my hands in a wave before slowly signing as I say, "Hi, Kyle. I'm Becky."

"You know sign language?"

I turn my attention to Rose, who seems genuinely surprised at the prospect. I shrug nonchalantly. "Know would be a stretch, at best. I just started learning it recently." I look back at Kyle and sign, "Want a cupcake?"

Those big eyes shine brighter at the prospect as he looks toward Rose pleadingly, his little hands flying as he signs.

She lets out a sigh but nods her head. "Fine, but just one."

Kyle claps his hands excitedly.

Damn, he's cute.

Grabbing the tongs, I take one chocolate cupcake and show it to him, slowly mouthing, 'Good?' I didn't think it was possible, but his eyes turn even bigger as he nods his head, moving closer to the counter, his little palms wrapping around it the moment I place the cupcake on the counter.

Before either of us can react, he lifts it to his face and takes one big bite, all of the chocolate coating over his face.

My mouth falls open, but Savannah just laughs as he looks up, the chocolate smeared all over his nose and cheeks as he flashes us a big grin.

"Slow down, little man," Savannah chuckles.

Rose lifts her hand and runs it over her face. "I swear he usually behaves better than this."

"Oh, please, he's just a kid. Let him enjoy it."

Our eyes meet, and a smile slowly spreads over her mouth as a silent understanding passes between us, a genuine smile. It's been ages since Rose Hathaway and I shared anything authentic.

We used to be friends when we were kids. We would hang out all the time, having playdates either at her house or mine, but then, over time, things slowly changed.

My dad died in a car accident when I was nine, and life as I knew it fell around my family like a house of cards. We were all devastated by the loss, and it was around that time that I gravitated more toward the boys. They became my rocks, my protectors. They would come to my house at random times of the day and pull me out to play. All I had wanted was to cry in my room. But they didn't let me. And somehow, we became inseparable—the three musketeers, as people around town affectionately referred to us. And it was around that time that Rose started to throw snarky comments our way, and that division that appeared only grew exponentially. Maybe I should have tried harder, but we were kids, and I was hurt, so I gave back as good as I got.

"You want something?"

"Oh, no. That's it. How much do I owe you?"

I wave her off. "It's on the house."

Rose's eyes widen. "What? No, you can't do that, it's..."

"It's fine, really. Don't stress about it. You guys are here for the reading group?"

187

"I... Yeah." Rose nods, tucking a strand of hair behind her ear. "Mom mentioned there was one happening here today, so I figured I'd bring Kyle so he could meet some new friends."

"That's amazing. We love to meet new readers." Savannah winks at Kyle, who's happily munching on the last of his cupcake. Rose pulls out some wet wipes from her bag and hands them to the boy to clean himself. Once he's done, Savannah asks, "How about we go and you help me pick out the story we'll read today?"

Kyle glances from Savannah to Rose, his little brows furrowed in confusion. Rose repeats the question in sign language, and Kyle nods enthusiastically.

Savannah jumps from the chair, and together, they go off toward the back, Rose's eyes following the two of them.

"Savannah is the one who leads the group," I explain, drawing her attention. "But I give them space in the back. Recently, the library got more books, but that meant losing the reading space for kids. Not that anybody wanted to lead it. Mrs. Parker retired a few years ago, which left Mrs. Kenny all alone in the library, and she just doesn't have enough time."

"I see that you've got your hands full."

"Not as much as you, I'd imagine. Kyle seems like a really nice kid."

Rose's mouth falls open, clearly shocked by my statement. I guess I shouldn't be surprised. The last time we were together was back during high school, and we were constantly at each other's throats. But we grew up since then, and those girls were gone.

"Thank you." The corner of Rose's mouth lifts, and I can see all the love she has for her son. "He really is amazing."

I grab Savannah's mug from the counter and place it into the dishwasher. "You guys here for a visit?"

"Umm..."

The bell chimes, drawing our attention. Two kids come rushing inside, followed by their mothers. They wave at me as they make their way to the back of the shop.

"We moved back, actually," Rose continues once we're alone again. "John started to work for his dad."

My brows shoot up. John O'Neil was one of the guys on our football team back in high school. Although he wasn't nearly as talented as Emmett or Miguel, he was decent enough to get a scholarship to continue playing in college, and Rose decided to go with him.

"It's just temporary," Rose explains quickly. "John was injured last year and missed the draft, but he'll reapply next year once he's at one hundred percent."

"I'm so sorry to hear that, Rose. I didn't know."

One of those shapely brows quirks up. "You? Didn't know something related to football?"

I could see how she'd think that. Football used to be the center of Emmett and Miguel's lives, so it became the center of mine. I knew everything about the game, and you could usually find me on the sidelines cheering my friends on, but it was just one more thing that had changed after Miguel and I broke up.

"There were more important things I had to focus on." I shrug.

"I guess that's true."

Laughter comes from the back of the room, drawing Rose's attention. "I guess I should go make sure Kyle is okay. Thank you for the cupcake."

"Of course. I'll see you around?"

With a nod, Rose walks away. Over the next ten minutes, more parents and kids come. Some people stop to grab coffees before they, too, disappear down back. I handle the usual walk-ins as I listen to Sav read the kids a story. These were the moments I liked the best. When the shop was filled with people, laughter, and good stories, it reminded me of why I wanted to open this café in the first place. The hour passes in a flash, and some people linger around, chatting and buying treats for the kids.

"I'm out of here. I called Grams, and she told me she was going to the store. On her crutches! I kid you not that woman will take me to an early grave."

I wave her off. "Go, save the day. I'll clean up later."

"You're the best. I'll take you out for drinks when you find five spare minutes for little ol' me." She gives me a pointed look. "Maybe then we can finish the conversation we had earlier."

Of course, she'd want that.

"I don't know what you're talking about."

"Mhmm... We'll see about that. Later, Becs."

With a wave over her shoulder, she disappears out of the café.

Shortly after she's gone, the crowd starts to die down, so I use the opportunity to start cleaning. There isn't much of the treats left tonight, but I pack it regardless so I can drop it off at the police station.

I hated throwing the leftovers away, so instead, I would usually take whatever wasn't sold to somebody who I knew worked the night shift and could use it.

I scan the street as I pass by. I wave at a few people that I know before passing the street in front of The Hut. Today, the place is relatively quiet, just a few regulars, and that's about...

Only it's not.

I catch the group sitting in the booth by the window. Lucas and Kevin, a few of the guys I went to high school with, are sitting along with Mary Sue, Lauren, and Miguel.

My stomach twists into a knot as I watch Lauren laugh exaggeratedly at whatever Miguel says. Her hand falls on his forearm.

My gaze is glued to that one point of contact, and I can feel the blood starting to buzz in my veins as I watch her finger rub little circles over his skin. Irritation springs to life, but it's not the only thing either. Jealousy, hot and heavy, slams into me like a tsunami, making me stumble back.

He's not yours, I remind myself. *That kiss yesterday didn't mean anything.*

You don't want it to mean anything.

My jaw clenches as I stare at them for a heartbeat longer before turning on the balls of my feet and continuing my way to the police station on autopilot. My mind is still going over what I just saw, which only makes me more irritated with myself.

Molly is at the front desk when I arrive, and her smile spreads when she sees me. She's in her late thirties and the only female police officer in Bluebonnet.

"Are you bringing some baked goods?"

"You know it."

Molly gets out of her cubicle, her blonde ponytail swaying with movement. "Nico will be so pissed he missed you." I hand her the box, and there is no missing the giddy twinkle in her irises.

"He's not working tonight?"

"Oh, he is, but we just got a call, so he went out on patrol." She opens the box and peeks inside. "Carrot cake cupcakes!" Molly pulls one out immediately and takes a bite, letting out a happy sigh. "How you make something that has a vegetable in it taste so good, I'll never understand, but these are divine."

"I'm so happy to hear that. Anyway, I have to go, but you guys enjoy those and say hi to Nico."

"Thanks again, and will do."

With a wave, I get out on the street. I was so ready for today to be over.

Making a point to avoid The Hut, I walk back to Reading

Nook, where my truck is waiting for me. Unlocking the car, I toss my backpack onto the passenger seat and slide the key in place, starting the ignition. I expect the familiar loud rumble of the engine roaring to life, but there is nothing.

What the...

My brows pull together as I turn the key and try again to start the car, but once again, only silence greets me.

"Perfect, just freaking perfect," I mutter to myself as I pop the hood and get out of the truck.

I pull the hood up and turn on the flashlight on my phone as I illuminate the engine and poke around, not that I know much about cars. Between Chase, Emmett, and Miguel, I learned how to change the oil and change the tire if I ever needed to. I also took my car to the shop religiously to make sure it was working properly. But recently it started to make some weird noises. I was planning to check it out, but these past few weeks were just so busy I barely had enough time to breathe.

"What's going on?"

The fine hair at my nape rises when a warm breath tickles my skin. I jump at the sudden question, my back colliding with the hard chest behind me. My heart is beating a mile a minute as I turn around and come face to face with the last person I want to see.

"Miguel."

CHAPTER

17

MIGUEL

Rebecca turns around, and those big, hazel eyes meet mine like a deer caught in the headlights.

"Miguel."

My name is a whisper, and I can feel it all the way to my bones. My stomach tightens as I just stare at her, drinking her in. It's the only thing I can seem to do—taking her in, exploring every little detail of the woman who used to be my world, and noticing the smallest of changes that happened since the last time I saw her. The way her red hair is pulled in a high ponytail. A few runaway strands curled around her face. Those slightly parted pink lips just beg me to lean down and press my mouth against hers.

Fuck.

It's like now that I've kissed her, I couldn't think about anything else but how good it felt and how much I wanted to do it again. How much I wanted to touch her. Feel her. How—

"Are you trying to give me a heart attack?" she hisses softly, breaking me out of my thoughts.

"No. I was walking back to my car when I saw you crouched down in front of your truck, muttering to yourself."

nce Mom and I came back home, I tried focusing on work

but then my dad came, and my concentration went to shit. The tension in the room was palpable to the point you could cut it with a knife, so when my phone buzzed with the incoming call from Lucas, I didn't think twice before agreeing to meet him and another one of our friends for a drink. Anything to get out of the house.

Then, as I was driving into town, I might have seen the lights still on in the Reading Nook, and I might have parked close by so I could have an excuse to walk by the café later to check if she was still there.

Rebecca looks over my shoulder. "Where's your date?"

My date? My brows pull together. "What are you talking about?"

She shakes her head. "It doesn't even matter. You can go on your way. I'm fine here."

"You didn't look fine just a moment ago. What's going on with your truck?"

"It won't start, but like I said, it's fi—"

Before she can finish, I gently move her out of my way and pull out my phone. Turning on the flashlight, I illuminate the interior of the hood.

"Did you leave any of the lights on?"

The silence stretches as I poke around the engine, trying to figure out what's going on, but it's too damn dark for me to see anything properly, even with the flashlight on.

Why the hell does she park here anyway? The side alley was in total darkness, with no light in sight. It could be dangerous.

When I look up to point that out, I find Rebecca glaring at me, her arms crossed over her chest. "Did I leave my lights on? Who do you take me for, Fernandez? A freaking fool?"

"It was just a question, Red. I think it could be your battery or your alternator. Did the car make any noise when you tried turning it on?"

"Nothing. Seriously, it's fine. Just leave it. I'll call the mechanic tomorrow so they can come and give it a look. You can go. It's nothing I haven't done a hundred times before myself."

The way she brushes me off so easily annoys me to no end, but I don't let her see it. Instead, I cross my arms over my chest.

"And how did you plan to get back home?"

"I..." My question clearly catches her off guard because it takes her a moment to answer. "I'll just call my brother."

My jaw clenches in irritation. Because seriously, how stubborn can she be?

"And you'll wait for him to drive all the way back from your place and sit here in the dark?"

"Yes. I don't see what the issue is."

"The issue is that it's late, and it's pitch black here. Why didn't you install a light if you're parking here every day?"

I don't need light to see the anger flashing in Rebecca's irises. Her fingers curl into a fist as she glares at me.

"This is Bluebonnet, not Austin. Besides, I don't remember asking for your opinion."

"Well, I'm giving it to you anyway. This might be Bluebonnet, but it doesn't make it safe. There are bad people everywhere."

Her chin lifts up a notch. "Yeah, I learned the hard way that there were bad people everywhere. Including where you least expected to find them."

So we were back at it again.

I suck in a long breath, biting my tongue so I don't say something I'm going to regret.

"I'll call Chase."

Rebecca uncurls her arms and unlocks her phone. I wait as she pulls out her brother's contact and presses the call button. I can hear the phone ring, but it goes straight to voicemail. She tries again, but the result is the same. Before she can try one more time, I grab her hand.

"Just let me drive you home," I whisper softly. "It's late, and I'm going there anyway."

Her tongue darts out, sliding over her lower lip. I watch that little movement as she weighs her options, and I can see the moment in which she finally gives in.

"Fine, but only because I'm getting worried. Chase is home alone with Mom, and I don't want to wait for Emmett to get here."

Because God forbid, I'd think she was doing this to willingly be in my proximity.

"Whatever you wanna tell yourself, Red."

Rebecca shoots daggers at me as she walks to the passenger side and grabs her stuff. We walk in silence a little way down the main road to where I left my SUV. My fingers itch to slide over her lower back as I pull the door open, but I force myself not to do it. Instead, I walk to my side and get in, just as Rebecca does the same.

Turning on the ignition, I pull out from the parking lot. Soft music plays in the background as we drive away through the streets of Bluebonnet, but it doesn't help with this building tension that only seems to grow stronger by the second.

I try to keep my attention on the dark roads. It's not an easy task now that she's sitting next to me, her presence, her scent overwhelming in the small confines of the vehicle.

I'm just turning onto the gravel road that leads to our place when my phone starts to ring. My gaze darts to the screen to find a picture of a brunette staring at me. Julia.

And I'm not the only one who notices it either.

Rebecca lets out a strangled sound.

I reject the call, my eyes meeting Rebecca's in the darkness.

"You didn't have to hang up on my behalf."

"It's fine," I say non-committedly, shifting my attention to the road.

Rebecca snorts. "Is it? Or were you too afraid I'd tell your new girlfriend you were out on a date tonight?"

My fingers clench around the steering wheel. "What the hell are you talking about? I wasn't on a date."

"I saw you at The Hut with Mary Sue and Lauren. What would you call that, if not a date?"

This whole nonsense was about that?

"I was there with the guys," I grit through clenched teeth, irritated that I have to explain myself. "The two of them came later and joined us. That's it."

"Mhmm... Y'all seemed awfully cozy tonight."

I turn toward Rebecca, but she's looking out of the window, her fingers curled around the door handle.

What is she planning to do? Jump out of the car?

"So what if we were on a date? What does that have to do with you?"

She presses her lips together but doesn't bother turning toward me. "You're right. It has absolutely nothing to do with me."

Her voice is even, and I swear I could see the walls surrounding her quickly start to rise, tall and impenetrable.

Fuck!

I run my fingers through my hair, pushing it back. This was so not what I wanted at all.

Then what did you want? A little voice at the back of my head challenges.

Wasn't that a million-dollar question? The one I didn't have an answer for.

"What were you even doing out?" I ask, trying to change the subject and ease some of this tension between us.

Rebecca is quiet for what seems like an eternity. Just when I think she won't answer, she surprises me.

"I went to the police station. I usually carry the leftovers from the café to shelters or places I know where they have a night shift."

"Police station?" I repeat, my fingers curling around the steering wheel.

"Yes, Nico gave me the idea a while ago, so it's just been something I do. There is no sense in throwing away perfectly good food."

"Why am I not surprised?"

I bet he gave her the idea. Anything so he could spend time with her.

How many moments like this did the two of them have? How many times did she bring him food? Or did she just stop to see him at work? Did she ask him to try out her new recipes like she did with me when we were dating back in the day?

"What does that mean?" she asks, some of that anger back.

"Just that you and Nico are awfully close, that's all."

"We're some of the rare people who stayed in Bluebonnet. So we hang out." She shrugs.

Fucking shrugs.

"Is there something going on between you and Nico?" I ask, my voice deadly low. The muscle in my jaw flexes as I stare intently at the road, waiting for her answer. The last thing I needed was to crash us into a tree.

From the corner of my eye, I can see her turn toward me. "What?!"

"Is. There. Something. Going. On. Between. You. And. Nico?" I grit through clenched teeth, each word feeling like it was ripped from my mouth.

I glance toward her. The surprise disappears from her face, and instead, rage slowly starts boiling to the surface. If I wasn't so angry—so jealous because that's what this was, red hot jealousy at a man who used to be one of my friends—maybe I would have seen this coming, but I was too focused on the anger and keeping this damn car from swerving.

"Stop."

"What?" I glance quickly toward her before returning my attention to the road. We were almost at her house, but not just quite.

"I said, stop."

Before I can say anything, she unbuckles her seatbelt and reaches for the door handle.

I press my foot against the break, and the car jerks forward as it comes to a sudden stop. Rebecca doesn't seem the least bit fazed as she pushes the door open and jumps out of the car.

"*Shit.*"

Putting the car in park, I fiddle with my belt for a second before it finally gives, and I get out of the SUV. Thankfully, she didn't get far, so I can catch up to her easily. My fingers wrap around her wrist, and I tug her back.

"What the hell do you think you are doing? You could have broken your neck!" I yell at her, my breaths coming out in ragged pants.

"You have no right, Fernandez!" Rebecca shouts, jabbing her finger into my chest. "No fucking right."

"Oh, no? I don't have the right to ask if one of my friends is dating my ex-girlfriend?"

"No!" This time, her fist connects with my chest. "Because it's none of your Goddamn business who I'm hanging out with or sleeping with, for that matter."

My teeth grind together as my brain focuses on one thing, and one thing only: Rebecca in bed with another man. His hands on her body. Her whispering his name.

Before she can punch me once again, I grab her hand. "Do I

need to remind you that you were the first to ask about my dating life?" I ask softly, leaning down so we're face to face. "If you can ask, so can I. Two can play this game, Red."

"Oh, no, you don't. You lost the right to ask those kinds of questions when you left." She tries to pull her hand out of mine, but I'm not budging. "And the only reason I asked was because there was a girl calling you just after I saw you having drinks with another woman. Not that that's anything new for you. As we established, you're used to dating multiple women at the same time."

"Left?" I growl, taking a step closer, so close she has to tilt her head back so she would be able to look up at my face. My voice drops deadly low as I whisper, "You're the one who left."

She presses her finger against my chest, tilting her chin up. "What did you expect me to do? Stay around and watch you fuck your side-piece for kicks and giggles? Join in on the fun? What, Miguel? What did you want from me?"

CHAPTER

18

REBECCA

Three years ago

"I don't know what to do, Mrs. Santiago." I shake my head as I pace around the room. My fingers are intertwined so tightly that my knuckles have turned white. "We're losing her. More and more each day, and I don't know..."

A sob tries to rip out of my lungs, but I cover my mouth with my hand to stop it from coming out.

I hate this.

I hate my mother's illness. I hate the fact that we're losing her slowly but surely. I hate feeling this weak and helpless. Because no matter what I do or say, it won't change a thing. There are no trials. No medications. Not anything that could help us. Nothing that could stop the inevitable from happening. Soon, she would be gone, all the memories we had together would be erased, and I would have to sit there and watch it all unfold.

"I know, Becky." Mrs. Santiago moves closer, wrapping her arms around my shoulders. "And I'm so sorry you have to deal with that, honey."

"If I didn't come when I did, the house would have burned to the ground."

I still couldn't believe she left the food in the oven while she was watching TV. She was fine this morning. A little tired, but she was my mom. I thought things would be okay, but then I came home because I realized I had forgotten some papers and found smoke coming from the house, and the oven was on fire.

How didn't she notice something was off? How didn't she smell the food burning, see the smoke?

But I knew how. She was lost in her own head, and when that happened, it was like she completely tuned out. There could be an earthquake outside, and the house could be falling apart or burning down, and she wouldn't have noticed.

"I'd tell you it'll get better, but we both know it would be a lie."

"It's just not fair." I stomped my foot, feeling like a petulant child, but I couldn't stop myself. "After losing my dad in the car accident, why do we have to lose her too?"

When would it be enough?

When would our family's debt to the universe be paid off, and we'd be left to live our lives in peace?

"I don't know, baby." Mrs. Santiago places her chin on my shoulder, her hands giving me a reassuring grip. "But I know you'll figure it out."

A knot forms in my throat, making it hard to breathe.

"I don't know if I can," I croak out, shaking my head. "It's all just too much."

"Hey, now." Mrs. Santiago turns around. "You *can* do this. I know you can. You're way stronger than you give yourself credit for, Rebecca."

She was wrong, though. I was falling apart. The ground was collapsing under my feet, and there was nothing I could do to stop the destruction. Chase was away in the military doing God knows what, God knows where. Matthew was a mess in school, and I could barely keep him in line as it was. Mom was getting worse, and I...

"How about this? How about you let me help you for a few days so you can go visit that boyfriend of yours and decompress a bit?"

"I can't." Even before she finishes, I'm shaking my head. "I can't leave Mom and my brother alone. I can't ask you..."

She slides her palms down my arms and takes my hands in hers. "You're not asking. I'm offering. You've been here for months taking care of your family. You're running yourself too thin. Don't think I didn't notice the bags under your eyes or how pale you've been lately."

I open my mouth to protest, but Mrs. Santiago shoots me a death glare that has me biting the inside of my cheek. I knew that look all too well. My mother sent it my way one too many times. When she still knew who I was.

Besides, what should I say to her? I certainly couldn't tell her the truth. While, yes, the bags under my eyes were partly due to everything that had been going on with my mom, there was another reason for my sleepless nights, and I had yet to decide what I'd do.

No, I couldn't tell her that.

I didn't want to worry her more than I already did.

"You can't take care of others if you don't take care of yourself, Becky. Go and take care of yourself, and let me help you out."

"He's on the other side of the country. What if something happens?"

I wanted to go and visit Miguel. God knows he asked me to come, but I only managed to do it once. It was months ago, a few weeks after the semester started. I drove there all night and got to spend one magical weekend with him. But since then, things have been tense. It was hard for us to talk because we were always busy. Between work, our classes, football, and my family, we were lucky if we managed to exchange a few texts.

I tried calling him a few times in the evening, but he was always with the guys, either in the gym or outside partying. Although he tried to move away so we could speak, it was pointless. I could hear the music, his friends calling him, and the girls. I tried to reason with myself that it was all a normal part of the college experience. He was there with his friends and teammates, but I couldn't deny that the more time passed and the more we were pulled in different directions, the more my uncertainty grew, which didn't help at all.

The time was never right. Besides, Miguel didn't go to college nearby. No, an over twenty-hour drive separated the two of us. There was no way I could drive home in case something went wrong and Matthew or Mom needed me. I couldn't do that to them.

"Well, then, I guess it's a good thing I booked you a flight for today."

I'm pretty sure my eyes bug out at her statement.

"No, you can't. That's too much..."

Mrs. Santiago's hold on me tightens. "Well, tough luck, I already did it."

Tears burn my eyelids as I try to keep my emotions under wrap. But there is no fooling Mrs. Santiago. She frames my face and runs her thumb over my cheekbone.

"You're family, Rebecca. Family helps family. You don't have to do it all on your own."

This time, I really do break. A loud sob comes out of my lungs as I pull my hands and wrap them around her neck. Mrs. Santiago returns my embrace, her sweet scent reminding me of my childhood. Of the countless times she hugged me, helped me get up when I fell, and cleaned my scratches and wounds. "Thank you so much."

"There is nothing to thank me for." She rubs her hand up and down my back. "You just go and have fun. We'll be here once you get back home."

So that's what I did. I went back home and quickly packed a bag for a weekend trip before informing Matthew about what was happening. He wasn't happy, but he didn't put up a fight. By the time I was packed, Mrs. Santiago was knocking on our door.

After a quick goodbye, I drove all the way to the airport. I was anxious to get into the air and finally see Miguel. I tried calling him, but when he didn't answer, I figured it was for the best and decided to surprise him instead.

There was a slight delay, but I finally landed in Michigan just after eleven in the evening. Since nobody is picking me up, and it's late, I decide to splurge and rent a car.

By the time I make it to Miguel's campus and find a place to park close to his building, I'm wiped, but even that doesn't stop the excitement coursing through my body. After months of long-distance, I'll finally get to see Miguel.

I quickly check my reflection in the rearview mirror. My eyes are still slightly puffy from crying earlier, and there are dark bags under my eyes.

Maybe I should have tried to put on some makeup, but I didn't have it in me. I just wanted to come here. I needed to see Miguel. I needed to feel his arms wrapped around me and hear him say everything would be okay. I didn't even care that it would only be temporary.

I needed somebody to hold me before I started to fall apart under all the pressure of what's been happening in the last few months.

Grabbing my bag, I get out of the car.

I'm just getting out my phone to call Miguel when somebody exits the dorm. I give the guy a small smile as I slip inside. By some miracle, there is nobody sitting at the front desk, so I use this opportunity to slip toward the stairs, climbing two at a time. I'm slightly winded when I get to the third floor and see Miguel's door at the end of the hall.

I lift my hand and knock, the sound echoing down the silent hallway. I bite the inside of my cheek, shifting my weight from one foot to another.

Maybe he's out with the guys? I should have probably called a few more times, but I just wanted to get here as soon as possible. He's been telling me he's busy with a project for one of his classes, so I just assumed—

The door pulls open, and a gorgeous blonde appears in the doorway. Eric's girlfriend? I think Miguel mentioned that his roommate was seeing somebody. Or was it one of his teammates? With so many new people in his life, it was hard to keep track of everybody.

Her brows quirk up, "Can I help you?"

"I—"

My gaze falls down as I slowly take her in. My stomach sinks, my mouth turning dry before I even register what I'm seeing.

I blink once, but no, the image in front of me is still the same.

This unfamiliar, stunning girl is standing in the doorway of my boyfriend's dorm, wearing nothing but his shirt.

And not just any shirt.

His jersey.

She's wearing his freaking jersey.

The one he wore and gave me before I went home so I could have something of his with me.

The one that made me feel loved and cherished like I belonged.

The girl flips her hair over her shoulder. "Did you need something? Because we're really busy here."

Oh, I had just the idea of what they were busy with.

How is this my life?

This can't be real. It can't be happening. Miguel wouldn't do that to me.

But he did.

There is no denying it.

This half-naked girl standing in his doorway is proof I haven't been imagining things these past few weeks.

No, Miguel is cheating on me.

"Are you mute or something?" the girl barks out.

Bile rises, burning my throat.

"I... No," I shake my head, which only makes the nausea worse.

You'll not throw up in front of this girl.

My fingers are clenched into a fist so tight I can feel my nails bite into my skin. "I have the wrong room, so—"

"Who was knocking, Marie?" Miguel's gruff voice comes from inside the room.

Shit.

I take a step back, trying to get the hell out of there, but I'm already too late.

Miguel's gaze finds mine over her shoulder, and I clearly see the moment the realization of what had happened hits him.

"Rebecca? What are you doing here?"

Something inside my chest shatters at the sound of his voice, gentle and caring.

Then why the hell did he do this to me? To us?

Tears blur my vision. With a soft shake of my head, I turn

and storm out of the room. I can hear Miguel call my name, but I don't slow down. I take two steps at a time, needing to get away.

Between trying to run as fast as I can and tears gathering in my eyelids, I stumble over the last step. Cursing, I trip forward and bump into a woman, almost falling on my nose, but I steady myself at the very last second.

"Slow down!" she yells after me, but I'm already running toward the door.

Just a little bit longer.

I try to pull my keys out of my bag, but of course, this is the moment when I can't find them.

"Becky! Wait."

The sound of Miguel's voice has goosebumps rising on my skin. The tears that I've tried to hold at bay come rushing out, and this time, there is no stopping them.

"Dammit, Rebecca!"

Calloused fingers grab my upper arm and turn me around until I'm facing Miguel. He's breathing hard, his clothes rumpled, and his hair messy. Seeing him like that breaks my heart all over again.

"Let me go," I whisper, trying to tug my arm out of his hold.

"I'm not letting you go until we talk."

"There's nothing to talk about." I yank harder until he has no option but to let go. "I think I've seen enough."

Her dressed in his jersey with nothing underneath it.

Her hair and makeup messy.

Him standing bare-chested in his bedroom.

With *another woman*.

My fingers wrap around the keys.

Finally.

"You have no idea..."

I have no idea?

"Did I or did I not see another girl standing in your doorway

208

who looks like she just jumped out of your bed?" I yell at him, the accusation ringing loudly in the quiet night.

He lifts his hand and runs it through his wild curls. The motion I did so many times. Did she do it too? Did her fingers sink into his hair while he whispered sweet words into her ear?

"I, well yeah, but..."

I shake my head.

"There is no but. This..." I point between the two of us. "We're done."

And then, I walk away.

This time, he doesn't try to stop me.

Now

"I wanted you to believe me." Miguel's fingers wrap around my wrist, snapping me from falling deeper down memory lane. "I wanted you to let me explain. But instead, you left without a backward glance. You condemned me without a flicker of doubt."

I blink a few times, unsure if I heard him correctly.

He's trying to blame this on *me*?

After everything that had happened?

After I saw them with my own two eyes?

"I *saw* you," I protest, trying to tug my hand out of his grasp, but his hold is unyielding, and the only thing it does is bring us closer together.

Miguel lets out a humorless chuckle. "You saw what you wanted to see."

I stagger back, or I would if he wasn't holding me. It's like he slapped me. It would have hurt less if he did. At least then, the pain would be physical. Instead, he was tearing up the carefully put-together pieces of my heart with his words, bit by a tiny bit.

"So you're telling me you'd have been totally chill if you gave me a surprise visit and I opened the door wearing nothing but another man's clothes?"

Miguel's jaw clenches, and I can see that I hit a nerve. There is no mistaking the anger boiling in his dark eyes.

Good, let him be angry. Let him hurt; After all, he was hurting me just the same.

"It wasn't like that!"

"You keep saying that, and yet the evidence tells a different story. Although I'm not sure why I was surprised. At that time, you'd been pulling away from me for months. I tried calling you to let you know I was coming, but you didn't answer, and later I found out why—you were too busy screwing your side-piece."

"She wasn't my side-piece; she was just a friend who was there because we were working on a school project together!" Miguel grits. "Not that you stayed long enough for me to tell you that."

I just stare at him for a moment, unsure if I heard him correctly, but Miguel doesn't budge or back down.

"Are you seriously going with that excuse? I *saw* you. Hell, I saw *her*." Even saying that out loud felt like I was thrown back to that day. I could feel the ache squeezing my stomach as all the feelings were building inside me. Surprise, hurt, betrayal, heartbreak... Remembering it felt like I was riding on a rollercoaster I never signed up for, and there was no way out. "She opened your fucking door in the middle of the night wearing one of your shirts and nothing else. I don't know what kind of 'friend' she was, but that ain't friendly, Miguel. She almost ripped me a new one because I was interrupting you while you were 'busy.'"

Miguel's eyes narrow at me, those dark irises sucking me in, making me fall into their depths. My throat bobs as I swallow, but there is no getting rid of the knot that formed there. I start to turn away, but Miguel's hand slips under my chin, forcing me to look at him.

"I don't know what happened while I was in the bathroom, but if you would have just let me fucking explain. But no, you had to run out of there and push me away."

"Because it hurt too fucking much!"

My fingers clasp together in a fist, and I jam it against his chest, but he doesn't even react.

He wants to rehash the past?

Fine, we would rehash the past.

"I accepted a plane ticket I got as a gift from Emmett's mom because she saw how much I was struggling to take care of everybody in my life, so she wanted to give me a breather, and after a lot of convincing, I finally agreed to accept it. I flew across half the country so I could see you because I fucking needed you. I needed my best friend, my boyfriend, to wrap me in his arms and tell me everything would be okay. I needed you to reassure me that I was not making a mistake and that I could actually do all of this. I just needed you" — with each new sentence, I jab my finger deeper into his chest, angry tears burning my eyes — "But what did I find instead? I found another girl in your room, dressed in your clothes, with no idea of who I was!"

"She didn't know you because she hadn't met you. She knew I had a girlfriend."

"Then why did she put on your jersey?"

"I don't fucking know, Rebecca." Miguel runs his free hand over his face, and I can see the frustration building inside of him. "We got stuck in the rain on our way to the dorm. She was my partner for the project, and the library was closed, but we weren't done yet, so we came to my place. I went to put on some dry clothes in the bathroom, and I guess she took one of my shirts to change into so she wouldn't be sitting there all wet."

"Are you seriously going with that?"

Miguel blinks, and I can see fury and irritation rising to the surface. "I'm not 'going' with anything. That's what happened. Something I would have told you three years ago if you just fucking gave me time to do it.

"Well, she wanted something more. No girl in their right mind would take another guy's jersey if she knew he had a girlfriend."

"So this whole thing was about a fucking shirt? That's why we broke up? Because a girl was wearing my shirt?"

"No, we broke up because you betrayed me, because you cheated... You know what? It doesn't even matter. What happened happened, and there is no changing the past." I shake my head. "I can't keep doing this."

I start to turn around. I needed to get out of here. I needed—

Hands wrap around my wrists, and I'm tugged back. Before I know it, my back is pressed against the car, Miguel's hands caging me in. His breathing is heavy as he looms over me.

"Miguel, let me g—"

"I never cheated on you."

I shake my head, my eyes searching for a way out. "It doesn't even matter what happe—"

"It fucking matters." Miguel's hands slap against the roof of the car, making me jump in surprise. "I never cheated on you. Not once," Miguel growls. "Not back then, and not since. There has *never* been another woman for me."

My head whips in his direction, my mouth falling open. "W-What?"

Miguel leans closer, so close his nose is brushing against mine, those dark eyes holding me hostage.

"There hasn't been anybody else, Rebecca," he repeats slowly. His hand rises, those calloused fingers cupping my cheek, the touch of his skin against mine making a zap of electricity shoot down my spine.

He can't be serious.

My heart is beating wildly in my chest, the strong beat echoing in my eardrums as I try to grasp his words.

My mouth falls open, tongue darting out to slide over my lower lip. "You're lying."

There were girls before me. I knew he was occasionally hooking up with them, and I hated every single one of them for having something I couldn't have, for having a part of him that didn't belong to me.

Until it finally did.

Then, I never asked. There was no sense in torturing myself with the thoughts of Miguel with another girl. He was mine, and that was the only thing that mattered.

Until he wasn't.

Anger flashes in his eyes, and for the first time in my life, I'm scared of him. In all the years we were together, all the fights we had, I was never afraid of Miguel until this very moment.

"I'm not lying," he whispers each word slowly, making sure there is no misunderstanding. "Were there a few girls before you? Yes, but they were just random hookups that didn't mean shit. That's all they were; hookups. You were my first."

I sink my teeth into my lower lip. I want to look away from the intensity in his eyes, but there is nowhere to look but at him. And I don't know what to say, what to think about this whole situation.

What was the truth, and what was the lie? Did it even matter at this point?

Miguel's gaze falls down, zeroing in on my mouth, and his

voice turns husky. His fingers slide to my chin, his gaze holding me hostage.

"Since the day we got together, you've been the only woman I've touched." His grip on me tightens. "The only woman I've loved." He lifts his gaze to meet mine. "The. Only. One."

Before I can say anything, he leans down, and his mouth captures mine.

I suck in a breath in surprise, my body going completely still.

Miguel is kissing me.

Again.

A shudder goes through my body as that talented mouth slides over mine.

There is nothing gentle about the way Miguel kisses me. His grip on me is strong, the hard press of his mouth over mine relentless. He tilts my head to the side, nibbling at my lower lip and demanding entrance.

My lips part, his tongue sliding into my mouth and twining with mine, taking my breath and any rational thought away.

Miguel is kissing me.

I sway a little on my feet. My fingers grab onto his shirt to steady myself, but the only thing it does is bring us closer.

And it's like my body comes alive at his nearness, at his touch.

Every nerve ending in my body is sizzling to life as I return his kiss.

And holy shit, there was nothing that could ever compare to kissing Miguel Fernandez. Those long fingers cradling my face. The determination in every swipe of his tongue. The gentle nibble at my lower lip that always had me melting in his arms.

One of his hands slides down my side, his fingers digging into my waist as he pulls me closer. My chest brushes against his, my nipples turning into hard pebbles that press against the material of my shirt.

I tilt my head to the side, my tongue meeting his swipe for swipe.

His palm slides lower, fingers dipping under the hem of my shirt and making goosebumps rise on my skin at the touch. His fingers sprawl over my lower back as he brings me closer, and I can feel his hard length pressing against my soft belly.

"Fuck, Red," he rasps against my mouth, breaking the kiss. "You still taste the same."

I can barely catch my breath before he kisses me again, and I get lost in everything that is Miguel Fernandez.

My hand slides up his chest and around his neck. I push him back, and he doesn't try to protest. In the distance, I can hear the sound of the car door opening, and then he sits down, pulling me into his lap.

I let out a shaky breath as my palms brace against his pecs. I can feel the strong muscles of his shoulders flex under my touch. My fingers sink into his wild curls, and I tug at his strands, bringing him closer to me and deepening the kiss as my hips roll against his hard cock.

The motion is instinctual, each slow movement making my core clench with need.

We're a frenzy of limbs. It's like now that we've finally given into this attraction that's been building since the moment he stepped into this town; there was no stopping us.

I try to slide my hand under his shirt to explore his hot skin, but my fingers get stuck in the material. I let out a muffled sound in protest. Miguel pushes my hands back and grips the hem of his shirt, pulling it off in one swift movement, tossing the shirt out of the way before he pulls me back to him.

His skin is scorching hot under my palms as I explore the

215

lines of his chest in the darkness. He was always fit, but right now, every muscle of his torso is clearly defined.

"You're so fucking perfect, Red." Miguel slides his mouth over my chin, his stubble scratching my jaw and leaving goosebumps in his wake as he kisses his way down my neck, his hands slipping into my shirt.

He tries to unhook my bra, but his hand bumps into the steering wheel.

"Fuck," he mutters and just ends up pushing my shirt and bra out of his way before bending down and sucking on one of my nipples.

"Miguel..." My fingers grip his hair as I pull him closer to me.

He hums against my skin, his tongue flicking over one hard bud. Then, his other hand slides between our bodies and under my skirt.

"Fuck, you're so wet for me, baby," he groans as his fingers slide over my panties, feeling the wetness of the material.

I roll my hips against his hand. "Miguel, I need..."

I bite into my lower lip, feeling the color rise up my cheeks as I rub myself shamelessly against his fingers, the pleasure building in my core.

"What?"

"I need to feel you inside of me."

Even in the darkness, I can see his eyes shine with desire.

He doesn't need to be told twice. Miguel pushes my skirt up. I raise a little so I can sneak my hand between us and unzip his jeans. His cock springs free between us, my hand wrapping around his hot length. He hisses softly as I give him a few slow strokes just as his fingers push my panties to the side, the tips of his fingers rubbing against my clit.

My eyes fall shut as the first shudder runs through me.

Miguel's nose brushes against mine. I blink my eyes open to

find him staring at me. My grip around his cock tightens, and I position him at my entrance, lowering myself over him.

His fingers dig into my hips as he helps guide my movement. My teeth sink into my lower lip to stop it from wobbling as he stretches me slowly until he's fully seated, pain and pleasure mixing together.

It's been long, too long, since somebody made me feel this way.

Miguel's eyes hold mine as I pull back, only to sink down deeper.

His hand cups my cheek, brushing my hair back. "So fucking beautiful."

The softly whispered words make my heart skip a beat. A kaleidoscope of emotions is shining from his eyes, making it hard to breathe, so instead of focusing on that and trying to figure it out, I lean down and press my mouth against his.

Miguel lets out a low groan as we slowly find our rhythm, years of being together coming back like we were never apart. His hand cups my breast, fingers tweaking my nipple. I shift my weight, changing the angle as my movements become faster.

"Red," Miguel breathes, breaking the kiss. "Slow down, or I'll—"

But I didn't want to slow down. I was so close, and I could feel he was too. His hands slide down, gripping my ass, as I sink lower, his cock hitting just the right spot. My whole body tenses as the orgasm rips through my body.

I can feel Miguel come along with me, his hard muscles sleek with sweat as my weightless body falls over his.

I press my forehead against his, our ragged breaths mingling together as we come down from the high.

Miguel's still inside of me, his warm palm gently rubbing against the small of my back as his mouth brushes against my forehead.

We just sit there, neither of us moving, when the soft buzzing breaks through the post-sex haze.

Holy shit, I just had sex with Miguel.

I jerk back as if somebody threw a bucket of ice-cold water over me. My eyes land on Miguel's before I quickly look away.

"That's my phone."

I pull away, my head bumping into the top of the car as I scurry back into my seat.

Seriously, what was I thinking?

Not only did I have sex with my ex, but we did it in a car? What were we? A pair of horny teenagers?

"Rebecca…" Miguel calls out my name, but I'm too busy tugging down my skirt and trying to make myself presentable.

"What are you doing?"

Whatever, it's a lost cause anyway.

"Trying to find my phone."

I finally spot it, along with my bag, on the floor. I pick it up and turn the screen to find Chase's name on it.

Shit.

I answer the call, but before I can utter a word, Chase's gruff voice stops me.

"Why are you breathing so hard?"

I sink my teeth into my lower lip as my eyes meet Miguel's, who looks almost as panicked as I am.

"Becky? Where are you?"

"I-I…" My voice stutters as the panic sets in.

Shit, get a grip, Becky.

"I'm on my way. My car didn't want to start."

"What? Wait there, I'll co—"

"No!"

My hand flies to cover my mouth so much for being subtle.

"What do you mean no? How are you planning to come home?"

"I got a ride from..." My eyes fall on Miguel. His hair was mussed from when my fingers ran through it just minutes ago. His lips were swollen from our kisses. "I got a ride. I'll be home in a bit."

"What do you mean—" Chase starts, but I interrupt him. "See you soon."

Not giving him a chance to ask any more questions, I hang up the phone and run my hand over my face.

I was so freaking screwed.

The car comes to life, startling me. I turn toward Miguel, only to find him put together. Like nothing had happened. He checks the mirrors, although the road is completely empty given the time of the night, and starts driving.

Neither of us says a word until he pulls in front of my house.

"Thanks for the ride." I reach for the door handle, but Miguel's hand grabs mine before I can slip out.

"We have to talk about what happened."

I shake my head before he can even finish. "There is nothing to talk about."

His brows pull together, irritation flaring in his irises. "Rebecca..."

"No, Miguel. Tonight was a mistake." One big fucking mistake. "It shouldn't have happened."

I pull my hand out of his grasp. "Thanks for the ride."

His jaw clenches, but this time, he doesn't try to stop me as I slide out of the car and walk up the porch just as the door opens and Chase steps out. He looks me up and down, his sharp gaze not missing anything. Shifting his attention over my shoulder to Miguel's car that's still sitting in the driveway, before his focus is back on me, one brow rising in a silent question.

"Don't you even start," I mutter, as I push past him and up the stairs.

Everything that just happened is still playing in my head in vivid color.

I climb to the second floor, the reflection in the mirror hanging in the hallway catching my attention.

My hair is a mess, and my lips and neck are red and swollen from Miguel's stubble.

My hand rises, tracing the faint marks.

What the hell have I done?

CHAPTER

19

MIGUEL

"So what's the verdict?" I ask, crossing my arms over my chest as I watch the older man stick his head under the hood of the truck.

Last night, after I dropped Rebecca off at her house and returned to my parent's place, I found her keys on the passenger's side floor. They probably ended up there somewhere between our fight and sex.

Off-the-charts-I-couldn't-get-it-out-of-my-mind sex.

Not that I was surprised. Rebecca and I always had chemistry, even when we were just two stupid teens trying to figure out what the other person needed. And some of our best moments were after a fight.

Mr. Dalton mumbles something to himself, breaking me out of my musings. He pokes around for a moment longer before straightening and pulling the rag out of his back pocket to wipe at his oil-stained hands.

"Her alternator is dead. Not that her battery is any better. It's also time for an oil change."

I nod, having already figured out as much myself. "How fast can you do it?"

Mr. Dalton turns his attention to me. "It ain't gonna be

cheap. I can't believe she's still driving this old thing. I tried to tell Becky the last few times she came over that it would be much cheaper for her to simply buy a new car. More reliable too, but she wouldn't listen."

Of course she wouldn't listen. Rebecca loved that fucking truck. It was one of the last things of her dad's that she had.

"I don't care about the money. Can you fix it?"

His brows shoot up. "I can try, but it might take a while."

"Do that."

We go back to the front desk together, where I leave him my contact info so he can call me once he finishes with the truck and go to my SUV that's parked outside.

Jumping into the driver's seat, I start toward the ranch.

I was too restless to sleep after everything that happened last night and how we left things, but finding those keys was exactly the excuse I needed.

She could try to run away as much as she wanted, but she couldn't avoid me forever.

Not after everything that had happened.

"I can't believe this; I told you weeks ago!"

I slow down my jog when I hear an irritated female voice coming from the office at the front of the barn.

"What do you want me to do, Cheryl?" Aaron asks, clearly exasperated.

"I want you to stay with your son."

"I just explained to you that I have to go out in the fields with Dad. The fence is broken, and if we don't fix it, we risk losing some animals."

"It's always something with you. I had this trip planned with the girls for weeks, and you want me to cancel it at the very last minute? Can't your mother watch him?"

"She's not home. I think she mentioned a hairdresser appointment. I don't know."

"See! Even your mother has a life outside this ranch. You can't expect me to be stuck here all day."

I bite the inside of my cheek, weighing my options. I should probably leave. Nothing good will come from Aaron knowing I'd overheard his discussion with his wife.

Aaron lets out a long sigh. "I'm not asking you to stay here all day. You could take Gage with you."

"It's a girl's day, Aaron. Excuse me for wanting to go and have a few hours with my friends, and at the same time, get a dress for the wedding that's happening *next* week. You should just take Gage with you. He loves to ride."

The door creaks and I turn around to see a young boy, five or six maybe, slipping into the barn. He looks up, his light eyes widening in surprise when he sees me. The last time I saw my nephew, he was just a baby, but now he was an actual tiny human being. His dark hair is a mess of locks sitting on top of his head that reminds me so much of Aaron and I when we were kids. He's dressed in a pair of jeans and a plaid shirt, a little Stetson sitting on top of his head. He is like a mini version of my brother. The only thing he got from his mother was his green eyes.

"It's too far for him. He's too young," Aaron mutters, reminding me of the conversation going on.

"Of course he'd be too young to go with you, but you expect me to bring him with me everywhere."

Gage's gaze darts toward the shouting coming from the office, and I see his smile slip from his face.

Shit, he doesn't need to hear this.

"Cheryl—"

I step into the doorway. "He can come with me."

Both heads turn in my direction, matching surprised faces glancing at me. "What?"

"Gage." I give him a pointed look. "If you both are busy, he can come with me. I was planning to go to town anyway."

"See?" Cheryl lets her arms fall by her side. "Miguel will take him, and we can both do our thing."

"Gage doesn't even know him!" Aaron protests at the same time the little voice joins our conversation.

"Miguel? As in Uncle Miguel?"

I turn around to find Gage standing behind me, an unreadable expression on his face.

"Hey, buddy. Remember me?" I ask, crouching down so we're at the same level.

I might not have seen my nephew these past few years, but I had some experience dealing with kids. Lonestars wanted their players to do some PR and volunteer with kids, which, in all honesty, was the best part of the job, and I never minded doing it.

Gage's brows pull together. "Not really, but Dad sometimes talks about you. You play football?"

Aaron talks about me?

I wasn't sure what surprised me more. The fact that my brother mentioned me to his kid or that he told him about football.

"Yes, I do. You like football?"

He shakes his head, giving me an apologetic smile. "Not really."

I let out a soft chuckle. "That's fine."

"I like riding horses. I'm going to be a rancher just like Daddy one day."

"That's amazing, pal. You wanna know a secret?" I lean closer and whisper softly, "I love riding horses too."

Those green eyes turn into saucers. "You do?"

"Sure do, but I think I'm rusty since I've been gone so long. What do you say, wanna hang with me today? You can tell me all you know while we do some chores."

Gage glances from me to Aaron. "Can I?"

My brother's gaze shifts to me, and I just shrug, leaving it up to him. Aaron lifts his hand and pinches the bridge of his nose. "Sure thing, buddy."

"Give me ten so I can take a shower, and I'll come pick you up?"

Aaron nods, and Cheryl shoots me a big smile. "It's good to see you, Miguel. Thanks for doing this."

"Of course. I'll be back in a bit."

"So where are we going?" Gage asks a little while later from the back of Aaron's truck. He insisted I take it, so we didn't have to deal with changing the car seat.

"I have to return something to one of my friends in town."

"But you don't live here."

I look up in the review mirror to find him watching me intently. "So?"

"So, how do you have friends here? I usually see my friends every day when I'm in school."

I let out a soft chuckle at his serious expression. "I used to go to school with my friends too. But now, we usually talk on the phone."

Gage tilts his head to the side as he thinks about my answer. "I guess that makes sense. I don't see my friends that often now that it's summer."

"No? What do you usually do then?"

Gage lifts his shoulders. "Play on the ranch. Daddy and Papaw let me ride a horse, but only if I take care of it afterward."

"You like horses a lot?"

"Horses are the best. I could ride *all* day long and never get tired of it." His whole face lights up, and the sheer joy of it reminds me of my own childhood—the good times, at least.

"I bet you wouldn't."

Spotting an open parking space, I pull the car to a stop. "C'mon, we're here."

Unbuckling my seatbelt, I get out of the car, but before I can open the back door, Gage's already running out.

"Where are we going?"

"To the Reading Nook."

"Really?" He fist pumps excitedly. "Yes!"

I don't get a chance to say anything because he's already running toward the café.

Shit.

If I lose this kid, Aaron will kill me.

Rushing after him, I push open the door of the café only to come to a stop at the sound of Rebecca's laughter.

"We missed you the other day for the reading club," Rebecca says to Gage, who's already sitting on the barstool next to the counter.

"I missed you too, Miss Becky, but Mom said she was busy and she couldn't take me."

Rebecca brushes one wild strand out of Gage's face. "Are you with her today?"

"No, I'm with my Uncle Miguel!" Gage starts turning around as if he just remembered we came here together, his eyes light up when he spots me standing in the doorway. "Look! He's here. Did you know he's a famous football player?"

Rebecca's head whirls in my direction, her wide eyes

landing on mine, and I swear, it's like all the air is kicked out of my lungs at the sight of her.

I could still hear her soft moans, feel her warm breath tickling my skin, and her palms skimming over my muscles. Fuck, she was stunning. And last night just confirmed it all over again. There was just something special about Rebecca when she let her walls crumble and allowed people to see her just the way she was.

For a moment, we just stare at one another, neither of us saying a word. Her eyes roam my face before her gaze falls to my mouth. My tongue darts out, sliding over my lower lip, remembering the taste of her on my mouth, reminding me of all the other things I haven't tasted in a while. Just thinking about it has my dick twitching in need.

As if she can read my mind, color creeps up her cheeks.

"Miss Becky?" Gage nudges her hand.

"Hmm?" With a shake of her head, she looks down at the boy.

"Did you know my uncle plays football for a living?"

She tucks a strand of her hair behind her ear. "Yes, I know that."

Gage nods his head, a serious expression on his face. "I still think horses are way better."

Becky chokes on her laughter. "Horses are amazing, Gage."

"They sure are." Gage turns to me. "Can I go look at the books in the back?"

"Sure, just don't run out of the café without me knowing."

I barely get to finish before he's jumping off the chair and rushing toward the back.

"This kid will be the death of me," I mutter, my eyes following his every movement.

"Gage's a good kid."

"Yeah, he is."

Content that he seems to be entertained, at least for the moment, I turn my attention to the woman standing next to me.

Today, her makeup is minimal, her hair twisted in a braid of some sort that's falling down one shoulder. She's wearing a plain black tee with the café's logo on it along with the cutoff shorts, leaving what feels like miles of tanned skin exposed.

I was completely screwed when it came to this woman.

Rebecca notices me staring. Her throat bobs as she swallows. "What are you doing here, Miguel?"

"I wanted to let you know that I found your keys in my SUV last night. I guess they fell down when we..."

Before I can finish, she presses her hand against my mouth.

"Not so loud."

I look left and right. "There are legit three people in here," I mumble, my voice coming out muffled from underneath her palm.

"People in this town like to gossip," she hisses.

I gently wrap my fingers around her palm, pulling her hand away. "So what? It's not like it would be the first time."

"They're gossiping enough as it is. We don't need to give them any more ammunition."

I guess she was right about that one.

Rebecca pulls her hand from my grasp and walks behind the counter. "Where's my truck?"

I take the chair that Gage was sitting in only moments ago. "I took it to the shop."

Surprise flashes on her face. "You did what?"

"I took it to the shop." I shrug. "They'll call once the truck is fixed."

I don't bother pointing out they'll call me when it's done. There were some things she didn't need to know, and this was one of them.

"Oh." she tucks a strand of her hair back in place. "You didn't have to do that."

"I didn't mind."

Her teeth graze over her lower lip, drawing my attention to her mouth. The same mouth that I kissed last night, the little moans that came from those lips as I devoured her. The image was so vivid in my mind, and I couldn't get it out of my head.

"Miguel..." Rebecca sighs.

I look up to find her eyes narrowed at me.

"What?"

"Stop it."

I flash her my most innocent smile. "I'm not doing anything."

"You know exactly what you're doing." She crosses her arms over her chest. I know she's going for a scary look that should deter me, but the only thing it does is push her tits up, making me want to bury my head in her cleavage and show her just how much she wants me.

The corner of my mouth tips upward. "And what is that, pray tell?"

"We're not playing this game."

"Oh, I don't think this is a game at all." Leaning closer, I drop my voice so only she can hear me. "We have to talk about what happened last night."

Rebecca shakes her head immediately. "There is not—"

"We didn't use any protection," I point out, not giving her a chance to finish.

It's like I dropped a bucket of ice water over her head—her lips part, something that looks a lot like horror flashing on her face.

"It was stupid, I know, and I'm sorry."

"I..." Her tongue darts out, sliding over her lower lip. "I'm on the pill. And I'm clean, so you're good."

Some of the weight that's been on my shoulders since I realized what had happened last night falls off. But there is something else, something that feels a lot like disappointment.

"Do I have to worry about something?"

Worry about something? My brows pull together as her question registers in my head. "Hell, no. I told you last night..."

Her phone rings before I can finish. She lifts her finger as she picks it up and turns her back to me. "Yeah?"

My fingers clench into a fist by my side as the irritation builds inside of me.

Was she not listening to a word I told her last night?

She thought I was fucking around in Austin, and she had to go and check if she was clean?

"What?" I blink, my gaze falling on her squared shoulders. "But I told you Linda has to leave early, so I needed you to pick me up," Rebecca says to whoever is on the other side of the line. She listens for a moment. "I know, but somebody has to take care of Mom. Fine, I'll figure it out." Silence. "No, I'll figure it out."

She hangs up the phone, letting her hand drop.

"What's going on?" I ask, my voice coming out gruff.

I was still pissed as hell that she thought so little of me. Not just that, that she didn't believe a word I said. What did that say about last night? What did I want it to say?

I had no fucking clue.

"Chase was supposed to pick me up from work, but he got a call from the shelter."

"Shelter?"

"He volunteers. He helps them catch the runaways, and he even started training some of them to see if any have working-dog potential. Which is great. At least he leaves the house to go somewhere. I just wished he'd come when I needed him."

"You going home?"

"I—"

"What are you still doing here?" A short brunette comes from the kitchen, a tray in hand. "Didn't you say you have to go home early?"

"I do, I just don't have..."

"I'll take you home."

Rebecca turns around. "You don't have to do that."

"I'm going there anyway."

The same words I said last night echo in the space between us. Rebecca remembers it too. Her throat bobs as she swallows, but I can see some of that resolve crumbling.

"C'mon, Red, you said you were in a hurry. I can get you there in no time. And I promise, no sidetracking."

Her cheeks turn beet red. The other woman glances between the two of us with interest.

"Fine, I'm just going to grab my stuff."

Nodding, I watch her slip through the door behind the counter, my eyes falling on the curve of her ass peeking from underneath the shorts. Raising my hand, I rub at my chin.

Get a grip, dude.

Of course, the girl catches me staring, a knowing smirk on her lips.

"Gage!" I yell, turning toward the back of the café. "We're leaving."

The boy comes rushing back just as Rebecca joins us, a bag in hand.

"Thanks for doing this, Jessica," Rebecca says as we start toward the door.

"You know it. I'll see you tomorrow."

Pulling the door open, my hand slides to the small of her back. I can feel her shudder at my touch, but she doesn't say anything as we make our way to the car.

"You okay?" I ask, glancing around at Gage, who strapped himself in the car seat.

"Fine." He glances at Rebecca as I start the car. "Miss Becky, are you coming home with us? Maybe I can show you my horses. Uncle Miguel promised he would let me teach him how to take care of them. He said he forgot."

"Did he now?"

Rebecca and I exchange a look as Gage continues to chat away.

"He did! He doesn't have horses where he lives now." He shakes his head as if the idea itself is preposterous.

"He doesn't?" Rebecca surprise mocks.

"No! Can you believe it? But I'm going to teach him. We can go to the barn once we get back, right? I can teach you today."

"Sure thing, buddy."

Just then, my phone starts to ring, cutting off the music that's been playing.

From the side of my eye, I can see Rebecca's body stiffen. I glance at the screen, pressing the answer button.

"Yo, Monk, what's up?" my teammate's gruff voice fills the cabin of the car as I take the turn onto the gravel road. "You wanna come with us? We're planning to hit a few bars tonight. I know it's not really your scene, but I figured maybe you pulled that stick that you have shoved so far up your ass now that it's off-season, and you'd relax a little bit."

"Hello to you, too, assh—" My gaze darts to the rearview mirror to find Gage listening intently. "Butthole," I correct at the very last minute.

Rebecca shakes her head, giving me a side-eye.

"Butthole? What are you? Five?"

"No, Gonzales, but I have little ears in my car."

There is a pregnant pause. "You have a kid?"

"I have my nephew with me," I clarify. "And you're on speaker."

"Oh, shi— shoot. Sorry, I forgot Walker mentioned something about you visiting your family. I thought you came back already."

"Not yet." Rebecca's house comes into view.

"Well, once you come back to town, the offer still stands. You can't live off of practice and those protein shakes, Monk."

"I don't think I heard you," I yell loudly. "The connection sucks here. I'll have to catch you later."

"You sound fine to me."

"I'm losing you. Later!"

I disconnect the call just as we pull in front of Rebecca's house.

"What is a monk, Uncle Miguel?"

Rebecca and I exchange a look. I'm pretty sure I look like a deer caught in the headlights. Rebecca bites the inside of her cheek, and I can see the amusement dancing in her eyes as she waits for my answer.

"Umm... A monk is a religious person."

His little brows furrow. "Like preacher Jamison?"

"Yeah, just like that." I nod my head. "Wait a bit in here. I'll be right back and then we'll go look at the horses."

Pushing the door open, I get out of the truck. Just as I'm rounding the hood, Rebecca's door opens.

"I could have done that."

"It's fine." She looks toward her house. "Thank you for the ri—"

She tries to walk past me, but I corner her against the truck, my hand slipping under her chin as I lift her head up so her eyes meet mine, those pretty pink lips parting in surprise.

Screw it.

Leaning down, I press my mouth against hers. Rebecca's

palm lands on my chest. I can feel her uncertainty there for a moment before her fingers grip my shirt, pulling me closer. I nip at her lip, my tongue slipping into her mouth. My body hums in agreement, blood pumping through my veins. The need to be closer to her, to explore every inch of her body and hear her call out my name, is overwhelming, but I force myself to take a step back.

"The. Only. One."

Rebecca blinks her eyes open, a confused expression flashing on her face. "Huh?"

"Gonzales is full of shit, but what he said is true. There is a reason my teammates call me Monk. I don't go out. I don't party. I don't drink. I don't do hookups. There hasn't been anyone else. Not one single person since you walked out of my life three years ago."

Lifting her chin, I rub my thumb over her lower lip one last time. Then, although it physically pains me, I force myself to drop my hand and take a step back.

"I'll see you later, Red."

CHAPTER

20

REBECCA

"Thanks for picking me up," I say in a way of greeting as I slide into Kate's SUV.

"What happened to your car?"

"Alternator. I think?"

Kate glances at me as she starts driving. "You don't know?"

"I wasn't the one who took the car to the shop."

Her brows draw together at my confession. "You didn't? Then, who did?"

The image of Miguel flashes in my mind. Those calloused fingers cupping my cheek as his brown eyes stared into mine so intently, I could have sworn he could see to the very bottom of my soul. Even just thinking about it makes my stomach squeeze tightly.

I don't go out. I don't party. I don't drink. I don't do hookups. There hasn't been anyone else. Not one single person since you walked out of my life three years ago.

Was he telling the truth? And if so, did it change anything? Did I want it to change anything?

After everything that was revealed in the last few days, I didn't know what to think about this whole situation between the two of us.

Did I overreact back then? Should I have stayed and listened? Would I have listened if he had tried harder to explain what had happened?

Did it even matter?

It's been three years. Three long years since we broke up. Was there even a point of thinking about the what-ifs?

Three years, and yet, you jumped into his arms the first chance you got, a little voice reminds me.

"Becky?"

I blink, Kate's curious face coming into focus. "I..." I tuck a strand of my hair behind my ear, looking out the window, and lie, "Chase. He's been driving me around, too."

At least, that last part was true.

Partially.

I couldn't exactly tell her it was Miguel, out of all people, who was the one who took my car to the shop. She'd have a gazillion questions and make a way bigger deal out of it than it should be. Not that I could blame her. I had all those questions myself and no answer in sight.

"Mhmm... I heard somebody else gave you a ride the other day. Care to comment on that?"

Shit, I was so caught.

"I don't know what you're talking about."

"Rebecca Allison Williams!"

"You're pulling out the middle name? I think that's the proof that we've made a southern lady out of you after all."

"Don't you try to change the subject, Becky. Did you or did you not ride in Miguel's car?"

Biting the inside of my cheek, I look out the window. "Look, we're here."

"Do not force me to drive around the block one more time. You know I'll do it."

"Fine," I let out an exasperated sigh. "It was just a ride.

Chase was busy, and I needed to get back home. Now, can we get inside and try those dresses, please?"

Thankfully, Kate listens and parks her car in front of the shop. Killing the engine, she turns to me. "You know you can talk to me, right?"

"I know," I whisper softly, my throat feeling tight.

And I did. The problem was that I didn't know *what* to tell her. How do I explain all the conflicting thoughts and emotions that were fighting inside of me? Besides, she had enough on her hands as it was.

Kate nods after a moment of silence. "Let's get inside."

Not needing to be told twice, I push my door open and slide out.

After a lot of searching, Kate finally found her wedding dress in a little boutique in the next town over, and it was perfect for her.

The smiling attendant greets us as we walk into the cool shop.

"I'm so happy to see you both again. I have your dresses ready for you. Would you like a glass of champagne or a mimosa before we start?"

Kate shakes her head. "I'm good, thank you."

Her attention shifts to me, but I wave her off. "I'm good, too."

"Okay, then. Let's get to work." She leads us toward the back of the store, where there is an empty loveseat and an armchair. We leave our things there as the attendant motions toward the changing rooms.

"Which one do you want to try first?"

"You go," I tell Kate as we follow the attendant.

Kate takes off her clothes, and the attendant helps her into the dress. I watch as she expertly works, buttoning a gazillion tiny buttons on her back.

"Emmett will have a field day with these," I chuckle softly, trying to imagine my giant of a friend trying to get Kate out of the wedding dress with those big-ass hands of his.

"There you go. What do you think? Does it fit better? We loosened it a little bit in the mid-section area, just like we discussed the last time.

Loosened it? My brows pull together in confusion. *I don't remember anything about that. Why would they need to loosen it?*

Kate steps onto a little stool in front of a big three-way mirror and does a little twirl, checking out her reflection. Instead of going for a traditional white dress, hers was pale beige, almost champagne color. Thin spaghetti straps cover her shoulders. A heart-shaped bodice accentuates the curve of her cleavage, and a row of tiny buttons goes down her back. Her skirt is falling down in a straight line with a layer of tulle and lace over it.

"Yes, I think this fits better now." Kate slides her hand over her side; her eyes meet mine in the reflection. "What do you think? Will he like it?"

"He won't know what hit him," I tell her honestly.

Even pale and with bags under her eyes, there was just something so radiant about Kate in her wedding dress. The dress was made for her, and I knew she would look stunning on her wedding day. Not that Emmett would care one bit either way. Kate was his whole world. He was so goddamn in love with her he would have married her in her PJs with messy hair and no makeup while they sat in their living room. But wearing that dress? He'll be a goner.

"The only question is, how quickly will he start to cry."

Her eyes meet mine in the mirror. "Oh, shut up. He won't cry."

"I wouldn't be so sure about that," I sing-song. "Wanna place a bet?"

"I'm not betting against my fiancé!"

"You're no fun." I slide my hand around her waist. "I mean it, though. He's one lucky guy to have you."

A soft expression passes over her face as she leans her head against my shoulder. "I'm the lucky one to get all of you. And to think I thought it would be Penny and me forever, and now we have this big, nosy town all having our backs." Her eyes mist, and she sniffles softly.

"Hey." I turn around, poking her gently in the side. "No crying."

Kate tilts her head back, sliding her finger under her eyes. "I don't know what's wrong with me. I've been a mess lately."

"You're about to marry the love of your life while setting up your business and future, all while you were sick. It's normal that you're overwhelmed."

"I know, but my mood swings have been all over the place, and I hate it. I'm not a crier."

"No, you're not, but every girl needs a break occasionally. How about you take that dress off before you get it all wet?"

With the help of the attendant, we get Kate out of her dress, after which I try my own gown. Happy with the final result, we wait for the woman to pack our dresses in bags and get out of there.

I listen to Kate tell me about dress shopping with her aunt, Penny, and Mrs. Santiago as we make our way back to her place. Kate insisted that she wanted her dress to be a surprise for everybody, so she only asked me to come dress shopping with her.

Later on, Kate admitted that the pressure from her aunt and Mrs. Santiago was getting to her, and while she didn't mind giving in too much when it came to the party, she wanted to choose the dress for herself. So the two of us went shopping alone, but that meant that Kate also had to go shopping with her family, too.

Kate's phone rings as we get out of the car at her house. I go toward the back seat, pulling out the bags with dresses, when I overhear Kate's side of the conversation.

"Right now?" She chews on her lip as she listens intently to whatever the other person is saying. "Yeah, of course. I understand. Okay, I'll be there."

With a goodbye, she hangs up and runs her hand through her hair, letting out a long breath.

"Is everything okay?"

Kate jumps a little at my question before turning around to face me. "No, well, yes, but I have to go and take care of something." Her gaze falls on the bags. "Can you take those upstairs to the guest room? Just make sure to lock the door." She pulls the key out of her purse and hands it to me. "I wouldn't put it past Emmett to go snooping around."

I let out a strangled laugh. "You know it. Anything else? When are your college friends coming?"

"Their plane will land in a couple of hours. I hope this won't take too long, and I'll have enough time to set everything up."

"What do you need to do? I can help."

"Really? I've already put so much on you."

"That's what maids of honor are for. Spill."

I listen carefully as Kate tells me everything that needs to be done before the party tonight, already mentally cataloging where to start.

"Shit, I really need to go. Will you be okay?"

"Perfect, don't worry about anything."

"You're the best." With a quick hug, Kate dashes for the car. "You know where the front door key is, right?"

"Yeah, yeah." I wave her off.

I shift the bags with the dresses to one arm as I climb the few steps to the front porch. Rising on the tips of my toes, I reach for the shelf above the door to grab the key the two have stashed there. Not really original, but then again, the crime rate in Bluebonnet was minimal, so rarely anybody, especially somebody living on the ranch outside of the town, bothered with locking the door.

The weight of the dresses makes me wobbly on my feet. Cursing quietly, I feel my muscles strain as I try to reach further, but just when I'm about to get it, the front door opens, and I stumble forward.

"*Holy shit...*"

A wall of muscles greets me, and I clutch the person's shirt, trying to steady myself.

"Trying to break in, Red?"

The low, husky voice has the hair at my nape rising.

My fingers clench around the material as my heart does a little flip inside my chest. I slowly raise my gaze until I meet familiar chocolate eyes observing me with the same silent intensity that was focused on me the last time we were together before he turned around and walked away, leaving me with words that have haunted me for the past forty-eight hours.

There hasn't been anyone else.

Not one single person since you walked out of my life three years ago.

And now we were alone once again.

CHAPTER

21

MIGUEL

"Are you trying to scare me to death?" Rebecca lets go the moment she realizes who she's holding onto, like she's been burned.

Her reaction shouldn't sting, but it did.

I lean against the doorframe, trying to hide the fact that feeling her hands on me unnerved me unlike anything else.

I tried to stay away the last couple of days, giving her some time to think about what had happened and all the things that were said. What I expected it to accomplish, I wasn't sure. But I couldn't take her looking at me with so much distrust.

"If I remember correctly, you were the one trying to break in."

She crosses her arms over her chest, clutching two long white bags. "I wasn't breaking in. I was trying to get the key so I could take this inside. The better question is, what are *you* doing here?"

"Emmett called me and asked if I could pick up some stuff at the store for the party later tonight and start the barbecue since he was called out to the fields. There was some issue with the cattle or something."

I didn't ask too much; I was just grateful for the opportunity to finally get out of my parent's house and from my dad's disapproving gaze.

"He..." For a while, her mouth hangs open, but then she presses her lips together and shakes her head, looking away. "Of course he did."

"He said Kate should be home, but the place was empty, so I looked around until I found the key. Not that it was hard to find it."

"Well, Kate got a phone call, so she asked me to put these away and help set things up."

Her gaze turns to me, finally meeting mine. I take in her face and the silence stretches between us as the realization sets in.

"So it's just the two of us," I whisper, my voice coming out raspy.

"Yeah."

I watch as her throat bobs, and my gaze zeros in on the motion. I could still remember how soft the curve of her neck was, the intoxicating scent of roses that clung to her skin as I buried my face in her neck, the warmth of her skin.

I shift my weight from one foot to the other as my body starts reacting to the memory of her in my arms.

"You don't have to stay," Rebecca points out.

The muscle in my jaw twitches in irritation at her comment.

She expected me to leave?

"Yeah, because my family is crazy about me hanging around the house."

An understanding flashes on her face, her eyes softening slightly. But I didn't want her pity. I wanted... I don't even know what I wanted, to be completely honest.

So much was said between us, and yet, at the same time, nothing was actually resolved, and it irked me to no end.

It's like the divide between us was bigger than ever, and I didn't know what to do about it.

Should I talk to her? Figure out what went wrong between us? Why, after everything that played out three years ago, she still kept it a secret this whole time? Ask her why she never told anybody what had happened the day we broke up? Ask her why she didn't even give me a chance to explain what had happened? Why she didn't trust me? Trust in us? Would it even matter? Would going back change anything? Did I want it to change?

"Fine," Becky mutters, breaking me out of my thoughts. "I'm going to take the dress inside before Emmett gets home. Kate made me promise I'd make sure he doesn't see it before the wedding day."

She squeezes the bags closer to her chest and starts for the door. Her body brushes against mine as she slides past me. The damn bag is almost as big as her, and it's dragging on the floor.

"Give me that before you trip over it and fall." I slide my hand under the bag, our skin brushing together as I pull the dress out of her arms.

A frown appears on her face as she tries to tug it back, but I hold it out of her reach. "I can do this myself, thank you very much."

"I didn't say you can't. I just don't want you to break your neck in the process. The last thing I need is for Kate to want to murder me any more than she already does. Where do you want this?"

"Fine," she huffs. "She said to put it in the guest room."

Without another word, she turns around and starts marching up the stairs. I watch her stiff back as she climbs up, my gaze falling down her body. She's dressed in another plain tee and a pair of cutoff jean shorts that hug her curves like a second skin. Her legs have a golden hue to them, her hips swaying softly with every step she takes. My mouth goes dry as I watch that slow movement, my pants growing tighter by the second.

I know I should look away, but I can't. It's almost like I'm transfixed. No, there is no almost about it. I'm transfixed by her. There always something about Rebecca that drew my attention from the time we were kids. It was her natural beauty and the determined way she walked through the world. I had an opportunity to meet my fair share of beautiful women, but none of them held a candle to her.

Rebecca stops in the middle of the staircase and looks over her shoulder, her eyes narrowing on me. "Were you staring at my ass just now?"

I pinch the bridge of my nose, muttering silent curses at being caught staring. Of course, she'd have no problem calling me out on it, either.

"It's a nice ass."

A flicker of surprise flashes on her face, but she stifles it quickly. "Hurry up, we have work to do." Not waiting for an answer, she turns around and continues marching upstairs.

Seriously, this woman is giving me whiplash.

"I'm coming."

I take two steps at a time, catching up to her once she gets to the second floor and unlocks the first door to the right. The room is simple. A queen-sized bed occupies most of the space, with a nightstand on each side. Opposite of the bed is a small armoire with a TV hanging above it and another door that leads to the bathroom.

"Just put it on the bed."

Wordlessly, I do as she says. One of the bags unzipped slightly, giving me a peek at the golden gown sitting inside.

"Is this Kate's?"

My throat bobs as I swallow. I don't know what it was about the whole situation that made me unsettled. Maybe it was the fact that I never thought about Rebecca and a wedding dress in the same sentence, but now that the image crossed my mind, I couldn't get it out of my head. What kind of dress would she pick? One of those princessy, over-the-top gowns? No, that wasn't Rebecca. She'd go for something simple and elegant. Something—

"No, that's mine." Rebecca glares at me, pushing my hands away. "The no-snooping rule goes for you too, mister."

She firmly puts the zipper in place, making sure both bags are lying flat against the mattress. Only when she's happy does she take a step back and bump into me.

My hands grab her hips, steadying her.

She sucks in a breath at the contact, looking over her shoulder. Our gazes meet, and the air crackles with pent-up tension as my gaze falls to her face, lowering to her parted lips.

My tongue darts out, those hazel eyes fixing on my lips, and I can see her swallow hard.

"Rebecca..." I groan, my fingers digging into her hips.

Her eyes linger on my mouth for a moment longer before she slowly lifts them to meet mine.

"I can't be responsible for what I'll do if you keep watching me like that."

"I don't watch you in any way," she whispers softly.

"Liar." Her eyes widen in surprise at the accusation. Unclenching my fingers, I skim the back of my hand over her cheek, brushing her hair out of her face. My eyes trace my movement, taking in every little detail about her. The way her lips part. Her chest rises at the soft intake of breath. Color floods her cheeks at my touch. Goosebumps rise on her skin.

Sliding my hand to her stomach, I pull her flush against me, my head bending down, lips brushing against the shell of her ear. "You can say anything you want, Red, but your body will always reveal the truth," I whisper, my voice coming out husky as I fight the surge of lust cursing through me. "Always."

A shudder runs through her body at my words, her eyes squeezing shut. "Miguel..."

Whatever she wanted to say was lost when a loud bang came from somewhere in the house, making us both jump in surprise.

"Miguel?" Mrs. Santiago calls from downstairs.

"Shit."

Rebecca's eyes shoot open, panic flaring in her irises. She quickly pulls out of my grasp, her hand reaching out to smooth her hair.

"Are you in here?"

"Go," she whispers.

"Rebecca..."

"Go," she hisses softly. "I have to lock up, and then we have things to do."

I rake my fingers through my hair, my jaw clenching. "Fine."

With one last look at her, I step out of the room and take a deep breath to collect myself. My gaze falls down to the bulge in my pants.

"Miguel?" Mrs. Santiago calls again, then mutters more quietly, "Where is that boy?"

You know how screwed you are when not even the fact that my best friend's mother almost caught us helps with my hard-on. Rearranging myself, I quietly move down the stairs. Following the sound of rustling, I find Emmett's mother in the kitchen placing plastic containers into the fridge. She must hear me because she looks over her shoulder. "There you are! I've been looking for you."

"Sorry, Mrs. S., I was in the bathroom," I lie.

She waves me off. "It's all good. C'mon, help me get all the food from the car."

I follow her as she marches out of the kitchen like a woman on a mission. "Kate hasn't been feeling well lately, so I decided I'd make some side dishes for you kids so she doesn't have to worry about it. Becky, what are you doing here?"

Mrs. Santiago opens her arms and wraps them around Rebecca. Her gaze meets mine over her shoulder.

When she had the time to sneak out, I had no idea.

Rebecca pulls back. "Kate mentioned needing help with the party, so I decided to come early."

"That's so nice of you." Mrs. S. pats Rebecca's shoulder, her gaze moving between the two of us. "C'mon, you two, we have a lot of work to do."

"Well, well, well, if it isn't the hotshot defenseman himself, and here I thought you were too good for us now that you're a big star." A hand slaps me over the shoulder as Timothy and Jamie come into view.

"I was always too big of a star for you, so I don't see how a new address changes that," I throw right back.

"Maybe you had too big of a stick stuck up your ass," Timothy chuckles as he pulls me into a half-hug. "It's good to see you, man."

"You too," I agree, shifting my attention to Jamie, who extends his hand. "How have you guys been doing? What are you up to?"

"Prepping to go to law school," Jamie says.

My brows shoot up. "No shit?"

"Yeah, busted my knee up freshman year, so I tried a few different things to figure out what I wanna do with my life, and I ended up really enjoying the debate team, so here we are."

"I can't say I'm surprised. You always liked to argue."

"Oh, shut up." Jamie elbows me, unsuccessfully trying to keep a straight face.

"That's so cool, man, really." I turn toward Timothy. "What about you? Still causing trouble? Chasing girls around the town?"

Timothy chuckles lightly and lifts his hand, a wedding band shining on his finger. "Hardly. My version of trouble these days is not putting my dirty clothes where they belong, so I must find different ways to apologize to my wife."

"Wife?"

Well, I didn't see that one coming. Timothy was one of the biggest playboys when we played together in high school. I was certain he'd stay single forever.

"And a kid on the way." He looks around and points toward the tables. "She's there."

A little brunette looks our way and smiles at him which has a big, goofy grin spreading over his face.

"Who'd have thought? The biggest playboy from our class has turned into a sap," Jamie teases. "Not just that. Can you believe he's teaching the new generation? We're all screwed."

"What?"

Timothy shrugs. "I'm working as an assistant coach for the high school. It's actually been pretty cool. You should see some of the boys play. They're so fucking good. I can't wait to see what they can do in the next season."

"That's amazing. Who'd have thought that you, of all people, would end up being a pillar of respectfulness?"

"I think calling him a pillar of respectfulness is pushing it a little," Jamie laughs.

"Fuck off, you're just jealous I get to play when you have to deal with people's bullshit all day."

Jamie takes a sip of his beer. "I'll remind you of that when you come complaining to me about one high school drama or another."

"It'll keep things interesting." Timothy turns to me. "But seriously, if you have time, you should stop by the school. It's technically off-season, and we can't practice, but I've seen some of the boys working out alone on the field. I'm sure they'd appreciate you coming. Everybody went crazy last year when they found out a Bluebonnet native got into the NFL. It gives them hope that they can do it too."

"I'll try to drop by the school." I knew better than most how meeting somebody you admire can change your life for the better and give you the motivation to keep working hard. "A high school coach, married with a baby on the way." I shake my head. "How things have changed."

Just then, a flash of red catches my attention. I glance toward the house where Rebecca is talking to a group of women.

She went back home to change after we set everything up and fuck me. If I thought she looked stunning in a simple tee and shorts, it had nothing on Rebecca in a dress. Especially not this tight-fitting, straps crisscrossing-over her back kind of a dress. At first, the tension between us was almost palpable, and having Mrs. Santiago around didn't help much either. I wanted to talk to Rebecca about what had happened, but she did everything in her power to ignore me, and she only talked to me when she was bossing me around on where to set things up. Then Emmett and Kate came, along with their college friends, and things became even crazier if possible.

"And I guess some things never change," Jamie snickers.

"What?" Lifting the beer, I take a long sip as I turn my attention back to the guys.

"You and Becky?" Jamie nudges my shoulder with his. "Is that still a thing?"

"They broke up, asshole," Timothy chimes in. "I told you that."

"So what? You'd never think it by the way he looks at her."

My fingers grip the bottle tighter, and I make a point to keep my eyes on him even though every fiber of my body wants me to seek her out. "And how is that?" I ask as casually as possible.

Although I avoided alcohol for the most part, I needed something to ground me tonight, but now I had a feeling this one beer wouldn't cut it. I feel the itch to turn around and seek her in the crowd, but I force myself to stay still. I didn't want to draw any more attention to myself than I already had.

"Like you did when we were dumb high schoolers."

"What did we do as dumb high schoolers?" Emmett asks as he joins our group, Lucas, Kevin and his college friends following behind him.

"What we didn't do is a better question," I mutter as my gaze meets Hayden Watson's.

He tips his chin in my direction, the corner of his mouth lifting in a smile. "What's up, Fernandez? Long time no see."

I met Emmett's friends once when we were playing against one another back in college, and just this spring, Hayden entered the draft early, just like I did, and he was lucky enough to stay in Boston.

We exchange a handshake as Emmett makes the introductions around the group. "These are Nixon and Hayden. You guys remember Miguel, my best man, and these are Jamie and Timothy, our high school buddies."

The introductions are made, and we chat a little bit about their trip as we finish our beers.

"What did I hear about some kind of famous football game y'all play here?" Nixon claps his hands together, a big grin on his face.

Emmett's eyes narrow. "Your southern accent sucks, Cole. Don't do that shit again."

The quarterback shrugs. "Hey, when in Texas."

"We can't play since we're missing...." Timothy looks around, his gaze fixing on something over my shoulder. "Oh, no, he's here."

My muscles stiffen at his words because only one person is missing, and that's...

Emmett turns around, so I do the same, my gaze finding Nico standing next to the tables.

Talking to Rebecca.

There is a soft smile on her face as she listens to whatever he has to say.

What is so fucking funny?

"They got pretty close," Emmett's comment has me gritting my teeth in irritation.

What they were, was standing too fucking close. Rebecca was leaning against the table, that damn dress raised high up her thigh, and his knee was brushing against hers.

"Yeah. I guess it makes sense considering they were some of the rare people who stayed back and didn't go to an out-of-town college."

That was the second time somebody mentioned the two of them being all alone here. Did they know something I didn't? Did something really happen between the two of them? And why did the thought make me want to pummel my fist into Nico's stupid face?

A loud whistle spreads through the backyard.

"Yo, Nico!" Jamie yells loudly, drawing his attention. "We playing football or what?"

"I'm coming!" Nico shouts back before turning his attention to Rebecca and saying something only she can hear.

Whatever it is must be comedic because she bursts into laughter.

My fingers clench tightly into a fist by my side.

You don't want to attack one of your high school friends and make a scene.

But I did.

I so fucking did.

"Okay, then, let's assemble the teams." Emmett nudges me with his elbow. "I think I'll take my best man. Just like in the good ol' days."

"We'll see if you can catch up, old man," I say, glancing at him. Emmett chuckles, "We'll see about that."

They go back to dividing the teams, and my attention darts back to Rebecca and Nico. Who are *still* talking.

"I guess we're one person short," Hayden comments.

"Becky!" Emmett yells. She turns around, clearly rolling her eyes. "What?"

"Wanna play with us?"

Even from here, I can see the excitement shine in her eyes. Rebecca was always our biggest supporter, being at almost every game and practice. I saw first-hand how people brushed her off because she was a girl, but she put them in their place really quickly because that girl knew her football.

"Yes!" She does a little excited dance before she and Nico finally decide to join us. "Who are we playing with?"

"You are with Hayden, and Nico is with us," Emmett points out.

"Perfect." She rubs her hands together. "I get to kick your asses."

Just then, she looks down at herself. "Shit, I guess I should get rid of this."

Before my brain realizes what she's saying, she grabs the

hem of her dress, pulling it over her head, and leaving her only in a freaking black bikini.

Fuck. My. Life.

REBECCA

"Okay, let's do this," Hayden says, and we all clap hands together as we turn around to take our positions.

Kate cheers loudly from the sideline with Penelope and Henry next to her, grinning at me. The rest of our friends have grabbed blankets and moved closer to our makeshift field so they could watch the show.

Turning forward, I almost stumble over my own feet when I see the man standing on the other side.

Miguel.

Seriously, it's not fair how good that man looks. His skin has a golden hue from being in the sun. His shoulders are wide, each muscle and line defined to perfection. He ditched his shirt at some point earlier today and is showing off his naked chest, narrow waist, carved abs and that deep V that leads to a pair of bright red swim trunks that hang low on his hips.

My teeth graze over my bottom lip as my gaze falls lower.

Way too low.

I shift my weight from one foot to the other, but it doesn't help relieve the ache rising between my thighs.

How is it that it's barely been a few days, but I already wanted to jump his bones? You'd think I didn't have practice staying away from the man. Only now that we crossed that line and had sex, I couldn't stop thinking about the way his hands felt on my body or how much I craved his kisses.

Get a grip, Becky, before somebody realizes where your head's at.

I force my gaze up, but not fast enough.

Miguel's eyes meet mine, and if I'm to believe the dark, hungry look shining in his irises, he's thinking about the very same thing. One dark brow quirks up almost imperceptibly, and I know he caught me checking him out. His eyes slowly take me in from head to toe, and he likes what he sees.

"Was that really necessary?" he asks in that husky voice of his that I swear I can feel to my very core.

"Was what necessary?"

"The bikini."

The...

I prop my hands against my hips. "Miguel Luis Fernandez, you did not just tell me to go and cover up!"

"Shit, she pulled out the middle name," somebody chuckles softly.

"It's never good when they bring out the middle name. That's when you know you really fucked up."

Ignoring them, I keep all my focus on the man in front of me.

"I just figured it'd be easier."

Bullshit.

My brow quirks up. "Easier for who exactly? Because this is perfect for me, and if you have a problem with it, well, tough luck, buddy. You didn't hear me complain because all of you boys are walking around half-naked."

The muscle in his jaw twitches, eyes narrowing, so I know I've hit a nerve.

"Fine, whatever. Are we playing or what?" Miguel asks just as Nico appears by his side.

"I figured I'd take this spot," Nico says, glancing between Miguel and me.

Miguel snorts. "Sorry, but this one works better for me." He rolls his shoulder. "Can't risk injuring it, or my coach will get an aneurysm, you understand that, right?"

Nico opens his mouth, but before he can say anything, Emmett claps his hands. "In positions people."

With an apologetic smile on his face, Nico goes to the other side to take his place.

"That was mean," I say, crossing my arms over my chest.

Miguel smirks and bends down. "No, what was mean was that he tried to butt his way in here."

His eyes zero in on me and don't let go as everybody around us gets into position.

"Stop it," I grit through clenched teeth so nobody else can hear.

"I'm not doing anything."

"You're staring at me like..." My tongue darts out, sliding over my lower lip.

Miguel's eyes roam over my body, and a shiver passes down my spine at the intensity of his stare. I swear I can feel his gaze like an actual touch.

"Like?" he prompts, all innocence.

Like you want to devour me. The words are on the tip of my tongue, but I swallow them back. There was no way I'd admit it out loud.

"Somebody will notice."

"You started it when you took off that dress." Miguel leans closer, so close I can smell the spicy scent of his cologne. "And there was no fucking way I'd let another man put his hands all over your naked body. Especially not a man who clearly has a crush on you."

"Game time, baby!" Emmett yells, startling me.

I pulled back immediately, realizing how close we were together, but thankfully, nobody else seemed to have noticed.

Since we're starting on offense, when Callie blows the whistle, Jamie calls out the play. From the corner of my eye, I can see the ball fly into Nixon's awaiting hands. I start to move, but Miguel's arms wrap around me, pulling me into his chest in a stronghold.

"What are you doing?" I ask, looking over my shoulder at him as I try to get out of his grasp.

"What does it look like I'm doing? Defending my territory."

My stomach twists in a knot at the possessiveness of his words. Something tells me that this doesn't have anything to do with football, and I'm not sure how to feel about it.

Contrary to me, Hayden didn't have any problem getting through the defense, gaining us ten yards.

The first quarter is so intense I wonder for a second if we somehow ended up in the NFL instead of Emmett's backyard, but nope, we're still where we're supposed to be. We're the first one to score a touchdown, but by the end of it, Miguel's team has evened the score.

The second quarter is much of the same. Miguel moves past me and scores on the first try, but then we manage to retaliate, thanks to Lucas and me. Lucas fist bumps me, and Nico gives me a high five, but when I turn around, I find Miguel scowling at us from a distance.

After that, things turn nasty.

Miguel's guarding me like a hawk. And he's touching me. Every chance he gets. Although I know it's coming, there is no bracing for the way those calloused fingers run over my skin. Or stopping the reaction of my body to him.

And he knows it.

He fucking knows it.

Miguel jumps to his feet, a pleased smirk on his mouth, after tackling me to the ground for the hundredth time. He offers me a hand, but I shoot him a glare and push upright myself, dusting the earth off my ass as I get back to my team.

"We've gotta get this one if we want to win," Hayden murmurs as our team huddles together.

"Good luck with that, Miguel's been a pain in the ass." Lucas glances over his shoulder, and I catch a sight of the other team discussing their strategy.

"The guy probably thinks he's playing in the pros."

"Well, he is playing in the pros," Jamie points out. "It's not his problem you've been out of the game for so long."

Lucas shoves him away. "Shut up, Jamie."

I get in between them. "Okay, just throw me the ball."

"You?" Lucas' skepticism is clear. "He's been riding your ass this whole time."

My lips press in a tight line, but before I can say anything, Hayden slaps him over the head. "If she says to give her the ball, give her the ball."

Callie, who's been somewhat of a referee this whole time, blows the whistle. "Last play!"

"Time to hustle people. I'm getting hungry," Emmett yells.

I roll my eyes, and a few people boo him as we get on the line.

Miguel flashes me a blinding smile. "Ready to lose, Red?"

"In your dreams."

"Mhmm... That could be arranged."

Arrogant asshole.

"You think you're the man?" I flash him a smile as I bounce on the balls of my feet.

Jamie snaps the ball to Nixon, and I start to run. Miguel lunges toward me, but I manage to duck to my right and slip out of his reach. Nixon throws the ball, which lands perfectly in my arms, so I run toward our makeshift end zone. People cheer for me from the sidelines, and my hair whips around me as I turn around to find Miguel just behind me.

"This is the best you can do, Mr. Hotshot Football Player?" I ask as I do a celebratory dance.

But then strong arms wrap around me, and my body collides with a hard chest.

Hard, *naked* chest.

All the air is kicked out of my lungs as he lifts me up, my feet dangling in the air.

"Miguel!" I yell in protest, but the only thing it does is make his grip on me tighten.

"I warned you," he whispers in my ear, his low voice sending chills running down my spine.

"I didn't do anything," I mutter. "Put me down."

"Can't do that, Red. You wouldn't want people to get an eyeful, now would you?"

"What are you..."

I suck in a breath as my ass brushes against him, his hard length nestling between my cheeks.

"Oh..." I look over my shoulder, my lips parting in surprise. Miguel's gaze falls on my mouth, and he curses quietly.

The next thing I know, he's running with me in his arms, and before I manage to grasp what's happening, we're airborne. My hands clasp around him tighter as we fall into the lake with a big splash. The cold water is a shock to my system. A shudder goes through me, but strong, warm hands don't let go of me.

Together, we swim to the surface. My hair plasters to my face as I suck in a long breath, kicking my legs so I can stay afloat.

"Are you crazy?" I push my hair back and turn around to face him.

"What?" Miguel laughs. "It was getting hot out there."

"I'll give you hot." I push him back, his laughter following after me as I swim to the shore and get out of the water.

"What was that about?" Kate joins me.

Shit. I knew this would happen. I will kill him.

Plastering an innocent smile on my lips, I grab my towel from the chair and wrap it around my shoulders. "What?"

She narrows her eyes on me. "You and Miguel?"

"Oh, he was baiting me about the game." I shrug, trying to play it off, but if it's based on the skepticism dripping from Kate's every word, she's not buying it.

"More like he was all over you since the game started."

The moment I get my hands on him...

"You're imagining things." I shake my head. "Can we talk about something else? I actually wanted to see what you think about the setup for tomorrow." I point at both sides of the pier. "I was thinking of placing the chairs here, and then..."

Kate shifts her attention to what I'm describing, nodding her head and giving a few of her own ideas. Her friends and Penelope joined us halfway through our discussion and offered to come tomorrow morning to help me with the setup.

Thankfully, none of them mention Miguel again.

Problem solved, at least for now.

CHAPTER

22

MIGUEL

"So, Miguel, do you have your speech prepared for tomorrow?" Timothy asks once we're chilling on the deck after dinner, the bonfire crackling brightly in the night, just like in the good old days.

"Yeah, what did you prepare? You know that's the most important part of the evening," Jamie chimes in when the balled up napkin hits him in the head. *"Ouch!* What was that for?"

"What most important part of the evening?" Emmett grumbles. "The most important part of tomorrow will be putting a ring on my fiancé and finally being allowed to call her my wife."

Guys start laughing. "You're such a sap, Santiago," Nixon chuckles.

"Says the guy who had us organize an impromptu wedding just a few days after he asked his girlfriend to marry him because he didn't want to wait."

"Touché." Nixon lifts his beer, a smile curling his lips. "But I get to call her my wife."

They continue talking about their girlfriends and wives, and I can't miss the fact that they look so... happy. More than that, they look content. Like they've finally found their place in life.

and it was next to these women. Nixon and Timothy were married, and now Emmett was about to get married, while Hayden was in a committed relationship.

Everybody was settling down—finishing their degrees, getting married, having kids. I did that too. Well, partly, and yet, the longer I was here, surrounded by my friends, the more unsettled I was feeling. Like I was missing an intrinsic part of me.

The laughter coming from the house draws my attention. Rebecca ushered the girls into the living room once we were done with dinner for what she called a bridal shower. I had no idea what it entailed, but they've been there for the last hour, if not longer.

I watch the brightly lit room momentarily, my mind swirling with different emotions, most of which I'm not sure I want to name. All I know was that my feet were bouncing with nerves, and I was feeling restless.

Before I can overthink it, I stand up.

"I'm off to take a leak," I say to no one in particular.

Maybe if I stretched my legs, some of this pent-up tension would leave my body.

"If I were you, I'd make sure to stay away from the bride because if she finds out..."

"If the bride finds out what?" Kate asks, joining us with the rest of the girls.

I scan over the group, holding my breath as I wait to see familiar red head, but she's not here.

Did she leave already?

"That I'm going to use the bathroom," I say quickly, shooting Timothy a death glare as his wife sits onto his lap, his arms slipping protectively around her middle. "Now, if you'll excuse me."

Thankfully, they're too distracted with their significant

others to pay me much attention. I walk toward the house and suddenly spot two figures standing on the back porch. The dim light coming from the living room gives just enough visibility to recognize the people standing there.

Rebecca and Nico.

I come to a stop, my fingers clenching into fists as I watch from the darkness the two of them talk, that restless feeling I've been fighting all day long becoming even stronger now. I try to listen in on their conversation, but their voices are too soft for me to discern what they're talking about.

The blood rushing through my veins echoes in my eardrums as I watch them together for what feels like forever. Seriously, what do they have to talk so much about? Then he leans in, his arms wrapping around Rebecca's shoulders as he pulls her into a hug.

I swear the moment lasts for an eternity before he finally lets go.

Thank fuck.

Then he descends the stairs, and I move out of the way so he misses me standing there. Only when he's far enough away do I get out of the shadows, my gaze finding Rebecca still standing on the porch, her phone on her ear.

I move closer, overhearing the conversation.

"I'm not checking in on you," she lets out a sigh, followed by a short pause, "I just wanted to make sure everything is okay, that's it." Another pause. "Fine, I'll go back to my friends. You try not to party too hard. God forbid you have fun."

Hanging up the call, she shakes her head and mutters to herself, "He'll be the death of me."

Slipping the phone into her bag, she lets it drop on the table before leaning her palms against the railing. I watch her observe the sky and just take her in.

The contemplative expression on her face.

The way the moonlight makes the red in her hair stand out.

The curve of her mouth as she chews on her bottom lip.

Pushing back, she gets off the porch.

I step in front of her just as she looks up, her lips parting in surprise. Reaching forward, my fingers wrap around her wrist. I look around, making sure we're alone before I pull her toward the side of the house and the trees nearby.

"Miguel!" Rebecca hisses softly once we're far enough from the house. "What are you doing?"

"We're going to talk," I say evenly, looking around us. Content with the spot, I turn to face her.

"Are you cra—"

"What the hell did Mr. Good and Reliable Guy want this time around?" I cut her off, the irritation that's been building since I got back to Bluebonnet finally boiling over.

"Excuse me?" She pulls her hand out of my grasp, her fingers wrapping around her wrist and rubbing at the skin.

"What did Nico want?" I repeat, slower this time. I cross the distance between us, which only makes her backtrack until she bumps into a tree.

"What's your deal with Nico, of all people? You guys used to be friends."

"That was before he wanted to take what's mine." The words are off my tongue before I can stop them.

"W-What?" Rebecca's eyes widen in surprise, her mouth falling open.

"I told you earlier I don't like seeing another man's hands on you."

I lean closer, bracing my palms against the tree on either side of her face. My heartbeat is racing inside my chest as that rose scent reaches my nostrils.

"Miguel..."

Rebecca extends her hand, her fingers brushing against my chest.

A part of me expects her to push me away, but instead, her fingers just linger there. Not fully touching, but not moving away either.

"Hmm?" I whisper as I lean closer, the tip of my nose brushing against the side of her neck.

Since we dove into the lake, her hair air-dried and was now a mess of curls spread around her head. Wild and untamed, just like the woman in front of me.

My throat bobs as I swallow, my mouth gently pressing against her pulse point, tasting her silky skin.

Rebecca lets out a shaky breath, her body shuddering in my arms.

Those slender fingers curl around my shirt. I can feel her heartbeat that matches mine as I press my mouth against it once again.

So fucking sweet.

"We shouldn't be doing this," she whispers.

Her words are like a bucket of ice water thrown over my head. My body goes still for a moment. "Why the hell not?"

She looks up, those beautiful hazel eyes heavy with need. "Because we're broken up."

Fuck this.

Taking a step closer, my body brushes against hers. "Does this feel like we're broken up?"

Her grip on my shirt grows stronger as her eyes move to my mouth.

"Because if it does, just say the word." My fingers slip under her chin, and I lift it up so her eyes meet mine. "One word, Red, and I'll leave you the hell alone."

The time ticks by as the silence stretches, the tension building between us so thick it could be cut with a knife.

When she doesn't say anything, I start to take a step back, but her fingers clench my shirt tighter as she pulls me to her, her mouth finding mine.

Fuck.

She tastes exactly like she did the very first time I kissed her.

Like she's the beginning and ending and everything in between.

Like fucking home.

Groaning softly, my hand slips to the back of her head, fingers tangling in her hair as I pull her closer to me, my mouth sliding over hers as I back her into the tree. Our bodies press together like two pieces of a puzzle falling into place.

It's always been like that, and the last three years hadn't made any difference. Rebecca Williams was made for me, and no distance or anything else will ever be able to change that.

Rebecca's arms wrap around my shoulders. For a moment, I think she'll push me back, tell me to go screw myself, but instead, she pulls me closer.

I let out a soft groan as her leg rises, hooking behind my knee, her palms sliding over my back as she returns my kiss.

I nip at her lower lip, my fingers tightening in her hair, and I tilt her head, my tongue swiping into her mouth.

"Fuck, how is it possible that you taste so fucking perfect? Feel so fucking perfect?" I whisper against her skin, my mouth peppering kisses down the side of her neck as her fingers rake through my hair, pulling me closer.

My teeth graze over the crook of her shoulder, and I can feel goosebumps rise under my palms as she lets out a shaky breath, "Miguel..."

She shifts, my leg slipping between hers, and I can feel her heat press against my knee as she rolls her hips, seeking her release.

I angle my leg higher, and my hand slips to the small of her back, fingers sliding between the tiny straps holding her dress in place so I can feel all that glorious, warm skin. I help stabilize her as she chases the high.

It's like high school all over again, but fuck it, there was nothing better than watching her come apart thanks to me.

Her eyes feel heavy, pupils dilated, and I know she's close.

"You can say whatever you want, Red," I pant, my forehead pressing against hers. I was so hard, I could barely see straight, but I wanted to see her come first. "You can try to reason, but you and I both know that you were made for me. This is inevitable. We're inevitable."

"Until the moment you leave."

There is no accusation in her tone, just the facts. And maybe that's what hurts the most. Because I would leave, and I knew that even though three years had passed, nothing had changed. She still wouldn't go with me, couldn't come with me. And yet, neither of us stops.

"But maybe we can have this moment," she says softly. "A closure of sorts. God knows we didn't get it the first time around."

I didn't want closure. I wanted her. All of her. But if that wasn't possible, I'd take the next best thing.

I'd take anything that she wants to give me because she's the only thing that matters.

"And how would that work?"

"Like this." She tilts her head, her mouth pressing against my neck as her leg wraps around my middle, bringing us closer together. Her dress hitches up, my hard dick nestling between her thighs. "Stolen moments where we lose ourselves in each other and forget the rest of the world."

That's what she had wrong. I was lost without her. These last three years have felt like I was walking alone in the dark, endless tunnel with no way out. Coming back. Seeing her again. It was like I finally could see the light at the end of it.

"I can work with that."

I lean down, ready to stop talking, but she presses her finger against my mouth.

"But nobody can know."

My brows pull together. "What?"

"Take it or leave it, Fernandez."

She wanted to hide this? Whatever this might be. After everything that had happened? Everything we've been through?

For all her bravado, I can see she's nervously chewing at the inside of her cheek as she watches me. "Which one will it be?"

But why would she not want to hide it? I was leaving sooner rather than later. Could I really judge her for it?

"Fine, nobody will know."

Pushing her hand away, I seal my mouth over hers in a hard kiss. We move frantically. Her hands roam my body as her hips meet mine, our tongues twisting together like we might be pulled away at any second.

Slipping my hand between our bodies, I tug her bottoms down and sink my fingers into her wet heat.

She sucks in a breath as my fingers slide inside her, with barely any resistance whatsoever.

"You good?" I ask gently.

Rebecca shakes her head. "Don't stop."

"No way, Red." I slide my fingers out before sinking them deeper, the heel of my palm pressing against her clit. "First, you're going to come on my fingers, and then I'm going to fuck you so deep you won't be able to walk straight."

If all we could have was a secret, then so be it, but I'll make damn sure she remembers it. I'll make sure even when I'm gone, she'll think about this moment. About us. About *me*.

Leaning down, I suck her nipple into my mouth as I thrust

my fingers inside her tight pussy. Rebecca meets my thrusts, her fingers digging into my back so hard I'm sure she'll leave marks.

I bite gently at her nipple, licking away the sting as I rub at the sensitive bud. Her pussy squeezes around my fingers like a vice grip, and she lets out a loud moan.

"Miguel, I'm co—"

Her eyes flare open as I press my hand against her mouth, muffling the sound as her body shakes with the orgasm.

"You don't want our friends to hear you and come looking, now do you?"

Her eyes widen, but that grip on my finger grows even harder at the idea of being caught. The corner of my mouth lifts in a smirk as I help her ride through it, my whole body taunt with the need to sink inside her.

Pulling my fingers out, I flip her over. My free hand slides to her stomach and pulls her flush against me as I lean my chin against her shoulder.

"See what you do to me, Red?" I ask, pressing my hard dick against the curve of her ass. "The power you have over me? Even after all this time, I'll do whatever the hell you ask me to, regardless of what I want, just to get you."

She looks over her shoulder, the heat still burning in her hazel eyes. "Then why are you not inside me?"

I don't need to be told twice.

I thrust forward, my cock sliding into her to the hilt. She groans at the intrusion, her ass pressing against me harder.

"Open." I press my fingers against her mouth. "I want you to taste yourself." Her lips part, her tongue sliding over them tentatively. "See how hot you are for me? How sweet? The next time, I'll bury my head between those thighs and won't stop until you come on my tongue." I thrust deeper into her, her legs shaking—from the words or the fact I'm nestled all the way inside her, I'm not sure. "But it'll have to be somewhere we're alone because I want to hear you scream my name. We can't have that here, now can we?"

Rebecca shakes her head silently.

I rub my cheek against her neck, my fingers sliding up and squeezing one of her tits. "Good girl," I rasp as my thrusts become harder.

My cock twitches, the pressure on the back of my spine building. I was close, so damn close, but there was no way I was cumming without her.

"Rub your clit," I growl against her ear as my fingers tweak her nipple.

Rebecca lets out a whimper, but she does as I say, her fingers rubbing at that bundle of nerves as I sink deeper and deeper.

My fingers slip from her mouth, her eyes falling shut as another wave of pleasure slams into her, making her body shudder in release. I cup her cheek, turning her toward me and sealing my mouth against hers, muffling our moans as I cum inside of her.

Breaking the kiss, I brace my hand against the tree, trying not to squish her with my weight. We stay like that, our sweaty bodies wrapped around one another as we catch our breath.

Rebecca's fingers twine with mine on her middle.

"We should go back before somebody comes looking for us," she whispers, breaking the silence.

I tighten my hold on her, not wanting to interrupt this moment, although I rationally know she's right. People would start asking questions if we didn't show up. We were gone long as it was.

Letting out a sigh, I press my mouth against the side of her face, allowing myself to inhale her sweet scent one last time before forcing myself to take a step back.

I turn her around and help her put her clothes back in place before I do the same myself. "You go first."

Rebecca nods, running her fingers through her wild hair. With one last gaze in my direction, she starts walking back toward the lights.

I stare after her until she's out of my sight.

Was this crazy? Were we crazy?

While a part of me felt satiated, the other part of me wanted to rush after her, grab her hand, and take her somewhere where it would be just the two of us and never let her go.

Tilting my head back, I rub my hand over my face, pinching the bridge of my nose. I could still smell her on my hand. Still feel how she gripped me so tightly, like she never wanted to let me go.

"*Fuck.*"

How the hell was I supposed to go back to our friends now and pretend nothing happened? Pretend I wasn't just minutes ago buried so deep inside her that you wouldn't be able to tell where one of us ended and the other one began?

Shaking my head, I try to push the thoughts out of my mind. Joining our friends with a dick tenting my swim trunks won't help one bit.

Figuring I've given her enough time, I go after her. The closer I move to the clearing, the louder the music is, and so is the light. I lift my gaze as I step into the backyard, only to find Rebecca standing there. Her back is to me, so she doesn't notice me, but Kate does.

She slowly shifts her attention over Rebecca's shoulder. Her brows rise, the corner of her mouth twitching as she glances from me to Rebecca and back. "Well, hello, Miguel. We were just wondering where you two were."

Shit.

We were so fucking caught.

Plastering a neutral expression on my face, I lift my shoulder. "I went to take a leak."

271

Kate smirks knowingly. "In the woods?"

"Yeah, the bathroom was occupied."

"Mhmmm, the bathroom was occupied," Kate repeats. "Funny how I didn't see either of you here a few minutes ago when I came to use the bathroom."

"You're imagining things, Kate." Rebecca shakes her head. "I'm off to grab something to drink."

My gaze is glued to her back as she all but runs toward the rest of our group. When I turn around, I find Kate watching me intently. "You better know what you're doing, Fernandez, because if you break her heart..."

With one last warning glare, she follows after her best friend.

I could understand her worry, but there was no need for it.

We both knew what we were getting into and what the stakes were.

CHAPTER

23

REBECCA

"You look like shit."

I jump at the sound of my brother's soft voice and turn to find him standing in the doorway. For a man who was a six-foot-five wall of pure muscle with a ginormous dog standing by his side, they moved like two ghosts.

"You scared me. What are you doing up?"

Chase's brows pull together as his eyes zero in on my mouth, his head tilted just right so the ear on which he hears better is turned toward me.

Chase lets out a grunt, his shoulder shrugging. "The better question is, what are you doing up? You didn't come home until two."

Meaning he was probably up because he couldn't sleep. Again. But then, I had the exact same problem, although for vastly different reasons.

"There is a lot that has to be done before the ceremony, so I'm going out there to help."

I look over his shoulder toward the quiet hallway before returning my attention to Chase. "Will you guys be okay?"

These past few days, I felt like I was barely present, and I hated it. Chase wasn't still fully healed, and Mom was... Well, Mom. She was lost in her own mind more often than not.

"Go." A hand lands on my shoulder, giving me a firm squeeze, but then, almost as quickly, he pulls it away. "I have this under control."

"Okay, but call if you need anything." I grab my to-go cup filled with coffee and bag before slipping out the door.

Since my truck is still at the shop, I decide to walk to Kate and Emmett's. Thankfully, it's still early, so it's not too hot yet. I guess there was something positive about being unable to sleep.

You'd think that having sex would ease some of that pent-up tension that's been building inside of me for the last few weeks, but it only made me more wound up. The whole situation was unnerving. The way Miguel knew my body. How good he could make me feel with the barest of touches. How he knew just how far he could push me to get what he wanted.

It's been years. He shouldn't know me that well, and yet he does, and I don't know how I feel about it. Should I even think about it this much? He said it himself: he's here for the wedding, and then he'll be gone, and my life will go back to what it was.

Kate and Emmett's house finally comes into view, so I push all those thoughts to the back of my mind and focus on what's essential—the wedding.

Thankfully, we cleaned most of the remnants of last night's party before we left, so everything was ready for the setup.

I slip into the shed, pull out boxes of decorations we've made, and get to work.

I figured I'd start with the arch since it's the most important part of the ceremony. Dragging the box after me, I put it on the dock and start pulling the tulle out of it. The pale yellow material has just a little bit of glitter, so it shines prettily under the bright light. For a moment, I look at the arch, trying to figure out the best plan of attack, as I check the inspo image Kate put on her Pinterest board.

"Let's see how this goes," I mutter to myself, tucking a strand of hair behind my ear.

Since Emmett was the one who built the damn thing, I had to rise on the tips of my toes, and even then, I had to toss the tulle over.

"I should have gotten a damn chair."

Only now, I'm too lazy to go and get it, so I repeat the process, grabbing the piece, stretching up, and tossing it over the arch. By the time I'm done with the top part, my breathing is labored, and my shins are burning. Taking a step back, I look at my handiwork, noticing a few sections that need fixing.

Sucking in a breath, I rise on my toes again to do just that, but suddenly I lose my balance.

"Shi—"

Just as I start to fall forward, strong arms wrap around my middle, and I'm pulled into a firm chest.

"You looking to go for a swim before the ceremony?" Miguel's rough voice tickles my neck.

I look over my shoulder, my eyes meeting the dark depths of Miguel's gaze. My heart is racing from the almost fall, or maybe because of Miguel and his nearness.

"Don't you dare let me fall."

I didn't have time to go and change now. There was way too much work that had to be done.

Miguel's chest rumbles with laughter. "That could be arranged. But seriously, what were you doing?"

"Trying to decorate this arch, but the damn thing was built with giants in mind, apparently."

Miguel glances up. "Hardly, it's not that tall."

He shifts a little, one hand rising to touch the top of the arch which only has a couple of inches on him. "See?"

No, I didn't see anything because the fingers of his other hand, the one still wrapped around me, had slipped under my shirt, rubbing at my belly.

My stomach clenches, and I have to bite the inside of my cheek to stop myself from making a sound.

"How do you want it?"

"W-what?"

"The arch? How do you want it?"

Color floods my cheeks.

Of course he's asking about the arch, Becky. He isn't asking how you want him to devour you. Don't be silly.

"Umm... It should be slightly tighter on the top."

"Like this?" he murmurs, his fingers tracing circles over my skin while he fixes tulle with his free hand.

"You should let me go."

Miguel's eyes meet mine. "You just said not to let go."

"Not to let me drop in the lake," I correct. "But I'm good now. Besides, somebody could come."

The last thing we needed was for somebody to see us like this. It was bad enough that Kate caught us as we were coming back to the party after what happened in the woods. She was already suspicious enough as it was.

A flicker of irritation flashes on his face, but it's gone as soon as it appears. "Fine, but you have to kiss me first."

My mouth falls open. "What?"

Which part of nobody can see us does he not understand?

"Kiss me," Miguel repeats, challenge shining as clear as day in his irises. "A payment of sorts, so I can keep behaving nicely today. That's what you want, right? For me to be on my best behavior, so nobody would suspect we're hooking up behind their backs."

"Miguel..."

He turns me around, his hands gripping my hips. "There is nobody here, Red. Just you and me, but if you don't hurry up..."

This man really liked to play with fire.

But did I really have a choice?

Excuses, excuses, the little voice at the back of my head chants, but I ignore it.

I rise on the tips of my toes, planning to give him a small peck at the corner of his mouth. After all, he didn't specify how or where I was supposed to kiss him, but the moment my lips brushed against his mouth, he turned his head, his mouth falling hard on mine.

My knees wobble from the intensity of his kiss, the pure need screaming from every swipe of his mouth. I brace my hands against his chest, needing to steady myself as he pulls back, leaving me breathless.

My eyes blink open, and I catch his tongue sliding over his lower lip as if he's trying to savor the feel of our kiss.

And damn him, now I want more.

I want to rip that shirt and feel the firm muscles under my fingertips and cash on that promise he made me yesterday in the woods. Then I wanted to get down on my knees and drive him crazy with need, just like he made me. Wanted to feel his le—

"You're here early."

Miguel and I jump apart at the sound of Kate's voice.

What is it with people sneaking up on me today?

I turn around, plastering a severe look on my face as I cross my arms over my chest. "And what are you doing outside?"

"I saw you from the window and figured I'd come to see if you needed help."

"What I need is for you to go inside and relax." I place my hands on her shoulder and turn her so she's facing the house, giving her a slight push. "I've got this covered, and we can't have Emmett seeing you before the wedding. It's bad luck."

Kate looks over her shoulder. "You know we live together, right?"

"I don't care. He's not seeing you before the ceremony." When we get to the house, I spot Penelope coming down the stairs, Henry, her guide dog, by her side. "Hey, Pens, keep an eye on your sister? I don't want to see her outside."

"You know it."

Stopping in the doorway, I cross my arms over my chest. "Don't make me lock you inside the house."

Kate gives me a pointed look. "You can lock me in all you want, but there are still windows from which I can see."

Her words make me pause for a moment, but I try to keep a neutral expression. "There is nothing to see."

"Mhmm..." Kate looks pointedly over my shoulder. "Nothing at all."

With that, she closes the door behind herself.

Did she see the kiss?

Dammit, I knew we shouldn't have done it.

No matter how good it felt.

I don't get a chance to obsess over it because a truck pulls by the side of the house, and soon enough, the sound of various doors opening and closing fills the yard before Emmett and his friends join us.

"How do you want the chairs, Becs?" Emmett asks.

Letting out a breath, I start directing the group, pointing out where each thing needs to go before I return to the arch.

Miguel's eyes take me in from head to toe as I close the distance between us, but I shoot him a warning glare before switching to all-business mode.

It takes us three long hours, but it's totally worth it because the whole place looks like it's out of a fairytale.

The guys go to the porch to grab a drink while I walk

through the setup, ensuring everything is in place. Content with how it all looks, I approach the house, checking my phone.

No messages or calls. How surprising.

"So, Miguel, did you end up writing the speech or not?" Nixon asks.

My head snaps up just as Miguel shrugs. "I'll just wing it."

"You will what?" I cross my arms over my chest as all the guys turn toward me.

Miguel lifts his arms in defense. "Hey, don't look at me. Emmett said my speech isn't important."

I glance from one man to the other, my teeth grinding together. "You better be joking. And you," I jab my finger into Miguel's chest, "better have that speech ready because if you mess it up, I might just strangle you. Now, if you'll excuse me, I have a wedding to get ready for. And y'all should go to Emmett's and start getting dressed." My nose furrows as I pass by them. "And maybe take a shower."

The makeup artist is just putting final touches on Kate's face when there is a soft knock on the door, and Kate's aunt peeks inside, a tentative smile on her lips. "You all about ready?"

Kate waves her inside. "Come on in. I'm just about to put on the dress."

Mabel looks over her shoulder. "Oh, I'll go and get your mo—"

Before she can even finish, Kate shakes her head. "I want you, Aunt Mabel."

Kate didn't have the best relationship with her mother, so much that when she was a junior in high school, she decided to move to Bluebonnet with her sister, so it wasn't surprising that she preferred her aunt to help her get ready instead.

Mabel enters the room almost tentatively, closing the door behind her. "Are you sure?"

"I'm sure." Kate takes her hand and pulls her inside. "You've been more of a mother to Penny and me in the last few years than Mom ever was."

Biting the inside of my cheek, I monitor their interaction from the side, not wanting to interrupt their special moment. Emotions swirl inside of me as I watch Kate take her aunt's hands in hers. I feel grateful for this woman who opened her door and gave me one of my best friends. I was also happy that Kate had somebody like Mabel Adams in her corner. But, if I was being truly honest, there was also jealousy because I knew if the day came that I would get married, I'd never have this moment. Mom won't get a chance to help me put on my wedding dress. Dad won't walk me down the aisle or dance with me.

Feeling like an intruder, I turn around, blinking the tears that have gathered in my eyes as I go toward the wardrobe, pulling out the bag with the wedding dress.

Kate must hear me because she turns around, and I force out a smile, "You ready?"

She nods and lets out a shaky breath. "I'm ready."

I hold the bag while Miss Adams unzips it and pulls out the dress. Tears glisten in her eyes as she takes it in for the very first time.

"Kate, this is beautiful."

Between the two of us, we helped Kate get into the dress and slip all the little buttons in place. All the while, I could hear the familiar *clicking* of the shutters as Jade, another of Kate's Blairwood friends, took the photos.

Once we're done, I take a step back and almost bump into Penny. "I'm sorry, Pens."

"No worries."

Kate turns around and takes in her sister, grabbing her hands to pull her closer. "You look beautiful, Penny."

"Well, you're the one who needs to look beautiful today, not me," Penny lets out a soft chuckle as Kate places her hands on her waist, letting her feel the delicate design of the lace.

"Oh, she looks stunning. All eyes will be on her today," I chime in, flashing a knowing smile at my best friend.

"The dress is beautiful, just like I wanted it to be. And the hairdresser and makeup artist did an amazing job. They put my hair in a low bun and added that hairpiece you found," Kate explains.

Penelope tilts her head to the side, her fingers skimming over the delicate lace of Kate's dress, trying to imagine how it might look.

"Do you like it?"

"I love it."

"Emmett is going to flip one way or the other. You could come out in a potato sack, and that man would marry you."

"Penelope Adams!" Miss Mabel chastises.

"What?" Penelope shrugs, not in the least bit fazed. "It's true, and you know it. He would still think she's the most beautiful woman in the world."

She was totally right about that one. Emmett didn't care one bit about what Kate would be wearing; he just wanted them to tie the knot already.

Kate leans her head against Penny's shoulder, letting out a soft sigh. "He's the best."

The shutter keeps going off in the background, capturing the moment, but then, there is another knock on the door.

"Who is it?" I ask immediately. "I swear if it's Emmett, I'll...."

"Bradley."

"Oh." Rushing to the door, I peek outside to make sure Kate's dad is alone before I let him enter.

I move to the side as I watch Kate share this moment with her family, that vice grip squeezing around my heart as I fight with the little green devil sitting on my shoulder.

Instead, I try to focus on practical things. I take Kate in, making sure every hair is in place, that her makeup is impeccable, and that her dress is spotless.

Only then do I brush my hand against her elbow. "I'll walk with Penny downstairs."

Kate smiles at me. "Thanks, Becky."

Nodding, I wait for Penny to give Henry the command. Together, we descend the stairs, and I grab the harness I've decorated earlier. Everybody was dressing up, so of course, we had to do the same for him.

"You two look absolutely adorable," I tell her as I make sure everything is tied properly. "Are you nervous?"

"Thank you. And a little bit," she admits. "Hopefully, I won't have a blind-girl moment out in front of all the guests."

"You wanna walk it once again? We have time."

Penny shakes her head. "No, we'll be good." She rubs Henry's fur as we stop just before the door leading to the back porch. "Right, Henry?"

The dog licks her palm reassuringly.

Soon enough, Kate and Bradley join us, and it doesn't take long for the music to start. Penny sucks in a long breath as she lifts her chin and gives Henry the command to move forward.

"What's going on with you?" I ask softly.

Kate pulls her gaze from her sister. "What do you mean?"

"You know what I mean," I give her a pointed look. "Did

you seriously think I didn't notice you sneaking out to the bathroom earlier today?"

"What?" she turns her attention back to Penelope, but I don't miss the flash of panic on her face.

"And twice last night at the party," I point out.

"So what?" She shrugs, trying to play it off. But she's still avoiding my gaze. "I'm nervous."

Who was she trying to fool?

"Nervous to marry the love of your life who treats you like a freaking princess? Yeah, right. Try again."

"It's not the wedding. It's the fact that I'll be the center of attention." She gives me a little push as the music changes. "That's you."

My eyes narrow slightly. "We're not done, missy."

I clasp my hands tightly around the bouquet of flowers as I make my way down the makeshift aisle. The nerves hit me the moment I step in front of everyone. I'm not sure why because I already know the majority of them. Hell, they're not even here for me!

Still, my stomach didn't get the memo because I could feel it roll uncomfortably.

Get a grip, Becky. It's just a quick walk down the aisle among people you already know.

I put one leg in front of the other, my whole focus on the destination in front of me. Which turns out to be a bad idea because my eyes land on Miguel, whose gaze is already locked on me. The intensity in his eyes makes the knot in my throat tighten.

God, he looks so gorgeous; it should be illegal.

If he dressed like this for his games, I was surprised some city girl didn't already snatch him because that man definitely knew how to fill a suit.

The dark material is stretched over his broad shoulders, the crisp white shirt tucked into the waistband of the slacks that hug those powerful thighs, with a tie neatly wrapped around his neck.

The tie I helped Kate pick out for the best man.

My throat bobs as I swallow.

I know I should look away—the last thing I needed was for somebody to catch what was going on—but I couldn't do it. It's like those dark eyes held me hostage, and I couldn't avert my gaze even if I tried.

So, instead, my fingers grip firmly around the flowers as I move closer with each step.

After all, where was I supposed to look? He was the best man, and I was the maid of honor. That was all there was to it.

So why did it feel like my skin was burning under his gaze? Why did I want to squeeze my thighs together to alleviate some of the ache building inside my core?

I wanted this man, true. But simultaneously, I was afraid of the feelings he evoked in me.

He unsettled me, unnerved me to my very core. I had a feeling I would regret what was happening, but did it change anything? No. Because, just like he said, we were inevitable, and fighting this attraction between us was futile.

I could only hope that I'd come out of this whole thing unscathed.

CHAPTER

24

MIGUEL

Fuck, she's still the most gorgeous woman I've ever laid my eyes on.

It takes everything in me to keep a straight face as I watch Rebecca walk down the aisle. My stomach is wound up tight as I watch her move. Effortlessly like a fucking mirage.

Rebecca is wearing a golden dress that compliments her auburn hair. The material seems to shimmer in the late afternoon light as she glides down the aisle. Thin straps cover her shoulders and go into a heart-shaped bodice. The dress is hugging her every curve and falling all the way to the ground. There is a slit on the side, her leg peeking with each step she takes and shoving off fuck-me red heels. Heels I wanted to feel digging into my back as I got her all to myself once we were done here.

"That, my friend, is what you lost when you walked away." Emmett smirks. So much for being my best friend and taking my side.

A soft grunt is my only response, which only makes him chuckle harder.

Could I blame him, though? The whole situation was messed up. The three of us have been best friends since we were kids. I wouldn't want him to abandon Rebecca any more than she wanted to get in between the two of us.

That was the worst part of losing Rebecca. Not only did I lose my girlfriend, I lost my best friend.

But she's yours now.

Not entirely. I wasn't sure what we were or what would happen, but I knew I couldn't say no to her.

I loved her even before I fell *in love* with her. She had me wrapped around her finger, completely enticed, and I was starting to wonder if that was ever going to change. Will there ever be a woman I'd feel more for? Any woman that could ever top my feelings for Rebecca Williams? Did I even want there to be one?

The thoughts swirling through my mind make my head spin, so I push them to the back of my mind.

My gaze is glued to her as she makes her way down the aisle and takes her spot opposite me. The music changes, and I can hear people stand up and see Emmett's attention shift toward the front to watch his bride. From the corner of my eye, I catch the look of wonder and love, so much love, shining on his face. But even that doesn't stop me from staring at Rebecca over my best friend's shoulder.

Because while everybody else has eyes for the bride and groom, I can't stop staring at the woman standing across from me.

The ceremony passes in a blur. I don't hear half the things the minister says, barely catching the moment when I have to give them the rings.

Rebecca shakes her head almost imperceptibly, but I can see the corner of her mouth twitch upward. I zero in on that movement before returning my gaze to hers, and I'm pretty sure she can see all the dirty things I wanna do to her once this whole thing is over because a slight flush spreads over her cheeks.

"I now pronounce you man and wife, yo—"

Before the minister can even finish, Emmett pulls his wife to him, his mouth crashing over hers. He dips her back, and people start cheering all around us.

Looking up, I find Rebecca watching our friends, longing flashing on her face. It's there for a split second before she masks it, but I've seen it, and something about it sends a jab of pain going through my chest.

However, I don't get a chance to think too much about it because soon we're all swamped by the guests who come to congratulate the newlyweds, and then there are the photos. Tons and tons of pictures. As if the ones taken at Emmett's before the ceremony weren't enough. I don't even get to put my hands on Rebecca in them either because each one of us is standing on the opposite sides as we're arranged like mannequins by Nixon's sister Jade as different people come and go.

After more than two hours, Jade finally calls it quits, and we can join the rest of the party for dinner. The whole time I talk with Emmett and Kate, I keep sneaking glances at Rebecca, who's doing her best to ignore me.

Once the dinner is finished, I rub my hands against the sides of my legs and get to my feet, a glass in hand. "If I can have a moment."

People settle down, eyes turning toward our table as I clear my throat. "As the maid of honor kindly informed me, and if you know Becky, you know you don't want to get on her bad side. Trust me. I should know since I've done my fair share of doing exactly that." Soft laughter spreads through the room as I glance at the woman in question. Her brow is raised, her fingers playing with the champagne flute that was placed in front of her. "Anyway, apparently, as the best man, I am expected to give a

ANNA B. DOE

speech tonight, so if you're not in the mood to listen, I suggest you get up and leave."

"Will you finally get it over with, Fernandez?" Emmett asks, tossing a balled up napkin at me. "I want to go and dance with my wife. Not that you'd know anything about that since your ass is still single."

This time, people burst into laughter, and I can't help but join in.

"Oh, now you've done it. You know what's the first thing your golden boy did the moment he saw Katherine here? He fell on his ass, quite literally, and not at all spectacularly. It was just a random August afternoon; we were out on the field practicing when he spotted her. Just as I threw the football at him, it knocked him right in the head, but I guess we're all lucky he's got a really thick skull on him, right?" More laughter. I glance at my friend to find him shaking his head at me, so I continue, "Makes one wonder if he'd have fallen so hard so fast if it weren't for me, so I guess I'm also part of the reason for their love story. Wouldn't you say?"

Cheering erupts from the crowd, and somebody even whistles, everyone is smiling widely. I see Emmett grab Kate's hand in his, his finger caressing over the ring he put on her finger.

"I know, I know. I'm the best friend he could have asked for."

"Oh, I got so lucky with you," Emmett comments dryly.

"Of course you did. But joking aside, I've never seen two people more perfect for each other. Most people are kids when they're seventeen, and hardly anybody thinks about life outside of high school, but even then, Emmett knew Kate was his future, his life, and he didn't waiver from his path, not once. He fought for his girl, and he got her in the end." My gaze goes to Rebecca, and I find her smiling softly. Once again, I can feel that ache

288

building inside my chest. We stare at one another, but then I remember all the people watching and the promise I made her, so I give my head a little shake and lift my glass, turning back to the crowd. "To Kate and Emmett. To many more years together, filled with love. I wish you all the best, guys."

People join in, lifting their glasses in congratulations. I take a sip of my drink as I sit down, and the music starts playing once again.

"You okay?" Emmett asks Kate. "You look a little bit pale?"

I turn toward them, taking Kate in, and he's right. Even with the makeup, I can see that color drained from her face.

She nods and pushes back her chair, hurrying toward the house. Emmett curses and gets up, but Rebecca's already on her feet.

"I'll go make sure she's okay," she says, squeezing his shoulder as she walks by.

"Do you think it's something she ate?" I ask, my gaze still glued to Rebecca's retreating back.

"Nah, she's been feeling off for a while now. I thought it was the stress, but now I'm not so sure."

I turn toward my best friend, noticing the frown etched between his brows. "She's going to be okay."

"She has to." Emmett's lips press in a tight line, determination clear on his face. There wasn't anything he wouldn't do to make sure she was okay. "She's my whole fucking world."

REBECCA

"Kate?" I call out as I run after her into the house. I know where I have to go even before I hear it. The faint sound of somebody throwing up.

Lifting my hand, I knock against the bathroom door. "Kate, are you okay?"

A muffled 'fine' comes from the other side of the door, followed by more retching.

"Bullshit," I shoot back immediately. "What's really going on? You're clearly not fine."

I had a sneaking suspicion about what was happening here. What I couldn't understand was why she didn't want to say it. Did she not recognize the signs? Hardly unlikely. Which meant that either she knew it and she tried to ignore it, or she was simply keeping it a secret from me.

"Just had to use the bathroom, that's all."

"That's why you left in such a hurry?" I roll my eyes at the absurdity of it. "Because you had to pee?"

"Yup."

I open my mouth to call her on it, but the water starts running.

"I don't believe you," I yell so she can hear me over the noises, my palm banging against the hardwood. "What's really going on? This is the second time today you've run off like that."

Either she didn't hear me, or she chose to ignore me. I have my suspicions, but I decide to play along and wait her out.

"I could say the same," Kate says as she turns off the water. *Finally.*

"Did you see me running away today?"

"No, but I did see the looks you and Miguel were giving each other. When did you start sleeping with him again?"

"W-What?" I croak out, my mouth falling open.

Fuck.

How much did she see? I thought we'd be safe with all the attention on Kate and Emmett, but I guess I was wrong.

"Oh, don't act like a prude. I know you very well, Rebecca Williams, and you have that recently fucked glow around you."

"You're imagining things," I say immediately. I'm grateful that the door is still closed because I can feel the flush spreading over my cheeks.

"Mhmm... If you say it enough times, you might even believe it yourself."

"I do believe it! Besides, we were talking about you, and you're evading my question."

"Am not."

"Liar."

The door pulls open, and Kate appears in the doorway, arms crossed over her chest. "Well, I guess that makes two of us."

"I guess it does," I huff.

"Soon." Kate takes my hand in hers and gives it a firm squeeze. "I promise. I have my reasons."

So she does know, but she's keeping it a secret.

I could deal with that.

"I know. I just worry."

"I worry about you, too," Kate whispers softly. "Are you sure you know what you're doing? You were..."

"I know how I was. But things are..." I let out a sigh. There was no sense in keeping it from her when she clearly figured it out. "Complicated."

"Aren't they always? I just don't want to see you get hurt again."

"I'm not. I'm not the girl I was back in high school. This time around, I know exactly what I'm getting into. At the end of this, he's going to go back to Austin, and I'll stay here, and I'm fine with that."

Kate watches me for a moment. "Are you really?"

No, I wasn't. But what choice did I have?

"I am." I force out a smile, but I don't think she believes me. "This is our goodbye. A real goodbye." Needing to change the subject, I tighten my hold on her. "C'mon, let's get you back to your groom before he sends out a search party."

Together, we join the others. Kate spots Emmett, who's talking to his college friends, almost immediately.

"You coming?"

"I'm going to check my phone. I'll find you later?"

With one last look in my direction, she nods her agreement and goes to her friends. I walk to our table and grab my champagne flute before pulling out my phone—no new text messages. Taking a sip of my drink, I look up. People are dancing and laughing all around the backyard, clearly having fun.

My attention goes to my friends. Emmett takes Kate's hand and pulls her on the dance floor, and his friends follow suit.

I spot Miguel on the other side of the room. Our eyes lock for a moment, and I can feel that familiar warmth spread inside my belly.

Until Kate's words flash in my mind, so I turn back to my friends.

Kate noticed something was going on. I didn't need somebody else to question it, too.

Taking another sip from my drink, I feel a stab of envy as I watch Kate and Emmett dance.

It should have been us.

This moment.

It should have been us.

But our lives went in separate directions a long time ago.

Maybe it was time to let go.

"Dance with me?"

The softly spoken question has the faint hairs at my nape rising. Slowly, I turn around to find Miguel standing next to me, watching me.

This whole day, he has been watching me, his eyes silently telling me things he wanted to do but couldn't.

I glance around the backyard, but nobody in particular seems to be paying us any attention. Still...

"I don't think that's a good idea."

Something dark passes over his face. "C'mon, Red. It's one dance between old friends. Nobody will question anything. After all, we're the maid of honor and best man."

I knew he was probably right, but that wasn't what worried me. Not really.

I was scared that if I let him pull me into his arms, I wouldn't want to leave.

Letting out a soft breath, I nod slowly, giving in. "One dance."

Extending my hand, I place it into his outstretched palm. A zap of electricity goes through my body as my fingers slide into his, intertwining tightly. Together, we make our way to the dance floor, where he pulls me closer, his hand settling at the small of my back as he starts moving to the gentle beat.

At first, my body is stiff against his, but little by little, I can feel my muscles relax. His warmth seeps through the jacket of his suit, and all I want to do is lean against him. The last few days were chaotic, and now that the wedding was over and everybody seemed to be enjoying the party, the tiredness finally caught up to me.

For a while, we just dance, neither of us saying anything. But that was the thing about Miguel and me. We didn't need to talk to understand each other. There were countless times when we'd just be together, fingers clasped tightly, my head resting on his shoulder, and it was enough.

"They didn't have their first dance," Miguel says, breaking the silence. "Don't people usually have one of those?"

I hum in agreement. "Kate wanted them to have the last dance. Just the two of them when everybody else leaves."

She suggested it just a short while ago. At first, I found it strange, but the more I thought about it, the more I liked the idea. It felt special and intimate—a moment just for the two of them where they get to unwind and enjoy their day without the curious eyes of everybody on them.

I look around until I find Kate and Emmett dancing together in the middle of the dance floor. His arms are wrapped protectively around her, and I can see his mouth moving as he whispers something in her ear. The love the two of them shared was so strong it was palpable.

Tears burn my eyes, my throat growing tight the longer I stare at them.

"She's pregnant," I voice out my suspicion.

I watch as Emmett spins her around gently, and Kate is smiling brightly. It's like they're all alone. I'm so damn happy for them. They deserve their happily ever after.

"What?" Miguel asks, pulling back so he can look at me.

Blinking the tears away, I turn my attention to him. "Can you keep your voice down?"

"Not when you drop a bomb like that!" he hisses.

"Well, try to keep your mouth shut, Fernandez." I jab him in the chest. "She doesn't want anybody to know. My guess is she hasn't told Emmett yet."

"But she told you?"

I shake my head. "She didn't have to tell me."

Once again, my eyes find their way to my best friend, who seems to be radiating with happiness despite the fact not that long ago she was throwing up.

She thought she was being sneaky, but it was hard to miss

how exhausted she looked in the last few weeks, and then there were her very often disappearances to the bathroom. Coincidence? I think not.

"Just pretend like you're surprised when they tell you, that's all."

Miguel looks at Kate, a frown appearing between his brows. "I don't get it. She looks completely normal. How can you be sure?"

"Because I was once in her place, okay?"

"W-what?"

Shit.

The words slipped from my tongue before I could think them through. And if Miguel was surprised at the revelation about Kate, it has nothing on the shock that's currently reflected on his face.

"Forget I said anything." I try to pull out of his hold, but he isn't letting me go.

"You were pregnant?" Miguel slowly repeats as if he can't wrap his head around the words. Those brown eyes stare at me blankly, his face devoid of any emotion.

I wasn't sure what I was expecting.

Why did I even say it?

I should have kept my mouth shut, but I was tired, and being in his arms felt so familiar, so... safe.

Stupid, stupid, stupid.

"It doesn't matter." I shake my head, trying to divert the situation. "Let's just forget I even said anything."

There was no sense in opening up old wounds. Especially not this wound. Not after all this time.

I start to walk away, but Miguel tugs me back to him. "Like hell."

"Miguel."

The previously blank expression is replaced by the fire

blazing in his dark eyes. Anger, hurt, and something that looks a lot like jealousy play on his face, each emotion shifting in quick succession.

I should have known he wouldn't let this go easily. Now that the confession was out in the open, there was no taking it back. He wouldn't let this go until he got to the bottom of it.

"Don't you Miguel-me, Rebecca. Not after you just dropped this bomb on me. Pregnant?" he hisses. "You were fucking pregnant? When? When were you pregnant?"

I look around, noticing a few people giving us curious looks. The panic seizes my throat, making it hard to breathe. Taking one deep breath, I try to calm myself. "This isn't the time nor the place," I say slowly, trying to keep my cool when all I want to do is run away from here. "If you ruin this for Kate and Emmett, I'll never forgive you."

He just watches me for a moment, those dark eyes staring into mine. "Fine," he grits.

Fine?

I expected him to protest more, but this is good. I didn't want to cause a scene at the wedding and ruin my friends' day. And maybe, just maybe, Miguel will forget I said anything.

I should have known better, though. Miguel's grip on my arm tightens as he starts pulling me away. "Let's go."

"Miguel, what are you doing? Where are we going?" I ask, looking around, but we're already too far gone, and nobody is paying us any attention.

Miguel chooses to ignore me. His full focus is getting the hell out.

Even in the darkness, I can see the hard line of his shoulders and his rigid posture. He was pissed, and there was no way I was getting out of it.

Shit, this shouldn't have happened.

Why couldn't I have just kept my mouth shut?

The noises die down a little when we get between the trees next to Emmett and Kate's house, only slowing down when he's sure nobody will interrupt us. It was the same place where we were yesterday, only now circumstances were much different.

"When were you pregnant, Rebecca?" He lets my hand drop, turning around so he can face me. The anger reflected on his face has only grown vehement in the last few minutes. His chest is rising and falling rapidly, fingers curled into fists by his side.

An icy chill runs through me, making goosebumps appear on my skin. "Miguel, just let it—"

"I'm not fucking letting it go until you tell me. *When?*" he yells, making me stumble back a step. Miguel has never, *ever* yelled at me, not like this.

"Three years ago," I whisper softly, my eyes falling shut.

The silence that settles over us is almost deafening. My heart is beating violently in my chest as I wait for his reaction. I expect more yelling, but instead, his words are so soft it's somehow worse.

"Where is our baby, Rebecca?"

I squeeze my eyes, feeling the burn of the tears gathering behind my eyelids.

Fuck.

All this time, and the mention of one of the darkest days of my life still hurts just the same as it did the day I lost everything.

The day my heart shattered when I lost the boy I'd loved all my life, only to lose the last part of him I had in the very same breath.

Three years ago

It takes me hours and a big chunk of cash, but I somehow get a seat on the next flight back to Austin, which is early the next morning. So, instead of being with my boyfriend, I spend the night at the airport, my arms curled around my knees as I reject every single call and message he sends me.

MIGUEL:

Where are you, Rebecca?

You just ran away?

Like wtf?

You didn't even give me a chance to explain what happened!

Just come back so we can talk.

Red, please, it's not what it looks like.

Not what it looks like, my ass. Could he be any more cliché? I saw them! I saw them with my very own eyes. God knows what I would have walked into if I had come a few minutes earlier.

Although I wanted nothing more than to turn off my phone, I couldn't do that. I couldn't risk not answering the call from Mrs. Santiago or Matthew, so I sat there and tortured myself every time my phone buzzed, the images of Miguel and that girl flashing in my mind like snapshots every time the screen would light up until I was forced to turn the phone off.

The whole flight home isn't any different. It was like my mind was on a loop, and the only thing I could think about was Miguel. His hands on that girl. Him looking into her eyes. Him kissing her.

How did this happen?

Why did this happen?

Was he that unhappy?

Why didn't he just say something instead of hooking up with somebody behind my back? And not just with anybody, the girl looked like a freaking model. She was everything I was not, and I couldn't stop comparing us. Thinking of what I did, considering what I could have done differently to prevent this.

There are so many questions swirling inside my head, but no answers.

By the time we land, my head is pounding, and my stomach is rolling with unease. Although I tried to keep quiet, there was no hiding my tears. I think my seatmates were grateful to be able to get away from me as soon as we landed.

I make my way out of the plane and find my truck.

Only then do I turn my phone on, and my heart twists inside my chest as I wait for the messages to come through, and they do.

Dozens of them.

I bite into my lip as I watch them pop on my screen.

I couldn't do this.

It hurt too fucking much to do this.

So I did the only thing I could: I blocked his number and deleted all the messages without opening them.

My heart sinks into my belly, and I can feel a dull kind of pain spread through my middle. I slide my hand over my stomach, willing it to settle down.

This is for the best.

Since it's still early, the drive home is relatively quick.

Once I pull in front of my house, I check my reflection in the mirror. My face is blotchy from crying, the circles under my eyes are even darker than before I left, and my cheeks are beet red. No matter what I do, there is no hiding what had happened.

Unbuckling my seatbelt, I get out of the car. Sharp pain

slices through me. I bite the inside of my cheek, as I grip the door handle.

It takes me a few moments to regain my composure, but when I do, I see the front door open, and Mrs. Santiago steps out on the porch. She gives me one look, and I can see the worry in her eyes. "Rebecca? What are you doing here? You weren't supposed to come home until tomorrow."

I shake my head, "I'm so sorry to put this on you when you went out of your way..."

"Nonsense." Mrs. Santiago waves me off, her arm curling around my shoulders. "What happened? Why are you crying?"

Her kindness and that familiar scent of wildflowers and sugar undoes something inside of me. I turn around, burrowing my head into the crook of her neck as I let the tears flow.

"Oh, honey..."

She rubs her hand up and down my back, whispering soft encouragements as she lets me cry. "It's going to be okay. You'll see. Everything will be fine."

But she was wrong. Nothing will ever be fine again.

"C'mon, let's get you inside. I'll make you some tea so you can calm down and tell me what happened."

I pull back, rubbing my forearm over my face. "I'm sorry for crying like this. I'm a mess."

"There is nothing wrong in crying. But I swear once I get my hands on that boy..." She ushers me in front of her. "C'mon, I'll make you— Rebecca, there is a bloody stain on your jeans."

I blink, trying to process her words. My gaze falls, and for the first time, I notice the red stain. A very big, red stain.

"Did you get your period?"

"No." I bite the inside of my cheek, my hand pressing against my stomach. "I can't get my period. I'm pre—" my voice stutters as I shake my head, more tears falling down.

This couldn't be happening.

Not now.

But it was.

Mrs. Santiago helped me change and took me to the hospital, where she held my hand, but it was pointless as the doctor confirmed it with a pitying look on her face not even an hour later.

The last connection I had to Miguel Fernandez was officially gone.

Now

"Rebecca," Miguel's hands land on my shoulders, giving me a little shake and snapping me out of my thoughts. "Where is our baby?"

"I lost it," I croak out the words, that familiar ache spreading inside my chest. "I lost our baby."

"Fucking hell," Miguel curses.

He runs his fingers through his hair before he suddenly turns around and slams his fist into the nearby tree.

"Miguel!" I run to him, wrapping my arms around his middle and pulling him back to me before he can do it once again and hurt himself. "Stop it. You're going to injure yourself."

"I don't fucking care!" He turns to me, his eyes blazing with anger, but deep down, I can see something else. Something I've become very acquainted with in the last few years. Pain. "What the hell, Rebecca? Why didn't you tell me?"

I stagger back, his accusation like a slap to my face. "What?"

"Why didn't you tell me anything? Did you plan to keep the baby a secret even if you had it?"

He did not just go there.

"I came to tell you!" I jab my finger into his chest, pain shooting through my arm. "When I found out, I was alone and scared. We were miles apart. The whole situation was tense as it was. I had just found out there was a reason my mom had been acting weird the past couple of years, and the woman I knew, the woman I needed, was gone and would never be the same. And then I got a positive pregnancy test and got scared shitless of what it would all mean. I wasn't ready for a baby, and you weren't here, and still... *Still,* I flew all the way to Michigan to tell you, and what did I find? Some girl standing in your doorway, dressed in your fucking shirt."

Miguel grits his teeth. "You know what happened. I explained it to you..."

"*Now,*" I interject. "You explained it to me now. Three years ago, you let me walk away."

"Because you didn't want to listen! I tried talking to you. I asked you to stay so I could explain. I tried calling and texting you, but you blocked me. You, who promised always to take my side and be there for me, turned your back and thought the worst of me!"

"And I'm not denying that!" I lift my hand to poke him once again, but he grabs my wrist to stop me from doing it. "I never denied that. I was a stupid kid who had too much on my plate. A kid who was physically and emotionally exhausted trying to keep everything I loved from drowning. My family, us, everything was falling apart, and I couldn't do anything to stop it. I needed you, Miguel. I needed you to help me deal with all of it. I needed you to tell me things would be alright, but instead, I found you with another woman."

"Would you have kept it from me?" Miguel asks again, enunciating every word.

I let out a shaky breath, feeling all the fight leave my body.

"I don't know what I would have done," I admit softly. "I never got a chance to think about it."

"Rebecca..."

I shake my head. "I lost the baby on my way home from Michigan State. I didn't even notice I was bleeding until Mrs. Santiago pointed it out. I thought I was cramping because of all the stress. It was just another blow in a row, but this one felt fatal."

"Mrs. Santiago? What does she have to do with any of it?"

I lift my shoulders in a shrug. "She was the only person who knew. Everything. She knew about Mom. She knew about the stuff with Matthew. She was the one who got me the plane ticket and offered to look over my family while I went to see you. She knew about the baby. She was the one who took me to the hospital and held my hand through it all. I'll never be able to repay that woman for all she did for me these last few years."

Mrs. Santiago was my surrogate mother in all the ways that counted. She stepped in when I needed her the most and didn't accept no for an answer, no matter how much I insisted I was fine. That woman was an angel, and I knew I wouldn't have been able to survive the last few years without her help and support.

"Rebecca, I..."

I shake my head, the regret for all that was lost slamming into me. All the things that could have been, should have been ours, but we never got to experience them.

Miguel runs his hands over his face, messing his hair as he looks around us. I should have never said anything. Should have never admitted what had happened. There was no point to it. It only brought him pain, and I didn't want that for him. There was nothing that he could have done to change what had happened. Nothing that would have changed the outcome. It took me a while to accept it, but now I knew better.

"I have to go."

My heart squeezes at his words. Go? He wants to go? Now?

"You're leaving?"

His Adam's apple bobs as he swallows audibly, his gaze darting away from me as he repeats, "I have to go."

With that, he turns around and runs toward the party.

This time, he's the one walking away, and I let him.

CHAPTER

25

MIGUEL

I lost it.

The words play on repeat in my head, over and over and over. It seems like an endless loop, and I don't know what to do to stop it.

I lost our baby.

I run my fingers through my hair, fisting the overgrown strands and tugging at them. That feeling of tightening around my heart keeps growing, making it hard to breathe.

I lost our baby.

Letting out a frustrated huff, I grab the comforter and shove it back. The early morning light barely peeks through the curtains, but I don't care. If I stayed one more second in this room, I was pretty sure I'd go crazy.

No, I needed to get the hell out of here.

Quickly, I put on some clothes and quietly descended the stairs, going straight for the door.

The cool early morning air makes goosebumps appear on my skin, but it's the only relief during the long summer months, so I embrace it as I make my way to the barn. The mix of hay and animals hits me in the face the moment I open the door.

The horses look up from their stalls, letting out irritated huffs at the sight of me.

Ignoring their judging stares, I push up my sleeves.

I lost it.

Gritting my teeth, I grab the shovel and get to work.

There was always something about physical labor that appealed to me. There was solace in it. You didn't have to think about it too much. Even after years of being away, the movements came mechanically to me. It was so easy to slip back into my place like no time had passed. My muscles strain every time I lift the shovel, and beads of sweat start appearing on my forehead.

I hoped that physical labor would help get this restless energy out of me, but no matter how hard I work, I can't get what happened out of my head.

I flew all the way to Michigan to tell you, and what did I find? Some girl standing in your doorway, dressed in your fucking shirt.

It was stupid.

Everything that had happened. All the time we could have had. All of it was lost.

And for what?

I lost our baby.

Because of me.

Because of what had happened.

Because I didn't try harder.

Maybe if I had jumped on the plane, I could—

"What the hell do you think you're doing?"

The hairs at the back of my neck prickle at the sound of my father's deep voice. I stop mid-motion and glance over my shoulder. He's standing in the doorway of the stall, his hands propped on his hips as he glares at me, that perpetual frown etched between his brows.

"What does it look like I'm doing? I'm working."

Shaking my head, I shift my attention to the task at hand. Seriously, there was no pleasing this man. I'm not sure why I'm surprised. He's always been that way. No matter what I did, help or no help, stay or leave, he would have found something to bitch about.

I'm just dipping my shovel into the ground when fingers wrap around my arm, and I'm tugged back to face him.

"I can see that. Why? I thought you were here for the wedding, and then you were leaving."

I grit my teeth, my fingers clenching around the wooden handle. "Is that what this is about? You want me to leave?"

"That's not what I meant..."

"Then how did you mean it, Dad? Because to me, it sounded pretty much like you're kicking me out of the house. Again."

Fire blazes in his dark eyes. They're so similar to mine. It's almost like I'm looking at my reflection in the mirror. And just the thought of it has me taking a step back.

I was *nothing* like my father.

"I didn't kick you out of the house. You were the one who chose to leave."

"Because you gave me an ultimatum!" I yell, pointing my finger at him. My heavy breathing is the only sound filling the room. Even the horses have calmed down, sensing something's going on. "I could either stay and bend to your demands, or I could go and play football. You can't deny that's what happened."

Dad's jaw clenches, the vein in his forehead throbbing visibly. "Don't you dare talk to me like that, young man. I'm still your father."

"Well, I'm not the eighteen-year-old kid who's afraid of you any longer, and I don't have to take your crap."

307

Dad snorts. "As if there was a day in your life when you were afraid of me."

My throat bobs as I swallow the knot that seems to be perpetually stuck there when I'm around my father.

That's where he has it wrong. I was always afraid of him; always afraid of the reaction to something I did or chose would cause, always afraid to tell him exactly how I felt because of the fear that I'd be rejected, or deemed not good enough. Because that's always been the case. I was never good enough.

Not for my family.

And certainly not for my father.

"You don't know shit, Dad." And if that wasn't the saddest truth, I don't know what was.

Turning around, I grab the pitchfork and pick up another bunch of dirty straw, tossing it into a wheelbarrow as I quickly scan the space for any other spots that need to be cleaned but come out empty. Tossing the pitchfork into the wheelbarrow, I grab the handles and start for the door, but Dad gets in my way.

"You can't do the job half-assedly, Miguel." He grabs the pitchfork, shaking his head in that disapproving manner that makes me feel like I'm ten again.

Never good enough.

Not at school.

Not at the ranch.

And the only thing I was good enough at, he never cared to learn or give two craps about.

"Whatever," I mutter letting go of the handles. The wheelbarrow falls on the ground with a loud *thud* as I stomp toward the door.

I was so done with all of this.

"Leave, of course! Because that's what you're a master at, Miguel. Leaving."

Clenching my hands into fists, I turn around to face him.

"Because you made me, Dad! You are the reason why I left! And I'm starting to regret coming back at all."

If I hadn't come back, I would never have seen Rebecca again.

I'd have never found out what had happened.

I'd have never had to face my father and his disdain ever again.

If only I stayed away, like I promised myself I would do, none of this would have happened. I'd still be happy and focused on football back in Austin.

For a split second, I see something flash on his face. Regret? Doubt? Surprise? The fuck if I know. It's not like this is the first time we've had this exact same fight.

But then, quicker than you can blink, it's gone.

Dad's fingers tighten around the pitchfork, his knuckles white. He raises his free hand to his chest, rubbing at the middle.

He thinks he's hurt by my behavior? Let him trade places with me for a day, then he'll know what real hurt feels like.

With a shake of my head, I turn around and get the hell out of the barn.

One more day.

Post-wedding brunch at Emmett's, and then I'm done. I'm getting out of this godforsaken town, and this time, I'm not coming back.

The step creaks as I climb to the back porch of Emmett's parent's place. The tall, two-story house is the same as I remember it from my childhood. I've lost count of the number of times I've been here. Emmett and I'd run through the back door after school without a care in the world, only to be greeted by Mrs. Santiago's smile and food. This was my happy place, a home away from home, but today, I hold my breath as I push the back door open, unsure of who I'll find inside, but the only person there is Mrs. Santiago.

She looks up from the pan, a smile forming on her lips. "Miguel! Did you get some rest?"

"A little. How are you doing, Mrs. S.?" I tip my chin in the direction of the stove and quickly change the subject so she can't detect the lie. "Need some help?"

"Oh, please." She waves me off. "I'm the happiest when I get to cook for a big group of people."

That much was true. The Santiago household was very much like my own. People were always mingling around the house. The ranch hands were more like a family than workers.

Laughter comes from the living room, drawing my attention.

"You should go back there. Some of Emmett's friends have come down already. Hopefully, Emmett and Kate will be here soon, because breakfast is almost ready."

"Mrs. S., do you nee—"

My heart does a little summersault at the sound of her voice. My eyes fall shut as that grip around my chest tightens.

I guess my fight with Dad did one good thing after all. It pushed my conversation with Rebecca out of my mind, if only temporarily.

"Miguel."

That one softly spoken word is like a punch to my gut. My Adam's apple bobs as I swallow the knot lodged in my throat. My eyes snap open, zeroing in on her pale face.

Any trace of makeup is gone, leaving visible dark circles under her eyes. Her hair is piled up on top of her head in a messy bun. She's dressed in a simple maxi dress, her hand gripping the doorway so hard her knuckles have bleached of color.

Not even a foot separates us, and my fingers itch to reach out and touch her.

I press my lips together, the events of last night flashing in my head.

The wedding, the dancing, her confession.

I lost our baby.

My fingers curl into fists by my sides. The silence stretches as we just stare at one another, the tension filling the air sizzling with all the things neither of us wants to voice out.

"Great, you're just in time," Mrs. Santiago says, snapping me out of my thoughts. "You can take this out to the table. And Miguel can help you."

"Oh, no." Rebecca shakes her head, turning her attention to Mrs. Santiago. "I can—"

But the older woman is having none of it.

"I'm sure it's not a problem." She turns toward me, a sweet smile on her face, but I don't miss the determined expression in her eyes. A look that's not leaving any room for me to tell her no. "Right, Miguel?"

"Of course."

"Perfect!" Mrs. Santiago claps her hands before grabbing a bowl and handing it to Rebecca while I get a tray with a different assortment of meats and cheeses.

I follow after her into the dining room where, just like Mrs. Santiago said, a few of Emmett's friends are already chatting softly amongst each other.

Hayden sits with his girlfriend Callie on his lap, a coffee mug clenched between her palms as he whispers something in her ear. The opposite of them is Nixon, along with his wife. His arm is thrown over her shoulders as he plays with a strand of her hair almost absentmindedly while she types something on her phone.

"Morning."

All heads turn toward me, smiles forming on their faces as they echo back the greeting.

"I hope you didn't make those," Hayden jokes, pointing at the food I'm carrying. "If I remember correctly, the last time you cooked, one of your teammates ended up sick."

"I wasn't the one cooking," I protest, remembering that incident a couple of years ago just before my team played against the Ravens. "The asshole raided my fridge and made himself mac and cheese." Hayden opens his mouth, but I give him a pointed look. "With the cheese that was sitting in there for God only knows how long. It served the idiot right for stealing my food. But no need to worry, Hades. Your ass is safe. It's all Mrs. S."

"That's good to know."

"I just don't get it." Nixon tilts his head to the side. "How didn't he see that the cheese was molded?"

"That's what I asked him too, but the idiot thought it was some gourmet cheese or something like that," I snort. "As if I had money for shit like that."

While my family had enough money, after leaving Bluebonnet, I had to rely on my scholarship. Because I was playing football, I couldn't work. Not that I actually had time to work for the most part, so I lived off the cafeteria food for the three years I was in college. And the little I managed to scrape by with an odd job here and there, like helping people move or cutting grass, was spent on bare necessities.

"As if a country bumpkin like you knew anything about gourmet shit even if it bit you in the ass," Emmett chuckles, and all heads turn toward the doorway where he's standing with his arm wrapped around his wife, a big grin on his face. Completely and utterly ecstatic.

Why wouldn't he be? Just last night, he married the woman he'd been in love with since he was seventeen.

As if they have a mind of their own my eyes scan the room, until they settle on Rebecca, who's just coming in with Mrs. Santiago behind her. The older woman slaps her son over the head. "Emmett James Santiago, I taught you better than that!"

"What?" Emmett raises his hand, rubbing the back of his neck. "I'm telling the truth."

"You're being mean. Now get your ass inside and sit down. The food is getting cold, and I'm sure your friends are hungry."

Nobody needs to be told twice. People take their seats, leaving the one next to Emmett open for me, and right across from me is none other than Rebecca.

Because of course she is.

She's the maid of honor, and I'm the best man.

Just until this brunch is done, an hour tops, and then you're leaving this place behind, and this time you're not coming back, I remind myself.

Wiping my sweaty palms against the sides of my legs, I pull out my chair, making a point of looking anywhere but at her.

Even if I didn't just have a fight with my dad, I didn't know how to deal with everything that had happened last night. Everything that I found out.

I wasn't even sure what I was angrier at. At her, for keeping it a secret for so long, or at myself for not being there when it all played out.

Both.

I was angry at both of us, but there was nothing that I could do to change it.

What would be the point, really?

I had one foot out of Bluebonnet, and Rebecca had to stay.

I should have never started... Well, whatever the hell this thing between the two of us is.

I eat methodically, stuck in my own thoughts as people around me chat about God only knows what, and it isn't until a chair scrapes against the hardwood floor that my head finally snaps up.

"We have an announcement to make!" Emmett yells, getting to his feet and pulling Kate along with him.

Everybody quiets down as we turn our attention to the newlyweds. The pure happiness radiates off the two of them, and I can't help but feel a twinge of envy at seeing my two best friends so in love. But this was more than that. Watching them... They felt complete, like two halves of a whole.

"What's with the theatrics, Hulk?" Hayden asks, a grin on his face.

"Right?" Nixon chimes in readily. "We know you got hitched yesterday. We were there, remember? No need to look so smug about it."

"Shut up, you two. This isn't about the wedding." Emmett glances down at his wife, his smile growing even bigger, and Kate isn't much different.

"Okay, lovebirds, spill it. What's the big news?"

Emmett pulls his gaze from his wife and turns to face the room. "We're pregnant!"

For a split second, nobody says anything, but then all hell breaks loose. Somebody cheers loudly, and everybody starts talking at once. People jump out of their seats and go toward Emmett and Kate, pulling them into a big hug.

Even through all that cacophony, my eyes still find Rebecca easily. She, just like me, is still sitting in her chair, her eyes watching me intently.

"She's pregnant."

The words that set everything in motion last night come

rushing back. But it's not those words that have my heart beating wildly in my chest as the knot forms in my throat, making it hard to breathe.

I lost it.

I lost our baby.

Rebecca was right, after all.

Happiness for my friends fights with the jealousy brewing inside of me at the announcement, and I hate myself for feeling this way. Hate myself because no matter how much I want to, I can't be happy for them wholeheartedly like they deserve.

Blinking, those hazel eyes come into focus.

All the unsaid things passed between us with that one glance.

It should have been us.

Maybe in another lifetime, it would have been.

But not now.

Looking away, I shift my gaze just as Emmett lets go of Nixon, his eyes meeting mine. Forcing a smile, I push from my chair and go to one of my oldest friends. Swallowing down the lump in my throat, I pull him in a one-sided hug. "Congrats, man. That's amazing."

"Thanks." Emmett slaps me on the back, his eyes narrowing slightly. "You good?"

Shit, so much for pretending.

"Why wouldn't I be?" Plastering a smile on my lips, I let go of him and wrap Kate into my arms, quickly changing the subject. "Let's just hope the baby takes after you and not his ugly mug."

Kate starts giggling as Emmett slaps me over the head. "Who are you calling ugly?"

"I just call it as I see it, man. Kate is the one carrying the good genes around here."

Just as I step back, an arm brushes against mine, and a zap of electricity goes through my body at the point of contact.

Rebecca.

I don't even have to look down to know it's her. She's been the only woman who has ever been able to affect me this way.

Going back to my seat, I grab my glass. It's not alcohol, but it'll have to do.

"A toast," I say as I take in the room, waiting for people to join me. The last person my eyes land on is Rebecca. Although a smile is plastered on her face, I can see the pain shining in those hazel depths as she watches me, so I look away. "To a new Santiago coming our way. Congratulations, you guys."

People cheer in agreement, lifting their glasses. I take a sip of my drink, wishing it was something more potent. Something that could erase this pain growing inside my chest.

For the rest of the brunch, I immerse myself into a conversation with Hayden, who wants to know everything about my rookie year so he can prepare for what's coming his way in a few short weeks. Thankful for the distraction, I immerse myself in talk about football, the only thing that has ever been a constant in my life.

It's not long after that the Blairwood crew declares they should hit the road, which is a blessing, really. The moment their truck pulls out of the driveway, I spot Emmett pressing a kiss on top of Kate's head. A knot in my throat grows thicker the longer I watch them. The protective way his hand is spread over her lower back, their hushed voices, him gently pushing her hair behind her ear...

I clear my throat. "I think I'll be going if you guys don't need me."

Emmett and Kate turn toward me, a frown appearing between my best friend's brows. "No, it's fine. Are you okay? You seem off."

Shit.

"Yeah." I run my hand over my face. "Just tired. Didn't get much sleep last night. I'll be better once I crash."

"Okay. How about we grab an early lunch at Letty's one day next week so we can talk in peace? These past few days have been crazy."

"I... shit."

I didn't want to do this.

Emmett just watches me for a moment, contemplating my words. "You're leaving."

His voice is even, almost like he expected it, but at the same time, I don't miss the disappointment on his face.

I shrug my shoulders, trying to seem as nonchalant as possible. "That was the plan all along."

"So you're just... sticking with the plan?"

"Yes, you know this place isn't home any longer."

"Bullshit. Home is a place you create. You can't tell me that Austin feels like home."

Maybe not, but at least they wanted me there.

They respected me there.

And the same couldn't be said for Bluebonnet.

"Austin is my home." Taking a step closer, I pull my best friend into a hug. "Take care, okay? I really am happy for you."

Emmett shakes his head, but whatever he wants to say, he bites his tongue. "Thanks. Good luck with football. How about we try to drive down and catch a game?"

"I'd love that."

Kate shoots me a soft smile when I pull her into my arms. "Try to keep him on his toes. Just because he got the girl doesn't mean he has to stop working hard, okay?"

"Will do." She pulls back, slipping under Emmett's arm. "We'll miss you around here."

They might, but they were a family now, and soon they'd

have a little boy or a girl added to the mix. We were growing up, and going in different directions was just a part of it.

"I'll talk to you guys soon."

With a wave, I go toward my car. My fingers curl around the door handle when something urges me to look up. And that's when I see her.

Rebecca is standing in the doorway, her arms crossed over her chest, watching me.

I allow myself a second to take her in for the last time, just one more second, and then I slip into my seat.

On the drive back to my parent's place, I mentally go over all the things that I'll need to pack before I can hit the road. I already dreaded telling my mom, but there would be no avoiding it.

I'm just pulling up their driveway when a flash of light has me looking up.

Red and blue.

I barely get a chance to register what it is when the sirens start wailing, and the ambulance passes by me.

Dread shoots through me, and I sprint toward the house in time to see my brother bending down to console Gage. I look around the room, but Mom and Dad are nowhere in sight.

I come to a stop just as my brother pats his kid on the shoulder and straightens to his full height.

"What the hell happened?" I pant, my breathing heavy from the running.

Aaron grits his teeth, the motion so similar to Dad's you'd think they're one and the same. Then he says the words that rattle me to my very core. "Dad just had a heart attack."

CHAPTER

26

REBECCA

Yes, you know this place isn't home any longer.

I couldn't erase the determined look on Miguel's face from my mind. Nor the sorrow that flashed there before he finally got in his SUV and drove away.

For good.

He was gone for good this time.

They thought I didn't overhear the conversation, but they would be wrong. It wasn't my intention to listen in on them, but I just caught the end of their discussion and heard enough to put the pieces together.

Miguel had left.

And I just knew he would not be coming back again.

I saw it on his face.

Miguel Fernandez was done with Bluebonnet Creek.

"You've been awfully quiet."

I blink, my focus once again on Savannah who's carefully watching me. She tilts her chin in my direction, those crystal blue eyes not missing anything. "What's up with that?"

I place the cup I've been drying down and take another one. "Nothing, just lost in my thoughts."

She crosses her arms over the counter, her laptop and any

ANNA B. DOE

work that she's been doing forgotten. "Thoughts about what exactly?"

Miguel.

All my thoughts lately have been surrounding him.

The way he kissed me.

The feel of his hands as they explored my body.

The anger that flashed in his eyes when he found out the secret I'd been keeping from him.

The ache in my chest as I watched him drive away.

Miguel. Miguel. Miguel.

I'm not sure why because he sure as hell wasn't thinking about me.

On the contrary, really.

He had no problem leaving as if nothing had happened.

Which, granted, might be the truth.

We made no promises.

We had no future.

Then why the hell could I still feel the press of his lips against mine? Sense those calloused fingers skimming over my flesh? Feel his fingers dig into my skin as he sinks into me, making me experience passion like no other man ever could? Making me feel like that young and careless girl I used to be when we were together?

"Earth to Rebecca." A hand appears in front of my face as Savannah waves at me, and I can feel the color rise up my cheeks. "Are you blushing?"

"I'm not blushing; it's just warm in here." I feel bad for lying to her, but I couldn't tell her any of what's really been on my mind because that would lead to more questions, most of which I don't have an answer to.

"The AC is working just fine," Savannah points out.

"Maybe I'm coming down with something?" I offer weakly. Seriously, some days, she's like a dog with a bone.

"Oh, no, you don't. You promised me we were going to hang out once the craziness of the wedding was done, and I'm keeping you to it."

"And we will."

"Promise me, Becs." She points her finger at me. "You and me and drinks and The Hut. I wanna hear you say it out loud."

I roll my eyes. "Fine, I *promise*. Happy?"

"I would be if that gloomy look wasn't on your face."

I let out a sigh. "Just thinking about Mom's next appointment."

This part was the truth, at least. Mom has an appointment planned in a few weeks, and I was dreading it merely because I could see she's been deteriorating lately, and I hated it. I hated this disease, and I hated that my hands were tied, and I couldn't do anything to stop this.

Savannah's smile falls. "How is she doing?"

"On and off," I let out a sigh. "Off more and more these days."

"I'm so sorry to hear that. Do you think there is something they can do?"

I shake my head. That was the saddest part. There wasn't anything anybody could do. There wasn't a medicine or a treatment that could give me my mom back.

The bell jingles, and I look up to find Mrs. Smith and Mrs. Winters enter the café, their heads bent close together as they chat. Based on how animatedly they're talking, today's gossip must be really good.

Savannah and I exchange a silent glance as the two of them join us at the counter, so immersed in their conversation they barely pay us any attention.

"Good afternoon, Mrs. Smith, Mrs. Winters," I say, smiling brightly at them. "What can I help you with today?"

"Hey, honey." Mrs. Smith turns to me. "I'm here to get a

half-dozen chocolate cupcakes for my grandkids. And can I also get one of those vanilla lattes?"

"Sure thing. Anything for you, Mrs. Winters?"

"Get me one of those lattes, too."

"Two lattes and half a dozen cupcakes, coming right up."

Placing two cups under the espresso machine, I start the coffee as I grab the box and start putting the cupcakes inside.

From the corner of my eyes, I can see Mrs. Winters turning to Mrs. Smith. "Poor Margaret. I can't believe she has to go through all of this. She must be devastated."

"He's so young, too, and in such good shape. You'd never think something like that could happen to him."

Young? Good shape? I glance toward Savannah, who just shrugs, clearly as confused as I am. *What the hell's going on?*

Placing the lid on the cupcakes, I put them next to the register and turn to the coffee machine so I can finish the order.

Mrs. Winters hums. "It's so sad. It really is."

Sad?

"I know. I hope he recovers quickly."

I turn toward her, unable to stop the question from coming, "What's going on?"

I hadn't heard anything, but then again, my mind was all over the place between the wedding, helping Kate clean up, and trying *not* to think about Miguel, everything that had happened, and the fact that he left without saying a word.

The two women exchange a look. "You didn't hear?"

I carefully place a lid on the cup and put it on the counter, an uneasy feeling starting to brew in my stomach at the serious matching look on their faces. "Hear what?"

Mrs. Winters shakes her head, "Luis Fernandez had a heart attack."

I blink, unsure if I heard her correctly. She couldn't mean...

"Yes, they even called the ambulance." Mrs. Smith nods, her lips pressed in a tight line. "He was taken to the hospital."

Mr. Fernandez.

As in Miguel's dad.

Taken to the hospital.

Because of a heart attack.

A freaking heart attack.

"It's such a shame. I tried calling Margaret to see how they were doing, but nobody picked up the phone."

Mrs. Winters elbows her companion. "That's because they're probably still at the hospital. That poor, poor woman!" Her attention shifts to me. "Did you talk to her maybe?"

It takes me a moment to hear her from the ringing in my ears.

Mr. Fernandez. In a hospital.

"No, I..." I shake my head, my mouth suddenly feeling dry. Did somebody call Miguel? Tell him what happened? "I didn't hear anything."

"Well, if you hear something, do let us know. Maybe we can prepare them some food for when they get back from the hospital so Margaret can focus on helping her husband get better."

"Of course."

Mrs. Smith pats my hand, giving me a sad smile. On autopilot, I finish and process their order, and soon enough, they leave the café.

"Are you okay?" Savannah asks, snapping me out of my thoughts. "Do you need to go?"

I wanted to. I wanted to so badly, but Jennifer was off today, so I couldn't leave before closing time. "I have to finish here first."

"Nobody will blame you if you want to close the shop early and go check if he's okay."

I shake my head. "I will do that once I'm done here."

Once I had enough time to process what I had just heard and get a grip on my emotions, the last thing Mr. and Mrs. Fernandez needed was for me to start crying when I saw them.

I can see that Savannah wants to protest, but she changes her mind at the very last moment. She stays for a while longer, most likely waiting for me to come around, but in the end, she has to leave because she has to take her grandmother to see her doctor.

"It's going to be okay," she whispers, pulling me in a tight hug.

A heart attack didn't seem like an okay thing, but I just nodded since it seemed easier than to fight her on it.

After that, the shop picks up, so I'm busy for the next couple of hours, but the moment things wind down, I pull out my phone and call Mrs. Fernandez. The phone rings a few times before I'm directed to her voicemail.

Worry niggles at me, but I try to push it back. Mrs. Smith said they were at the hospital. Mrs. Fernandez probably had her hands full trying to take care of her husband, and answering her phone was the last thing on her mind.

That left the other thing.

Chewing at my lip, I pull open my contacts—or, more specifically, my blocked list and one name on it.

Somebody should call him to make sure he knew what was going on. No matter the relationship between Miguel and his dad, I knew that deep down, he'd want to know what had happened.

Slowly, I press the unblock button and just stare at the screen.

What I expected to happen, I didn't know.

I let out a shaky breath. "Get a grip, Becky."

My finger hovers over the call button when my phone

suddenly rings in my hand, startling me so much that I almost drop it.

"*Shit.*"

Tightening my grip on the device, I check the screen before quickly pressing the answer button. "Linda?"

"Where are you, Becky?" Linda's question is muffled by the yelling coming from the background.

"Reading Nook. Why? What's going on?"

"Can you come home? Your mom's extremely distressed, and nothing's working."

My stomach sinks with dread. "I'll be home soon."

Brushing Mom's hair out of the way, I give her sleeping face one last look before I slip out of her room as quietly as possible. She had one of her episodes, searching for my dad, and it took a good hour until she finally calmed down, and I managed to reassure her that everything would be fine.

Running my hand over my face, I slowly make my way down the stairs to find Linda in the kitchen, putting away the last of the food since Mom barely touched anything.

"Is she asleep?"

"Yeah," I make my way to the fridge and grab a bottle of wine.

"I'm so sorry I had to call you. I tried to calm her down, but she didn't recognize me, and..."

I shake my head. "It's not your fault."

We knew this would happen. We knew that she would keep deteriorating, but I never imagined it would be this fast.

Was I doing the right thing? Keeping her here?

It felt right, and I was grateful for it because of the little glimpses I got of my mother every now and again, but then, on days like today, I couldn't help but wonder...

"You can go now, Linda."

"Are you sure? Chase won't be back until tomorrow afternoon at the earliest."

In all the craziness that was this weekend, I completely forgot that Chase has his specialist's appointment regarding his leg, and then he was supposed to visit an army buddy of his. Thankfully, when I got up this morning, I found my truck sitting in the driveway and waiting for me because otherwise I'd be screwed. But when I tried calling to see who brought it and how much I owe them, they told me it was all taken care of. Which only meant one thing—Miguel paid to have it repaired.

Was it before our fight or after? Why did it even matter? I had my truck, and Miguel was gone.

Which reminded me...

"We'll be fine," I reassure her.

The older woman nods.

I grab a wine glass from the cupboard and fill it as she picks up her things. I walk her out the door, making sure it's locked and the house is still quiet as I make my way to the back porch.

I don't bother with the lights as I sit on the swing, taking a sip of wine. Putting the glass on the table, I grab my phone and pull out Miguel's contact.

Maybe I should just shoot him a message instead? Or call Emmett, but he and Kate went out of the town for a short honeymoon. I didn't want to interrupt them. They deserved some rest, which meant this was on me. I had to put on my big girl panties and—

The sound of feet pounding against the gravel snaps me out of my thoughts. I look up just in time to see a tall figure running toward me.

My heart speeds up as I watch the person move closer, fear setting in.

People don't go running around these parts.

There was an odd animal here or there, getting lost and moving too close to the house, but never people.

What if...

The person comes to the stop a few feet away, the soft moonlight illuminating the tall form just enough. I let out a shaky breath as I stared at his rapidly rising and falling chest.

I push to my feet, my legs feeling wobbly underneath me. "Miguel." His name is a soft whisper coming from my lips.

Miguel lifts his hand, running it through his hair as his eyes meet mine.

Mere feet separate us, but it feels like an ocean. There is so much that has happened between the two of us, and I have no idea where we stand. Does he hate me for the secrets I've kept from him? Are we friends? Are we lovers? Are we nothing like we were before he came back to Bluebonnet?

His hair is a mess, dark curls going in different directions from where he ran his fingers through it. His shirt is plastered to his chest, patches of sweat visible even in the darkness.

"Rebecca," he rasps, his gravelly voice sending tingles running down my spine.

He was running.

Here.

He hadn't left just yet.

He's still here.

Quietly watching me.

How was it fair that even after everything that had happened, after all the insecurities and doubts and hurt we've inflicted upon each other, this man still affected me this way?

I didn't know what was going on or where we stood.

The only thing I knew was that there was a haunted look blazing in his dark eyes, and I itched to make it go away.

I'm not sure which one of us makes the first move. But suddenly, strong arms wrap around me. Miguel's hand falls on the small of my back, his other one slipping to the back of my neck, holding onto me for dear life.

"My dad, he..." Miguel rasps, his voice muffled.

He knew.

That's why he was still here.

He knew what had happened.

"Shhh, I'm here."

Miguel's arms tighten around me, squeezing me for dear life. He buries his head into the crook of my shoulder, and I let out a shuddering breath. The scent of citrus, sweat, and hay surrounds me, and my eyes fall shut as I let myself inhale everything that is Miguel.

The boy I remember from my childhood mixes with the man standing in front of me, so different and yet the same. In this moment, the past doesn't matter. Everything that has happened, all the words exchanged, they're meaningless. The only important thing is that he's here, and he needs me.

I slip my free arm around his waist. My face is burrowed into his chest, the warmth of his skin seeping through the thin cotton of his shirt.

For a second, it feels like I remember to breathe for the first time since I've heard the news, but then I feel Miguel's body shake against mine.

"Miguel?"

I try to pull back, but he's not letting go of me. If possible, his hold on me tightens, and that uneasy feeling is once again swirling inside my stomach.

"Is everything okay? Is your dad..."

I don't let myself finish the question. Because what if he's not okay? What if something happened and his condition worsened? What if...

"He's still in the hospital. They wanted to keep him there to make sure he was going to be okay," Miguel says into my shoulder, his voice coming out muffled. "But if everything works out, we should be able to bring him home soon."

Home.

He's coming home.

"Thank God." I let out a long exhale as my fingers gripped the worn material of his shirt.

Mr. Fernandez was okay.

At least one of us will have both parents alive and well.

"That's good news, right? If he's going home, that means he's doing better?"

"Or maybe he just pissed the nurses off so badly they are more than ready to discharge him just so they don't have to be in his presence for much longer."

A strangled sound comes from my lungs as the image of Mr. Fernandez's grumpy face pops into my mind. I could totally see him annoying the nurses and doctors just so they'd let him leave as soon as possible.

"That does sound like something he'd do."

"That's Dad. Stubborn like a mule."

I knew another man just like that. Not that I thought Miguel would appreciate the comparison. But I could see it. They were more alike than either of them wanted to admit. I think that was part of the reason why they didn't get along to begin with.

"I'm so happy to hear he's doing better. When I heard he had a heart attack..." I shake my head. "I was just about to call you, but then you appeared and..."

Miguel pulls back, those exhausted eyes scanning my face. "You were planning to call me?"

"You said you were leaving, and I didn't know if anybody told you. So, yeah, I was planning to make sure you knew what's going on." I shrug. "No matter what happened between you and your dad, you'd never forgive yourself if you didn't come back, Miguel."

A lot of things might have changed about Miguel, but at the core, he was still that boy I fell in love with. The boy who loved his family above all else, the boy who'd do everything to make them happy.

Miguel stares at me, different emotions playing on his face.

I look away, unable to stand his probing stare.

There was no sense in making a big deal about this. It's something any of our friends would have done. Because this is just the way our community was. We took care of one another.

"It was all my fault." The words are whispered so softly at first, I think I imagined them. I turn around to find Miguel's gaze fixed on me, but it's clear his mind is miles away.

"What are you talking about?"

Miguel lets go of me, his hand running through his already wild locks.

"The heart attack." His hand falls down his side. "It was my fault."

"It was a *heart attack*," I point out. "How could it have been your fault?"

"We had a fight. I couldn't fall asleep after..." He shakes his head, but I don't need him to finish that sentence to know what he meant.

After what happened the other night.

After what I told him.

The secret I revealed.

"Anyway, he found me in the barn where I was trying to busy myself with work, and we got into a fight like we always do."

I take a step closer, my palm brushing against his arm. "People fight. That doesn't mean that what happened was your fault."

Miguel's fingers clench and unclench by his side. "He didn't get a heart attack in any of the years I've been away."

"He didn't get a heart attack the day you got here either, did he?" When he refuses to turn to me, I close the distance between us, my hands cupping his cheek and forcing him to look at me. "What happened was a freaking accident. It didn't have anything more to do with you than it did with me. People get sick, Miguel. Young and old. There is, unfortunately, nothing that we can do about it."

"I just hate this so fucking much."

"I know." I push a strand of hair out of his face, pressing my forehead against his, and repeat again, softer this time, "But this wasn't your fault."

We just stare at one another for a moment, breathing each other in.

"Why are you so nice to me?"

"What?"

"Fuck it, Rebecca." He shakes his head but doesn't pull away. "I was a jackass to you, and still, you're here comforting me."

My heart does a little flip inside my chest as his fingers slide to my face. "I'm so fucking sorry," he whispers, his voice coming out hoarse. "I yelled at you. I wanted to leave. I *would* have left if this whole thing didn't happen, and now you're trying to make sure I'm okay. After everything that has happened."

"It doesn't matter."

"It *does* matter. I was a complete asshole the other night. I'm sorry for what I said. It was totally uncalled for, but fuck it, it caught me by surprise. I never expected..." He shakes his head, his Adam's apple bobbing. "Yes, I think you should have told me, but I blame myself more than anything. I keep going back, thinking of what I could have done to change what had happened. I keep thinking if things would have played out differently, if I hadn't let the fear and anger get the better of me. If I had grabbed your hand and pulled you into my chest, demanding you listen to me, to let me explain. Hell, I should have jumped on the next plane to Texas and locked you in a room if that's what it took. Maybe then things would be different. Maybe then... What if everything that had happened was my fault?"

"No." I place my hands over his. "Losing our baby was nobody's fault. Trust me when I say it. What happened... There was no reason for it. No way we could have known the outcome, and there was nothing that either of us could have done to change it. What I know is it wasn't either of our faults. It just wasn't meant to be. It took me a long time to come to terms with what happened, a long time to stop feeling guilty. What if I knew sooner that I was pregnant? Would I have done something differently? What if I wasn't under so much stress? What if I did something unconsciously that hurt the baby? What if I somehow, unknowingly hurt our baby?" I shake my head. Even now, years later, it was hard for me to think about what had happened. "There are so many what-ifs, but at the end of the day, none of it matters. That baby is gone, and nothing will bring it back, and we're the people we are because of it. There is only one reality, and this is it."

"It wasn't your fault." His fingers slide into my hair, those intense chocolate eyes staring into mine. "You hear me?"

"I know that now. It just wasn't meant to be."

And if that wasn't the story of our lives, I don't know what is.

Our paths keep crossing, only for us to be pulled in different directions.

Miguel presses his forehead against mine. "I'm still sorry for what happened. I'm sorry for not fighting harder. Sorry that I wasn't there for you when you needed me. I'm so fucking sorry, Rebecca."

"I'm sorry too," I whisper softly, staring into those brown eyes. Up close like this, I can see the tiniest speckles of gold shining in the brown depths. "I should have trusted you and not let my insecurities get the better of me."

"I'm not sure if I would have trusted me." Miguel's thumbs swipe over my cheek, making me realize a tear had slipped down. "I should have never let her stay. I should have walked her home, and things would have played out so much differently."

But would they really?

Everything that Miguel ever wanted was to play football professionally. And if things happened differently, that would have never happened. If I told him that day that I was pregnant, he would have left everything to be with me. I just know it. Miguel would have given up his dream for our baby, and it would have crushed him.

"Maybe they would have," I say softly. "Maybe they wouldn't. At the end of the day, it doesn't matter. Who we are today is because of the choices we made in our past. But one thing I know is that I don't want to be angry any longer, Miguel."

"I don't want to be angry at you either."

Miguel's eyes bore into mine before they dropped down to my mouth. A rush of tingles goes down my spine from the intensity of his stare. My tongue darts out, sliding over my lower lip.

"Rebecca..." My name is a low growl sending tingles down my spine.

"Yeah?"

There is a beat of silence where he just stares at me, and I hold my breath as I wait to see what he'll do.

"I should go home," he whispers but doesn't attempt to move. "But I don't want to. I don't want to go back to that empty house and remember the last words I said to my father in anger before I stormed away."

His pain and frustration are so strong they're almost palpable. I hated it. I hated seeing him so conflicted, hated to see him hurting.

Slowly, I take his hand in mine. "Then stay here."

His eyes widen slightly in surprise.

"Stay," I repeat.

My eyes hold his as I take a step back, giving him a chance to change his mind, but he doesn't. Miguel follows after me into the house.

"Where is everybody?" he asks softly.

"Chase isn't here, and Mom's asleep, so we need to be quiet."

Making sure the door is locked, I lead him up the stairs and into my bedroom.

Slowly, I turn around to find Miguel taking in the space, although not much has changed since the last time he's been here.

I tuck a strand of my hair behind my ear, suddenly feeling nervous. "Do you want to..."

I don't get to finish because Miguel's eyes meet mine, and he closes the distance between us.

His palms cradle my cheeks as he leans down and kisses me. I wrap my fingers around his wrists, holding onto him as his mouth sweeps over mine, pushing me back until my knees touch the mattress, and I fall down, breaking the connection.

I tilt my head back to find those blazing eyes on me. He tugs his shirt over his head, tossing it on the floor.

"I want you," he whispers, his knee sinking into the mattress on my side. "That's the only thing I have ever wanted. You, Rebecca."

Placing my hand on his chest, I slide it onto his neck and pull him to me. "I'm yours. I've always been yours."

And a part of me worried, I always would be.

CHAPTER

27

MIGUEL

The bright morning light blinds me the moment I open my eyes. Cursing quietly, I turn around, burrowing my head in the pillow. The scent of roses reaches my nostrils.

Rebecca.

My eyes snap open, and I slowly notice little details around me: the desk on one side of the room with a pin board above it filled with photographs, the rose candle standing on the nightstand next to a stack of books, and the fluffy light gray rug on the floor. But the woman who owned all of it was nowhere in sight.

Groaning, I push into a sitting position and rub at my face. I didn't hear Rebecca get up, but it must have been a while ago because my clothes were neatly piled up on the edge of the mattress, along with my phone. Sliding out of the bed, I grab my clothes and put them on before checking the time—just past seven-thirty. I couldn't remember the last time I slept this long or this good. I quickly go to the bathroom to splash some water on my face and find a spare toothbrush in one of the drawers to brush my teeth.

Opening the door, I look up and down the hallway, only to

be met with silence. Still, I try to be quiet as I make my way down the stairs, searching for Rebecca.

Soft music is coming from the kitchen, so I follow the sound, and sure enough, there she is, quietly humming as she grabs a cup of coffee from the counter and takes a sip before she flips the pancake.

Moving into the kitchen, I slide my arm around her middle, pulling her body to me. "Morning," I whisper, pressing my mouth against the side of her neck.

Fuck, she smells sweet.

Like sugar, chocolate, roses, and everything good in my life.

Rebecca jumps a little in surprise. "Hey, I didn't hear you come in."

"That's because you were too busy singing."

"I don't sing," she protests, turning her attention to the pancake.

"I'd beg to differ."

I watch as she slides the pancake onto the plate before putting more batter on the pan. My stomach rumbles loudly, making its presence be known.

"You could have woken me up, you know."

Rebecca shrugs. "It's fine. I figured you should get some rest after everything that had happened."

The images of yesterday flash in my mind.

The blue and red lights.

Driving to the hospital.

The heartbreak and fear that were written all over Mom's face no matter how much she tried to hide it.

Dad's ashen face, and the way he suddenly seemed so small lying on that hospital bed.

How is it possible that all of that happened only hours ago?

I bury my head deeper into Rebecca's neck, pushing back

the thoughts of yesterday, and inhale her sweet scent, letting it ground me. "Why would I want rest when I have you?"

Color floods her cheeks, and I know she's thinking about last night. The way I focused all of my attention on her. On bringing pleasure to her body and losing myself in her velvet heat as I swallowed the noises she made so we wouldn't wake anybody up.

"I'll burn breakfast if you don't stop teasing me," she chastises, pushing me back.

"That's fine. I can always have you for breakfast instead."

She turns to glare at me. "Stop teasing me."

"Fine."

Chuckling, I grab her empty cup and search for one of my own, pouring us fresh coffees. Taking a long sip, I lean against the counter, but when I look up, I find Rebecca's mom standing in the doorway and watching us.

"Mrs. Williams, good morning." I straighten and give the woman a tentative smile as I take her in.

Rebecca's mom has adopted me into their family when we were kids, treating me just like she did any of her children. The last few years definitely had left their mark on her. Her usually vibrant dark hair was more gray than red now. And there were new lines surrounding her eyes and mouth.

Those hazel eyes that are so much like her daughter's stare at me, but there is blurriness to them that wasn't there before. She takes me in, a frown etched between her brows.

Rebecca looks up at her mom before she gives me an apologetic smile. Stirring the bacon in the pan, she places it to the side and wipes her hands on the towel before going to her mom.

"Hey, I didn't realize you were awake." She places her hands on her mother's shoulders. "C'mon, let's get you se—"

Mrs. Williams shifts her attention from Rebecca to me once

again. I start to think that this might be a bad idea and I should probably leave so I don't upset her when her words make my heart stop.

"Miguel?" Mrs. Williams tilts her head to the side, her eyes narrowing on me. "Is that you?"

It's like all the air is sucked out of the room. Rebecca's eyes widen as she glances from her mother to me.

"Yeah, sorry for intruding like this."

"Oh, nonsense!" She slips from under Rebecca's arms and slowly moves toward me, outstretching her hands.

Bending down, I gently wrap my arms around her fragile body, my chest squeezing tightly as her hands tap my back.

Damn, I missed this.

"Just look at you. How much you've grown since the last time I saw you."

Glancing over her shoulder, I catch tears glistening in Rebecca's eyes before she brushes them away. Turning her back to us, she goes back to the stove, but I have an inkling she needs a moment to collect herself.

Before I can say anything, Mrs. Williams pushes me at arm's length and just stares at me. "You're even more handsome than you were before. Not that I'm surprised."

"You're one to talk." I flash her a smile that she returns almost immediately.

"Oh, please! Are you staying for breakfast? It feels like I haven't seen you in forever."

"It's been a while."

I don't bother correcting her that we saw each other not that long ago. I looked up Alzheimer's online that day I helped Rebecca search for her mother, and I knew that she wouldn't remember anything.

"Becky, you should probably bake some eggs. You know Miguel can eat for three people."

"I know, Mom."

Mrs. Williams pushes me toward the table. "Come, you have to tell me everything. Becky is always so tight-lipped about you."

Mrs. Williams shoots a glare in Rebecca's direction, but she chooses to ignore it, instead focusing on finishing the breakfast.

"So, how are you doing? Did you come home for good?"

"Good, and no. I'm here for the wedding."

Her brows scrunch together. "Wedding?"

"Emmett and Kate's wedding, Mom," Rebecca reminds her gently.

That distant look is back in her eyes, and I can see the first traces of frustration showing on her face as she tries to remember something that's not there. "Right. Emmett and Kate's wedding. Not that I'm surprised. That boy really had it bad."

I chuckle softly. "That he does. He was determined to get the girl, and get the girl he did. I still can't believe Kate fell for his sorry ass."

Mrs. Williams nods her head. "There is nothing a man won't do for the woman he loves."

"I guess there is that."

Grabbing my coffee cup, I take a sip.

"What about you two?" Mrs. Williams shoots me a pointed look. "When will you make an honest woman out of my daughter?"

Well, shit.

Her question throws me off guard, making me choke on the coffee. I place the cup on the table and start coughing loudly.

Rebecca chooses that exact moment to bring food to the table. Putting the pan in the middle of it, she places her hand on my back and gives me a few robust taps.

"Are you okay?"

"F-fine," I croak out as I look up just to see Mrs. Williams observing us with watchful eyes.

"What? It's a legitimate question. You two have been dancing around each other for way too long. I think it's time for you to settle down."

"I..."

Not knowing what to say, I turn to Rebecca for any sign of guidance, but she pointedly ignores my gaze.

"Now's not the time, Mom. Miguel is busy playing professional football in Austin."

Pulling her arms back she sits down on the chair next to me and starts piling food on everybody's plates.

"Nonsense." Mrs. Williams waves her off. "If you wait for the right time, you'll always come up short. Perfect time is a phrase for people who aren't ready to settle down and are looking for excuses." Those hazel eyes meet mine. "I never thought you were the type of man who needs excuses, Miguel Fernandez. Quite the contrary, actually."

Although spoken softly, her words are like a kick to my gut. But I don't know what to tell her. Yes, I've always gone after what I wanted, but this was different. Rebecca and I broke up years ago, and as we've established recently, this thing between us couldn't work. Not because we didn't want it to work but because our lives were just too different.

"Mom," Rebecca chastises. "Can we all focus on breakfast instead?"

I don't miss the fact that she didn't correct her and tell her that we weren't together. I guess there wasn't really a point to it. Maybe Rebecca had told her already, and Mrs. Williams just couldn't remember due to her illness, so she didn't even try.

Mrs. Williams lifts her hands defensively. "I was just saying."

After that, we change the subject. Mrs. Williams asks me

about football, so I tell her about how I entered the draft early and about my teammates. She listens intently, a smile playing on her lips, and for the first time, I feel like I belong. Becky's family always accepted me just the way I was. They never complained about football. Never told me it was a foolish dream I should give up on. Hell, Mrs. Williams attended more of my football games than my own parents did until that last year. I guess that should have been a sign in itself.

Maybe if I paid more attention, I would have noticed something was off with her. But I was too immersed in my studies, too immersed in football and getting that scholarship, too enamored in Rebecca.

Once we finish, Becky gets up and starts collecting the plates, so I do the same. I'm going back for the second batch when I notice Mrs. Williams looking around, a confused expression on her face.

I lean down, trying not to scare her. "Mrs. Williams?"

She jumps slightly, her hazel eyes wide as she clenches her fingers together. "Where is Jackson?"

I blink a few times, thrown off guard by her question. Mr. Williams? Why would she... The realization hits me just as I catch the smile falling from Rebecca's lips.

"Jackson went out to work," Rebecca says softly, grabbing a towel to dry her hands. "He'll be back later."

Mrs. Williams looks around the room, completely confused. "Work. Right." Then her eyes land on me, and that scowl is back, but this time, there is no recognition. "And who're you?"

"I—"

"Are you bringing strange men home again, Gigi?"

Gigi?

Rebecca doesn't seem the least bit fazed by any of it as she makes her way to her mother. "Miguel is a friend. He'll be going soon. How about we get you to the living room?" Rebecca gently slips her hand under her mother's arm and helps her to her feet. "You can watch your favorite show."

Mrs. Williams nods. "Okay."

I watch as Rebecca leads her mom to the living room, murmuring something softly to her the whole time. My heart hurts watching them like this.

What must it be like? One moment here, like no time has passed, the other gone, back to the past to the point that she doesn't even remember her own daughter? I couldn't imagine it. And yet, this has been Rebecca's life for the last few years.

The TV turns on, soft voices filling the background. Then Rebecca appears in the doorway. Her gaze is fixed on the floor, and I can see her shoulders shake as she lets out a long breath before looking up.

Her eyes meet mine, and for a split second, she looks surprised to see me standing there.

"Is it always like this?" I ask, breaking the silence.

"Pretty much." Rebecca nods, joining me in the kitchen. "Although her lucid moments are far and few between. For the most part, she's stuck in the past."

Living in the time when her husband was still alive. Waiting for him to come back home, only for it to never happen.

Rebecca goes back to cleaning the table, but I pull her to me instead. My arms wrap around her middle, and I place my head against the top of her head.

"I'm so sorry, Red," I whisper softly.

Her body is stiff in my embrace. I expect her to protest, to push me away, but instead, her fingers curl around my forearms, holding me tightly.

"It is what it is."

"This is awful. This life..."

"Maybe. Maybe not. Some days, I hate it. Others I feel grateful that she lives in the world in which Dad's still alive. At least she has him. Even though it breaks my heart every time I have to lie to her and tell her he's coming home when I know damn well that'll never happen."

Rebecca's parents were so in love. I could remember it even though he died in a car accident when we were just kids. The Williams' were devastated by his loss. The whole town was really. Mr. Williams was a good man, and everybody loved him. In all the years after that, I never saw Mrs. Williams look at another man, much less show any interest in dating.

She focused on her children instead, and they were happy.

I couldn't imagine what it must be for Rebecca to have to go through all of this over and over again.

"I'm so sorry, baby." The endearment falls off my lips easily, like it always did.

Becky turns in my arms, her eyes meeting mine. I could see tears glistening in them. Lifting my hand, I cup her face, running my thumb over her cheekbone. "Don't cry."

There was nothing worse than seeing Rebecca cry. She was always so strong. So fierce. It hurt even more seeing her broken apart like this.

"Hey, it's going to be okay," I whisper, brushing away her tears.

Fuck this.

Leaning down, I press my mouth against hers. I can feel the salty taste of tears on her lips as I kiss her gently. Every swipe of my mouth over hers is a silent reassurance that things will be okay.

My hand slips to the back of her neck, my fingers tangling in her hair as I tilt her head. Rebecca lets out a shuddered breath, her lips parting as her fingers clasp around my shirt, pulling me closer to her.

So I give in. I let her take what she needs. I let her lose herself in me.

She nips at my lip, a soft growl coming from my chest as I cup her cheeks between my palms. Damn, she tastes so sweet. So perfect. So... mine.

"Oh, I'm sorry!" a female voice says, breaking through the haze that's Rebecca.

We pull apart, and I catch a glimpse of Linda as she scurries out of the kitchen.

"Shit," Rebecca mutters, pressing her forehead against my chest, her breathing heavy.

Shit, indeed.

Although I guess I should be happy it was Linda and not Rebecca's brother. I was sure that encounter would have gone much differently if Chase had caught us making out.

My hand tightens in her hair before I let my fingers slide out of her silky strands and take a step back. "I think I should get going. I promised Mom I'd bring her some fresh clothes in the morning."

"Wait, I have something for you."

She hurries toward the counter grabbing a plastic container and hands it to me. "You can take this to your parents. And before you ask, this is the healthy version of chocolate muffins, but they taste as good as the regular ones."

Muffins.

She baked muffins for my parents.

"What about me?"

Rebecca rolls her eyes. "Nobody said you can't eat them."

"That's not the same, and you know it."

"Fine," she lets out a sigh. "I'll bake you something too. As a thank you for getting my truck fixed."

"I don't know what you're talking about." Closing the distance between us, I press my mouth against hers. "Later?"

CHAPTER

28

MIGUEL

"Do I look like a damn invalid to you?" Dad grumbles as I try to help him into the house two days later after he was finally discharged from the hospital.

"What you look like is a grumpy man-child who doesn't know how to accept help when he clearly needs it," I mutter to myself, but of course, the old man hears me and shoots me a death glare.

"I'll give you a man-child."

He pulls his arm out of my grasp, but after barely taking three steps, his legs wobble, and he stumbles forward.

"*Fucking hell, Dad,*" I yell, wrapping my hand around his elbow to steady him.

His breathing is hard, a layer of sweat coating his forehead, and his whole body is shaking from exertion.

He's tired, not that the bastard would ever admit it out loud, especially not in front of me.

Dad's been protesting since the moment we got to the hospital, and all through Mom getting his discharge papers taken care of. The stubborn man tried to walk to the car on his own, but one look from an older nurse had him popping his ass into the wheelchair instead. There was at least one person in

346

that hospital who knew how to deal with him, so I guess there was that.

That compliance, however, didn't transfer to coming home because the moment the truck pulled to a stop, he was out of the car all on his own.

"Is your pride seriously more important? Do you want to end up in the hospital again? Just let me help you."

"I'm f-fine," he hisses. "I don't need help."

"Oh yeah, because nothing screams fine than a man barely standing on his feet after suffering a freaking *heart attack*."

"Pre-heart attack," Dad corrects.

He's been repeating those two words like a parrot. I don't know why he thinks there's a kind of difference to be made.

"Yes, a pre-heart attack. Meaning you were fucking lucky to be alive, and you're still able to move and do shit on your own."

Dad turns to glare at me. "Watch that mouth, boy."

"I'm not watching anything. You almost *died*, Dad. I know you don't give a crap about me and about what I think, but think about Mom. Think about how that would affect her. Think about Gage. What if he found your sorry ass dead in the barn? How would that affect him? Do you seriously want that?"

"Will you two stop it already?" Mom yells as she joins us in front of the house. She glares from Dad to me and back. "You're both acting like complete dumbasses. Too similar for your own good. You" — she gently jabs her finger into Dad's chest — "will stop grumbling and listen to what we tell you. You'll accept help, start eating healthy, and you *will* recover, or so help me God, Luis, I will be the one to kill you myself, and you" — she turns to me, her finger meeting the center of my chest — "Your Dad loves you. He might not be the best at showing it, but he does love you." Mom crosses her arms over her chest and glares at both of us. "I've let you two keep at this for way too long. It's time for you to get your shit in order and talk like two adults."

347

"Margie..." Dad starts to open his mouth, but Mom shoots him a death glare.

"I'm not joking, Luis. I let this go on for way too long. You have two amazing sons. One's working his ass off to keep the family business thriving, the other one is living his wildest dreams despite all the obstacles we put in front of him. It's time to let it go. I want all my boys home, and I want us to be happy and healthy so we can watch our grandchildren grow up. Is that too much to ask?"

"Fine," Dad huffs.

"I didn't hear you."

"I said fine."

"Perfect." Moving closer to him, she wraps her arms around him and presses her mouth against his cheek. "Now go and lie down. I'll bring you some soup in a little bit, okay?"

Dad grumbles something but doesn't try to protest when I take his hand. We make our way up the stairs in complete silence. The only sound is his heavy breathing that becomes more and more labored with every step he takes.

Neither of us comments on it, but I can hear him let out a long exhale in relief when we finally get to their bedroom, and he sits down on the bed.

Looking around, I spot a glass, so I go to the bathroom and fill it with cool water.

"Thanks," he says as I hand it to him. He drains it slowly, his hand shaking a little as he holds onto the glass. Once he's done, I go and refill it again and put it on his nightstand.

"Do you need anything else?"

Dad shakes his head. "I'm fine."

"Okay then." With a nod, I just stand there for a moment before turning around and going for the door.

"Your mom's right, you know."

I stop, my hand lingering on the doorway. "About what?"

"You have succeeded despite everything. I watched your game last season, and I felt proud, but then I remembered I had nothing to do with that. I didn't do shit to help you get there."

My brows pull together as I process his words. "You? Watched the game?" I ask. The incredulity of the situation wasn't lost on me. I turn around to face him and point at my chest. "My game?"

Dad didn't watch football games. Hell, I don't think I remember one instance when I saw the man sit down and watch any kind of sport, God forbid, actually going to a game. I think I was the only kid in my class who didn't have parents attending my games. Santiago's tried to come any chance they got, and Rebecca was there all the time. My parents? Not once.

"Yes, I watched your game. You've grown into a fine man, Miguel. And I'm sorry that I didn't do more to contribute to that."

A knot forms in my throat. I try to swallow it down, but it's like the damn thing is stuck there.

"I'm the man I am because of you."

Dad visibly flinches at my harsh tone, and a part of me feels bad about it, but that lonely boy who just wanted his dad to come and watch him play is screaming loudly from the back of my mind.

"I know I was hard on you growing up, but you were always so wild, so carefree."

I open my mouth to protest, but he shakes his head. "That's not your fault. I just didn't know what to do with you. I was raised by parents that lived from the land. It was the only thing I knew how to do. Aaron was the same. He was always so simple. But not you."

"If you want to tell me once again how difficult and how big of a disappointment I was and how much better Aaron is, you can save your breath. I already know that."

"You weren't a disappointment, Miguel. While your mother is right, and we're more alike in some ways, we couldn't be more different in others. You always dreamed big, and it scared me. You didn't just love football; you were obsessed with it. It was your only option; nothing else would ever measure up. And, while yes, a part of me was disappointed because I wanted both my boys to follow in my footsteps, I was also worried about you. Worried about what would happen if you didn't get a chance to live your dream. What if you weren't drafted? What if you got injured and could no longer play? There were just so many possibilities, so much uncertainty, and I didn't want that for you."

I just stare at him, at a loss for words. I didn't know what to do with what he said.

"I don't want anything from you. I just..." He shakes his head. "I wanted you to know that although I don't have the right to it, I'm proud of the man you've become and how far you've come."

"Then why did you tell me to leave?"

Dad lifts his hand and runs it through his hair, letting out a sigh. "I thought *you* wanted to leave. You were pretty adamant about not coming back in the first place. I thought you'd be gone as soon as the wedding was done."

"I was planning to," I admit. "But since coming back..." My gaze goes to the window. The barn is just on the left, with a glimpse of fields stretching out in the distance out front. Miles and miles of fields. "Just because I love football doesn't mean I don't like the land."

"I know." Dad nods.

For a while, we just stand there, neither of us saying anything. Our conversation didn't take away the years of hurt and distance, but the wound doesn't seem so fresh any longer.

Just then, the door creaks, and Mom peeks inside. "Oh,

good, you're in bed. I was getting ready to force you into it if necessary." Pushing the door wider, she enters, a bowl of soup in her hands, and goes straight for the bed. "I've got you something to eat, and then you can take your medicine." She glances from Dad to me. "I didn't hear any yelling."

"There was no yelling," Dad answers.

"Good. Now food. I want you to get better."

Mom lifts the spoon, which makes the frown between Dad's brows deepen, but he obliges her anyway. If Dad had one soft spot, it was Mom. I stay there for a heartbeat longer before silently getting out of the room. I pull my phone out of my pocket as I head down the stairs.

ME:

We just brought dad home.

Rebecca's answer is almost immediate.

RED:

That's amazing.

How is he feeling?

ME:

Like a grumpy asshole.

RED:

Miguel!

He's sick, you have to cut him some slack.

ME:

Heart attack doesn't give you an excuse to act like an asshole.

In his defense, he did just apologize for what happened four years ago.

Anyway, want me to come later tonight?

RED:

> Can't. I promised Savannah we'd hang out. Another day?

Dammit, I didn't want to hang out another day. We didn't get a chance to see each other since I left her house two days ago, or since I've spent most of my time helping Mom at the hospital. I missed her. But I couldn't say that, and it wouldn't be fair of me to ask her to cancel her plans now that I was here.

ME:

> Yeah, sure.

> I guess I'll go find something to do before I go crazy. Talk later?

I could always go upstairs and pull out my laptop to get some work done on my summer class. God knows I was behind, but the idea of staying inside after being in the hospital was suffocating.

No, I had to get out of here.

The outside is quiet, most of the ranch hands have already left to work out on the fields, but there is always something to do around this place, so I push my sleeves up and get to work.

"You're always working!"

At the sound of the slightly familiar and most definitely angry voice, my head snaps up.

"Because this is our livelihood, Cheryl," Aaron says softly. "What do you want me to do? Dad's sick, so somebody has to pick up the slack, and that somebody is me."

"This isn't about your dad. You've been doing this for months now, years, really."

"Of course I have. It's my job. More than that, it's my family's legacy."

I look around, trying to find a place to go. I was pretty sure that my brother wouldn't appreciate my eavesdropping on his fight with his wife—*again*—but the only exit was out in the barn where the duo was fighting. Yeah, no way in hell I was doing *that*. Maybe they'll leave soon so I can try and sneak out without them noticing me?

"What legacy? You're a *rancher*, Aaron! You've been working yourself to the bone, and for what? Maybe if you found a different job, you wouldn't have to work so hard. You're barely home. You're the first out of the house, and most days, you don't come home until late at night. You barely get to spend any time with Gage."

"That's bullshit. Gage comes to the ranch every day and hangs around the barn, helps me with some small tasks, and I take him out riding."

"But what about me, huh, Aaron? What about us? When do we get to do something?"

Fuck, this is not going well.

The tension coming from the two of them is so thick I can feel it out here. The silence stretches for what seems like forever before Aaron finally says, "I wanted to take you out to eat the other week, but you said no."

"You wanted to take me to The Rose Garden!"

"What's wrong with that?"

"It's the only restaurant in this godforsaken town!"

I wince as her words ring in the quiet barn.

The horse huffs next to me, so I place my hand on its neck and give it a soft rub to calm him down.

I honestly didn't know what to make of it. Aaron and Cheryl

dated all the way through middle and high school, and then they got married the summer after they graduated. They always seemed to be so united and happy together, but I guess something changed since then.

"This is what this whole fight is actually about. It's not about work, not about me not spending time with Gage. But *this*. You want things I simply cannot give you."

"Can't or won't, Aaron?" There is no missing the accusation in Cheryl's voice. I wait for my brother to say something, to reassure her, but there is only silence. "That's what I thought."

I hold my breath, listening intently, but there is only the sound of the horses until...

"*Fuck*," Aaron mutters quietly before something rattles.

The horse flinches, but I pull at his reins, trying to calm him down, and just when I succeed, a tall figure appears in the doorway.

Aaron's dark eyes meet mine, but there is no anger, just resignation. "How much did you hear?"

Shit. So much for sneaking out unnoticed.

"Enough," I admit. "I'm sorry. I didn't plan on listening, but the only way out was through that door, so..."

I lift my shoulders in a half-hearted shrug.

He looks around the stall, that impassive expression on his face. His marriage was clearly on the rocks, and yet he didn't seem to care the least bit. I couldn't understand it. The Aaron I remembered didn't give up on things that mattered to him, and family was one of the most important things to him.

"You want to go to The Hut?"

My brows shoot up at the unexpected suggestion. I couldn't think of the last time Aaron and I hung out. The two of us always ran in different circles since we were kids, and any time we were forced to be together, we'd get in a fight. "Like now?"

"Yes, now. I need something to drink."

My gaze goes over his shoulder as if I expected Cheryl to come back screaming.

"I'll be sleeping on the couch anyway. There is no sense in going back home now and upsetting Gage with another fight."

Another fight?

How many fights were there?

Mom didn't mention anything. Then again, would I have suspected something if I didn't witness it with my own eyes? Probably not.

I guess this was a common occurrence around here.

Was that the reason why he looked so resigned? Because he was used to it? And if Aaron and Cheryl couldn't make it, what did that say about the rest of us?

"Yeah, sure."

Aaron nods. "Rinse out and meet you in ten?"

I nod, and we each go our own way. The house is quiet when I slip inside. The door to my parent's room closed. I quickly take off my clothes and shower before meeting Aaron in front of the house.

"How's Dad?" Aaron asks as we climb inside his truck.

"Grumpy."

"Of course he is." Aaron shakes his head. "I still can't believe he didn't tell anybody that he wasn't feeling well for so long. I keep telling him he should retire, but he doesn't want to listen."

"Why am I not surprised? That man would die on top of the horse if he could."

"Yeah, I guess you're right."

Me? Right? I glance toward my brother, but his gaze is firmly fixed on the road ahead of him, his jaw pressed in a tight line.

We drive the rest of the way in silence. The parking lot in front of The Hut is packed.

"What's happening here? Are they giving away something?"

"No, it's live music night," Aaron says as he drives through the parking lot, searching for a spot. "I completely forgot about it. It's been a while since I've been here."

"So basically, this is Bluebonnet's equivalent of going to a club."

"Something like that. Finally."

Aaron makes a sharp turn, parking in the only available spot, and we get out of the truck.

The loud music comes from the bar even through the closed door. We slip inside, and Aaron immediately spots a few familiar faces as we make our way to the bar, where he orders whiskey.

"So what's your plan now that the wedding is done?"

"Me? That's what you want to talk about?"

Mick slides two shots of whiskey in front of us, and my brother nods his thanks. His fingers wrap around the glass as he swirls the amber liquid inside.

"Beats talking about my problems," he mutters, downing his drink and signaling for another one.

Well, if the last few days were any indication of how things were at his place, I couldn't blame him for not wanting to talk about it.

"No plans." I shrug. "I still have a few more weeks before I have to be at the summer camp, so I might as well stay here to help around if needed."

"That's your only reason for staying?"

I glance at him, my brows pulling together. "Should there be another reason?"

Aaron lifts his shoulder, downing his second drink. Apparently, tonight he was on a roll. "I don't know. You tell me."

What the hell was he talking about?

I shake my head at him. "There is no other reason."

His brow quirks up. "Not even your ex?"

His words make me pause. Aaron lifts his hand, ordering another drink.

"What does Rebecca have to do with this?" I ask slowly, making sure to keep my expression neutral, not that Aaron is interested in looking at me.

"People have been talking about you two."

My teeth grind together in irritation. "People need to find something better to do."

"So you wouldn't mind if she moved on?"

"Where is all this coming from?"

Instead of answering, Aaron turns around and tips his chin toward the dance floor. Annoyed with his cryptic comments, I turn around only to do a double-take.

Because Rebecca is there, dancing with some dude.

My jaw clenches, fingers tightening around the glass in my hand.

Aaron smirks. "No other reason, my ass."

CHAPTER

29

REBECCA

"So, how is Mr. Fernandez doing?"

Fernandez?

I look up from my glass to find Savannah watching me intently. "Miguel?"

How the hell does she know I saw Miguel? The only person who saw us together was Linda, and I didn't think she would go around town talking about what she saw. Not like there was much to see, but still.

The corner of Savannah's mouth tips upward in a knowing smirk. "I was asking about *Miguel's* dad, but sure, we can talk about your ex. It is still ex, right?"

Shit, I walked right into that one.

"Mr. Fernandez is doing better. From what I've heard, they held him in the hospital for a few days to make sure he's okay, but now he's home, which is a relief. I should probably stop by their house one day to see if I can help in any way."

"Heard?" Savannah quirks her brow, taking a sip from her beer. "As in from *Miguel?*"

I kick her under the table with my foot. "Will you stop it already?"

Savannah laughs. "No way, you were the one who brought

it up." Her phone buzzes on the table. She picks it up, her smile falling a little.

"What's up with that face?" I ask, grateful for the change of subject.

"Mark." She rolls her eyes. "He was supposed to come to Bluebonnet tomorrow, but apparently, something came up at work."

I bite the inside of my cheek, trying to hold back my tongue.

Sav mutters something under her breath as she turns her phone face down and shifts her attention to me. "Again. There, I said it so you don't have to."

"That guy doesn't deserve you."

"He's not that bad. Things are just different now that we're trying to do the whole long-distance thing." Sav tucks a strand of her hair behind her ear. "Anyway... Forget about Mark. I want to hear everything about Mr. Football Player. What else did you hear from him? Is he still here? I thought he was supposed to leave after the wedding?"

"He was, but considering everything that happened, he decided to stay."

"I guess that makes sense." She tips her beer in my direction. "How do you feel about him staying?"

Exhilarating, confused, scared.

There were so many emotions swirling inside my stomach at the thought of Miguel. I didn't know what to make of it. What to make of him or this situation we were in. Was he staying, and if so, for how long? Did he expect us to stick to the plan we originally made? Did I want that?

My body wanted it for sure. It craved him. I yearned the feel of those calloused fingers roaming my body and bringing me pleasure like I'd never experienced before. But my heart was another story entirely. It was screaming at me to stay the hell away from him because the only thing he could bring us was heartbreak.

"Ladies." We both turn around at the sound of a low baritone to find a couple ranchers in front of us.

"Would you like to dance?" the guy closest to me asks, flashing me a smile that shows off a dimple in his right cheek. There is interest shining in his blue eyes as he extends his hand toward me expectantly.

"I—"

I take him in as I try to come up with a way to reject him easily. He was cute; I'd give him that. Dressed in a pair of jeans and a white shirt with two buttons undone, he had a few inches on me, nowhere near Miguel's towering height.

And here I was again, just a couple of weeks since Miguel came back, and I was comparing every man to him, only to find him lacking.

I was in so much trouble.

"She would love to!" Sav says, nudging me forward.

I turn over my shoulder to glare at her, but she just smiles wickedly. "You said there is nothing going on between you and Miguel, so I don't see what one little dance could hurt," she whispers into my ear.

I was so going to kill her.

I tell her exactly that with my gaze before plastering on a pleasant smile and turning to the guy. "One dance."

I slide my hand into his warm palm, and together, we join the dancers. He turns me around to face him, his hand falling to my hips as he starts to move us together.

Why did it have to be a slow song, of all things?

He leans in so I can hear him over the loud music. "I'm Hardy, by the way."

"Becky."

"Nice name for a nice girl. You new here, Becky?"

"Hardly," I chuckle softly. "I was actually born and raised here."

His brows shoot up. "Really? How come I haven't seen you here before today, then?"

"I've been busy lately."

"Oh, yeah? What keeps a pretty girl like you so busy?"

Seriously? This is the best he's got?

"She was busy with the wedding."

The hair at the back of my neck stands on end at the sound of that deep, gravelly voice.

I'm not the only one who hears it. The guy looks over my shoulder, a trace of irritation showing on his face, but then his eyes slightly widen at the sight of Miguel.

"Sorry, dude." He lets go of me like I burned him. "I didn't know she was your girl."

His girl? He can't mean...

"I'm not..." I start to protest, but the guy's already lost in the crowd.

What the actual fuck?

Irritation slams into me. Which is crazy because I didn't even want to dance with that guy. But I also hate the fact that Miguel managed to scare him off so easily.

I turn around, raising my hand, but before I can jab my finger in Miguel's chest, his hand wraps around mine, and he pulls me into his chest.

The air is kicked out of my lungs as I connect to that firm wall of muscles, the heat of his skin burning me through the layers of clothes separating us. His other hand slides to the small of my back as he pulls me into him, those long fingers sprawling over the small of my back and sending shivers running down my spine.

"What do you think you're doing?" I tilt my head back to find those impossibly dark eyes staring at me.

"Dancing with you."

I grit my teeth. "That's not what I meant."

"You asked me what I was doing."

"You don't even like to dance."

"But you do, and I'd never leave you hanging."

The image of Miguel and I dancing at the homecoming, and later at prom pop into my mind. No, he wasn't much of a dancer, but he always made a point to dance with me.

"I had a partner. There was no need for you to sacrifice yourself."

"That tool?"

"Tool? You don't even know the guy!" I protest.

Seriously, how did we get here? It felt like being in high school all over again. I'd do something, and Miguel would throw a stupid comment, which would make me angry, and we'd get into a fight. A fight that later on would usually end with his mouth on mine and his hands on my body until fighting was the last thing on our minds.

Miguel's irises darken as if he, too, is remembering this exact same thing.

"Don't look at me like that," he growls, and I swear I can feel that sound all the way to my core.

It was stupid and primitive, but it was like my body didn't get a memo.

"I don't know what you're talking about," I mutter, making a point to look over his shoulder.

"Oh, you know *exactly* how you're looking at me." Miguel leans closer, his warm breath tickling the shell of my ear. "Like you want me to flip you around and fuck you so hard until I get that surly attitude out of your body."

I bite the inside of my cheek to stop any noises from coming out, but Miguel's relentless. His fingers slip under my shirt, rubbing circles over my skin.

"Is that what you want, Red? Because I'll do it. You just have to say the word, and I'll give you everything you want. And you know how fucking good I can make you feel."

My eyes fall shut, throat bobbing as I try to swallow the knot that's formed there, but it's useless.

I was screwed.

Completely and utterly screwed.

My fingers curl into a fist, nails digging into my palm so hard I'm sure I'll leave a mark.

His free hand cups my cheek, brushing my hair behind my ear and forcing me to look at him. "I bet there wasn't another man that was able to make you feel the way I did."

No, there wasn't.

Not for lack of trying, either.

I did go out on a few dates here and there.

I kissed other guys and even slept with one.

But there wasn't another man that could ever make me feel the way Miguel did.

"Miguel, we can't do this. Not here, not now."

I could feel people's gazes on us. I was pretty sure that tomorrow, Reading Nook would be full once again with people waiting for the latest gossip, and that was the last thing I wanted.

"There you are!" Savannah says, looking from me to Miguel. "Apparently, your *husband* came looking for you?"

"What?" I pull my hand out of his grasp and turn toward her.

Is she joking? Because this wasn't funny.

"That's what the guy said when he came back to grab his friend." She shrugs, shifting her attention back to Miguel, a sly smile on her lips. "I guess you're the husband?"

Miguel flashes her his most charming smile. "Miguel, and you are?"

363

"Savannah, Becky's bestie, and the one responsible for hunting down people who hurt her, so..."

Oh my God...

I grab her hand. "So we're leaving."

"But we just started chatting!" Savannah protests.

"Oh, you've already said too much," I hiss softly. "If the rumor spreads that Miguel is my *husband,* I will strangle you."

"I didn't say anything. I'm just conveying what I heard others say. There's a difference."

"I don't care." I grab her hand. "We're leaving. I've had enough of socializing for one day."

"Fine." Savannah looks over her shoulder. "It was nice meeting you, Miguel!"

"You too!" he shouts back.

"Seriously, Sav?"

"Hey, you were the one who was dancing with him. I didn't do anything."

"You pushed me to dance with that other guy, which in turn —" I bite my tongue, stopping myself before I can reveal too much.

Nobody was supposed to know!

And here we were dancing in public, people seeing us kissing. Before I knew it, the whole town would know that Miguel and I were together. Only we weren't, not really.

"Which in turn?" Savannah prompts, snapping me out of my thoughts.

"Nothing."

"Mhmm, that's what you said earlier, and yet it didn't look like nothing from where I was standing."

I let out a sigh. "Sav..."

She shakes her head, a smug smile playing on her lips. "Don't worry, your secret is safe with me."

CHAPTER

30

MIGUEL

I look up from the laptop when I hear soft muttering to find Dad slowly limping into the kitchen. His face was red, and even from here, I could see the droplets of sweat beading his forehead. The doctor said he should be using a walker so he could put some of his weight on it, but the mule that he is, refuses to do it because he wasn't a 'damn invalid'—his words, not mine.

Leaning back, I cross my arms over my chest, watching him go straight for the fridge. He opens the door, his head disappearing as he holds on to the handle.

He stays like that for a little while, before he finally pulls back, a plastic container in hand.

"What are you up to?"

Dad jumps and drops the container, his head whipping in my direction. "Fucking hell, Miguel! Are you trying to give me a heart attack?"

I shoot him an unamused look. "Seriously?"

Dad waves me off. "You know what I mean."

"I do, but you apparently don't need my help." Getting to my feet, I go to him and grab the container that fell on the floor, glancing at the baked ribs that were left over from dinner last night. "You know you shouldn't be eating this."

"Don't you start too," he grumbles, wiping the sweat from his forehead. "I finally got rid of your mother's nagging, and now you're all up in my business."

"You're lucky she's not here to hear you."

"I love that woman, but she's driving me bonkers with her worry." He looks at the container in my hand. "Gimme that."

I pull it out of his reach. "You know I can't do that. Your doctor said you should be eating healthy. No unnecessary spices, only soups, vegetables, and cooked lean meat."

"Might as well shoot me right now," Dad grumbles. "I wanted to eat potatoes, that's a vegetable, with the ribs last night, but your mother refused to give them to me. Now, stop telling me what I should do and give me that."

"I don't think baked potatoes are what your doctor had in mind when he said you should eat more vegetables."

"They're the only vegetable I eat."

"And that's why you had a heart attack."

"*Pre*-heart attack."

"The same difference. If you don't do something, you will actually have a heart attack, and then what will Mom do?"

Dad groans. "This conversation is tiring me."

Some of the color had drained from his face, but I had a sneaking suspicion that it had more to do with him being exhausted.

Moving closer, I slip my hand under his arm. "Let's get you to the couch."

Dad doesn't try to protest, which is telling in and of itself. Together, we slowly make our way to the living room, where I sit him on his armchair.

"You need me to bring you something?"

Dad looks up, a strained expression on his face. "Those ribs?"

"How about I make you a healthy shake instead? I think I saw some broccoli and kale in the fridge earlier."

Dad's face twists in disgust. "You know what? I think I just lost my appetite."

The door bangs loudly at the back of the house. "Papaw!" Gage yells, the sound of rushing footsteps echoing in the house.

"In here," Dad calls, looking up toward the door.

Gage rushes inside. "Hey, Uncle Miguel!"

"You should slow down, Gage. You don't want to fall," Dad reprimands, but the usual harshness in his voice isn't there when he talks to his grandson.

"I was in a hurry. Daddy asked me to come in and see if you needed anything."

"I'm good, but thank you." Dad ruffles his hair. "Wanna hang with the old man?"

Gage tilts his head to the side, his brows pulling together. "Can we watch cartoons?"

Dad chuckles, "Go for it."

I watch as he gives Gage the remote, and he quickly switches the program until he finds something he likes. It was so strange seeing Dad like this. He was never so complacent with Aaron or me. Even when we were kids, he'd find something for us to do around the ranch. But here he was now, watching cartoons with Gage like it's the most normal thing in the world.

"You don't have to stay here. You know that?"

I turn my attention to Dad, who's observing me intently.

"It's fine. I was working on something anyway."

"I mean in Bluebonnet. You don't have to stay in Bluebonnet. I'm sure you have more important things to do than to sit around the house and watch over me."

"You're just trying to get rid of me so you can sneak some unhealthy food when mom's not home," I joke, but Dad doesn't crack a smile.

"I'm serious, Miguel."

I lift my shoulders in a shrug. "It's fine. It's the off-season. Besides, I promised Timothy I'd stop by the school and work with some of his kids."

"Oh, that's good."

"Don't worry. I won't be hanging around here the whole time."

"That's not what I meant," Dad sighs. "I just don't want you to feel obligated to stay, that's all. You should go out and do something."

"Like what?"

"Daddy promised me he'd take me to the fair this weekend," Gage comments, his eyes still glued to the TV. How he caught what we were talking about when he was clearly immersed in his show, I'll never know.

"Fair?" I repeat, my interest piqued.

I haven't been to a fair since high school.

"There's a fair in the next town over. Maybe you should go and give it a look."

"Huh..." I rub my jaw, my mind already formulating a plan. "That's not a bad idea. Maybe I'll call a few of my buddies and go check it out once Mom's home."

"I don't need a babysitter, Miguel. Go." Dad pats Gage's shoulder. "I have my company right here. Right, Gage? You'll stay with Papaw until Granny comes home?"

"Will I get cookies?"

Dad chuckles, "I'm sure she'll have cookies for you."

"Just don't let Grandpa eat them, Gage. He can only eat veggies."

"Well, that sucks."

This time, Dad full-on laughs, and I can't help but stare at him. I don't remember the last time I saw the man laugh. "You're completely right, buddy. It does suck." He turns to me and finds me staring. "Go, your mom should be home soon, and I'm not about to get caught red-handed by her. She'll rip me a new one, and I'm in no mood for that."

Spotting an open space near the Reading Nook, I slide my car into it, killing the engine. Although it's late afternoon, the hot air slams into me the moment I open my door. Sweat appears on my skin immediately. My phone vibrates as I'm locking the door. I pull it out as I cross the street and see an e-mail sitting at the top of the screen.

My heart starts beating faster when I see the sender.

Kimberly.

She was working in Lonestars admin office as one of the people who took care of scheduling events and making sure the players got where they needed to be on time.

"Good afternoon, Miguel!"

I look up to find old Mrs. Timothy waving at me from her shop. Sliding the notification away to deal with it later, I lock my phone and lift my hand to wave back before continuing to Becky's café. I tried texting her to see what she was up to before I left my parent's place, but I have yet to hear from her.

Was the café that busy? I guess I could always sit around until she wraps up.

Looking through the floor-to-ceiling windows, I spot Rebecca standing behind the counter. My steps slow down as I drink her in. Her hair is down today, falling in loose waves around her face that I couldn't wait to sink my hands into before I claim that stubborn mouth of hers. There was nothing like messing that woman up a little so everybody knew she was taken.

But is she really?

Rebecca was pretty clear about what she wanted. A secret hookup. Closure.

She was mine now. That was the only thing that mattered.

Placing my hand on the handle, I start to open the door, but it won't budge. My brows pull together as I give the handle a little shake until my eyes fall on the sign hanging above the door.

Closed.

What the...

The motion on the other side of the window catches my attention, and I look up just in time to notice Rebecca's surprised expression as she turns the key and pulls open the door.

"Miguel? What are you doing here?"

"My dad was sick of me nagging him, so he shooed me away. I figured I'd stop by, but then, the sign says it's closed. Are you already done for today?"

"No, it's just..."

Before she can finish, laughter spills from the back of the room. I look over her shoulder, but the café is empty.

"And then, when he finally snapped, it was everything. The way he grabbed her and pressed her against the door as he devoured her was just so swoony," a woman's voice declares from the back before letting out a loud sigh.

My brows raise as Becky presses her lips together, her cheeks turning pink.

"Care to explain that one?" I ask, finding this whole thing extremely amusing.

"Umm." Becky tucks a strand of her hair behind her ear. "It's a book club."

My brows quirked up. "A book club, you say?"

"Yup, a book club."

"I think I liked it better when he put her on the kitchen

counter and got to his knees so he could show her just how a woman should be devoured," another voice adds—a somewhat familiar voice. "This woman knows how to write a really good steamy scene. I even showed it to my husband, so he could recreate it, and let me tell you..."

It takes me a moment to place the voice, but once I do, I'm pretty sure my mouth hits the ground.

"Mom?" I move Becky to the side and follow the sound of the voices until I get to the more private back part of the store.

Two dozen heads turn in our direction as I enter the room. And sure enough, my mother is one of them.

"Miguel? What are you doing here?" Her smile falls almost immediately as she gets to her feet. "Is something wrong with your father?"

"No." I shake my head. "Dad's fine. He's home with Gage."

Mom visibly relaxes. "Oh, you gave me a scare there for a minute. I thought something happened."

"No, just Dad being sick of me hovering over him. He said you'd be home soon."

Feeling everyone's eyes on me, I look at the women sitting in the room, spotting a few familiar faces. Mrs. Santiago flashes me a smile as Mrs. Smith leans close to whisper something in her ear. Then, other little details draw my attention. I knew there was a reading space in the back, but I'd never ventured to see it. The space had a cozy feeling, and while the front was more like a café, the back almost seemed like you were in a living room. Floor-to-ceiling shelves lined the walls, one of which had a little sliding ladder attached to it, and there was even a fireplace. Plush couches took up most of the space, with a big coffee table in the middle filled with... wine glasses?

"Are you ladies drinking back here?"

"We're not drinking," Mrs. Willow scoffs indignantly. "We're intellectually elevating ourselves."

Their earlier discussion pops into my mind.

"By reading..." My throat bobs as I look at the book they're all holding, only to be greeted by a cover of a shirtless dude.

What the actual loving fuck?

"Romance novels! What else?"

"What else, indeed?" I mutter more to myself, but it doesn't go unnoticed by others.

Mom's eyes narrow. "And what is that supposed to mean?"

"Nothing," I say quickly. "I just didn't expect..." I wave my hand in their direction. "Any of this."

I just couldn't wrap my head around the fact that my practical mother was a part of a book club. And not just any book club, but a romance book club where they discussed...

"Us to read romance novels? You can say it, Miguel. They're called romance novels. You should give them a try, learn a thing or two about how to grovel properly." She gives me a pointed look before shifting her attention to Rebecca. "Although by the looks of it, maybe you're not completely hopeless after all."

Shit.

Seriously, how did I get myself in a situation like this?

"I think I'll just go. Leave you ladies to your romance novels."

"No need!" Mrs. Willow gets to her feet, downing the rest of her wine in one go before pulling Mrs. Smith to her feet, which seems to cause a chain reaction. "We were just wrapping up. You ladies did a stellar job. Make sure to send out a newsletter with what we're reading next." She wiggles her brows pointedly. "The more spice, the better. Maybe even something kinky. My current bae will appreciate it a lot. C'mon, ladies, let's go grab a drink. I'm in the mood for something stronger."

Something kinky?

The woman is in her seventies, for fuck's sake!

Before either of us can say anything, we're left alone.

Well, except for Rebecca's friend.

"What the hell was that?" I ask, still a little dumbfounded by the whole situation.

"I think we scarred him for life." Savannah smirks, making Rebecca laugh.

"Oh, I think it'll take more than that to scar him."

"It's not funny, Red," I mutter. "You could have warned me."

"Oh, it *is* funny. And I did. I told you we were having book club."

"What kind of book club is this? Shouldn't you read, I don't know, biographies?"

"If you know a good, steamy biography, I'm sure they'd be game."

Steamy biography? I shake my head. "You'll be the death of me."

"Hey, don't knock it till you try it."

"Considering the only books I'm reading are for my class, I'll have to trust you on your word."

Rebecca pokes me in the chest. "Poor baby."

"You just keep on teasing, Red." I wrap my fingers around her wrist. "We'll see who'll be the last one laughing." I rub my thumb over the inside of her wrist, feeling the goosebumps rise on her skin. "When will you be done?"

Becky's pupils dilate, the pink of her cheeks growing darker. "Probably another thirty minutes or so. I have to clean—"

"Nope, you're off for tonight," Savannah interjects, reminding us we're not alone.

Rebecca pulls back, shifting her attention to her friend, who's smirking knowingly at us.

"What? No, I'll help you clean up," Rebecca protests, but Savannah is relentless.

"You set everything up because I was running late, so I'll stay here and clean up. You guys should go and have fun."

"You sure? We can stay and help," I offer.

"I'm positive. Go. Have fun."

"Thanks, I owe you." I grab Rebecca's hand. "C'mon, let's get out of here."

CHAPTER

31

REBECCA

"Miguel!" I yell at him as I try to keep up with his hurried steps.

He pulled me out of the café, barely leaving me with enough time to stop and grab my purse.

Tugging my hand, he finally pulls to a stop in front of his SUV.

"What are you doing?"

But instead of answering my question, he asks one of his own. "Is your brother home?"

"Chase?" He wants to talk about Chase? "Yeah, wh—"

"Great, that means I can get you for the next few hours to myself."

To himself?

"What do you mean?"

"I mean, I want to take you out."

My throat bobs as my brain processes his words. "Out? Like on a date?" My heart does a little dance of excitement before reality sets in, and I can feel my stomach sink. "You know we can't—"

"It's not in Bluebonnet."

"Oh..."

I blink, unsure of what to say. I knew this had 'bad idea'

written all over it. I wasn't blind. I saw the looks women gave me when Miguel walked into Reading Nook. They were already seeing us back together, and that could never happen. I should send him home and stick to the original plan. Hell, I should probably stop this whole thing altogether. But damn it, I wanted it. I needed to forget that this could only be temporary and that after a while, he would leave just like he planned to from the get-go. I wanted to use what little time we had left and spend a few hours with this man away from everything and everybody. A few hours where we could just be normal without worrying about what other people will think or say. I craved him.

Isn't that what it always came down to?

I wanted this man in any way I could have him. That was my biggest downfall from the very beginning.

Miguel's hand cradles my face as those dark eyes bore into mine. "Go on a date with me, Red."

Swallowing the lump in my throat, I nod my head. "Fine."

A smile flashes on his face almost immediately, and before I know it, his fingers slip to my neck, and his mouth falls on mine. The kiss is short, but the intensity of it leaves me breathless.

"Let's go."

He opens the door for me, so I slide inside. The door slams behind me, and I watch him walk around the front, taking the driver's seat.

"Where are we going then?" I ask, tucking a strand of hair behind my ear as he pulls from the parking space.

"That's for me to know and for you to find out," he says, his attention on the road as a smile plays on his lips.

"I don't like this." Pursing my lips, I lean forward to play with the radio until I finally find the station I like.

The corner of Miguel's mouth twitches upward in amusement. "You'll like this surprise."

I open my mouth, but before I get a chance to protest, his

hand lands on my thigh, giving it a soft squeeze. I suck in a breath as the zap of electricity courses through me—the song on the radio shifts to a familiar tune.

Kiss Tomorrow Goodbye.

Miguel's eyes meet mine, and for a split second, it feels like I've been transported in time.

It was one of those songs we listened to countless of times when we were sitting in his truck just like this. Back then, he drove an old beat-up truck, but we had fun. I would play with the radio until I found something I liked so I could hum softly to the tunes. He would protest about it, but he never forbade me to do it. His hand would find mine in between shifting gears because he didn't want to let go for more than it was absolutely necessary. That truck was our safe haven. We'd bring blankets and put them in the back of his truck's bed. He would drive us to a secluded area, and we'd climb up there. Talking, kissing, and making love under the stars.

His fingers sink into my skin, bringing me back to the present.

A soft, almost longing smile passes over his face as he turns his attention back to the road, and I look out the window, neither of us saying anything as he drives us out of Bluebonnet. It takes us a good thirty minutes before he finally pulls into a parking lot, and I realize where he brought me.

"The festival?" I ask, my eyes glued to the tops of the attractions I can see in the distance. Tents. Ferries wheels. Even through the closed door, I can hear the loud music coming from outside.

"Yeah, Gage mentioned it earlier, so I figured why not go?" Miguel maneuvers the car in a parking spot, killing the engine. "When was the last time you went to one?"

His question brings back memories of the senior year of high school. Emmett and Kate, Kate's sister, Miguel and I, and a few other of our friends all together having fun at the festival just like this one. My hand clasped in his. His mouth on mine. So much laughter. It was a good night. A night I haven't thought about in years.

My throat bobs as I swallow. "It's been a while."

"See? C'mon, if you're nice, I might even win you one of those ugly stuffed animals you like so much." He opens his door and slides out, so I do the same, our gazes meeting over the top of the SUV.

"They're not ugly. Besides, what if I want to play myself?"

He clasps his hands, rubbing them together. His excitement is infectious, and I can't help but laugh. This was the Miguel I remembered from high school, the boy that made me smile, the boy that made me fall in love with him before I even realized what was happening.

"Then I guess you can win *me* a stuffed animal." He grins as he joins me. "But I'll warn you. I want the biggest one out there, so no slacking off, missy."

"I have you one better, a challenge, if you will."

His eyes crinkle with amusement, and the need to rise on the tips of my toes and taste his mouth is so strong it's almost overwhelming. "I'm listening."

"Let's see who can get the biggest stuffed animal."

Miguel tilts his head to the side, thinking about my offer. "And what does the winner get?"

"The bragging rights that you won?" I suggest, but he's already shaking his head.

"Screw bragging rights. I want something better."

"Oh, yeah?" I quirk my brow. "And, in your opinion, what is that 'something better?'"

He grabs my hand and pulls me into his body, his free hand cupping my cheek, the tip of his thumb skimming over my lower lip. My stomach squeezes as his hungry gaze falls on my mouth. "A kiss on the top of ferries wheels."

"Hmm…" I nibble at my lip, pretending to think over his suggestion. "I guess that's doable. What do I get if I win?"

His eyes lift to mine. "Whatever you want."

I jab him playfully in the chest. "That's a dangerous game you're playing, mister."

"Maybe, but don't think I'll just let you win. I want that kiss."

"As if you can't kiss me anyhow."

"But this isn't the same, and you know it." He lets go of me and slaps my ass playfully. "C'mon, Red, time to get your ass kicked."

"Promises, promises," I sing-song.

I'm still laughing at his silly demeanor as Miguel's hand slips into mine, and we join the crowd going toward the festival. The music and chatter surrounding us grow louder the closer we get. My eyes scan the space, taking in the people and attractions around me. There are a bunch of food stands and people selling little trinkets. Kids shriek as they ride the attractions. There is the car cart game on one side, and I can see the little swings on the other. Kids that are probably around four or five are spun in circles, their small fists clutching the metal strings.

"Fuck, look at all that cotton candy."

I shift my attention to Miguel. The colored lights hanging above us are illuminating the longing look on his face.

"How about a snack first?"

"Oh, no, you don't." I clasp my fingers tighter around his. "You talked a big game about kicking my ass only moments ago. I won't allow you to blame it on a sugar coma or whatever later. Challenge first, then you can come back and eat whatever you want."

"Whatever I want?" He wiggles his brows playfully, and there is no missing his innuendo.

"What are you, five?" I roll my eyes as I tug his hand and start walking toward the stands with the shooting range.

He laughs so loudly a few people start turning their heads toward us. Of course, the booth we need is packed, so I come to a sudden stop, and Miguel crashes into me, his arms wrapping around my waist and pulling me closer. He lowers his head, his lips brushing against the shell of my ear.

"I don't know any five-year-old who'd even know what I have in mind for my snack, do you?"

A shudder goes down my spine at the sound of that low, husky voice whispering into my ear.

"Miguel..."

"Because nothing can ever taste sweeter than that pussy of yours, Becs. And I could eat it *all* day long."

I bite the inside of my cheek—hard—my thighs clenching together to alleviate some of that ache building inside of me.

This man.

This freaking man will be the death of me.

And I don't even have it in me to be angry.

I look over my shoulder. He's standing so close his breath is tickling my face, the heat of his body seeping into mine through all the layers of clothes separating us.

"Stop teasing, Fernandez, because I might just challenge you to put your mouth where your money is."

"It'll be my pleasure, Red."

I shake my head. "You're inco—"

I don't get to finish because the man at the stand yells, "Hey, you love birds. You playing or what?"

Color floods my cheeks at the question, and what feels like a dozen pairs of eyes on us. I bite the inside of my cheek as I slide out of Miguel's grasp. "Let's see what you've got, hotshot."

"You're on."

Miguel pulls out a bill and hands it to the guy, who slides it under the counter and puts ten balls in front of each of us, explaining the rules. I listen with half an ear, my gaze on the ensemble in front of us. The moving plates take the central position with different stuffed animals sitting on the shelves above it.

"You have to hit eight targets in order to get a small stuffed animal, ten if you want to win a big one."

Miguel quirks a brow. "Ladies first?"

"Oh, no, you go on ahead. I think I wanna watch you get a feel for it," I say, batting my eyelashes innocently.

His gaze narrows slightly, but finally, he shrugs. "It doesn't matter in which order we play. I'm winning this thing."

I hum non-committedly as he cracks his fingers before grabbing one of the balls. He tosses it in the air a few times, testing its weight before he shoots. The plate loudly cracks as it shatters, and a few people cheer around us. Miguel glances at me and flashes me a smile. "You were saying?"

"Impressive." I nod, biting the inside of my cheek as he turns his focus on the panel once again, picking a new ball and shattering another plate. I watch as each ball hits its mark until he grabs the very last one.

"Oh, shit." Bending down, I make a show of tying my laces when I hear Miguel curse loudly.

Straightening, I look at the last plate standing, and it takes everything in me to keep a straight face.

Miguel's eyes narrow at me, not missing a beat. "You did this on purpose."

I bat my eyelashes innocently. "What?"

"You know what."

Laughing, I pat him on the shoulder, "C'mon, don't be a sore loser, Fernandez."

"I'll give you a sore loser. We'll see how you play right now."

"I guess we will."

With a smile, I hand him my bag before moving toward the counter, where the guy is already placing another set of balls with new plates already rolling on the panel.

I grab one of the balls, letting my fingers curl around it.

"You sure you wanna play?"

I glance at him over my shoulder, "What? Is a big, bad football player afraid he'll lose?"

Before giving him time to answer, I shift my attention to the panel and throw the first ball. The glass shatters loudly, and somebody whistles. Not letting it deter me, I grab the second ball. The plates start crashing down one by one in quick succession until there are no more left.

Dusting my hands off, I turn around to face Miguel, who's watching me with wide eyes. "You were saying?"

"You tricked me," he accuses, but amusement is dancing in his eyes.

"I didn't. I let you assume. I do have two brothers, you know."

"You said you hadn't played in ages."

"And that's the truth. Doesn't mean I don't know how to throw a ball. I think you owe me, Mr. Fernandez. What shall I collect?"

His pupils dilate, the corner of his mouth curling in a sexy smile as he watches me. "What shall you collect, indeed?"

His intense gaze sends a wave of heat cursing through my body and making the pulse between my thighs intensify with the need to feel his hands on me.

"You can each pick your toys," the guy says, reminding us that we're not actually alone.

Breaking my eye contact from Miguel, I turn toward the stuffed animal section, scanning the selection.

"I'll get that dog over there."

Miguel's body brushes against mine as he reaches for it, the older man's attention turning to me. "And you lady? Want that bear?"

"Nah, I'll have the sloth one."

The guy's brows shoot up, but he doesn't comment as he hands me the toy. With a thank you, we move away from the stand.

"C'mon, I'll carry it for you."

I clutch the stuffed animal closer to my chest. "I can carry it myself."

Miguel rolls his eyes at me. "I'm not going to steal it. For that matter, you can take this one too."

I eye him carefully. "I was wondering why you'd pick that one."

Miguel looks at his stuffed animal. "Because you'd pick him. You always asked for the most hideous one on the shelf."

"Because nobody ever picked them. I always felt bad, so I'd take them home with me."

"You always did have a soft spot for misfits." He gives me a knowing look, and that tightening inside my chest grows stronger.

"I guess I did."

Not only did I have a soft spot for misfits, I had a soft spot for *him.*

Don't go there, the little voice at the back of my head warns me. *He's leaving soon.*

I knew that.

But I also knew there was no stopping this thing between us. It was foolish to think otherwise.

Foolish to believe I stood any chance of protecting my heart from falling all over again for Miguel Fernandez.

"Can we have that food now?" Miguel's question breaks me

ANNA B. DOE

out of my thoughts. He bats his eyelashes exaggeratedly, and I let out a soft chuckle.

"We can have food now."

So that's what we do. We get food from what feels like every stand out there, so we can try a little bit of everything and eat to the point I might actually puke, but since everything is so tasty, I just can't help myself. I had to try it all. Then, we stroll through the fair for a little while longer. Miguel challenges me to drive the bumper cars, after which I insist that I want to ride on the merry-go-round, and finally, when the night descends, we go on the Ferris wheel, my head resting on his shoulder as we watch the faint lights of the surrounding area illuminate the earth the higher we climb.

"Today was nice," I admit softly. "Thank you for taking me."

His thumb skims over the back of my hand in soothing circles. "You're welcome. I had fun, too."

"Even when I beat your ass?"

"Even when you beat my ass." Miguel's chest rumbles with laughter.

I glance up at him, our gazes meeting. He lifts his free hand, cupping my cheek, as his mouth falls on mine. The kiss is slow and tender. It's a kiss of two lovers who've known each other for a long time. Two soulmates who know the deepest, darkest parts of the other person, and they love them regardless.

With one final swipe of our mouth, we pull back. I graze my teeth over my lower lip, still able to feel the taste of him on my tongue.

"This doesn't mean I won't collect on my reward."

"Oh, I know." Miguel flashes me a smile. "Actually, I'm counting on it."

CHAPTER

32

MIGUEL

RED:

You home?

ME:

No, I'm at the school. I promised Timothy I'd stop by and check out the kids.

Why?

The knock on my window has me looking up to find the man in question on the other side. With one final glance at my phone and no new messages, I lock it and push open the door.

"Hey, man!" Timothy slaps me over the shoulder. "Thanks for doing this."

"Of course. I'm sorry I couldn't come sooner, but things have been crazy lately."

Between helping Aaron on the ranch, taking my parents to Dad's follow-up doctor's appointments, and sneaking in every chance I can get with Rebecca, I've had my hands full. Still, I meant what I said. I didn't mind stopping by and seeing the kids Timothy was coaching. After all, this was where I started too. My coach was my biggest support and influence at that time, and it was nice seeing that Timothy was following in his footsteps. So, if I could help even one of them get the chance I did, I would gladly do it.

"No worries, I completely understand. How is your dad doing?"

"The usual. He's complaining because we've been annoying him with our constant nagging and worrying."

Timothy laughs as we make our way to the field. "Why am I not surprised? My dad would be the same way."

I shake my head. "That man will be the death of me, I swear. But then, on the other hand, I have Mom worrying about him. She's putting on a brave face for the most part, but I can see how the whole situation unsettled her."

"That's normal. A heart attack is no joke. It's nice of you to have stayed."

"I don't really mind it." I shrug, and that much was true.

Yes, some of Dad's comments and brushing off his health concerns annoyed me to no end, but staying here wasn't as awful as I thought it would be.

When we step on the sidelines, I see a group of boys running around the field.

"It depends on a day-to-day basis, but these four are practically glued to the field. The one at the front is Austin. He's the team quarterback. Next to him are Michael, the wide receiver, and Kenny, the running back, and finally, we have James, our star defensive end. I swear that boy doesn't let anything past him."

Just then, one of the boys, Kenny, lifts his head and spots us. His eyes widen, and his mouth falls open. "*Holy shit!*"

The corner of my mouth twitches upward. Although I was pretty new to the pros, since Lonestars had a good last season, I've gotten my fair share of fans already, but nothing beats meeting kids and seeing that look of wonder and excitement on their faces when they realized their idol is standing in front of them.

"Language," Timothy reprimands, crossing his arms over his chest, but I don't miss the note of amusement in his voice.

"What?" his friends ask, looking up to see what had his attention. The tallest of the four, James, loses his footing for a second.

"*Holy shi— shoot!*" the quarterback comes to a sudden stop. "You're Miguel Fernandez! Like *the* Miguel Fernandez!"

I chuckle softly. "That would be me."

"That's fucking insane!"

"Do I need to make you do twenty pushups for every curse word that leaves your mouth, Austin?" Timothy asks sternly.

It was amusing seeing one of my friends, who used to be a laidback jokester, in this new authoritative role.

"But this is *Miguel Fernandez*, Coach!" Austin protests.

Timothy nods. "I'm aware of that. We used to play together in high school."

"You used to play with him?" I didn't think it was possible, but his eyes widened even further. "He was in the *Super Bowl*."

"We were in the playoffs," I correct. "I'm currently prepping for the next season and summer camp, so I figured I might come here and work out a little. You guys game?"

There is a beat of silence as the boys exchange a look.

"You wanna practice? Here? With us?" Austin asks, clearly the leader of the group.

"If you're interested." I shrug. "It sucks practicing alone."

"Hell yeah!" Michael nods. "I'm game." He nudges James with his elbow. "You swallowed your tongue or what?"

James lets out a grunt, red creeping up his neck.

"He's a *huge* fan," Michael explains, which earns him a slap on the head, followed by a low, "Will you stop it?"

"How about we let the football talk?" I drop my duffle on

the grass on the sidelines and crack my fingers. "You guys ready?"

A chorus of agreement spreads through the group. I join them on their run before we work on some drills. Timothy was right; there was some pretty raw talent that he was working with here. I make a mental note to check what's happening with them in the future or if there is any way I can help the Bluebonnet team.

"Good job, you guys. A break before we play a little friendly scrimmage?"

"Yes!" they all agree in unison.

I grab the water bottles, handing them out to the boys before taking one for myself. I'm just turning around when I see a flash of red from my peripheral vision. My fingers clench the bottle as I slowly turn around, and sure enough, Rebecca is right there, sitting on the bleachers.

The wave of longing slams into me like a freaking train wreck, leaving me breathless in its intensity. It was like I fell through time or some shit, and we were seventeen again, and Rebecca came to cheer me on during my game.

Fuck, I missed this.

I didn't even realize how much until this very moment when I laid my eyes on her. I didn't have a lot of people sitting in my corner at the games, but Rebecca always made a point to be there for me and cheer me on. She was my person. Sun or rain, win or lose, I knew I'd find her waiting for me after the game.

I didn't have that these past three years.

I didn't have her.

Her mouth curls in a smile as she spots me watching her. The soft breeze is making her auburn hair fly around her face. She tries to tuck it behind her ear, but it's useless.

"Mr. Fernan— Miguel?" one of the boys asks, correcting himself at the very last moment.

"Give me five?"

My heart is racing as I jog toward the bleachers—toward *her* —as if an invisible string is pulling me in her direction.

Rebecca gets up, running her fingers through her hair.

"What are you doing here?" I ask, taking her in.

"I stopped at your place, but you weren't there."

My brows shoot up in surprise. "You came looking for me?"

"Well, technically, I stopped to check in on your dad, but I did have something for you."

She turns around and grabs something from the bench—a box, I realize—handing it to me.

"What is that?" I poke at the box, my finger slipping under the lid so I can peek inside.

"It's the—"

"Holy shit." I glance at her before ripping into the box. "Is it those peanut butter cookies you make?"

"Umm, yeah. It's a thank you. For the, umm..." She clears her throat. "A thank you for the date the other day."

My head snaps up at the word 'date,' my heart doing a little flip inside my chest. Rebecca's looking down at her clasped hands, clearly nervous about the whole thing for whatever reason.

Shifting the box to one hand, I slip my finger under her chin and lift it so she's looking at me.

"I'm not going to say no to your treats. Thanks for bringing them over."

"Of course, I tweaked the recipe a little, so hopefully, you'll still like them."

"I don't think there was one thing you made that I didn't like."

Pink spreads over her cheeks at the compliment, her eyes darting away for a second. "I guess I should—"

"What are you doing later today?" I ask before she can

389

finish. I wasn't ready to call this quits just yet and watch her leave.

"I have to go back to the café, but after I close, I'm going back home, why?"

"How about you meet me at the treehouse?"

Rebecca's tongue darts out, sliding over her lower lip. "The treehouse?"

"It's still there. I saw it when I went for a jog one morning."

It was the treehouse that her dad built for her before he passed away, but somehow, over the years, it became *our* place. A place where we used to talk. A place where we had our first kiss. A place where we made love for the very first time.

"It is." She nods.

"So meet me there tonight."

"I..." Her throat bobs, but she nods. "Okay. I'll see you there."

Hell yeah.

"Okay," I agree. My gaze falls to her mouth and lingers there. I wanted to lean down and kiss her, but we were out in the open. Besides, we weren't alone. "Tonight."

"Tonight."

With one last glance, she turns around, almost bumping into the bench in the process, but she quickly steadies herself before walking away.

My gaze stays on her until she's out of view. Running my fingers through my hair, I let out a shaky breath and rejoined the guys, who were standing by the sidelines, watching the whole interaction.

"Who was that? Your girlfriend?" Austin snickers, wiggling his brows suggestively.

"That's none of your business."

"What do you think, dude? Of course it's his girlfriend, or he wants her to be. He was smiling like a fool at her," Kenny adds. "Something like when James smiles when he talks to Millie."

James shoves him away. "Shut up."

"Hey, if she brought me food, I'd be smiling like a fool at her, too." Austin tries to reach for the box. "That was Miss Becky, right? The one from the Reading Nook? She has some pretty sweet goods. What'cha got here?"

I slap his hand away. "That's mine, dude. But how about this, if you win a game of scrimmage, I might be tempted to share?"

The boys exchange a look. "Game on."

Toeing off my shoes in the mudroom sometime later, I step into the kitchen only to be greeted by the scent of tomato, ground beef, and spices hanging in the air. Mom's humming softly to a country tune playing on the radio, but she must hear me enter because she looks over her shoulder. "There you are! I was wondering where you disappeared to."

"Timothy asked me to stop by the school because some of the kids from the football team practice there during the summer."

Mom's brows quirked up. "That was nice of you."

"It's not a big deal." Moving closer, I grab one of the nachos and dip it into the sauce before tossing it into my mouth. Fuck, that's good. "They seem like really great kids," I mumble as I pick more food. "I'll have to keep an eye on them. The quarterback has a good arm, and the Smith kid is a force to be reckoned with."

She turns back to the stove and stirs the vegetables. "You sound like you had fun."

"I did. Then again, hanging with kids is the best part of this job."

"Well, we had fun too. We had company earlier." The hair at my nape rises because I know what's coming before she even finishes. I watch as she tilts her head, those sharp eyes looking at me and waging my reaction. "Rebecca stopped by to see your father."

I try to keep my face neutral as I clear my throat. "Did she?"

"Mhmm... She baked some muffins for your dad. And he liked them too. Just don't tell him they were carrot muffins because he'll throw a fit."

I snort out a laugh. "I'll keep that in mind."

"You do that." She nods. "Such a nice girl."

"Mom..."

She blinks, a picture of innocence. "What? I just say it as I see it. It was nice of her to visit and bring him something, was it not?"

"It sure was," I agree, taking a step back. "I think I'll go and take a shower."

"Don't take too long. Dinner will be ready soon."

"Actually." I rub at the back of my neck. "Would you mind packing them to go for me?"

"I didn't realize you had plans." She turns toward the stove, grabs the pot with the vegetables, and slides it into the meat, all innocent. "Should I just make enough for you?"

She was fishing for information, and she was shit at hiding it.

"As if you don't know that I need enough for two."

"Me?" Her brows rise. "And why would I know that? It's not like my son shares anything with me, now does he?"

Her words are a silent jab, and not just about Rebecca either. It was about me leaving for college and not coming back. It was about me avoiding her phone calls because I didn't know how to talk to her. Because I didn't want to make her choose.

But in the process, I only ended up hurting her more.

And still, *still*, she told me to come back home and didn't say one word about it until now.

Shit, I really am an asshole.

I let out a long breath and closed the distance between us. Wrapping her in my arms, I press a kiss against the top of her head. "I'm sorry, Mom. I'd appreciate it if you could prepare enough for two."

She tilts her head back and gives me a knowing look. "You know I can. Now, off with you." She waves me off, her nose furrowing. "You really need to take that shower before you leave."

"Are you telling me I stink?"

"I'm telling you that I raised you to be a gentleman and to put in some effort when you're taking a woman out on a date."

"It's not a date, it's..."

My words trail off, and Mom just raises her brows as she waits for me to finish, but nothing comes.

Mom shakes her head. "You two can tell yourself whatever you want, and you can try to sneak around all you want, but we all know better than that."

"Oh, is that so?"

"It is so." She cups my cheek, a soft smile playing on her lips. "You and Rebecca were inevitable from the time you were kids. Even when you were just friends, I could see the special bond you two shared. No matter where you went, she'd follow. Like the Moon and the Earth, always circling around each other. Now, off with you. I'm going to finish this so it's ready when you come out of the shower. Don't mess this up again, okay?"

I absentmindedly nod as I make my way out of the kitchen and up the stairs, my mind still mulling over her words, unable to let them go as I go through the motions of taking off my clothes and getting into a shower.

Like the Moon and the Earth, always circling around each other.

She was wrong, though.

Rebecca wasn't the Moon; she was the Sun, and I was the one circling around her this whole time, needing her warmth and her light.

Her love.

I needed her love like I needed air to breathe.

"Fuck." I run my hand over my face. "I'm totally screwed."

It takes me ten minutes to finish with the shower and get ready. I was anxious to get to her. You'd think I hadn't seen her in ages when it's only been a few hours.

A few fucking hours that seemed more like an eternity.

How did I survive without her for the past three years?

Movement from the living room catches my attention. Dad is stirring awake from his nap, his eyes darting to me.

Instinctually, I brace for some kind of reproach as he takes me in, but it doesn't come. "You going out?"

"I... yeah."

Dad nods just as Mom appears in the doorway, a basket in hand. "There you are! Here, I prepared this for you."

I peek inside the basket noticing way more stuff than the burritos I asked for.

"You didn't have to do all of that."

"Oh, please. I even packed some of those cookies Rebecca loves."

"Thanks, Mom."

Mom pats me on the shoulder. "You two have fun."

Nodding, I glance toward my dad, who surprisingly keeps quiet. "I'll see you guys later."

Turning around, I get out of the house and jump inside my

SUV. The drive to Rebecca's property and the treehouse is short, and thankfully, she's not here yet. Grabbing the basket Mom prepared, I slide out of the car and climb inside the treehouse, taking in the space around me.

Nothing much has changed, but the place looked clean even now. Somebody has been using it. Lace curtains hang above the window, and there is a wooden box situated on the other side just underneath it. A small shelf is filled with books and little trinkets Rebecca's gathered through the years, which she lined up next to a few of those ugly-ass stuffed animals.

I'm just pulling out the blanket Rebecca keeps in a wooden box when my phone rings.

I take it out of my pocket and find Big J written on the screen. Answering the call, I put it on speaker.

"Hey, what's up, Big J?"

"Yo, asshole, where the fuck are you?" Big J asks, barely waiting for me to finish. The guy wasn't one for pleasantries, not off the field and certainly not on the field.

James "Big J" Callahan is one of my teammates on the Austin Lonestars. The dude is enormous. We're talking six-six, three hundred pounds of a linebacker that you pray doesn't crash into you if you don't want him to rearrange every single bone in your body.

"I'm home. Where should I be?"

I move the basket closer and start pulling out the containers with food, and there is even a bottle of red.

"The fuck you are. I tried stopping by your house earlier this week, but you weren't home."

I come to a sudden stop as the realization hits me.

He's not talking about this home.

He's talking about my place in Austin.

Why would he—

I try to remember what day it is, as Big J continues talking in the background about some party the guys wanted me to come to, but I'm barely listening.

Kate and Emmett's wedding was the first weekend in July, and it's been a... couple of weeks since, then? No, it couldn't be, could it?

My screen lights up as I pull my phone from my ear, noticing the date in the corner.

July 20th.

"Fuck."

"She sure was a great fuck. Seriously, that woman knew how to blow—"

"Not that, asshole," I run my fingers through my still-damp strands. "I completely forgot what day it was."

"What do you mean, you forgot? Training camp is starting in a few days! Didn't you get the e-mail with all the info?"

The e-mail from the Lonestars that landed in my inbox a few days ago, that I swiped away, flashes in my mind. I had the best of intentions of checking it out later, but then other things occupied my mind.

Rebecca.

Rebecca occupied my mind.

"I wasn't really checking my phone." I rub my hand over my face, feeling the headache brewing behind my temples. "The service is spotty here."

"Wait, you're still at your parent's place? Weren't you supposed to come back weeks ago?"

"That was the plan."

A stupid plan. I don't know how I could have even thought I could just come back, only to leave Bluebonnet without a backward glance. Maybe if Rebecca had moved on and didn't live here. Maybe...

"Fuck, man. Well, you better get your ass here before Coach decides to give your spot to somebody else."

"Shut up. He's not giving my spot away."

"I don't know. They brought up that new defensive end from Penn State. I saw a few of his games, and he's fucking good."

I grit my teeth. He was riling me up, and it was working.

"Nobody is taking my spot because I'll be there, asshole."

The floorboards creak loudly. I whip around, my eyes landing on Rebecca's pale face.

Time seems to slow down as we just stare at one another.

Shit.

Through the buzzing in my ears, I can hear Big J clap his hands.

"That's the spirit. I'll see you in a few days, Monk. And remember, the last person who gets to training camp has to treat the whole team after the first game of the season."

The call disconnects without a goodbye, but I don't have it in me to care because my full attention is on the woman sitting on the other side of the treehouse.

"Rebecca..."

Her throat bobs as she swallows. "You're leaving."

CHAPTER

33

REBECCA

Nobody is taking my spot because I'll be there, asshole.

Miguel's words still ring in my head as I stare at him.

He's leaving. He's leaving. He's leaving.

Those three words roll around my mind on repeat. I'm not sure why I'm so surprised. This was the plan all along. So why does it hurt so much?

Because I didn't expect it, that's why.

In the last few weeks, we've fallen into a routine of sorts, and nothing except the two of us existed. These little dates, sneaking around any chance we got so we could be together. Talking late into the night.

And I forgot.

I forgot that this whole thing was supposed to be temporary.

Forgot that at the end of this, he'd go back to Austin so he could play football, and I'd stay here.

Tears prickle my eyelids, but I bite the inside of my cheek to stop them from falling.

Stupid girl, you can't cry. You knew the deal all along. You were the one who proposed it in the first place, and now he's leaving just like he planned.

I blink a few times, clearing my vision. Miguel is staring at me, the lines on his face hard.

"When?" I ask softly. My fingers are clenched into fists, nails digging into my skin.

He flinches back slightly, a guilty expression crossing his face. "Tomorrow."

"Tomorrow," I echo, my voice coming out shaky.

I sink my teeth into my lower lip as I nod.

How can one small word make the earth shatter beneath your feet?

He's leaving tomorrow.

And then it'll be over.

Officially over.

No more grudges. No more second chances. No more Miguel.

"Hey..."

Miguel's hand cups my cheek, startling me out of the spiral. Those dark eyes lock onto mine with such intensity and something else, something that looks a lot like pain.

But he couldn't be in pain.

Because we both knew what the deal here was.

We knew this could only ever be temporary.

But the longer he stares at me, the knot in my stomach grows tighter because I can see his mind working, and I know what's coming even before he utters the words.

Or at least tries to.

"Come with—"

I lift my hand, pressing it against his mouth. His warm breath tickles the tips of my fingers.

"Don't."

Please don't say it.

"What?" he asks, his lips brushing against my fingers.

ANNA B. DOE

"Don't say it." I move my hands to his cheeks, pressing my forehead against his.

"Don't say what, Rebecca? That I'm falling in love with you all over again? That I've *been* in love with you for as long as I can remember? That I can't imagine my life without you?"

"Miguel…" My eyes fall shut, each of his words like a kick to my gut. "Don't ask me to do something you know is impossible."

"It doesn't have to be impossible." His palms slide over mine, our fingers intertwining. "We could…"

I shake my head. "We *can't.*"

"We could find a way," he insists.

The frustration rises inside of me. But I would rather deal with frustration than face the fact that my heart is breaking apart because I have to watch the man I love walk out of my life.

Again.

Because that's what's happening.

Despite everything I did to guard my heart, somewhere along the way, I'd fallen in love with Miguel Fernandez once again.

Or maybe I never actually stopped loving him to begin with.

"How?" I slide my hands from under his, pulling back. I needed some space. I needed to put some distance between us before he broke the neatly patched scars on my heart. "How exactly are we supposed to find a way? Your life is in Austin, and mine is here. I have a business here. A family. My mom is sick, Miguel. She needs more care every day that passes. Chase is good at playing pretend, but he's not doing well. I can't leave them, and for what?"

I can see the vein in his forehead twitch.

I've struck a nerve.

Good.

I wanted him to be angry. Just like I was angry at everything, but most importantly, at myself.

400

"For me. For us. Hell, you could ask me to stay! Tell me to stay."

No, he couldn't be asking that of me.

He couldn't mean it.

But he meant it.

I could see it on his face.

He was serious.

If I said the word, he would stay.

For me.

He would stay.

"You can't stay."

"Why not?"

Because you love football. Because if I asked you to give it up for me, you'd eventually start to resent me, and I couldn't deal with that.

"Because there is no us!" I lift my hands in exasperation. "That's what we agreed on, didn't we? We agreed to have this time together, get some closure after everything that had happened."

He opens his mouth to protest, but I lift my hand to stop him.

"Don't do this, Miguel. Not now that our time is running out. We knew exactly what would happen going into this. We knew why, more than ever, that now would never be possible. We're not Emmett and Kate." I lift my hand, tracing the line of his jaw.

It should have been us. In another world. In another place. It might have been us too.

God, I'm going to miss him once he's gone.

Don't think about it. He's still here.

For a little while longer.

He's still here, and he's mine.

"We don't have forever, but we have right now. That's the only thing we can have."

My thumb slides over his lower lip, and I can feel him suck in a shaky breath.

"I hate this."

I hate this too, but there is no way out of this. No choice either of us is willing to make, at least.

"Tomorrow is out of our control. So hate it tomorrow," I whisper, moving closer. Our lips brush together, eyes locking. All the feelings brewing inside my chest are reflected in those dark eyes, and it pains me, but I can't look away. I refuse to. If tonight is all we can have, I'll spend what little time I have with him. "But tonight..." My hand slides around his neck, fingers tangling in his soft strands. "Make love to me tonight, Miguel."

Desperation and need flash in his eyes. They're the last thing I see before his mouth crashes over mine.

The kiss is fervent. We're holding onto each other like our lives depend on it, like the other person might slip through our fingers if we don't hold on hard enough.

But no amount of holding tight will ever be able to stop the inevitable from happening.

Don't think about that.

Not tonight.

Not when you have this one last time.

I tighten my grip on the back of his head, pulling him closer to me as my tongue finds his. Miguel's hands slide over my body, those calloused fingers slipping under my shirt and pulling it over my head. We break the kiss just enough for us to rip the clothes off our bodies and fall into the blankets he's already spread over the floor of the treehouse.

Our safe haven.

Our refuge.

Ours.

I straddle his lap. His hard length is pressed between my thighs, sucking all the air out of my lungs. Then his mouth devours mine, swallowing any sound that falls off my lips. I roll my hips as his tongue tangles with mine, his hot skin burning me with every touch, sending shivers down my spine.

"M-Miguel," I breathe as his mouth moves to my jaw. His teeth scrape down my neck, a couple of days old stubble making goosebumps appear on my skin. I rake my hand through thick strands, tugging his head back and exposing his neck. I nibble and suck as his hands shift to my ass, squeezing it tightly and pulling me closer. His cock settles between my lower lips, his tip brushing against my clit.

My hips move searching for more, a soft moan ripping out of my lungs.

"You're so fucking beautiful," he murmurs as his mouth worships every inch of my body. He nibbles at my skin, his tongue sliding over my nipple before he sucks it into his mouth.

"I need you inside me," I whisper softly, my fingers sinking into his shoulders. My hips move down as he lifts his, and his cock sinks into me in one swift thrust, kicking all the air out of my lungs as he slowly fills me to the brim.

Miguel's hand grips my cheek, pushing my hair back. He wraps his fingers around my hair, tugging it back as he stares at me wordlessly.

The love shining from his eyes makes my heart ache, and I know the words that'll come out of his mouth before he says them out loud. "Rebecca, I—"

I can't hear him say it.

Because if I do, I might change my mind. I might ask him to stay. And I couldn't do that. I couldn't be the person who he left his dream job for that he worked so hard to get. And it isn't just any job. He got into the freaking NFL, something most people can only dream of. I wouldn't; couldn't be the reason for him leaving it. I would never forgive myself, and eventually, if he did leave, he wouldn't forgive me either.

So I pressed my mouth against his, swallowing the words he wanted to say. He softly groans as he sinks deeper inside me, hitting just the right spot. My pussy clenches around his hard length.

So close.

"Rebecca," Miguel groans as he thrusts harder.

I suck in a breath, curling my leg around his waist and changing the angle so he's rubbing against my clit with each thrust.

"Harder," I pant, tugging at his strands. "I need..."

The words are cut off when his hips meet mine just as his mouth presses against the side of my neck, his warm breath tickling my skin. Then his teeth graze over my flesh. "I know what you need, baby." His hand slides between our bodies, his fingers finding that bundle of nerves. "So hot for me. So wet." He rubs his fingers over my clit. "So fucking tight, like you were made for me. You *were* made for me. Me and nobody else."

"Miguel, stop—"

"Say it, Red," he grits, his whole body coming to a standstill as his teeth sink into my neck. A bite of pain sends tingles running down my spine. "Say that you're mine, or I won't let you come."

Stupid, infuriating...

I try to move my hips, but he's pinning me to the floor with his weight, a wicked smile on his lips.

"I'll just keep teasing you until you relent." He licks over the place he bit, his other hand cupping my breast and tweaking my nipple. I close my eyes, the motion sending a ripple of sensation all the way to my core and making me shake with need.

Shit...

"Yours," I whisper, my hips buckling under his.

"What was that?" He shifts his hand, tweaking my other nipple almost in warning. "I didn't hear you?"

I open my eyes so I can glare at him. "I'm yours."

"Me too, baby." He pulls back, and in one swift movement, he's back inside me. His thumb pinches my clit as he fills me wholly. "Always have been."

With that, his mouth devours mine, our bodies moving in sync as we chase that high. My nails dig into his skin as the wave of pleasure ripples through my body, just as Miguel slams into me with a loud groan, his whole body going taut above me.

His body falls over mine, our sweaty skin pressed together as we both try to catch our breaths. He feels heavy laying like that on me, but I don't have it in me to push him away. Instead, I smooth my palms over his back, feeling his muscles quiver with aftershocks.

Ruined.

I was completely and utterly ruined for any other man, and I couldn't even care at that moment.

"I'm sorry I'm squishing you," Miguel softly whispers.

I shake my head. "You're not."

My fingertips skim up his back until they're playing with the curly strands of his hair at his nape. They've grown longer once again over the last few weeks, making it hard to resist the pull to run my fingers through them.

Miguel tilts his head back. His dark eyes have a sleepy look to them as he stares at me.

"I could never be sorry about anything that brought you to me," I admit softly, my finger skimming over his cheek, that lush lower lip surrounded with just the perfect amount of stubble.

"Rebecca..." He starts to push upward, but I stop him.

"Promise me one thing?"

"Anything."

"Promise me there won't be a goodbye."

I could take a lot of things, but I wasn't sure I could willingly let him go. Not now. Not after this. Not after feeling so vulnerable with him. Not when he was the only man that ever understood me.

Miguel starts to shake his head. "You can't ask tha..."

"Well, I am," I cut him off. "Promise me."

"Fuck, Rebecca."

I place my palms against his chest and push him back. He doesn't resist but falls onto the blanket. I straddle his hips, my lips brush against his neck, nipping at his ear. "No goodbyes."

He lets out a frustrated groan. "No goodbyes."

Placing a kiss on the side of his neck, just behind his ear, I feel him shiver. "Only tonight."

I pepper kisses down the side of his neck and over his chest until I come to his already rising cock. My fingers wrap around him, and I give him a slow stroke as I lower my head down and take him into my mouth. I hum happily as I taste us on his cock, my tongue darting over the underside of his shaft.

"Fucking hell, Red," Miguel hisses, his fingers sinking into my hair and pulling it back. His irises turn glazed as he glances at me. "Fine, you want tonight? I'll give you tonight. I'll mark you so hard you'll never be able to erase me from your memory like I'll never be able to get you out of mine." His grip on my hair tightens, and I feel a sting shoot right to my core, making me wet. "Now suck that cock like a good girl, so I can fuck that tight pussy of yours until you scream my name."

So I do. I lick and suck at his length until he's hot and hard in my mouth, and I can feel him throbbing with need. Then I climb into his lap and sink onto him, his length stretching me to the fullest, his name an echo on my lips that lives long into the night.

The soft creak of the floorboards wakes me up from my slumber. His fingers brush against the side of my face gently, as if he's trying not to wake me up, and it takes everything in me to stay completely still.

"I love you so fucking much, Rebecca. More than I ever thought possible." He rubs at my cheekbone. "Why can't it be enough?"

Pain shoots through my heart at the sadness in his words, pain so raw it leaves me breathless.

Leaning down, he presses his mouth against the top of my head, and then his touch is gone, and so is he.

Just like he promised.

Just like I asked him.

Only once I'm sure that he's gone do I let out a strangled sob. I tried to brace for the pain, but there was nothing that could prepare me for the wrecking ball that came swinging at me.

I don't try to stop it.

Instead, I embrace it.

Pulling the blanket to my face, his scent still lingering on the material, I bury my head in it and let it all out.

CHAPTER

34

MIGUEL

Promise me.

My throat bobs as Rebecca's words ring in my head.

No goodbyes.

The broken look in her eyes that she tried to hide. The soft feel of her fingertips skimming over my skin. The scent of roses and sugar and sex filled the small treehouse as I pulled back and forced myself to make good on my promise.

A promise I wanted to break so bad, but I couldn't.

Because I didn't want to be the reason for any more of her pain than I already was.

No goodbyes.

I hated her for it, though. I hated her for making me do this, for making me walk away.

Is she though? a little voice at the back of my head taunts me. *Is she making you walk away, or are you choosing to do it yourself?*

Grabbing the doorknob, I twist it open and enter the quiet house. It's early—or late, depending on how you look at it—and the place is clouded in darkness as I walk down the hallway.

No goodbyes.

My fingers clench into fists by my sides as I power toward the stairs.

Go. I need to go. To pack my shit and get the h—

I suck in a sharp breath as I bump into something. No, not something, a freaking side table that's been standing in the hallway since I can remember. I bite my tongue, trying to hold back from muttering the curses and waking up half the house, but it's hard when all I can focus on is the blinding pain shooting through my leg.

"Fucking shit..."

I press my hand against my hip, where I connected with the edge of the table. There is buzzing in my ears that matches the pulsing feeling spreading through my leg.

Holy shit, that hurts.

I'm so focused on the pain that it takes me a while to notice the shadow falling over me, and the sound of a gun cocking breaks through the buzzing in my ears.

The hair at my nape stands on end as I look up to find no one other than my father standing in the doorway of the living room, a shotgun in his hand.

His bushy brows connect over his forehead. "What the hell are you doing, Miguel?" he grits out as he glares at me.

"Me?" I hiss, my gaze still on the stupid gun. I knew he had one. Hell, he was the one who taught Aaron and me how to shoot when we were teens, but the last thing I expected was for him to pull the damn thing on me. "What the hell are *you* doing with a freaking gun in your hand? Are you crazy? You almost gave me a heart attack."

"I gave *you* a heart attack? I thought somebody was trying to break in!" He slaps the barrel of the gun over his palm.

"Why would anybody bother? You leave the door unlocked all the damn time! Besides, you live in the middle of fucking nowhere." I glare at the gun. "Can you put that away, please?"

His eyes narrow at me. "Fine." Turning on the balls of his feet, he slowly makes his way back into the living room.

Letting out a long sigh, I follow after him. I didn't know if I actually scared him, but the last thing I wanted was for him to have another heart attack.

"What are you even doing up so late?"

He looks over his shoulder, those sharp eyes sending daggers my way. "Considering dawn is breaking, I'd say it's early."

"Same difference."

Dad makes his way to the China cabinet and puts the gun inside the safe, closing the door before he straightens to his full height with a groan and turns to find me watching him.

"What?"

"Seriously? A China cabinet?"

"It's handy." He waves me off. "What's up with you?"

I blink, surprised at the change of subject. "Nothing."

"Oh, please, you look like your puppy died, and you were all chipper when you left a few hours ago."

"I..." I lift my hand and rub at my jaw, feeling the stubble scratch my fingertips.

Dad makes his way to his trusty old recliner and slowly takes a seat, but then his attention is back on me. It's unnerving, the way he looks at me, like he's actually waiting for my answer. Like he's... listening.

I wasn't quite sure what to do about it.

He quirks one of his brows, crossing his arms over his stomach. "So?"

"My teammate called earlier. He..." I clear my throat. "He reminded me I should get back if I don't want to miss the beginning of training camp."

There is a beat of silence as Dad watches me. I shift in my seat, uncomfortable under his scrutinizing stare. My whole body is stiff, muscles taunt and bracing for whatever he's about to dish at me.

Probably one of his many complaints about me leaving and betraying my family, how I'm a grown-ass man playing a game and refusing to grow up or—

"I was wondering when you'd get your ass back to Austin."

I square my shoulders, my lips parting...

"It was about damn time. I didn't want to have to be the one to remind you of your job. I wanted to, trust me, but your mother threatened I could move my ass permanently to the couch if I chased you away again, so..."

Wait...

"What?"

"You know your mother. She can be nice as a kitten, but if you piss her off, you better be prepared to duck from her claws."

"Not that, but..."

I shake my head unsure of what to say, *how* to say it.

"What?"

"This is the first time you've acknowledged the fact that football is my job."

"Ah." He nods. "That."

"Yeah, that."

What the hell was going on here? It felt like I entered a parallel universe of some sort.

All the years of dealing with my dad and having to fight him about football have done a number on me, and I had a hard time believing that Dad might have changed.

Dad lifts his hand and runs it through his hair. "I know I've been hard on you in the past."

I snort, the need to tell him exactly what I think is on the tip of my tongue, but I bite the words back, giving him a chance to finish.

"You might think I don't realize it, but I do. I'm a hard man in general. I was hard with Aaron, too. Just in a different way, but you..." He looks away, a distant expression passing over his face. "I never quite knew what to do with you. You loved football from a very young age. I knew that. It was so obvious in the way you played. But I worried about you. I worried about your dreams crashing down if you didn't succeed."

"But I did succeed."

Dad turns toward me. "You did. And I'm happy for you. I genuinely am. I hate it because there is nothing I'd love more than for you to be here, but I can see that you're happy and doing well. I know I don't say it nearly enough, but I am proud of you, Miguel. I'm proud of the man you've become."

A knot forms in my throat at his words. It takes me a couple of tries before I can rasp, "Thanks, Dad."

"There is nothing to thank me for. It was all you. Your hard work, your stubbornness, and your determination lead you to where you are." For a moment, he just observes me. "But you don't seem happy to be going back."

Placing my hand on my knees, I push to my feet and walk to the window. That anxious feeling that was brewing inside me since the moment I left Rebecca curled on the blankets in the treehouse is making me feel unsettled. "I am happy for season to start. I'm excited to get back on the field, it's just..."

I look toward the woods.

Is she still there? Still sleeping? Or did she wake up to find me gone? If so, how did she react? Was she happy? Sad? Relieved?

Shit, maybe I should just say screw it to her wishes and—

"Rebecca."

That one word snaps me back to the present. I turn my back to the window, closing the door to all the crazy ideas swirling through my head. Ideas I shouldn't be thinking about.

I nod my head. "Yeah."

"She doesn't like the idea of you going back? I'm sure you guys could make it work. Austin isn't that far..."

"It's not far, but she doesn't want to do this thing between us." My father's brows shoot up in surprise. "She has a lot on her plate with her mom, and so do I. It's just better this way for everybody involved."

Is it really?

"Well, if you guys think that's for the best."

"It is." I nod. It has to be. What's the other option? "I think I'll go up and pack my things so I can go first thing in the morning after Mom wakes up."

In reality, I wanted to get the hell out of here as soon as possible, but I knew better than that. If I left without a proper goodbye, Mom would kill me.

At least, there was one person who wanted to say goodbye to me.

It wasn't fair to Rebecca. I knew that, but I was feeling bitter. So sue me.

A hand falls on my shoulder, drawing my attention. "Things will work out."

I wasn't so sure about that, but I nodded regardless.

This was for the best.

Maybe if I repeated it enough times, I would believe it.

CHAPTER

35

REBECCA

"You were made for me. Me and nobody else. Say it, Red." His teeth sink into my neck, a soft sting shooting all the way to my belly as his tongue swept over my flesh. "Say that you're mine."

"Yours..." I cup his cheek, turning his face to me. "I'm yo—"

When his eyes meet mine, they're devoid of any emotion. He pushes my hands back as he gets up, leaving me all alone on the floor. I pull the blanket over me to hide my naked body from his icy stare.

"If you wanted to be mine, you'd have come with me."

I suck in a breath, my body startling awake. My heart is beating hard against my ribcage as my mind replays the dream in my head.

I run my shaky hand over my face, wiping away the sheer layer of sweat.

"It was just a dream."

More like a nightmare.

A nightmare that's been haunting me ever since Miguel left.

More like ever since you chased him away, the devil at my shoulder mumbles, but I push that little voice away.

I did the right thing. I did what I had to do. There was no going around it.

Miguel belonged in Austin, playing in the NFL. Me? My life was in our small town, taking care of my family.

Pushing away the covers, I slide out of my bed and do exactly that.

The bell chimes and my head snaps up immediately, only for the disappointment to slam into me the moment I see the person standing in the doorway. The person that is not, in fact, Miguel.

Of course, it wouldn't be.

Miguel was gone.

By now, he was back in Austin.

Playing football and living his life.

Something that I should be doing too.

Why couldn't my stupid heart get the memo?

It's been a week.

A week of doing things on autopilot. A week of jumping at every little sound. A week of looking around Bluebonnet with a constant ache in my chest, waiting to spot him somewhere, anywhere.

But he wasn't here.

I force out a smile as I greet the two teens who are barely paying me any attention. They place their order before returning back to their conversation, which works just fine with me. The last thing I want to focus on is small talk.

Handing them their order, I grab a towel and wipe my hands. I turn around to find my two friends watching me intently.

"Do you see what I see?" Kate asks quietly, but not so quiet I can't hear her.

"Mhmm..." Savannah hums softly. "I see it. Do you see what I see?"

"Yup."

I cross my arms over my chest. "Will you two stop it already? You are as subtle as a pair of elephants walking around in a pink tutu."

"Seriously?" Kate purses her lips, her hand sliding over her still-flat stomach. "I know I'm pregnant, but I didn't think I'm that fat already."

And now I feel shitty as hell for making her feel self-conscious.

"You're not fat." Kate's lips curl in a smile, making my eyes narrow at her as I finish, "but you aren't subtle either."

Kate nudges Savannah with her elbow, "Somebody's touchy."

"She's been like that the past few days. All gloomy and snappy at people."

Snappy at people?

My mouth falls open. "Am not."

I barely talked to anybody!

"Are too." Savannah points her finger at me. "Yesterday you snapped at that group of teens because they were listening to some music too loudly."

"Well, they were!"

"It was one of your favorite songs," Savannah counters without missing a beat. "Don't even try to deny it. I've heard you humming to it so many times in the past."

My cheeks heat in embarrassment.

Chewing at my lip, I shift my attention to rearranging the coffee station.

Savannah was right. It was one of my favorite songs. A song that the last time I heard it, I was with Miguel. Hearing it yesterday, after everything that had happened these past few days, triggered something in me, and I just couldn't stand to listen to it. I was afraid if I did, I was going to break and start crying, and I couldn't do that. I couldn't have people looking at me like I was crazy.

They're doing it anyway.

I wasn't dumb. I could feel their curious stares and hear their soft whispers. They tried acting inconspicuously, but the people of Bluebonnet wouldn't understand what inconspicuous meant, even if it bit them in the ass.

"Did you and Miguel have a fight again?"

Kate's question startles me out of my thoughts, and I almost drop the bottle with vanilla spice. "No..."

"Because if you did, I'm sure you guys will make up," Kate continues without missing a beat. "It's what you two do. You fight, and then you ma—"

"We didn't have a fight," I shout, putting the bowl down on the counter with more force than necessary, the loud bang drawing the attention of people around me.

Shit.

Closing my eyes, I let out a soft breath, trying to rein in my emotions. Only when I'm sure I have myself under control and know my voice won't break, do I admit softly, "Miguel left."

The heavy silence stretches between us as the girls stare at me, their mouths agape, matching shocked expressions on their faces.

At least it's out.

"What do you mean he left?" Kate's the first to break the quiet. "When?"

"Just like I said, he left." I shrug, feeling the tightness of my shoulders. I look away, unable to stand Kate's scrutinizing stare. "A few days ago."

"A few..." her voice hitches, and I can hear her suck in a

sharp breath. "He left? Without saying a word? He just up and left?"

"Hey, are you okay?"

At Savannah's soft question, I turn around to find Kate's cheeks red, her lips pressed in a tight line.

"What I am is *livid*. I swear I'd kill him if he were here." She curls her fingers into a fist and pounds it against the counter, almost knocking her coffee cup over in the process. Her blazing gaze turns toward me. "How can you be so calm? What's going to happen with you guys now that he's gone?"

"Nothing."

Kate's eyes narrow. "What do you mean, nothing?"

"Exactly that, nothing."

"But you guys were together." I open my mouth, but she gives me a warning glare. "Don't you even try to deny it, missy. I know you better than you give me credit for, and I know you guys were hooking up again. In reality, I was surprised it took you that long to get back together in the first place..."

I fist my fingers, feeling the bite of the nails as they sink into my skin. "We were never together, Kate."

Kate is on a roll, and there is no stopping her now, but the more she talks, the more my anxiety grows.

"You guys were destined to be together. I've known it since the very first time I saw you, and I had a feeling you'd figure things out if you just stopped for long enough to *talk*, but—"

"We're not you and Emmett!" I yell, feeling the tears prickle my eyelids.

I needed her to stop, and I needed it now. I was so close to breaking, and if she mentioned him one more time, I'd...

"We're not you two. We'll never be you guys. I'm so happy you're married and living your best life. I truly am. But I need you to understand this isn't my life. It never will be. We never got back together, and we never will. His life is in Austin, where he's working his dream job, and I'm here."

"Becky, I'm..."

"I can't." I shake my head, biting the inside of my cheek. "Not now."

I couldn't deal with this right now.

The wound was still too fresh, too raw.

My friends exchange a silent look.

I suck in a breath. I needed a moment to compose myself. More than anything, I wished I could just go back home and close myself in my room and stay there until this pain disappears and I feel like me once again. Since that wasn't an option, I decided to do the next best thing.

"I need to grab something from the kitchen," I mutter to nobody in particular as I push from the counter and slip behind the closed door.

My breathing is heavy as I press my back against the hardwood and squeeze my eyes shut as I try to calm down.

You will not cry.

You will not cry.

You will not cry.

I chant those words like a mantra until the burning behind my eyelids subsides, and I can suck in a long, slow breath.

A soft knock makes me jump in surprise. "Becky?"

Shit.

Kate pushes the door open, her head peeking inside as she takes me in. "Do you mind if we talk?"

"Will you leave if I say I do?"

Kate gives me a sad smile. "Not really."

Letting out a sigh, I move from the door so she can enter. The last thing I wanted was to make an even bigger spectacle out of myself then I already had in front of all the patrons in the café.

"I'm sorry for being nosy like that. It was wrong of me to put my nose in your business."

"I'm the one who's sorry. I shouldn't have yelled at you."

Kate shakes her head. "You had every right to yell at me. I never thought or wanted you to feel like this. I never wanted you to think I'm comparing Emmett and me with the two of you."

"I know that. And, like I said, I'm really happy for you guys. I genuinely am. But if I'm being truly honest, some days it's hard to watch you two."

"I get that. It should have been you guys. I always thought it would have been. You always seemed so solid, even when you were fighting. I was always kind of jealous of that. Of the bond you two have. Of the kind of relationship you had with him and Emmett, too. But you and Miguel were just built differently. You two were in perfect sync. Like two halves of a whole. You didn't have to say something, and he knew what you needed, and vice versa." Kate takes my hand in hers, giving it a squeeze. "But you changed. And looking back, it didn't start after you two broke up. It started way before that. It was subtle. That's why we didn't notice. You put a wall between yourself and the rest of us. And I get it. I get the need to protect yourself and your family. I did the same with Penny when we first came here, but we love you, Becky. And we want to help you. I know you're used to dealing with things on your own, and I understand why you did what you did. But we're here now, and we can help."

Her words have a chokehold on me. I press my lips together, my throat dry as I try to fight the emotions rising inside my chest. All the years and secrets I've kept, to protect myself and the people I love, weighing heavy on my shoulders.

But she was right.

I didn't have to do it any longer.

"I worried what would happen if anybody found out. Matthew was still underage, and Chase was gone. Would they take him away? Would what little I had of my family be ripped away from me?" I shake my head. "I couldn't risk it."

"I know." Kate's fingers squeeze mine. "Nobody blames you for wanting to keep your family together, but we aren't those kids any longer. Let us be there for you like you've always been there for us."

Sucking in a shaky breath, I nod. "I can try."

"I guess that's a start," Kate chuckles softly.

Yeah, I guess it was.

Kate and I stay in the kitchen for a little while longer, changing the conversation to a slightly lighter topic before she leaves to meet Emmett for her doctor's appointment.

Checking my face with the camera of my phone to make sure I don't look like a hot mess, I leave the kitchen. There are a couple of people waiting to be served, so I prepare their orders before grabbing a tray to clean up the tables.

I'm just finishing with the last one and look out the window to spot a family standing across the street. Something about them feels familiar, and it takes me a moment for the recognition to set in.

It was Rose and Kyle. And John.

I knew that he was also in town, but this was the first time I saw him in a while. His hair was a mess, thick stubble covering his jaw. Even from here, I could see that his face was red, and his mouth was moving quickly. They were clearly fighting about something. Rose opens her mouth, but he steps closer, and she flinches at the movement.

What the hell is going on there?

The doorbell chimes, drawing my attention. I look over my shoulder and find my brother's surly face. He limps toward me, his brows furrowed, Shadow at his side.

"Here."

He pulls a phone out of his pocket and hands it to me.

"Thank you so much! I don't know how I took the wrong one." The lie slips easily from my lips as I slide my hand into my back pocket to pull out his phone and hand it to him.

Chase grunts something undefined as he glances over his shoulders. His whole body is stiff, shoulders set in a tight line as if he's bracing for trouble.

I follow his line of sight, noticing a few curious glances focused on us.

Or maybe he's just annoyed with the attention that's on him.

But people wouldn't be staring if he showed his face in town every once in a while. Not that he would listen to what I was saying. If I had to keep making up excuses for him to leave the house, so be it. I was so sick of his grumpy, reclusive ways.

"Want me to make you a coffee?"

He shakes his head. "I'm good."

"How about these new cupcakes I made?"

If possible, Chase's face turns even grimmer than it was before.

"What? You're here now. Might as well get something out of it. So, cupcakes?"

"I want you to stop losing your shit, so I don't have to go out of my way to bring it to you."

Well, I guess it was only a matter of time before he said something. These past few days, I've tried to come up with different reasons to get him into town. My car was making strange noises. It wasn't. I was running out of milk, and the shop was busy, so I needed him to go and pick some up at the store. There was an extra carton out back in the storage.

I was so sick of his sulking. And while there wasn't anything that I could do to change my shitty life, there was something that could be done about getting Chase reintegrated with the town.

I wave him off. "My mind's been elsewhere."

"Like on Miguel?"

My eyes narrow at the mention of Miguel. This was the first time Chase brought him up since that day he found us kissing on our front porch. I guess I was too hopeful to think he wouldn't have noticed us sneaking around.

Still, I keep a cool face. "What would that have to do with anything?"

Chase just watches me for a second, his fingers sinking into Shadow's fur. "Just because I don't bring that shit up, doesn't mean I don't know what's happening under my roof, Becs."

Yup, definitely too good to be true.

I open my mouth to answer, just as the doorbell chimes.

"Next time you lose something, you're getting it yourself." With that, he turns around to leave.

"Cha—" I try to warn him, but it's already too late.

In his hurry, he bumps into Rose. I watch the surprise flash on both their faces at the collision. Rose stumbles back, but before I can blink, Chase's hands are on her arms, steadying her. Rose's lips part, her hand flying to her chest.

"Oh, my God, I'm so sorry."

Chase's breathing hard as he just stares at her for a heartbeat.

Rose tilts her head to the side, her hand reaching for his. "Are you okay?"

Chase's brows pull together as he stares at her mouth, trying to figure out what she asked him.

Then Kyle appears from behind her, only to come to a sudden stop when he notices Chase and Shadow. I watch the color leave his face, his eyes turning into saucers as he takes a step back, clinging to Rose's legs.

Rose places her hand on Kyle's shoulder reassuringly.

Hurt flashes on my brother's face for a split second before it's gone. "Sorry." He moves to the side, and Shadow follows,

Kyle's eyes keeping track of their movements as they enter the shop.

"It's fine. Kyle just isn't used to such big dogs."

Chase nods dismissively, his gaze darting to me. "I'll see you at home."

Neither of us gets a chance to answer before he all but runs for the door.

"Did I do something wrong?" Rose asks, rubbing at her arm.

"No," I shake my head, turning my attention to her. "Chase is just being... Chase." It was the best way I could explain my brother without giving away his secrets.

Letting out a sigh, I crouch down and wave at Kyle before signing, "Cupcake?"

He nods eagerly, peeking from behind Rose.

I wave him over. "Come with me."

Straightening, I catch sight of Rose looking over her shoulder, nervously nibbling at her lip. I remember the interaction I'd caught before Chase came over.

"You okay?"

Rose turns toward me, shaking her head. "Yeah, of course." She plasters a smile on her face. "Everything is perfect."

CHAPTER

36

MIGUEL

"You think you're the man?" Becky flashes me a smile, her hands gripping the ball tightly to her chest.

I pretend to go for her, but she moves to the right and slips out of my reach, rushing for our makeshift end zone with me jogging after her. I put in just enough effort so the guys wouldn't bitch about it, but not enough to catch her.

"This is the best you can do, Mr. Hotshot Football Player?" she asks as she twirls that sweet ass in a celebratory dance.

I speed up, my arms wrapping around her and lifting her over my shoulder.

"Miguel!"

"Fernandez!" Coach yells, breaking me out of my thoughts just in time to see yet another player get past my defenses and into the end zone. "Where the hell is your head at?! Because it sure ain't in this game!"

Shit.

I rub the back of my neck, my muscles tense, that familiar pressure weighing on my shoulders. I didn't even have somebody to blame but myself. Ever since I got back, I've been playing like shit, and Coach has every right to rip me a new one.

"I'm sorry, Coach."

His bushy brows connect over his forehead as he frowns at me. "I don't need your excuses. What I need is for you to pull your head out of your ass and pay attention to what's going on around you! Can you do that, or do I need to send you to warm the bench? Maybe if you feel it digging into your ass long enough, you'd consider what you're missing."

Benched?

My eyes meet Blake's over Coach's shoulder. He shakes his head, his lips pressed in a tight line.

Fucking hell.

"No, Coach," I say quickly, turning my attention to the man who has my career in his hands. "I'll do better. I promise."

I hold my breath as he just glares at me for what feels like forever. The whole field is eerie quiet as they all wait for the verdict. I can feel the eyes of all my teammates as they stare at me. Some are probably trying to figure out what happened to me, and others are weighing how they can use this opportunity to get ahead.

I'm so fucking screwed.

I want to let out a frustrated scream, but I hold it back.

"Fine, but this is your last warning. The next one, and you're getting the boot."

"Yessir!"

Pushing my teammate's curious looks and the thoughts of Becky and my family to the back of my head, for the next two hours. I give my best to keep my head in the game and do the job I'm paid to do—keep the offense out of our side of the field as much as possible. And I do it well. The anger coursing through me definitely helps.

When the whistle pierces the air and Coach calls the practice to an end, I'm a sweaty, panting mess. Tugging my helmet off, I shove my damp hair out of my face as I listen to

Coach's post-game wrap-up. He makes a few comments about the last play before turning to the assistant coach, his trusty clipboard in hand. The guy was probably already preparing the plan of torture for tomorrow.

I grab a bottle of water on my way to the locker room just as Walker joins me.

"What the hell was that about?"

"Came to yell at me, old man?"

Blake glares at me, clearly not amused by my comment. "No, I didn't come here to yell at you. What I want to know is, what's making you play like shit?"

"Why don't you tell me how you really feel?" I mutter dryly, quickening my pace, or at least, I try to, but Blake puts his hand on my shoulder and tugs me back.

"In the last year, I've known and worked with you. I don't think I've seen you distracted once. When you're on the field, one hundred percent of your focus is on that game, on the next play. But ever since camp started, you've been a mess. So don't be a smartass, and tell me what the hell's going on, Fernandez." He tips his chin in the direction of my hand. "Is it your shoulder? I thought the PT helped."

"It's not my shoulder." Instinctively, I roll them back. The sting is there for sure, but there is no pain. "It's just an off day."

For whatever reason, that makes his expression turn even more gloomy. "You don't have off days."

"Everybody has an off day." I shrug. Turning around, I push the door to the locker room open. The chatter dies down, all eyes turning to me.

"What?" I lift my arms in the air, irritated my teammates are acting this way. "Nobody died. It's just a freaking off day."

My hands slap against my sides as I let them fall and march to my spot.

"Try like freaking two weeks off," Big J chimes in, helpful as always.

I give him a warning glare; Big J doesn't seem the least bit fazed by it. "What? It's the truth. Ever since you got back, your game's been off. And people are starting to notice when Mr. Perfect messes up."

"Perfect," I scoff. "Hardly. Besides, I do have off days."

"Not you, Monk."

The throbbing behind my temples intensifies. I hated it when they used that nickname. I don't even know when it started. College? Or just after I got to the pros? The fuck if I know. Those early days were so overwhelming it was hard to pinpoint what was what.

What I do remember vividly is that nothing would help me forget her. I even tried hooking up with a girl once, just after Rebecca and I broke up. I was angry at her and at the world, and I just wanted to forget, so I drank my weight in alcohol, thinking it'd help. Thinking it might erase the look on Rebecca's face from my mind. But my stomach revolted at the idea of making out with another girl, much less trying something else. And I mean it quite literally. Granted, it might have been the alcohol too. I think I traumatized the girl for life.

But that wasn't the moment that snapped me out of my self-destructive ways. It was when the coach benched my ass for being sloppy on the field. I worked so freaking hard, and I was about to lose it all because I was being a heartbroken idiot? Would have to go back home with my tail tucked between my legs? Face *her*? Hell to the no. That's when I swore off all of it— the girls, the booze, the parties—and the nickname was born.

"You have an off-game, sure, but this is different. You're distracted. It's like your body is here, but your mind is only God knows where."

I clench my teeth, irritated with this whole conversation. Mainly because he's right. Not that I'd ever admit it out loud. "My mind is here," I bite out, spinning on my heels.

I open my locker and shove my helmet inside before tugging my shirt over my head and tossing it toward the hamper closest to my locker.

"Then why are you so irritated? Wait, I know." He claps his hands together, the sound echoing in the quiet room. "Does it have anything to do with that girl from a couple weeks ago?"

The hair at my nape stands, my fingers curling around the waistband of my pants.

"Wait, what? Monk has a girl?" Franco asks, the surprise evident in his voice.

"Yup, I'm pretty sure I heard a girl there when I called him to ask him when he's planning to get his ass to summer camp," Big J chuckles. "What happened? Did you finally get some pussy, and it messed with your mojo?"

I turn around and lunge at him, my fists wrapping around his jersey. "You don't talk shit about her, you hear me, Callahan?" I growl into his face.

From the periphery, I can see my teammates shift closer as dead-quiet settles over the room. Well, apart from Big J's laughter, that is.

"Oh, shit! You did. Didn't you?" He laughs even harder, his arms slapping against his side. "You finally wet your dick after how many years again? It doesn't even matter. Now she's messed with your head, and you can't play."

"You're playing with fire, Callahan," Blake says next to us, the warning as clear as day.

"What? You can't deny this is amusing. There is Monk no more. Now we'll have to find you a new nickname."

Sucking in a long breath, I force my fingers to uncurl, but

before I let him go, I connect my palms to his chest and give him a not-so-gentle shove. "Just fucking stop it."

A hand slaps me on the shoulder as Kyle, our safety, goes to the bathroom. "Don't get your panties in a twist, Fernandez, and overthink it. This is a good thing. A good tumble in the sheets usually helps me chill after a hard day at work. You should try it. I'm sure it'll be better next time."

There will be no next time. There can't be. My life is here, and hers is back in Bluebonnet. And after everything that had happened, everything that I know about her and about her mom, there is no way that I can ever ask her to leave. No matter how much I want to.

His comment makes a few people snort out a laugh.

What the hell is this? Junior high?

"Will you stop talking about her that way? She's not just some groupie."

"Damn, Fernandez." Franco places his palms on my shoulders and shakes me. "You can't go falling in love with the first girl you sink your cock into. You're a Lonestar. Own it, man. There are a bunch of girls out there who'd kill to be with you."

"Will you leave him alone already?"

Franco glances at Blake. "What do you know that we don't?"

"He went back to his hometown." This comment comes from Big J. I whip my head in his direction to find him drying his hair.

"What?" He shrugs. "You were back home when I called you the other day."

Seriously, guys bitch about girls being gossips. Yeah, right.

"Oh, damn," Franco groans. "You didn't."

"What?" I grit through clenched teeth, so sick of playing their games.

"This is even worse than I thought."

I suck in a breath trying to keep my cool. "And how, pray tell, is this worse?"

"You hooked up with the one who got away. The one who messed you up in the first place."

Becky's face as we lay in the treehouse that last night pops into my head. The sorrow in her eyes as we said our silent goodbye one last time.

Shaking my head, I push the memory away, locking it in the box stashed at the very back of my head.

Screw the shower.

"I'm getting out of here," I mutter, as I pull out my bag and grab my shirt.

I'm done with this conversation.

So freaking done.

Thankfully, my teammates are smart enough not to say anything else as I quickly put on my clothes, before I march out of the locker room.

My feet pound against the ground as I make my way out of the building. Their words still swirling inside my mind, fighting with the image of Rebecca in my head.

The one who got away.

The ironic thing was they were right.

She got away.

And I let her.

Twice.

"Fernandez, wait!" A hand grips my shoulder, tugging me back.

"I'm not in the mood, Walker. Get the fuck out of my way."

"Fat chance of that happening." Blake's dark eyes take me in slowly. "Are you okay?"

"Fine."

He watches me for a moment before shaking his head. "You're not fine."

"Walker..."

"Get your head out of your ass, Rookie." He slaps me over the head.

I rub at my nape. "Hey, what was that for?"

"Because you're acting like a spoiled brat. C'mon, now. Get in your car, and let's go."

"I'm really not in the mood to go to a bar, Walker."

What I want is to go back home, shower, and crash face first. All so I could repeat this all over again tomorrow, but unfortunately, Blake is having none of it.

"Good, 'cause we're not going to a bar." He pushes me toward my car. "Let's go, Rookie."

"You really need to ditch that nickname."

Walker just raises his brow. "Should I go with Monk instead?"

"Y'all really have a death wish."

Blake slaps me over the shoulder. "Don't worry, I think they'll come up with something new."

That's what I was afraid of.

I don't know where I expected Blake to take me, but his house definitely wasn't it. While I've been here a few times in the past, for the most part, we hung out with the guys either at the facilities or at our favorite bar close to the stadium. If they managed to drag me there, that is.

Pulling in front of a big, two-story colonial house in a suburban part of Austin, I get out of the car just as Blake comes swaggering from his garage. Before the sound of the garage door closing stops echoing, the front door bursts open and a small figure rushes out, throwing his arms around Blake's legs.

"Daddy!" Levi yells, his voice muffled as he burrows his head into Blake's legs. "You're late."

"I know." Blake ruffles his son's unruly hair. "I'm sorry, buddy. I got side-tracked at work, but look who I brought to see you."

Levi doesn't make any attempt at letting go as he peeks from around his father. That is until he spots me. "Miguel!"

His whole face lights up, a smile flashing on his face. Levi lets go of his dad and rushes toward me, his small body crashing into mine with the force of a linebacker.

"Hey, there, champ." I place my hand on his shoulder to steady him. "Did you practice your tackling skills recently?"

"Duh! I have to practice if I wanna be good like Daddy," he rushes out, but before I can answer, he just continues chatting away. "Where have you been? We haven't seen you in *ages*! Dad told me you went home to visit your family, but I said he was being silly because we're your family."

His words throw me off for a second. Did I hang out with Blake and his boys? Sure, but there was something on his face that I couldn't place. My eyes meet Blake's, but he just shakes his head silently.

Levi nudges me. "So, where were you?"

I turn toward him and crouch down so we're at the same level. "I was, in fact, visiting my family."

"Where is your family?"

"They live in a small town down south. It's called Bluebonnet Creek."

His little brows pull together. "Like the flower?"

I let out a chuckle. "Yes, like the flower. I'm sorry I didn't call more. I was a little busy."

His little arms clutch me tighter. "But you're here now? You're not going anywhere?"

Your life is in Austin, and mine is here.

"Miguel? You're staying?"

There it is again. That look.

What the hell was going on here?

Levi was a good kid, a happy kid. But today, he seemed worried. Not just that, there was a weird mix of desperation and anxiousness surrounding him that I didn't understand at all.

I place my hand on top of his head and ruffle his hair. "Yeah, buddy, I'm staying here."

"Good." A bright smile that I'm way more familiar with flashes on his face. His fingers wrap around mine, and he tugs me toward the house. "Come, I wanna show you the new Lego set I built with Dad."

"Hey, buddy, how about we give Miguel some space?" Blake asks, snapping me out of my thoughts.

"It's fine. I don't mind going with him."

"Yas!" Levi fist pumps. "Can we, Daddy? Can we?"

Blake lets out a long sigh. "Fine, but just for a little while. Then we'll sit down and have lunch, okay?"

His warning glare turns from his son to me, silently telling me he didn't miss what I was doing and that I couldn't postpone our conversation forever. But I'd take any reprieve I could.

"Fine," Levi drawls out. "Come, Miguel. There was this Spider Man set Dad got me recently, and it's really big. But Daniel tells me it's lame."

"It's most certainly not lame," I chime in as he pulls me into the house and down the hallway toward the game room. "That's what I told him! He's just being all grumpy all the time."

Considering Daniel was about to turn fifteen in a couple of weeks, I could see how that might be the case. I was grumpy when I was a teenager too. Always fighting with my brother and my dad. The only person that understood me and could calm me was Rebecca.

And there she was again, sneaking into my thoughts. No

matter how much I tried, I couldn't erase her from my mind. It was like the woman was etched into every fiber of my being, and now that she was gone, I didn't know how to move on with my life without her in it.

"Look!" Levi tugs at my hand, drawing my attention. I shift my gaze to the Lego set and listen patiently as Levi explains every little detail about the set and the new movie.

A lock of his hair falls in his face, and instinctively, I push it back. My heart squeezes tightly in my chest at the sight of him. At four years old, Levi was way too smart for his own good. He could talk your ear off about anything and nothing.

Would Becky's and my child have been like Levi? Were we supposed to have a girl or a boy? Would they be interested in Lego sets? Sports? Dolls? None of it? I could have imagined a hundred different scenarios.

An ache I didn't know how to name spreads inside my chest, making it hard to breathe.

"Daniel!" Blake yells loudly. "Get downstairs, please. It's time for lunch."

There is a beat of silence before Daniel yells, "Not hungry."

"Well, I don't care. Mrs. Maxwell made lunch, so you better get your ass downstairs now."

"Uh-oh."

I glance at Levi. "That happens a lot?"

"Yup," Levi nods, his hands clasping together.

Just then, Blake appears in the doorway. "Levi, time to wash your hands."

Levi jumps to his feet and does as Blake says, so I straighten, running my hand over my face.

Blake watches me carefully. "You good?"

"Yeah, I'm fine."

"C'mon, let's go to the kitchen. Wanna beer?"

I shake my head. I had a strict no-drinking rule the moment the pre-season started.

"Mind if I have one? I have a feeling I might need it."

"It's your house, dude."

Just when we get into the hallway, loud footsteps echo as Daniel rushes down the stairs. Just like Levi, his dark hair is also longer. Even through an oversized black hoodie, I can see his shoulders are slumped forward, a grim look on his face, as if he's bracing for a fight. For all intents and purposes, he looks like a younger version of Blake. Both boys do.

"I told you I'm not hungry," he mutters, crossing his arms over his chest.

"And I told you I don't care. You can eat now, or you'll go hungry until dinner when you can eat the leftovers Mrs. Maxwell made."

"Whatever," he grits his teeth and marches into the kitchen.

I whistle softly. "You weren't joking about needing that beer."

Blake lets out a sigh. "I wish."

I could bet. I didn't envy him one bit.

"Hey, Mrs. Maxwell. How have you been doing?" I greet, as we enter the kitchen to find his housekeeper stirring something on the stove.

She glances up at us, a surprised look flashing on her face. "Miguel! We haven't seen you around here in a while." Then she turns to Blake. "Why didn't you tell me we had company?"

"Because you were busy telling me about what had happened earlier?" he reminds her, and I don't miss the frown he directs at his older son.

The woman visibly flinches, her gaze darting to Daniel's slumped form sitting at the dining table. "True. But still, you should have told me! I could have prepared more food."

"I'm sure whatever you made was more than enough."

"It'll have to be." She takes a towel and wipes her hands. "Miguel, I heard you went to visit your family."

"I did, yes. My best friend got married this summer."

"Well, that's nice. You finally got your head out of your butt, you've been sulking around for way too long as it is."

"I haven't been sulking around."

"Oh, please." She gives me a pointed look. "As if I don't know what sulking looks like when I see it. You know I raised boys of my own, right?"

In her late fifties, Mrs. Maxwell has been working for the Walkers since Daniel was born. She might look like a sweet grandma with her silver hair and glasses perched on top of her nose, but you'd be fooled. Deep down, she's a no-nonsense lady. Nobody in their right mind would dare cross her. I think that's why Blake loves her so much. With two boys in the house, they needed somebody to keep them in line. God knows Reina isn't the one who'd do it. Blake's wife is usually too busy shopping and hanging out with her friends to spend much time with her sons, any time with her sons, really.

And on that note.

"Where is Reina?" I ask, looking around the room, but I don't see any sign of his wife.

My eyes land on Blake, and I notice his back has stiffened at my words. Closing the fridge, he slowly turns to me, a beer bottle in one hand and a bottle of water for me.

"You haven't told him?" Mrs. Maxwell asks, a frown appearing between her brows.

Guilt flashes on Blake's face, his cheeks heating under Mrs. Maxwell's watchful gaze, like he's a kid caught with his hand in a cookie jar just before dinner. "He was busy!"

"Haven't told me what?" I ask slowly, shifting my attention between the two. "What's going on, Walker?"

Blake hands me the water before taking a long swig from his

own bottle. I start to do the same when my best friend blurts out: "Reina left me."

The cool liquid gets stuck in my throat, and I start to choke.

Reina left him?

Patting my chest a few times, I manage to suck in a breath so I croak out: "She what?"

"Don't look so surprised. I wasn't. Not really."

"She left you, and you weren't surprised?" My tone is more high-pitched than intended. I glance toward the table and spot the way Daniel's jaw clenches almost imperceptibly.

I guess that explains everything.

Daniel's sulking even more than usual. Levi's clinging and anxiousness.

It all made perfect sense now.

Mrs. Maxwell lets out a loud harrumph before turning her attention back to the stove and lunch.

Levi runs into the kitchen breathlessly, and I decide to drop the subject. For now, at least. I didn't want to talk about this in front of the boys.

We all sit down to eat, and Levi talks our ears off as he tells me about all the things they did over the summer, pointedly ignoring the topic of his mother the whole time.

Once the lunch is done, Blake makes both boys help Mrs. Maxwell with the cleanup before they can leave, and we take our drinks to the back porch.

"Seriously? You didn't think to mention that Reina left?"

Blake gives me a pointed look. "Says Mr. Closed Off and Broody."

"This is different."

"Yeah, how so?"

"She's not my wife," I point out.

"But you'd want her to be."

His words bring the image of Rebecca walking down that

aisle back to front and center in my mind, only this time she's walking to me.

My wife.

The intensity of it, knocks all the air out of my lungs. He's right, and until this very moment, I didn't even realize how much I wanted that very thing.

Sure, it was something that occasionally crossed my mind back in the day, when we were first dating. Not as much about how I wanted to marry her, but that she was my person. Then she was gone, and now... Now, we had a chance to be together, only to be torn apart again, but I couldn't stop thinking about it. About her. I couldn't stop wanting her.

Rebecca Williams was mine, and I wanted to make it official.

"Don't even bother to deny it. It's all over your face. That woman has you wound up so tight, it'd be funny to watch if you weren't messing your career up for it. Why not just go back and ask her to forgive your sorry ass for whatever you did?"

"Why do you think I was the one who did something?"

He lets out a sigh and rubs his hand over his face. "Trust me, Rookie. It's always something that we did. One way or the other, we're always to blame."

The way he says it, I know he's not talking just about Rebecca and me.

"What happened with Reina?" I ask, changing the subject.

He lifts his shoulders. "She left. She just packed her bags, and when I came home from the gym, I found a note on the fridge and all of her things were gone."

"Just like that?"

"Just like that. She left, and the boys were here. Not that I'm surprised. It was just a matter of time, I guess. She wasn't happy, and she made that loud and clear any chance she got."

I only knew Blake for a little over a year, and I knew Reina even less, but I'd heard the stories. They used to date in college, and Reina got pregnant her freshman year. They decided to get married and keep the baby, so she dropped out of classes to take care of their son, which quickly changed after Blake signed for the NFL straight out of college.

I don't know how things used to be between them before, but since I've joined the team, I've seen Reina on just a handful of occasions, mostly when I would come to their house, and she was... unpleasant, to say the least.

"When did that happen?"

"At the beginning of the summer, shortly after you left, actually."

After I left?

"But that was weeks ago! Why didn't you say something?"

Walker shrugs. "What was the point? She was gone, and there was no getting her back. Not that I wanted to, not really. Reina and I might have been married on paper, but we weren't an actual couple for years. The only thing that bothers me is how she managed the whole situation with the boys. Daniel blames me for what happened. He's been a nightmare to deal with, constantly trying to push my limits. And Levi..." He lets out another sigh. "He's been extremely anxious every time I leave. Mrs. Maxwell keeps telling me that he constantly looks out the window when I'm gone. It's like he's afraid I won't show up."

"That's fucked up on so many levels."

He takes a pull from his beer, a dark expression crossing his face. "When she left, she didn't just leave me. She left them. And that's one thing I'll never be able to forgive her for."

"Has she tried to contact them?"

Blake shakes his head. "Not a peep from her. How fucked up is it that I'm not even surprised? She barely talked to them even before, but to just up and leave?"

He was right, it was messed up. The boys did nothing to deserve something like that, and I couldn't even imagine what it must have felt like to be suddenly abandoned by their mother like that. No matter how sorry of an excuse of a mother she used to be before, at least she was present.

"I'm so sorry, Walker."

"I'm not." He finishes the beer, his fingers wrapping around the can and squeezing it tightly. "I'm sorry I didn't do something about this whole situation sooner. I'm sorry that my boys are suffering the loss of their mother. But in all honesty, it was inevitable. Reina and I were never meant to be. I tried. I really did. And in the beginning, it was working, but these last few years..."

His eyes shift forward, a distant expression flashing on his face.

"What are you going to do now? The season is just around the corner."

"Mrs. Maxwell agreed to move in and stay with the boys while I'm gone, but I've made my decision."

"You're retiring."

I could see it on his face, the resolution. No matter what I said, he wouldn't change his mind.

He nods. "It's time. My boys need me, and I'm planning to do right by them." His gaze meets mine. "What are *you* going to do?"

"There is nothing that I can do."

"Is that so? Or are you just afraid to do what you know needs to be done?"

"I wanted to, dammit. I wanted to ask her to come here with me. But she didn't let me. Her mom's sick, and..." I shake my head. "It doesn't even matter."

"It clearly does matter because you're a mess." I narrow my eyes at him, but he just glares right back. "Don't even try to deny it. Not to me, Fernandez. The real question is, are you going to give up or find an alternative way to get what you want? Trust me, you'll regret it if you let your hurt pride get in the way of getting the woman you want, and from what I've gathered, this one's worth keeping."

CHAPTER

37

REBECCA

"I'm home," I greet as I enter the foyer.

Making sure the door is locked behind me, I walk down the hallway until I get to the living room and spot Mom sitting on the couch.

"Hey, Becky."

Turning around, I find Linda standing in the doorway of the kitchen. "How was your day?"

"Good." I tilt my head to the side. "How is she doing?"

Linda gives me a soft, almost apologetic smile. "The same. She still hasn't eaten, and when I tried to get her to shower, she started to get agitated, so I figured I'd let her be."

"Shit." I run my hand through my hair, pushing it back as I try to reign in my own frustration. "Thanks for trying, Linda."

"Of course. If you don't need me anymore, I'll be on my way."

"Sure. I'll see you tomorrow."

Linda gathers her things while I go to the kitchen to find a prepared plate of food in the fridge. Taking it out, I grab one for myself, too, before making my way to the living room.

"Hey there," I greet as I sit next to her on the couch. "Linda told me you were here all day. Was there anything interesting on TV?"

The silence stretches for a few moments as I place one plate on the coffee table.

"How about we have dinner together? Linda made this delicious homemade mac and cheese." I lift the plate so she can see it, but her gaze doesn't waver.

Dammit.

"Mom, you have to eat something."

Leaning in, I place my hand on Mom's knee, giving it a soft squeeze. Her face is expressionless as she stares at the TV unblinkingly. Physically, she might be in the room, but mentally, she wasn't here. The pressure starts building inside my chest the longer I stare at her.

She's been completely and utterly absent for the last few days, and it showed. Her face is ashen, skin dry. Her silver hair was a greasy mess falling over her shoulders. She was waning before our eyes, and there was nothing that we could do to stop it. She refused to shower, she refused to eat, and we barely managed to get her to drink a little bit of tea.

"Mom," I try again, but she slaps my hand away.

Instinctively, I pull it to my chest, the sting of her hit burning my skin.

"I'm not eating until Jackson comes home."

I take a deep breath, trying to calm myself. Fighting with her won't help appease the situation.

"You remember that Jackson said he's coming home late. He wouldn't want you to stay hu—"

"Don't placate me, Gigi!" Mom glares at me. "I know what you're trying to do! I'm not stupid. And I'm telling you right now, it won't work."

"I didn't say you're..."

"You did! Why are you always like this? Jackson told me he's coming so he *will* come. My *husband* loves me. He wouldn't leave me hanging. He isn't like one of those losers you usually date." Her lips part as if something just occurred to her. "Is that it? Are you jealous? Are you trying to sabotage my marriage?"

I open my mouth to protest, but she's faster.

"You are." She points her finger at me. She's so thin I can see the bones peeking from under her skin. "You always tell me he's not coming, but he is. I know he is."

"That's not it." I shake my head. "I told you earlier. Jackson called, and said he's working late."

"Liar! He wouldn't do that. He always makes it home for dinner."

So much for calming her down.

"I know, but this time—"

"You're lying! Why are you being so hurtful, Gigi? Are you jealous that I'm waiting for my husband so we can have a dinner date when your boyfriend left you?"

Each word of hers is like a punch to my gut. Rationally, I know she isn't aware of what she's saying, and she probably doesn't mean it that way. She's just angry and frustrated, but that doesn't make her words hurt any less.

"Why did he leave you this time? It's always something with you. Maybe if you tried harder, he'd have stayed. Ever thought of that?"

"I-I..."

My throat bobs as I swallow, trying to come up with the right words to say.

"What's going on here?"

Mom looks over my shoulder, a beaming smile appearing on her lips. "Jackson!"

She rushes toward my brother and throws her arms around

his neck. Chase stiffens at the sudden contact and turns his head to the side. "I knew you'd come. Gigi tried to convince me that you wouldn't, but I knew you wouldn't disappoint me." She turns to me, a smug smile on her face. "Didn't I tell you, Gigi? Jackson loves me. He'd never go back on his promise. He'd never leave me."

Tears fill my eyes as my brother's gaze meets mine.

No, Dad would never have left her. Not if he had a choice, that is. But he didn't. And she doesn't remember it.

She doesn't remember any of it.

Spinning on my heels, I push the back door open and get the hell out. I bite the inside of my cheek, trying to stop the tears from falling.

I hate this.

I hate this so fucking bad.

But there was nothing that I could do about it.

I couldn't yell or scream or do anything really. She wouldn't understand it, and it would only get her even more agitated than she already was, which would just cause more problems.

How long?

How long could we keep going like this?

Brushing the back of my hand over my cheek, I pull my phone out of my back pocket and unlock it. My fingers are ready to type the message when the name on top of the thread catches my attention.

Miguel.

But Miguel is gone.

He left, and he wasn't coming back.

We weren't together.

I couldn't message him and tell him what had just happened. I couldn't tell him how Mom's words hurt, although, I knew they weren't directed at me. How seeing her act like this broke my heart, and I wasn't sure there would be any of it left by the time this was done.

I couldn't reach out to the only person I wanted to, the only person who understood me.

Not after I was the one who pushed him away. Not after I asked him to leave without saying goodbye.

My fingers clasp around the phone tighter as I stare at the screen, the words turning more blurry by the second.

"When are you planning to call him?"

Blinking the tears away, I tilt my head back at the sound of the low voice, to find my brother watching me. Chase moves closer, Shadow at his heels.

I lock my phone, turning it face down for good measure. "I don't know what you're talking about." I glance over his shoulder. "Where is Mom?"

"I put her to bed," Chase sits next to me, letting out a soft groan, and Shadow settles at his feet. "She was really upset about the whole thing."

"She was upset with me, you mean," I correct.

"She's upset because she's confused, and she misses Dad. She didn't mean what she said."

"I know," I whisper softly, focusing on the setting sun.

For a while, we sit in silence, the cricket's song the only thing filling the quiet. The events of the last few weeks play in my head as I focus on that steady sound until my heartbeat evens out.

Finally, I turn my attention to Chase. The good side of his face is closer to me, making him seem almost normal. Almost. If only there weren't dark circles under his eyes, and the demons dancing in his irises.

"She's getting worse."

Incidents like the one today were more common than not these days, but they weren't the worst part. The worst part was that no matter what we did, we couldn't reach her and meet her basic needs. There was nothing that we could do to help her. No medication, no therapy, nothing.

"We have to do it, Becky."

I close my eyes and press my lips together, my fingers curling in my lap. My initial reaction is to revolt at the idea, but deep down, I know he's right. We couldn't go on like this much longer. Linda was amazing, but Mom needed around-the-clock care. She needed people who understood her like we couldn't.

Chase nudges my foot with his gently. "She might hurt herself or somebody else."

"I know." I tilt my head back, blinking the tears from my eyes. "But it's hard. It feels like I'm betraying her."

"You're not betraying her. She wouldn't want this for you."

Wiping at my cheeks, I find Chase watching me. "She wouldn't want you to see her like that, and she'd hate herself for the words she said to you. But most of all, she'd want you to be happy."

"I know that."

"Do you?" The harsh note in my brother's voice has me turning my attention to him. "Why are you still here, Rebecca?"

I tuck a strand of my hair behind my ear. "I don't know what you mean."

"Bullshit."

"Seriously? You decide to be chatty now?" I push to my feet, wiping my suddenly sweaty palms against the sides of my legs. I needed to put some distance between us.

"It's my revenge for making me run your imaginary errands like a fool."

I turn around to face him so he can read my lips easily. "I don't know what you're talking about."

Chase just crosses his arms over his chest and shoots me his sternest look. I shift my weight from one foot to the other, my palms gripping the wooden railing behind me.

"Why are you still here?"

Is he for real?

"Oh, I don't know, Chase," I mutter sarcastically. I was so over everyone sticking their nose into my business. "Maybe because I have a life here? A job? A mother who needs care twenty-four-seven? Two brothers I constantly worry about because one all but locked himself in the house, and the other one never picks up his phone and only checks in via text often enough so I don't send out a search warrant for him? Take your pick."

Chase is quiet for a moment, and I finally think he's going to let it go when he speaks, "She used to write me letters."

Letters? What does that have to do with anything?

"Who? Mom?"

A dark look appears on my brother's face. Chase nods, his hand falling on top of Shadow's head as if seeking comfort only this dog could give him. Shadow licks his hand, and Chase blinks, coming back to the present. He clears his throat. "When I was away, she'd send me letters talking about you and Matthew, and people I knew from home. Mostly random stuff, updates, and funny stories. Then, one day, I opened the letter, and it was about you and Miguel."

"She wrote about us?"

I knew she talked to Chase. We all did whenever he got a chance to give us a video call from wherever he was stationed at the time, but I didn't realize she wrote him letters, too.

Chase nods. "She told me you two finally got your heads out of your asses and admitted what she and everybody else around you knew from the very beginning, and that is that you two belong together. And seeing you two look at each other these past few weeks, I know exactly what she meant."

Chase too? Like seriously, so much for keeping a low profile.

"Even if we remove everything else, we live in two different cities, Chase."

"It's not like he lives across the country." Chase gives me a pointed look. "How many excuses will you find just so you don't have to take a risk, Rebecca? I didn't take you for a coward."

"Says the man who's been hiding on this ranch since he got home," I throw right back, not about to pull any punches. The muscle in his jaw ticks. "You know I'm right."

"We're not talking about me."

"Of course, you'd get all quiet and broody when the tables are turned."

This was the most he'd spoken to me since he came home, but the moment I faced him with his misgivings, he closes up tighter than Fort Knox.

Chase gets up, so I rush to finish before he can cut me off completely. "You can't preach to me about finding happiness when you're sulking and hiding here forever."

"I'm not sulking."

"Of course not." *Infuriating man.* "Chase?"

He stops in the doorway, and I swallow the lump in my throat.

"Call that doctor friend of yours so we can see about making the arrangements for Mom."

Saying the words out loud leaves a bitter taste on my tongue, but this wasn't about me. It was about making sure Mom got the best possible care. My guilt had no place here.

With a nod, he and Shadow disappear inside the house.

Letting out a long breath, I walk back to the swing and drop into the plush pillows, needing a little peace and quiet after everything that had happened today.

But the quiet doesn't last long because my phone chimes with a text message.

Sighing, I grab it and unlock the phone.

I do a double-take, my heart racing inside my chest as I read the three words written on the screen.

MIGUEL:

I miss you.

CHAPTER

38

MIGUEL

"Yeah?" I pant as I answer my phone, my feet still pounding in a steady rhythm against the treadmill.

Now that the season is back in session, I've been spending more and more time in the team facilities. There were training sessions, tape watching and game prep, practices, and doctor appointments, plus they were feeding me. Besides, it's not like I had anywhere else to go.

She didn't answer my message.

After my conversation with Walker, I couldn't get his words out of my head. They were rolling on repeat until I finally caved and texted her.

Only she never answered me back.

She was pretty clear about not wanting to have anything to do with you once you were gone.

"Seriously, Fernandez?" Emmett asks, the irritation clear in his tone. "Leaving without saying a fucking goodbye?"

"I was kind of in a rush."

"In a rush to run the fuck away from Bluebonnet, you mean?"

"In a rush to get back to Austin so I could be here for summer camp, you asshole."

In a rush to get the hell away from Rebecca, more likely, the little voice in my head taunts me, but I push it back.

"Still, you couldn't even stop to say goodbye?"

Promise me, Rebecca's voice echoes in my mind, the image of her in my arms that last night etched into my mind. *No goodbyes.*

"No." My voice comes out rough, so I clear my throat. "I was already late as it was. I completely spaced out about the dates, and not making camp isn't an option."

"Mhmm... So this is just about the summer camp?"

I pinch the bridge of my nose. "Yes, Santiago. Honestly, don't you have anything better to do than to hassle me with this? I've got work to do."

"Don't get your panties in a twist, Fernandez. I was just worried about you. Okay, and a little bit pissed."

"Yeah, well, you can take it up with my coach."

Something bangs loudly in the background.

"How did the camp go?"

Shitty.

Not that I can admit that.

"It was fine. I'm still on the team."

Although barely, and Coach was pretty clear about that. I would either have to get my head out of my ass and focus on football, or I was getting the boot. So, I did my best to shove the thoughts of a certain redhead out of my mind and focus on what was in front of me.

"You don't sound too happy about it," Emmett points out.

"I'm happy about it. I'm just tired."

"Tell me about it," Emmett hums before suddenly changing the subject. "I stopped by Rebecca's place. She looks like shit."

The mention of Rebecca has me losing my footing. I stumble forward, and I'd face plant if I didn't catch the handle next to me to steady myself.

453

"Fernandez?" Emmett asks, and I'm pretty sure I can hear a smirk in his voice.

"I don't know what that has to do with me."

"Oh please, you didn't actually think that your little rendezvous would stay a secret, did you? You haven't been away from Bluebonnet for that long to be so naïve. I mean, not only did Kate catch you in the act, but I've heard from different sources about your little date to the fair."

"You're delusional."

"Mhmm... that's why you almost fell on your ass right now at the bare mention of her."

I press my lips together, refusing to take his bait, but Emmett doesn't seem to get the memo.

"She had to move her mom to the assisted living facility."

Assisted living facility?

My heart starts beating wildly inside my chest as I try to process his words. "What? When?"

Emmett sighs. "Just recently. She's been getting worse to the point that even having Linda's help wasn't much use."

"Fuck, that's..."

I run my hand through my hair, not sure what to say.

She looked fine that day I saw her, almost... normal.

"I know. Becs is devastated. She put so much pressure on herself to help keep her family together. For her to agree to this..."

It had to be bad.

Did something happen? Was Mrs. Williams okay? Did she have an accident of some sort? Did she run away like she did that day?

I still remember the look of utter devastation on her face that night on her porch. The tears. Those fucking tears that were my undoing.

Is she crying now? Who's holding her and comforting her now that I'm gone?

Just thinking about it makes me grit my teeth.

No matter what I said, he'd try to turn it against me, so my plan was simply to ignore it and change the subject. "How's Kate doing?"

Thankfully, that does the trick. "She's good. Feeling slightly better now that she's in the second trimester. The doctor told us we should be able to find out the sex of the baby at our next appointment."

"That's cool. What are you guys hoping for?"

"Kate insists she just wants the baby to be healthy, but I'm hoping for a girl."

I don't need to see him to know how excited he is. I could hear it in his voice as clear as day. Emmett was ecstatic with the idea of becoming a father, of being a husband.

"A girl-dad," I whisper softly, my mind going back to my conversation with Rebecca.

Because it always came back to Rebecca.

Would I have been a girl-dad or a boy-dad? Would the kid have had red hair or brown, straight or curly? Would they have had her hazel eyes or my brown ones?

What would it have been like?

There are so many what-ifs, but at the end of the day, none of it matters. That baby is gone, and nothing will bring it back. We were the people we are because of it. There is only one reality, and this is it.

"Can you imagine it?" Emmett chuckles, breaking me out of my thoughts.

"I can, actually." Raising my hand, I rub at the middle of my torso, where I can feel the pressure building inside my chest.

Deciding to call it quits, I turn off the treadmill, adapting my pace as the machine slows down until it comes to a complete stop. "But can you? Are you sure you're ready for that?" I ask, unable to stop myself from teasing him, although I could totally see it.

Emmett had a way with women. He might not have a blood sister, but in his heart of hearts, Rebecca and Penelope were it.

"I was born ready. Kate wants to do a gender reveal party for the family and a few friends. You should come."

No goodbyes.

"I don't know. I'll probably be busy now that the season is underway. I practically live in the Lonestars facilities now."

"That's bullshit, and you know it. You're just a couple of hours away, and that's if there is traffic."

Maybe, but she asked me to leave.

"You're not that kid that left for college," Emmett continues when I don't say anything. "Things are different now."

"Maybe."

But I couldn't change her mind. I tried. I tried asking her to give us a chance. I tried to reach out. I tried to make it work.

She was pretty clear she didn't want that.

REBECCA

"How is she doing?" I ask Monica, the head nurse, as I enter the foyer of the Helpful Hands. The assisted living facility came highly recommended from Chase's doctor, and when we looked into it, we found out they just had an opening.

The older woman beams at me. "Today's actually a good day. She is knitting out in the garden. Want me to take you there?"

"That sounds amazing." Monica smiles brightly and comes around the counter as I pull a box out of the bag I'm carrying. "This is for you guys."

"Oh, thank you so much. We really appreciate it."

"It's no trouble. Do you mind if I take this one to Mom?"

"Not at all. Come." She waves me to follow along, so I do.

The assisted living facility seemed more like a home than a hospital, which was the best-selling point. The whole place was decorated in warm, soothing colors, and there were dozens of different activity rooms on the first floor managed by the staff and little nooks where patrons could just hang out.

Monica nods at another nurse we pass by as she pushes the door to the back garden. The moment I step outside, I spot Mom. She's sitting on the bench under a big tree, a blanket thrown over her lap.

I thank Monica before making my way to her.

"Hey, Mom," I whisper softly as I come closer, unsure of how she's going to react.

Mom turns to me, a smile flashing on her face. "Rebecca! What are you doing here?"

My heart hammers in my chest, that familiar ache filling my lungs. It's been a while since the last time she's been lucid. Since that day Miguel stayed over at our place, which was weeks ago. And at this point, I didn't even allow myself to wonder when she might be herself again. I accepted that she was gone.

I think this was the cruelest disease of them all.

Having your loved one close, but at the same time, not having them at all.

Some of that weight that's been sitting on my chest falls away, making it easier to breathe. I slide on the seat next to her and lift the bag I've been holding. "I came to visit, and I'm bringing goodies. I've been working on some fall cupcakes. Wanna try?"

"You know it." She puts away her knitting material and grabs the box, opening it. "These look delicious."

"The biscuit is plain chocolate, but I did the cream with pumpkin spice and cinnamon."

Mom takes a small bite and nods. "They taste really good. How are things at home?"

"Good. Chase is still going to PT, and even Matthew called the other day. He's back in college now. I'm trying to convince him to get his ass home for Thanksgiving, but we'll see if that happens."

"Is Miguel coming for Thanksgiving?"

I blink, unsure of where she's going with this. "Miguel?"

"Yes, Miguel." She gives me a pointed look. "He was here..." Her brows pull together as she tries to place the moment and when it happened, but she couldn't do that. "A while ago, no?"

I let out a nervous breath. I never knew how she would react. In most cases like this one, she'd start to lose herself if she was hyper-focused on things that she couldn't remember. It was like her brain was pulling her back to the cocoon of information that she knew.

"Yeah, he was in Bluebonnet for Kate and Emmett's wedding a few weeks ago, but he left," I remind her gently. "He's in Austin now, playing football for the Lonestars."

Because you told him to go, that little nagging voice whispers. *He wanted to stay.*

But I couldn't let him stay. I couldn't let him give up his dream because of me. Eventually, he'd come to hate me. It was better this way. He could live his dreams without me and my problems getting in his way.

Mom shakes her head. "That boy, he always loved the game the most."

See? Even Mom remembered it. If she could remember it despite her Alzheimer's, it meant that I did the right thing.

Then why did I feel like I wanted to throw up every time he popped into my mind?

And it happened often.

Something would happen that I'd like to share with him, or I'd try making a new dessert, and I'd want him to try it out, but then reality would hit me.

He's gone.

You made him walk away.

"He does," I whisper absentmindedly.

"He loves you too, you know that, right?"

Don't say what, Rebecca? That I'm falling in love with you all over again? That I've been in love with you for as long as I can remember? That I can't imagine my life without you?

"I do, but sometimes love isn't enough."

"Love is *always* enough. But that doesn't mean it's easy. Or that it doesn't require any effort." She gives me a pointed look. "On both your sides. And I've seen you two since you were children. You love that man, Rebecca. You've loved him your whole life. I don't know what happened between you two, but I can see that you're hurting. I would hate for you to wake up one day and realize you've wasted all this time, and for what?" She places her hand on my knee, giving it a soft squeeze. "Don't waste the time you have with the person you love above all else on silly things, baby girl. I know what I'm telling you."

The knot in my throat tightens, and my mouth goes dry.

She looks toward the fountain, her expression going distant. "The man I loved was taken away too soon from me, and there isn't a day I don't wish we could have had more time. There hasn't been a day since he has gone that I wished I didn't have one more minute with him, hell, one more second in which he holds me close."

I lean my head on her shoulder. "I know, Mom."

That was the only saving grace in our situation I could find.

At least, Mom got to be stuck in a happy place. Before Dad died. When they were happy and in love. She forgot the accident and all the bad things after it, but she had him. She had her memories and the love they shared.

Mom skims her fingers through my hair like she used to do when I was a little girl. "Don't waste your time on things that don't matter, which, as you'll learn soon enough, are many, and just love him. Embrace every moment you have together like it might be your last. Don't hold back, Rebecca. Don't let the fear of losing the people you love stop you from living your life fully. I know everything that has happened with your dad and me made you close off and guard your heart more fiercely, but it's okay to let people in. It's okay to let people love you because you're so lovable."

"I love you too, Mom. I missed you."

"I love you too, Bug."

We stay like that, my head on her shoulder, her hand gently stroking my hair as we sit out in the garden watching the fountain, for I don't even know how long.

After a while, I wipe away my cheeks and get up, only to see the confusion on Mom's face.

Once again, she's gone.

"Gigi, are you okay? Why are you crying?"

I force out a reassuring smile, slipping back into my role. "I'm fine. How about we get you inside? It's getting late."

Mom nods. "Yes, I'm feeling tired."

Slipping my hand under her skinny arm, I help her to her feet and into the house. "Where is Jackson? When will he be home?"

"He's working late. He'll be home soon. He said you shouldn't wait for him."

"That man." She shakes her head. "Always working too hard."

After I help her into her room and say goodbye to the nurses, I get back into my car and drive to Bluebonnet. The facility was situated about an hour away from our small town, just at the halfway point between Bluebonnet and Austin.

Austin, where Miguel lives now.

And here I was, thinking about him again.

Don't let the fear of losing the people you love stop you from living your life fully.

My fingers curl around the steering wheel.

Was Mom right? Was everybody right? Did I let the fear of losing the people I care about stop me from living fully? From loving them fully?

After high school, Mom started to get worse, and then everybody left. And while sure, I stayed in contact with Emmett and Kate, sometimes we'd go weeks without talking. Then there was Miguel. We put as much effort into staying in contact as we could. But he was so freaking far away, playing football and going to parties while I was home. And then *she* happened. I was already growing insecure by that point, and seeing that girl in his room only messed me up more, so I walked away. Breaking up with him before he could realize I wasn't worth the effort and he could have any girl he wanted. Before he could break up with me. Before he could hurt me. Before he could *leave* me.

Like my Dad left.

Like Chase left.

Like Mom left.

So I pushed Miguel away first.

I don't know how I managed to get back to Bluebonnet in one piece, but I did. Only instead of going back home, I go to Reading Nook. Jessica was covering for me, but she had a class to get to, so I needed to be in the café.

My brain is still processing everything as I work.

Thankfully, the café is relatively quiet, which works just fine with my mood.

I'm slowly preparing to close for the day when the bell chimes, and Nico enters still wearing his police uniform.

"Hey, stranger." He flashes me a smile as he moves to the counter.

"Hey, just done with work?"

Nico shakes his head. "I wish. I'm about to go in for the night shift, so I came to get some fuel first."

Grabbing a to-go cup, I put it under the coffee machine and start it. "We can't have our law-and-order officers going around without coffee all night long."

Nico chuckles, "Definitely not. So what's up with you? We haven't seen each other since the party at Santiago's."

"Haven't we?"

I knew that he couldn't come to the wedding because he had to work the next day, but he must have come to the shop.

"Nope. Jessica is usually the one here when I come. If I didn't know better, I'd think you're avoiding me."

"No, of course not. I've just been really busy with everything, and Mom's been getting worse. We decided to put her in an assisted living facility, so I needed to get all the paperwork in order, and pack her things."

The coffee machine beeps so I grab his cup, placing a lid on it before I put it on the counter.

Nico places his hand on mine, giving me a soft squeeze. "I'm so sorry, Becky."

"Me too. Today was a good day, though, so I got to chat a little bit with her."

Don't hold back, Rebecca. Don't let the fear of losing the people you love stop you from living your life fully.

"Hey..." Nico lifts his hand, cupping my face. "Are you ok—"

His thumb skims over my cheek as his worried eyes meet mine.

"I..." I pull back instantly, my heart galloping against my ribcage. "I'm sorry, Nico. I..."

His hand falls, and Nico just stares at me for a moment before a sad smile spreads over his face. "You're still in love with him."

"I am," I admit softly.

I don't think I ever stopped loving him to begin with.

My throat bobs as I swallow. "I really am sorry, Nico."

Nico shakes his head. "Don't be. Deep down I knew that, but I had hoped." Another shake. "It doesn't even matter."

Taking a step back, he pulls out his wallet and places a five on the counter. "For coffee."

He starts to turn around.

"I know you probably don't want to hear this..." He stops just shy of the door, his back stiff. My tongue darts out. "I really do appreciate your friendship, Nico. I always have."

The silence stretches between us for so long I think he'll leave without saying anything, but then he surprises me by glancing over his shoulder. "Go to him, Becky."

"W-what?"

"Go to him. He's been playing like shit, and we both know that when he plays like shit, there is only one reason for it. You. There was nothing that could ever unnerve that man quite like you could."

I let out a strangled sound. "Was that supposed to be a compliment?"

"Go to him."

With that, he walks out of the café, the door closing softly behind him. I lean against the counter, my fingers curling around the hardwood as I let out a shaky breath.

Could I actually do it?

Could I go to him and ask him to give us a chance?

What would happen if we didn't succeed?

But what if we did?

Just the thought has my heart racing.

Grazing my teeth against my lower lip, I force myself to uncurl my fingers. I brush them against the side of my leg before pulling out my phone and dialing a familiar number. The beeping seems to go on for hours before the call finally connects.

"I need your help."

CHAPTER

39

"Fucking hell," I yell as the whistle blows.

The opposing team just moved an additional twenty yards before Walker managed to bring him down. Meaning if something didn't change and quickly, they would score another touchdown, which would give them a healthy advantage over us, and the clock was running out.

"What's wrong, Fernandez?" Gregory flashes me his teeth, menace shining in his eyes. "Sucks to be eating grass all night long, doesn't it?"

"Fu—"

Walker bumps my shoulder with his, pushing me away. "Ignore him. He's just trying to rile you up."

I knew that, but I hated myself more for giving him a reason to do it.

This whole game was a shitshow, and I couldn't stop thinking it was my fault. My head wasn't in the game like it should be, and my teammates were depending on me to deliver.

As if he can read my mind, Blake grabs the back of my neck, bringing us closer. "Get your head in the game. Right now, nothing else matters, just you and stopping those guys on the other side of the line with whatever means necessary. Got it?"

I nod, gritting my teeth.

"Good," Walker mutters, slapping me on the back of the head before we get to our positions.

I look toward the stands at the mass of people. Usually, I avoided glancing at the crowd, but tonight, my parents were in the stands along with Emmett and Kate.

So much for showing them this was the right career choice for me.

My eyes take in the family section out in the stands until they land on the familiar faces. They're standing on their feet like the rest of the stadium, waiting to see how this game was going to unfold.

If we can intercept the ball and run it into the end zone, the game will be tied, which would leave more than enough time for our offense to score a winning touchdown.

I'm about to look away when a flash of red catches my attention.

What...

My heart is beating a mile a minute as my brain tries to process what I just saw, and before I can do a double-take, Big J pushes me from behind.

I get in my position, bending forward. Stupid Gregory is muttering something, but I can't hear it from the buzzing in my ears.

It couldn't be her.

Seriously, how long will I let this go on? Now I was starting to see her in the freaking stands between sixty thousand fans, which was crazy. What would she be doing here when she was the one who told me to leave?

Walker was right. It was time to stop this shit and get my life in order. One thing at a time.

Win this fucking game.

And then, go back to Bluebonnet and get Rebecca back.

So, what if she told me to go away without saying goodbye? What if she ignored my texts? She won't be able to avoid me once I'm knocking on her door.

I should have told her to go to hell and make her listen. Convince her to be with me so we could find a way to make this work. No, it wouldn't be easy, and we both had a lot of shit going on, but we could make it work. I knew we could. For *her*, I'd find a way to make it work.

Because having Rebecca in any way, shape, or form was better than not having her in my life.

I didn't realize how much I missed her that first time around. Maybe it was the way we ended things then. I don't know. But what I do know is that I fucking miss her. And when I don't see her or talk to her, it's like I can't breathe.

I was done with this bullshit.

As soon as I'm done here, I'll get in my car and go back home to talk some sense into her.

Home.

Because to me, there was only one home, and that was Rebecca Allison Williams.

She was my home. My safe haven. Mine.

The quarterback calls the play, snapping me out of my thoughts. Gregory moves past me, and I curse under my breath as I run after him. The wide receiver catches the ball on my left, but Big J is on his heels, and more of my teammates follow suit. The guy looks around for an opening, but he must sense Big J coming. He throws the ball at the very last second before Big J takes him down.

My heart stops as I watch the ball fly through the air, almost in slow motion. Since the guy was in the hurry, the throw lacked force. I start running toward the ball, jumping to catch it before anybody else. My feet touch the ground, and I start sprinting toward the end zone, the ball tightly clutched to my chest.

No slowing down.

No looking back.

No wavering.

The cheers spread through the crowd as I run into the end zone, and my teammates come rushing toward me.

"That's what I was talking about," Walker says as we bump our fists together.

We take a moment to celebrate the touchdown before the offense takes the field. Time seems to slow down as they play, conquering yard by yard in a synchronized dance we've been working on until the ball finally lands in the end zone. One field goal later, and Lonestars had another win under their belt.

The whole team gets out on the field to celebrate and shake hands with our opponents before going back toward the locker room. My mind already coming up with a plan on how to get to Bluebonnet as soon as possible.

"Fernandez!" Coach barks, stopping me in my tracks.

Shit.

Slowly, I turn around to face the older man. "Yes, Coach?"

"Field interview."

Shit.

I so didn't need to deal with this shit on top of everything else, but I knew better than to object.

"Yes, Coach."

I move toward the press box by the sidelines, and one reporter spots me immediately.

"Fernandez, can we have a word?" the guy asks eagerly. I've seen him a few times before, even did an interview with him last season. So I nod, ready to get this over with.

"Sure thing."

The guy gives a signal to his cameraman before plastering on a big-ass smile as he rants his introduction before shifting his attention to me.

"We have Miguel Fernandez here with us tonight. Congrats on your win. It was an intense game. How are you feeling?"

"Like you said, it was an intense game. Rams are a good team, but we had more luck tonight."

"That you did. Although, you were responsible for that game-tying touchdown, I couldn't help but notice that your game has been off lately. Does this have anything to do with your injury from the end of last season?"

Fuck.

I guess I shouldn't be surprised he asked that, but I didn't want anybody to question if I was healthy or not.

"No, my injury has healed completely. The beginning of the season is always hectic as everybody tries to find their footing. That being said, I'm more determined than ever to work hard and make this season even better than the last one."

"That touchdown was definitely a good start. We're looking forward to seeing more of you as the season progresses."

The guy wraps the interview, and we shake hands.

I turn around, ready to find my escape when, for the second time tonight, I spot a flash of red. The hair at my nape prickles at attention as an invisible force makes me stop in my tracks. A couple of players walk toward the tunnel, and that's when I see her.

Rebecca's eyes widen when she spots me, and she comes to an abrupt stop. Her hair is a wild mess from running, her chest rises and falls rapidly as she sucks in big gulps of air.

I blink a few times, thinking I'm imagining it, but no.

She's here.

In Austin.

At the stadium.

On the freaking football field.

Dressed in Lonestars' jersey.

My Lonestars' jersey.

"Rebecca, what..."

She lets out a long breath as she closes the distance between us, a determined look crossing her face.

"I love you too," she says loud enough for the people around us to hear it. Somebody whistles, but she ignores them, her complete attention on me. "I'm so sorry that I let you walk away without saying those words back to you, Miguel. I'm so sorry that I told you to leave, period. I tried to convince myself it would be easier for me to push you away because then, you were leaving on my terms, and I wouldn't have to wonder when and how it would happen.

"I wouldn't leave you."

She shakes her head. "Everybody I love leaves, Miguel. Everybody I love is taken away from me, and there is always that fear inside of me that you'd leave too. Then, I'd be left more broken than I already was, and I couldn't take that. So I pushed you away. I thought I could go back to my life like it used to be, but since you left, I realized that it's an empty life, and I hate it. I hate that I can't call you and talk to you. I hate that I won't get a chance to kiss you or wake by your side. I miss you. I miss my best friend. I miss my lover. When you walked away, you took a part of me, and I feel hollow without you by my side. So I came to ask you to forgive me and give us another chance. I came to ask you to stay."

I just stare at her for a while. Her throat bobs as she swallows, her fingers clenching and unclenching by her side with nerves.

God, she looked beautiful.

And mine.

"Good."

Rebecca blinks, uncertainty flashing on her face. "Good?"

"Yeah, good."

Without missing a beat, I take a step closer and grab her face between my palms, pressing my mouth against hers. The kiss is hard. I can hear her sharp intake of breath as my mouth crashes against hers in a long kiss. I gently nibble at her lower lip, my hand sliding to the small of her back and pulling her closer to me.

If my pads are digging into her, she doesn't protest. Her arms slip around my neck as her tongue meets mine, making me groan softly.

Hoots and hollers break through the haze that's Rebecca, reminding me we're still on the field and there are people all around us.

With one gentle swipe of my mouth over hers, I pull back breaking the kiss.

"Shut up, assholes," I yell, not removing my eyes from Rebecca, which only makes them laugh harder.

Those gorgeous hazel eyes flutter open, an almost dazed look on her face as she watches me.

I slide my thumb over her puffy lower lip, wishing we were alone so I could devour her body entirely and remind her of how good we're together.

"You saved me the trip because I was on my way to get you."

"You..." Her brows pull together. "What?"

"Exactly what I said, Red. I just made a plan to win this stupid game so I could sit in the car, get to you and force you to listen to me by whichever means necessary."

Her brows shoot up, that snarky side of hers coming out in full force. "Force me by whichever means necessary?"

"We both know how stubborn you can be. You can't deny it."

She looks away, tucking a strand of her hair behind her ear. "I don't know what you're talking about."

My fingers slide to her jaw, turning her toward me. "Your stubbornness is one of the things I love the most about you, no matter how crazy it sometimes makes me."

"You were really planning to come?"

"Yes. I don't want to have any regrets, Rebecca. I don't want to wake up another day and think about might-have-beens and should-have-beens. I want you. I *love* you. I loved you when we were sixteen-year-old teenagers. I loved you when we broke up at nineteen, and I still love you to this day. I will always love you. I told you at our friend's wedding that it should have been us, but the truth is, it can still be us. We can still get our happily ever after. It won't be easy, but I know that we can make it work. I *want* to make this work because I don't think I can live in a world in which you're not by my side. If that means making sacrifices, so be it. I was never afraid of hard work, and I'm not going to start to be afraid now. You're worth it. *We*'re worth it."

"We're worth it," she echoes. "I'm sorry it took me so long to admit that."

"It doesn't matter. I'd wait forever if that's what it took. That's how much I love you, Rebecca."

"I love you too." Her fingers tighten in my hair, eyes dropping to my mouth.

Screw everybody.

I lean down, ready to kiss her again.

"See? I told you they made up." I look up at the sound of Dad's voice to see him walking hand in hand with Mom, Emmett a few steps behind. "It was about damn time they did, too."

"Fuck," I press my forehead against hers. "So much for that."

Rebecca chuckles softly. "It's fine, later."

"We getting out of here?" Emmett smirks. "I think you owe us a dinner to celebrate your double win, Fernandez."

I kiss the top of her head. "I'll hold you to that, Red. Now, let's go celebrate."

EPILOGUE

MIGUEL

Thanksgiving

"And that's a wrap! Lonestars have won against the Patriots 28 to 14, continuing their winning streak."

Slapping my teammates on the back, I walk around the field until I spot the person I've been looking for.

"Good game, Watson."

Hayden looks up, taking the hand I offered him and pulling him to his feet. "It was a good game, Fernandez. Congrats."

Somebody calls his name, so he looks over his shoulder. "I'll catch you later?"

"Sounds good."

With a fist bump, we go in different directions. I continue walking through the field, my eyes scanning the crowd of athletes, faculty members, coaches, reporters, and family members until I finally spot the person I've been looking for.

The moment Rebecca sees me, a beaming smile appears on her face, and she starts to run toward me. I open my arms, and she jumps into my embrace just like she did when we were teenagers.

"Great game, babe," she whispers into my ear as I hold her to me.

"Thanks." I press my mouth against the hollow of her neck. "It was a good game. No Emmett?"

Emmett said he'd try to make it to the game today, considering one of his college teammates was playing against us.

"He and Callie left to see Hayden. And then they're going to Santiago's to celebrate Thanksgiving."

"See, Fernandez, that's how it's done," Big J joins us, extending his fist to Rebecca. "Hey there, Red. Good to see you again. You keeping our boy in line?"

Rebecca connects her fist to his. "You know it."

I narrow my eyes at him. My teammates loved Rebecca, and they had no problem showing it. Or maybe it was the fact that they knew how it irritated me to no end. "I don't see why you're complaining since you're coming to my place today."

Big J scoffs. "I basically had to invite myself after overhearing you and Walker talk about it."

"Then don't come." I shrug.

"Hell, no. Did you try your mom's cooking? That shit is *good*. I'm not passing up on that."

"You're giving me a headache, man." I shake my head and place Rebecca on her feet. "I'm going to take a shower and grab my stuff. Meet you out in twenty?"

"Sounds good."

With a quick kiss to her lips, I disappear down the tunnel and into the locker room.

Since it's Thanksgiving, and we won, Coach doesn't keep us there long. After a quick shower and making sure Walker, Big J, and suddenly Franco, too, know how to get to Bluebonnet, I wave them goodbye and meet Rebecca, who's waiting for me.

"Ready to go?"

"You know it."

"I'm so sorry, Rebecca." Monica, one of Mrs. Williams' nurses, gives her a sad smile.

I slip my hand around her waist, pulling her closer to me as she shakes her head. "It's fine. We all knew it was the most likely outcome."

She put on a brave face, but I could see that this was hurting her, and I hated it. I hated there was nothing I could do to take away her pain.

Although her mom's been living in Helping Hands for the last few months, Rebecca's been talking about bringing her home for Thanksgiving. She was so excited about it. It was the only thing she talked about. And now this.

"Would you like to go in and say hi?" Monica offers.

"I..." Rebecca bites the inside of her cheek.

"We can go visit with her for a little while if you want," I offer, rubbing the small of her back.

Rebecca shakes her head. "Better not. Last time, she got really upset. I don't want that to happen again."

"That's completely fine. Would you like me to give you a call if she has a good day?"

"Please do."

"Okay, no problem."

"Thank you, Monica. Happy Thanksgiving."

With a goodbye, we head out of the building and walk to the car.

Rebecca is quiet the rest of the drive home, her gaze fixed out the window. My eyes keep darting to her every now and again. There was nothing worse than seeing her sad like this, knowing there was nothing I could do to help her.

Her mom was getting progressively worse and fast. There was only one occasion when she remembered Rebecca, but for the most part, she thought she was talking to her sister Gigi. Rebecca still visited her at least once a week, although, I could see the toll each visit took, since the two women didn't have the best relationship. Not that Rebecca ever complained.

I pull into the driveway, noticing a few familiar cars. Turning off the engine, I shift my attention to Rebecca. "You okay?"

She nods, her palm covering my hand resting on her thigh. "I will be."

With a squeeze, I pull back and get out, walking around the car to open her door. Hand in hand, we make our way into the house, the cacophony of noises assaulting us immediately.

Mom's head peeks through the kitchen doorway. "There you are! We were starting to get worried." Her gaze shifts to Rebecca, and then over our shoulders. I see the moment realization sets in. She knew we were supposed to bring Rebecca's mom for a visit. Thankfully, she collects herself quickly. "Your teammates are here, Miguel. They're all in the living room. You mind giving me a hand, Rebecca?"

"Not at all."

Rebecca starts to pull her hand out of my hold, but I tighten my grip. "I can help too, if you want."

I wanted to be there in case she needed me.

Rebecca gives me a small smile. "I'll be fine." Lifting on the tips of her toes, she presses her mouth against mine. "Go."

I want to protest, but I know better than to do that.

"Okay. If you need something, yell." I kiss her cheek. "I love you, Red."

"Love you too."

With one last look in their direction, I slip out of the kitchen and walk down the hallway, following the sound of voices when I spot my brother pacing in the dining room all alone. His phone is plastered to his ear, a grim expression on his face.

"Fucking hell, Cheryl, pick up."

Cheryl?

Aaron curses under his breath. He pulls the phone away from his face and hangs up, only to dial her immediately again.

"Is everything okay?" I ask, stepping into the room.

Aaron turns around abruptly to face me. "Oh, it's you."

He looks like crap. A few days' worth of stubble covers his jaw, his hair is a mess from all the times he's ran his hand through it, and there are dark bags under his eyes. He looks like he's aged ten years since the last time I saw him, which was barely a couple of weeks ago.

"We just got here." I tip my chin in his direction. "What's up?"

Aaron shakes his head. "It doesn't matter."

"It clearly does matter. You look like shit, and you're clearly upset. What's going on?"

"She left."

My brows pull together. "She left?"

"Yes." Aaron rakes his fingers through his hair, letting his hand drop by his side. "Cheryl left me."

REBECCA

Helping Mrs. Fernandez prepare the Thanksgiving dinner was exactly what I needed. Cooking was simple. I knew how to do it, and it required all of my focus, which gave me the excuse to push the pain and disappointment at not being able to spend the holiday with my mom at bay.

At least for the time being.

Miguel's teammates were nice. They told us stories of Miguel with the team and made jokes the whole evening as we finished dinner. Then everybody helped clear out the table before they went back to the living room to watch the football game.

Like seriously, not only did they *play* in a football game, but they had to watch it too.

Arms slip around my waist, and I'm pulled into a firm chest as Miguel leans his head against my shoulder, his lips pressing against the side of my neck. He hums quietly, his chest rumbling in pleasure, as his hold on me tightens. "Let's go out."

I look over his shoulder. "Now?"

"Yes, now. C'mon, Red. We don't have much time."

He was right about that one. He has to be back in Austin tomorrow morning for practice, and after that, the team was going on the road, so we wouldn't be able to see each other until they came back.

Wiping my palms, I put the towel on the counter. "Okay, let's go."

Miguel slides his arms over my stomach and to my hips before he takes my hand, our fingers interlocking as he pulls me toward the back door.

"Where are the guys?" I ask once we get out.

"They left a little while ago."

I nod my head. "Blake's kids are nice. Levi and Gage seemed to be having a good time."

"That's good. Blake's been adamant that he's retiring after this year, and he's been asking about the housing situation and schools and whatnot."

"Blake is planning to move here?" My brows shoot up as Miguel leads me through the trees. "As in, to Bluebonnet?"

Miguel shrugs. "That's what he's talking about. He thinks the boys need a fresh start after everything that had happened with their mother."

I look up to find him scowling.

"What's up with that look?"

Miguel shakes his head. "I'll tell you later. Now, I want to focus on us."

We walk the rest of the way until he comes to a stop in front of the treehouse. "C'mon, Red. Climb up."

I look over my shoulder as I grab the stairs. "You just want to look at my ass."

Miguel flashes me a grin. "It's one sweet ass."

Laughing, I start climbing until I spot a light peeking from the inside. "What the..."

I climb the rest of the way, and sure enough, the blankets are spread over the floor, a bottle of wine and two glasses sitting in the corner, and twinkling lights blink happily from the walls.

"What is all of this?" I ask as Miguel joins me.

"A surprise."

"When did you have time to do all of this?"

For all I knew, he didn't leave the house since we got here.

The corner of his mouth twitches upward. "I might have had a little help. I wanted to recreate the last time we were here. Give this place a happy memory."

"Miguel..."

He cups my face, his thumb skimming over my cheekbone. "You know how much I love you, right?"

"I do." I nod, placing my hand over his. "And I love you, too."

"These last few months have been amazing, and I've only fallen more in love with the woman you've become. I admire your strength and resilience and the way you love the people in your life with your whole heart. The more time we spend together, the more I wonder how the fuck did I manage to survive these past three years without you, and I know with certainty that I never want that to happen again."

"What are you..."

His finger slides to my mouth, effectively shushing me. "I can't imagine my life without you in it. I don't want to live a life in which you're not a part of."

Holy shit, he's go—

"Rebecca Allison Williams, will you spend the rest of our lives together as my wife?"

My mouth falls open as he pulls out a ring box from his pocket and opens it. The most beautiful princess-cut ring I've ever seen shining under the twinkling lights.

Tears prickle my eyelids, making my vision turn blurry.

"I..." Shaking my head, I jump at him. "Yes!"

We stumble back, falling into the blankets. Miguel lets out a laugh as I land on top of him. He flips us over in one easy movement, his body hovering over mine.

"You sure?"

"Yes."

"There will be no takebacks."

"I don't want any. I just want you."

"You're all that I need."

He takes my hand in his, picking up the ring.

"This is our time, baby." The ring slips into place, a perfect fit. "Our chance at a happily ever after until death do us part. No more secrets, no more running, just you and me."

I was ready for it, so damn ready.

"I wouldn't have it any other way."

BONUS EPILOGUE

MIGUEL

"Boys," Coach claps his hands, the sound echoing in the locker room. "If I can have a moment."

My teammates quiet down, all heads turning toward the man who had led us through the wins and the losses this past season all the way to this moment right here, right now.

The Super Bowl.

I was playing in the freaking Super Bowl.

It was mind-blowing to even think about it.

And yet, it was happening.

"This past year has been long and hard. We've had our fair share of losses." He glances toward Mike, our wide receiver, who's sitting on the bench, a brace adorning his leg. He tore his ACL mid-season, which was our biggest hit, and he was still recovering. But one of the rookies managed to step in, and after a few shaky games and a lot of work with the offense team and our quarterback, he finally found his footing. "But despite it all, you rose to the challenge of this game and managed to get to the end. Whatever happens out there tonight, I want you to know how proud I am of you all."

"That's all nice and well, but how about we go out there and give our best to kick some ass?" Big J asks, cracking his knuckles.

A few people nodded their agreement, and I could see determination written all over my teammates' faces. The same persistence that's been boiling slowly in my own veins the further the Lonestars progressed in the playoffs. Nobody wanted to say it out loud so as not to jinx us, but I don't think there was one player on our team who secretly didn't wish for exactly this.

A chance to play at the Super Bowl.

Not just that, but to lift that Lombardi Trophy up in the air and join the group of the greatest players of all time.

"Who are we?" Big J yells, jumping on the bench in the middle of the room.

"Lonestars!"

"I didn't hear you! Who are we?!"

"Lonestars!"

"That's damn right! Now let's get out there and show them what we're made of."

He jumps down, slapping people on the heads and shoulders as he makes his way out of the room, the rest of our teammates falling in line with him.

"You ready for this, old man?" I glance at Walker.

There is a distant look on his face as he rubs at his beard.

His gaze meets mine, and I know exactly what he's thinking. In all the years that he's been playing, not once did he win a Super Bowl. There were a few times he got close, only for it to slip through his fingers.

And this, right here, was his last chance.

The final play.

He hasn't said anything to our teammates yet, but he was planning to announce his retirement as soon as the season wrapped up, but we were far from done yet.

He wanted this.

Badly.

"I was born ready."

And so was I.

I extend my hand, and we bump our fists together. "Let's go kick some asses then."

Once we get out on the field, my eyes scan the crowd, but it's too damn busy to find any familiar faces. They were there, though. Rebecca, Emmett, Kate, my parents, hell, even Aaron decided to come with Gage. They were all there to cheer us on. Losing today isn't an option, but I knew, based on the first half, that they'd make us work hard for it.

The whistle blows, and the offense takes their position on the field. I'm pacing on the sideline, my gaze locked on the field as I anxiously wait for my turn. Each play seems to last forever. It's like time is moving in slow motion as both teams do their best to win.

If I was sitting at home watching the game, this would be the perfect, gets you sitting on the edge of your seat kind of game I'd love to watch.

"We need a break," I mutter to Walker as we run on the field after our offense scored a touchdown, evening the score once again.

It's the last quarter, with not even five minutes on the clock, and my muscles were starting to feel like jelly.

The Bears get past our defenses and manage to get twenty yards for the first down.

I curse under my breath as I get on the line and try to get back that focus, but my body is screaming at me to slow down, my muscles burning with exhaustion. The sweat is dripping down my face and into my eyes, blurring my vision.

The Bears call out the play, and I blink to clear my eyesight, my narrowed gaze on the guy across from me, determined not to let anybody through.

The quarterback throws the ball toward the wide receiver, and it takes everybody a moment to realize it's a fake toss. Instead, the running back is moving toward the end zone. I run after him, Big J on my other side a second later. The guy looks around as we corner him and throws the ball as we tackle him to the ground.

Cursing, I look up, only it's not the other team that got the ball.

It's Walker.

And he's making a run for it.

Our teammates quickly rearranged, making sure to keep a path open for him. But there is no need. The Bears are even more surprised by the turn of events than we are. The Bear's tackle dives toward Walker, trying to bring him to the ground, but he jumps over him and continues sprinting. And then he's in the end zone, and all hell breaks loose.

We rush toward him, jumping onto him to celebrate. For the first time tonight, Lonestars are in the lead.

Walker's touchdown is exactly what we needed because our offensive line decimates them. They run the plays we've practiced seamlessly, winning yards until our tight end catches the ball in the end zone.

One field goal later, and the game is over.

And Lonestars are the freaking Super Bowl champions.

"Holy shit." I run my hands through my sweaty hair, looking around the field as I try to take it all in.

My teammates and coaches are high-fiving and hugging each other with big grins on their faces. The confetti flies all around us. The fans are cheering. Family and friends running onto the field.

A hand grabs my shoulder, and I'm tugged back. "We did it,

man," Walker yells into my ear. His hands grip my shoulders, giving me a shake. "We fucking did it."

"We did."

"Super Bowl champions."

A smile slowly works its way to my lips. I shake my head, still unable to wrap my mind around it.

"Super-fucking-Bowl champions, baby!" Big J shouts as he jumps at us, bringing our heads together. "We did it, you assholes."

More teammates join us in a group hug. The champagne bottle pops open, and before we know it, we're covered in sweet liquid.

"Fuck." I wipe at my eyes with the back of my hand, laughing as Alvarez, one of our kickers, runs away spraying more people. I turn around, my arms falling open as I spot a flash of red. Rebecca comes rushing toward me and jumps into my awaiting arms, not caring one bit that I'm a sweaty, dirty, and wet mess. Her legs wrap around my middle as I lift her in the air.

"You did it!" Her hands cup my scruffy cheeks as she beams at me. "You won."

"We fucking di—"

Her mouth crashes onto mine as she kisses me deeply. I tighten my hold on her, nipping gently at her lower lip. She lets out a soft moan as my tongue meets hers, sucking and swirling together, and I can feel myself growing hard.

My teammates hoot and holler from the side, a loud whistle piercing the air.

We break the kiss, and Rebecca's eyes meet mine. Her breathing is heavy; her pupils are dilated as she just stares at me. That fire that's brewing inside of me matches the one in her eyes.

Her tongue darts out. She slides her palm to my chin, her

thumb swiping over my lower lip. "I'm so freaking proud of you, Miguel. You deserve this."

My heart swells with emotions. All my life, I was fighting for this moment, and now it's finally here.

"Thank you. I'm glad I get to share it with you, Red. This all is great, but it wouldn't be the same if you weren't here with me."

She shakes her head. "Miguel..."

"No, Rebecca. It's the truth. Thank you for standing by my side. Not just these past few months but before. If it weren't for you, I wouldn't have been the person I am today."

"Always."

I lift her hand and press my mouth against her knuckles, where her engagement ring is sitting on her finger. "Forever."

REBECCA

Soft tickling wakes me up from sleep. I slowly blink my eyes open to find Miguel's dark gaze watching me, a sleepy expression on his face as his finger traces over my skin.

"Morning," I whisper softly, stretching my stiff muscles.

The last couple of days have been crazy. First, Miguel spent hours wrapping up at the stadium with the winner ceremony, taking photos, doing interviews, and God only knows what else. Then, they flew back home, where the city of Austin prepared a parade to celebrate the team winning the Super Bowl. It was amazing to watch it all, and I was so happy for Miguel and his teammates. I got to know them pretty well in the past few months that we've been navigating this whole long-distance relationship, and they've accepted me as one of their own. All of them worked their asses off this season, and they deserved that trophy.

"Morning."

"Sleep well?"

"So-so... Now that the high is waning a little, I think I'm finally wrapping my head around what just happened, but at the same time, I'm so ready for things to calm down. I can't wait to go back home and relax for a little while."

I snort. "Because you're so known for relaxing. I bet you'll be out and about on the ranch in the first forty-eight hours after we get there."

His hand slips around my waist, pulling me to him. "Not if you agree to relax with me. Think about it." He wiggles his brows. "You and me." His palm slips against mine, our fingers intertwining together. "In bed, so I get to slowly worship every inch of your body and make up for all the time we were away from one another."

A shudder goes through me at the intensity in his gaze, at the low, almost sultry tone of his voice that's going all the way to my core. I shift a little, his leg slipping between my thighs, his knee finding just the right spot. I suck a breath as I rub myself against him. His eyes darken as he watches me.

"Screw waiting until we're ho—"

He pulls me to him just as my phone starts buzzing on the nightstand.

"I should get this."

"It can wait."

I shake my head. "Miguel, it could be important!"

Groaning, he rolls to his back, running his palm over his face. He had yet to shave his beard, but you won't hear me complain too much.

Scooting up against the headboard, I grab the phone, noticing Kate's name on the screen. "Hey, what's up?"

"Finally! I've been texting you. Did you guys get on the road?"

"Nuh-uh. Not yet."

"What are you waiting for? It's already past noon!"

Shit, really?

I pull the phone away from my ear and check the time, and sure enough, she's right. It is past noon. "We'll get on the road," I promise. "I'll see you soon."

"Who was that?" Miguel asks, turning toward me.

The sheet slips down, revealing all that glorious golden skin and the most perfectly sculpted chest. My stomach tightens as I stare at him, my mouth going dry.

"Red?" Miguel lets out a low chuckle. "My eyes are up here."

I was so caught, but sue me. I missed him. I missed his touch.

"It was Kate. She wanted to know when we would be back."

Miguel's brow quirks. "Why?"

Shit.

"Umm... She invited us for late lunch, so we should probably get going."

"Seriously?" Miguel rolls to his back and lets out a groan. "We have the whole summer to hang out, and she wants to do it *today* of all days?"

"Yes, seriously. C'mon, people have missed you these past few weeks."

It's actually been months. The last time Miguel was in Bluebonnet was for Christmas, and even then, he managed to stay only a couple of days before he had to go back.

"Well, I missed *you*. And I planned to have my way with you all day long. Screw them, let's just stay in bed."

"As tempting as that sounds, we have to get on the road."

"Rebecca..." his low growl sends shivers running down my spine.

Leaning over him, I press my mouth against his. "I promise I'll make it worth it tonight."

"I'm keeping you to your word."

Blinking my eyes open, I notice the familiar landscape around me. My back protests as I turn around, my muscles stiff from sleeping in a seated position.

Miguel's dark eyes glance at me, amusement dancing in his irises, "Good morning, sleeping beauty."

"Don't tease," I mumble, rubbing at my face. "Why didn't you wake me up? I could have kept you company."

I didn't even realize I'd fallen asleep. Then again, these last few days, weeks, if I'm being completely honest, were crazy. I was running on fumes, and it's not even surprising that I'd crashed now that the football season was over and the post-Super Bowl events were winding down.

Well, almost.

"Because you seemed like you could use it. Did you get some rest?"

"A little." I roll my head from one side to the other, feeling the tense muscles. "I swear if I could, I'd sleep for days."

"I could get behind that. We should be home soon, so we can jump straight into bed." A frown appears between his brows. "Well, after that lunch with Santiagos."

I raise my brow at him. "Your home or my home?"

Considering he's been busy with football, and I've spent my time between Reading Nook, visiting Mom, and being in Austin every chance I got, looking for a place of our own did not meet the criteria of getting on our current to-do list.

"I told you to point to the house you want, and I'll buy it for you. Then we'd have *our* home to go back to now."

"I know, but it'll be your home, too. I want you to like it."

"Baby." His hand lands on my thigh, rubbing at my knee. "The only thing that I care about is that you're in it. You're my home."

A knot forms in my throat as the emotions swell inside me, making my eyes mist. I didn't know if it was overall tiredness or what, but I've been more emotional than usual.

"Hey, no crying. You know I hate to see you sad."

"Those are happy tears." Still, I brush them away. "We can start looking at houses soon."

"How soon? Today soon? While I don't mind going back and forth, I want to have you all for myself."

"How about as soon as tomorrow?"

"Fine, tomorrow," he agrees, turning on his blinker.

"Oh, we're going to town."

Miguel's gaze darts to me. "Didn't you say we're having lunch with the Santiagos?"

"We are. But in town. They wanted to celebrate, so we're going out to eat."

His brows pull together in confusion, but thankfully, he doesn't ask any more questions.

"Fine," he grumbles. "An hour. I mean it, Red. They have an hour of our time, and then we're going back home."

"Okay."

There is a beat of silence. "Why did you agree so easily? You never do that."

"That's not true."

"It so is. You always want to bicker with me. Sometimes, I think it's because the idea of the sex afterward turns you on."

"What?" My mouth falls open. "You're delusional."

"Mhmm... You can admit it. I know that's the reason I like to bicker with you. You get that look in your eyes and..." His voice trails off as he takes the turn onto Main Street, only to come to a stop. "What is this?"

I look out the window to find a whole crowd gathered on the side of the road with more people waiting on the main square. The cheering grows louder when they notice us, and people start waving banners.

Miguel Fernandez, our Super Bowl Champion!

Welcome home, #67!

You've made Bluebonnet proud, Miguel!

I turn my gaze to him, watching as he takes everything in. Different emotions play over his face: surprise, disbelief, and excitement.

"It's your homecoming."

Miguel turns to me, his eyes wide. "Did you organize this?"

I shake my head. "People wanted to do it. They've been hinting about it since the playoffs started, but once they knew you were playing in the Super Bowl, it was a done deal. Everybody gathered together to do this for you. All I had to do was make sure you came here."

"But... what if we lost?"

I let out a small chuckle. "It wouldn't have mattered to them. Win or lose, you're their champion, Miguel." I place my hand in his palm, giving it a soft squeeze. "Let's get out."

He nods, almost on autopilot and pulls the car into the open space in front of Reading Nook. Unbuckling my seatbelt, I turn around and grab my bag, pulling out his jersey and handing it to him.

He just raises his brow but pulls it over his head before getting out of the car. Grabbing my own jersey, I put it over my shirt before slipping outside, too.

Miguel is already surrounded by kids of different ages, all of them asking him for photos and autographs.

I join them, standing a few feet away as he does his thing. There is a genuine smile on his face as he chats with the little ones. That's one thing I noticed about him in the past few months since we got back together. It didn't matter where we were or what we did; if a kid managed to gather the courage to come and ask him for a photo or autograph, he would gladly do it.

When he's finally done, he straightens to his full height and turns toward me, his dark eyes taking me in. I can see desire and possessiveness flare in his irises as he stares at me.

All those years, and seeing me in his jersey still does it for him.

"Miguel!" Mr. Hathaway, the mayor of Bluebonnet, breaks us from our little bubble. "It's so nice to see you, young man." He extends his hand and shakes Miguel's. "In the name of Bluebonnet and the town council, we wanted to congratulate you on winning the Super Bowl. You did the whole town proud."

"Thank you, sir."

"Come, there are a lot of people who want to see you!"

Miguel takes my hand in his, and together, we make our way toward the town square and the stage—yup, they lifted a whole stage. I guess they weren't joking when they said they were going all out.

Mr. Hathaway climbs up to the stage first and introduces Miguel, and the crowd starts cheering loudly, chanting his name.

I want to stay behind, but Miguel doesn't allow me to do it, so I climb up the steps and face the residents of our little town. Emmett and Kate are standing on the side, my friend holding his little baby girl up in the air. She's dressed in the cutest Austin

Lonestars onesie Miguel got her recently. Miguel's family is also here, along with the Santiagos, all of them wearing matching proud expressions on their faces.

Mr. Hathaway gestures for Miguel to take the microphone. Reluctantly, he lets go of my hand and moves to the center of the stage.

"Well, this was a nice surprise."

Laughter spreads through the crowd, and some people start to cheer again.

"I mean it, you guys. It didn't even cross my mind that you would prepare all of this for me. Thank you so much. I really appreciate you all cheering for the Lonestars throughout the season. It hasn't been easy, which makes this victory that much sweeter." He glances toward me, and I give him an encouraging smile. "I also want to thank my family and this gorgeous woman standing next to me. They've kept me grounded through the good times and the bad ones, and I'm so grateful to have them in my corner." He extends his hand. My fingers slip into his palm, and he pulls me into him, his mouth brushing against the top of my head. "I love you, Red."

"Does this mean you're finally locking her down?" Mrs. Smith yells from the first row.

We pull apart and laughter spreads through the crowd.

"That's the plan, Mrs. S. That's the plan."

With a wave at the crowd and one more thank you, we get off the stage. Fans swarm Miguel instantly.

"I'm going to find our friends," I whisper into his ear before disappearing into the crowd.

I greet a few people as I make my way through the throng until I finally spot Emmett and Kate talking to some of our high school friends.

Kate sees me coming first. "There she is. How are you holding up?"

"Barely." I look over my shoulder, but I can't even see Miguel from all the people surrounding him. "I can't believe so many people showed up."

I expected a small crowd for sure. Football's been the only thing people talked about these past few weeks, but this was on a completely different level. There were probably two thousand people here, if not more.

"Oh, please. They just waited for a chance to do something like this. And when it's for one of their own?" She gives her head a shake. "There is nothing they wouldn't do."

That much was true.

Baby noises coming from the crook of Kate's arm draw my attention. I take a peek at the small bundle, a smile spreading over my lips. "I can't believe you brought Kaylee, too!"

"She wanted to cheer for her uncle." She lifts her in the air, pressing her nose against the baby's middle. Her face twists in disgust. "I think she got a little too excited."

Emmett glances down at us, "You want me to take her?"

Kate shakes her head. "We're good. I'll just go and change her real quick." She turns to me. "Mind if we go to Reading Nook?"

"Of course. Do you need me to grab you something?"

"That bag over there?"

"Sure thing." I pick up the diaper bag, and together, we move through the people toward the cafe.

"How was Austin?" Kate asks.

"Crazy. This whole experience was. And that's coming from me, who was basically standing on the sidelines as a support system. I can't imagine what Miguel must feel like. The coverage, the reporters, the fans..." I shake my head. "It's unlike anything I ever witnessed."

"I know! You guys ready for things to calm down?"

I pull the key out of my bag and unlock the front door,

flickering on the light. "Yeah, I don't know if it's this whole thing or what, but I'm so damn tired it's not even funny. It'll be nice to just chill and lay back a little."

Kate places the bag on one of the tables and shifts Kaylee from one hand to the other as she starts pulling things out. I take the changing mat placing it over the table. Kate lowers Kaylee down, and I stand next to her, grabbing one of her toys. It's some kind of circle thingy that chimes every time you move it. Her little head turns toward me, those impossibly dark blue eyes gazing at me.

"She's so cute." I press my finger gently against Kaylee's little nose. "Am I right? Who's the cutest baby of them all?"

My heart swells as she blinks her eyes, a goofy grin spreading over her lips. Yes, I know she's too small to actually smile, but ask me if I care. In my head, she's smiling at me.

I expected I'd feel more unsettled around her, given everything that had happened in the past. And while, yes, there has been a part of me, a teeny, tiny part that was jealous of Kate when she announced her pregnancy, that feeling was fleeting. My friend looked gorgeous, and I was happy for her and Emmett. And then, when Kaylee was born a couple of months before, and I got to hold her for the very first time, there was nothing but love for this little baby, and a little bit of sadness for me. For Miguel. For the life that we could have had but was taken from us.

"Seriously, how perfect can one baby be?"

"Don't you start too," Kate says as she expertly takes off her diaper and starts cleaning her. For such a small thing, she sure made a big mess. "Emmett is already talking about trying for another one. I swear to you, if I agreed to it, he'd want us to have a whole freaking football team, and he'd get right to it."

I let out a soft chuckle. "I'm not surprised. That man is obsessed with his daughter."

It was funny, seeing my big giant of a best friend carrying that little bundle in his arms like a football. I kid you not. If he could, he wouldn't let her out of his arms.

An almost giddy expression crosses her face. "He is." With a sigh, she shakes her head. "But that doesn't mean we need more kids. At least not right now. Hell, I was bleeding for three weeks straight, to the point I called my OB to check if everything was okay, which it thankfully was, but I only recently got the all-clear from my doctor last week. I'm not even feeling like me again just yet. Besides, we should enjoy this time with her while she's small. Maybe in a few years."

"There is that," I nod, my attention still on Kaylee as my mind goes over her words. A frown appears on my face. Kaylee was born just around the holidays, and I had my period a little before that. Did I have it since?

"Do you mind taking her?" Kate asks, breaking me out of my thoughts. "I need to use the restroom, and then I'll meet you outside."

"Of course. You go ahead. Just lock up once you're done."

"Sounds good." I grab the diaper bag as Kate hands me Kaylee.

The little girl snuggles her head into the crook of my arm. Her hat is askew, so I pull it down, making sure to cover her ears. A little bit of dark hair is peeking from underneath the pale yellow fabric.

"You're so lucky. All you have to worry about is when you'll get to eat and play. That's all."

But seriously, when was the last time I got my period?

I must have gotten it sometime in January. Maybe I just forgot? God knows my life's been a whirlwind lately.

I drop my hand, pressing it against my belly. I can feel the nerves making my stomach clench.

"I'm just imagining things," I mutter to myself. Kaylee

makes baby noises, drawing my attention. "Right, Kaylee? It's all just in my head. There is no way I could be pre—"

"There you are. I've been looking for you."

I glance up at the sound of Miguel's voice. He's walking toward me, those dark eyes taking in the baby before they meet mine, and I swear I could combust from the heated look in his gaze.

"You look so fucking sexy right now," Miguel whispers as he frames my face.

I lean into his touch. "Oh yeah? You're probably confusing me with this little beauty."

"Hell, no. It's you holding this baby. It does things to me, Red. So many things."

A knot forms in my throat at his words and the look in his eyes.

"I can see us just like this in a few years. You pregnant. Seeing your body change. Seeing you holding our baby in your arms just like this. There will be nothing more perfect or beautiful. I just know it."

My tongue darts out, sliding over my lower lip. "What if it's not in a few years?" The words slip off my lips before I can think them through.

I watch his smile slowly fall as he processes what I said. His eyes widen, staring into mine. "What are you trying to say, Rebecca?"

I guess there is no going back now.

"I don't think I've had my period since December."

A confused frown appears between his brows. "You don't think?"

"I've been trying to remember, but I just can't pinpoint it."

"So you could be pregnant? That's what you're saying?"

I nod my head wordlessly.

"Right now?" His eyes drop to my stomach, before he lifts his gaze. "You're..."

"You're still here!" Kate joins us, her gaze going from Miguel to me and back. "Is everything okay?"

"We have to go," Miguel says, leaving no room for argument.

"What?"

Ignoring my question, Miguel gently takes the baby from my arms and drops a quick kiss to the top of her head before handing her back to Kate and grabbing my hand. "Let's go, Red."

"Where are we going?" I ask as he starts power walking away from the crowd.

"To the store."

"To the..." He can't be serious, but oh, he is. I tug my hand back, willing him to come to a halt. "Miguel!"

He looks over his shoulder. "What?"

"We can't go to the store."

"Why not? Isn't that how you usually do it? Go to the store and grab one of those tests or whatever?"

I tuck a strand of my hair behind my ear. "I mean, yeah, but..."

"So? Let's go."

He starts to turn around, but once again, I tug at his hand.

"What if I'm not?"

The question is softly spoken, but Miguel comes to a standstill. "If you're not..."

My throat bobs as I force down the knot. "Pregnant? What if I'm not pregnant?"

His smile slips as he stares at me for a moment before snapping out of it. "Hey," he moves closer, his arms wrapping around me. "It's okay. It's going to be okay."

I slip my arms around his waist, burrowing my head into his

firm chest and inhaling his clean scent, mixing with a dash of cologne.

"I'm sorry, Red." His hands rub up and down my back. "I just got so excited at the idea. The last time, you were all alone going through this, and I wanted to be there for you now. If you want to wait..."

I shake my head before he can finish. "No." The uncertainty was killing me as it was, and to wait would be torture. "I want to know, but I'm scared."

"I'm here, and we'll do it together."

Nodding, we stay like that for a little while longer before I pull back. Together, we make our way to the store. Thankfully, there is a kid behind the counter who rings our order, so I hope the gossip won't spread through the town too soon. Talk about mortifying.

Miguel grabs the paper bag, and we make our way to the car. A few people stop us, but we manage to sneak away easier than I thought and drive to my house. Chase is nowhere in sight, which works just fine for me as we climb up the stairs and slip into the bathroom. Miguel reads the instructions, and I have to force him out of the bathroom so I can pee in peace. But the moment I flush the toilet, he's back in the room.

I shift my weight from one foot to the other, the damn test sitting on the counter like a ticking time bomb waiting to explode. "What if it says no?"

"Nothing." Miguel shrugs.

"You won't be disappointed?"

"A little bit," he admits. "But you're what matters. You're always going to come first to me. If the test says no, that just means we're gonna have to try harder." He wiggles his brows, his lips curving in that mischievous smirk I love so much. "And you know what that means."

"What?"

"That we've got lots and lots of practicing to do."

"Oh yeah?"

"And you know me, I'm always up for a challenge." His hands cup my cheeks, and he tilts my head back. "You say the word, and I'll do whatever it takes for us to get our family, Red."

I look at the test. "Up until this moment, I didn't even realize how much I wanted this. It's crazy. We don't even live in the same house! How the hell are we supposed to have a baby?"

"We'll get a house."

"But you live in Austin half the year!"

"Then we'll get two houses. With big yards and lots of rooms. You say the number, and I'll get my assistant to start digging."

"Miguel..."

He takes my hand, interlocking our fingers as he reaches for the test.

"It's going to be okay, Red. We'll figure it out. Together. You're not alone in this. You'll never again have to do any of this alone."

That vice grip is squeezing me tightly, making it hard to breathe. His thumb slides over my cheekbone. "Ready?"

"No."

"Whatever happens, we've got this."

Letting out a shaky breath, I nod my head. "We've got this."

"Count with me?" Miguel watches me for a moment longer before starting the countdown, "Three. Two. One."

Slowly, we look at the test we're holding in our hands. My heart is beating a mile a minute, and it feels like it'll break out of my ribcage. Time seems to slow down as we both take in that white plastic stick.

Miguel lets out a loud whoop as his arms wrap around me and lift me in the air, but my gaze is still locked on that stick.

At the one word written on the screen.

"P-pregnant."

"Hell, yeah."

My hand is shaky as I lift it to cover my mouth. "I-I'm..."

"We're pregnant."

He places me on the floor, his hands framing my face as he leans down and presses his mouth against mine.

"I think it's time to get that housing situation in order, Red."

Holy shit, he's right.

"Hey." He tilts my head back. "Don't start stressing out. We have time. We'll figure it out before this baby comes around. I love you, Rebecca." He pulls back, sliding his palm to my stomach. "And this baby. I love you both so much."

"I love you too, but I'm scared. What if something goes wrong again? What if...?"

Miguel places his finger against my lips. "Shh... No negative thoughts. Nothing will go wrong. And if... *If* it does, I'll be there, and we'll get through it. One step at a time, together. But nothing will go wrong because this is it, baby. This is our time. Our moment. Our family."

"We're going to have a family."

It felt surreal; after all this time, all the years, and everything we've been through, we're finally here.

"We finally got our happy ending."

"Red, this isn't the end. This is only just the beginning."

SAVANNAH

"Double whiskey on the rocks," I say to the bartender as I slide into the first open barstool.

The guy gives me a curious look, but he doesn't comment as he grabs a glass, throwing a few cubes of ice in it before placing it on the bar in front of me and pouring my drink.

The moment he starts to lift the bottle, stopping the pour, I wrap my fingers around the cool glass, toss my head back, and down the drink.

My eyes squeeze shut as the alcohol burns down my throat, making tears prickle under my eyelids.

Shit, this is strong.

But I needed strong.

More than that, I needed to feel numb tonight.

And this was the only way I knew how to do it.

Blinking my eyes open, I wave to the guy for a refill.

I was determined to get drunk tonight.

Maybe that would help erase the last few days from my memory.

Or at least alleviate the ache inside my chest.

Because today was the day I put my grandmother, my only living family, to rest.

It still felt surreal. Even at seventy-five years old, Grams was one of the most vibrant people I knew. I loved her to pieces, although some days, she drove me crazy with how independent she was. How damn stubborn. That woman was energetic, opinionated, loud, and generally didn't take shit from anybody.

How could a person like that be gone?

One day she was here, telling me I should ditch my piece-of-shit boyfriend and find myself a nice man that would treat me well so I could focus on him and stop bossing her around already, and the next, I found her lifeless body lying in her bed.

A heart attack.

My throat grows tight as the image of her pale face flashes in my mind and more tears gather in my eyes.

She was right, though.

Mark was a piece of shit.

Not just that, he was a lying, *cheating* piece of shit.

Grabbing my glass, I down it, only to start to choke.

Shit.

I bend forward as I try to catch my breath when I feel a hand pat against my back. "Easy now."

The low, raspy voice has the hair at my nape standing at attention. Following the sound, I turn to the side, but my vision is too blurry to see clearly. All I can do is feel. Feel a big hand soothe up and down my back. Feel the warm body sitting next to me, his knee brushing against mine. Smell the spicy scent of an unfamiliar man's cologne.

Finally, I stop coughing and manage to catch my breath. Blinking a few times, the guy's face comes into focus, and my mouth goes dry, but for a completely different reason.

Holy shit, this man is gorgeous.

And tall. So damn tall. You could see it even when he was sitting. How did I miss him taking the chair next to mine? I have no idea. Because there was nothing subtle about this man. I was pretty sure when he entered the room, everybody knew it. My tongue darts out as I stare at him. It wasn't just his physical appearance either. There is a silent intensity shining in his light eyes as he watches me. Blue or gray? It was hard to tell in the dimly lit room. His dark hair is rich, the ends curling around his ears, and a neatly trimmed beard is covering his jaw. He's dressed in simple jeans and a blue polo shirt that reveals his firm bicep with a full sleeve of tattoos over his tanned skin.

His brows pull together, a few lines marring his forehead. "You okay, Blondie?"

Hearing that nickname snaps me back into reality. Feeling embarrassed, I look away, searching for the bartender. "Fine."

The guy is serving the customer on the other side of the bar.

I lift my hand, signaling for another round, and he nods in acknowledgment.

"Do you really think that's a wise idea?" my companion continues without missing a beat.

Seriously? Is this guy for real?

Annoyance rises under my skin. I tilt my head to the side to find him watching me, his fingers wrapped around a glass of rich brown liquid. "What are you? My dad?"

Those astute eyes lock on me, and it takes everything in me not to shudder. "I could probably be."

I let out a snort just as the bartender appears with my refill. "You're not that old, buddy."

At this angle, I could see a few more lines on his face, mostly around his eyes and on his forehead, but he was far from old. Older? Probably. He had what? Eight years on me? Ten tops, which would put him to be in his mid-thirties. Definitely not more than that.

What the hell was a guy like that doing at a random hotel bar in the middle of nowhere Texas? He didn't seem like the country type. Even with the beard and messy hair, he was still too clean-cut for this place. And there was no hint of a Southern accent either. A passerby. Maybe on business?

My eyes dart down to his glass and the hand wrapped around it. No ring. Or line where one was supposed to be.

Why the hell are you looking at his ring finger? I chastise myself as the bartender refills my glass. *Get a grip, girl.*

"Some days I feel that old." He tips his chin in my direction. "What brings you here?"

His question brings Mark back to the forefront of my mind, and the anger that's been simmering under the surface of hurt comes back swinging.

"Lying, cheating *ex*-boyfriend," I grit through my clenched teeth.

That's better, though. Because if I focused on Mark, I could forget the empty hollow losing Grams left inside of me.

"Huh, so I guess we're the same."

It takes me a moment to register his words. My head whips in the direction of the gorgeous stranger, my mouth falling open. "What?"

"Today, I signed two of the most important documents in my life. Including finalizing the divorce from my lying, cheating *ex*-wife."

Wife? He was married? Scratch that, she cheated on him? Was she nuts? Why would somebody cheat on a man like *that*? If I was coming home to that man every night, I couldn't imagine myself even glancing at another guy, much less cheating on him.

He lifts his glass before he downs his drink in one go. Contrary to me, he doesn't seem the least bit affected by it.

My throat bobs as I swallow, following his lead.

He waves at the bartender for another round. Once our glasses are filled, he clinks it against mine. "To better luck in love?"

I let out a strangled laugh, running my fingers through my hair. "Yeah, I think not. I've had my fair share of it, and I'm officially done with love. Hell, I'm done with *men*."

His brow quirks up. "That bad?"

I can feel his gaze roam over my face, taking in every little detail. I shift in my seat, suddenly self-conscious under his sharp eyes that don't seem to miss anything. Only in the process does my knee bump against his, and a jolt of electricity shoots through my body at the small touch.

He must feel it, too, because I can see his pupils dilate.

He lifts his glass to his mouth, not once breaking the contact between us as he takes a slow pull of his drink.

My gaze falls to his mouth. One amber droplet clinging to

that full lip. His tongue darts out, and I can feel my heart start to race inside my chest.

"We're closing in fifteen," the bartender says as he grabs our glasses, breaking us out of our staring contest.

I look down, a strand of hair slipping from behind my ear like a shield. "Well, that's a bummer."

Taking my bag from the table, I push to my feet. My belly feels warm from all the drinks I had. In hindsight, it might not have been the best idea to drink so much because I still had a good hour's drive in front of me before I got back home.

Home to my empty house and my memories of Grams.

The stranger gets up, too, and stops in front of me.

I tilt my head back to find him watching me quietly. Those light irises have grown darker, the shade of the sky just before the storm hits.

My stomach twists, warmth spreading through me, but it doesn't have anything to do with the alcohol and everything to do with this man standing in front of me.

He lifts his hand, and I suck in a breath, bracing for the contact. His fingers gently brush a strand of my hair behind my ear as his gaze falls on my mouth. His jaw works as he just watches me, and my thighs clench together as the need pulses through me.

"You want to get out of here?" he asks in that gruff voice that makes goosebumps rise on my skin.

My heart starts beating faster, my tongue darting out to slide over my lower lip.

He can't mean...

But he does.

Oh, how he does.

My teeth sink into my lower lip. I should say no. That would be the most logical answer. I wasn't one for hookups. I was a good girl who followed the rules. I was the type of girl who went on dates before sleeping with a man.

And where did that get you? A little voice at the back of my head challenges. *Dating losers who can't make you come, only to cheat on you and leave you brokenhearted, that's where.*

This man wasn't a loser. I don't know how I knew it. I simply did. And I was pretty sure he knew how to treat a woman. There was this air around him. Confidence oozed off of him in waves. Besides, what did I have to lose? I had nobody waiting for me back at home, only memories, and those I did not want to face. We were both available and newly single.

One night.

It would be one night where I could forget everything and just be.

What would be the harm in that?

"Okay," I whisper softly.

"You sure, Blondie?"

I nod softly. "Let's go."

He watches me for a second before his hand drops and takes mine, our fingers interlocking.

My heart starts beating a mile a minute as he leads me out of the bar and into the hallway. The elevator is just about to close when his hand shoots up, and we manage to scramble inside, along with an older couple. They eye us with interest.

Do they know? Can they see we're two strangers who are about to hook up? And if they do, why do I care? I'll never see them again. Just like I'll never see this man again after tonight. It didn't matter.

I look away, my eyes fixing on our reflection in the mirror.

Under the bright lights, he looks larger than life, towering over me for a good foot, his wide shoulders taking a good portion of the tight space. His warm fingers are safely clasped around mine. He's dark to my light. He runs his fingers through his hair, making the thick locks unruly around his head, and his skin has a glow to it of a man who spends time out under the sun. Nothing like my fair skin that burns easily if I, by accident, forget to put SPF on before leaving the house to pick up mail.

We look good together, more than good really. We look like a couple.

Don't go there, I remind myself. *You're not a couple. You're just hooking up, that's all.*

He must feel me watching because his gaze meets mine, and the fire blazing in his irises makes me shudder. It's like he's devouring me with his gaze alone, and suddenly, the elevator seems too small.

The ride to his floor seems to last forever, but when the bell finally chimes, I barely get to say goodbye before he pulls me out of the elevator and marches toward his room. He presses the card against the lock, and the light barely shines green before I'm ushered into a dark room.

The door falls shut, and he spins us around. All the air is kicked out of my lungs as my back touches the hardwood. Soft light is peeking through the curtain over his shoulder, but then he's in front of me, and he's the only thing I can see. The only thing I can *feel*.

"You're so fucking gorgeous, Blondie," he rasps. Those large palms frame my face, tilting my head back as his thumb skims over my lower lip. "I saw you the moment I stepped into the bar, and I couldn't take my eyes off of you."

He leans down, but before he can press his mouth against mine, I turn my head to the side so his lips brush against my cheek, his beard sending shivers as he kisses down the side of my neck and back up. My arms wrap around his neck, fingers sinking into that lush hair to pull him back.

"No kissing on the lips," I whisper softly as his eyes meet mine. "One night. No names. No kissing."

Get ready for Blake Walker. The single dad will move to Bluebonnet Creek, and find the surprise of his life—his kid's new teacher is his one night stand he couldn't get out of his head, and, more importantly, she's pregnant with his baby! Pre-order Need You To Choose Me, coming spring 2024.

Thank you so much for reading It Should Have Been Us! I hope you enjoyed Miguel and Becky's story as much as I did. If you have a moment, please consider leaving a short review.

ACKNOWLEDGMENTS

What a ride! I've been getting questions about Miguel and Becky since March of 2021 when I published *Kiss Me First,* and these two made their appearance for the very first time as bickering best friends to Emmett, who helped him find his happily ever after. By the time I was done with it, I knew there was a possibility for a story there, and since you guys kept asking, I couldn't say no.

Writing this book was hard, honestly, this whole year was hard. I don't know if it's the fact that I barely stopped since I wrote my first book, or real-life events and everything that's happening in the world and book community that are affecting my creativity.

Plotting the story is usually the most fun part for me, but there are instances when sitting down and actually writing it is hard. Which is what happened with this book. However, now that I've finished it, and got to read it from start to finish, I have to admit, I've fallen in love immensely with these two characters, and this whole new world I built in Bluebonnet Creek, and I can't wait to give you more stories featuring some of the side characters.

I want to give a shutout to my amazing alpha team—Nina, Melody, Carrie—thank you for listening to me complain and worry when I didn't know how to proceed with the story. You girls deserve a medal for dealing with me!

A big thank you to my team—my editor Kate for fitting me in her schedule at the very last minute (per usual), my lovely designer Najla and her team for giving me the most stunning covers I could have asked for, Wander for some stunning images and, of course, my street team and all the bloggers who have worked tirelessly to help me promote this book.

But, most importantly, thank you to YOU, my readers, none of this would be possible or made any sense without you. I'm so grateful for every single one of you, and I hope you enjoy Becky and Miguel's story as much as I do!

Until the next book.
    Xoxo,
    Anna

PLAYLIST

Olivia Rodrigo – drivers license
Lauren Duski – I Would For You
Ryan Hurd (with Maren Morris) – Chasing After You
Lauren Weintraub – She's Mine
Seaforth – Breakups
Tyra Madison – Right Girl Wrong Time
Madeline Merio – If You Never Broke My Heart
Avril Lavigne – Tell Me It's Over
Colbie Caillat – Never Getting Over You
Adeline Hill – The Things I Didn't Say
Mimi Webb – I'll Break My Heart Again
Anna Graceman – Runnin' to Me
Kelsea Ballerini (feat. Kenny Chesney) – half of my hometown
Zoe Wees – Hold Me Like You Used To
Olivia Rodrigo – good 4 u
Christ Young, Cassadee Pope – Think of You
Tokio Hotel – Easy
Matt Hansen – without you with me
Camylio – sometimes
Olivia Rodrigo – traitor
Christ Moreno – It Was You
Mitchell Tenpenny – Truth About You
Jake Scott – Texas Girl
Munn – the reason i hate home
Frawley – If I Don't Laugh, I'll Cry
Luke Brzan – Kiss Tomorrow Goodbye
Sadie Jean – Locksmith

Taylor Swift – You're On Your Own, Kid
Clara Mae – Loved You Once
Taylor Swift – Last Kiss (Taylor's Version)
Taylor Swift – The Story Of Us (Taylor's Version)
Taylor Swift – Mine (Taylor's Version)
Alexander Stewart – i wish you cheated
Taylor Swift – If This Was A Movie (Taylor's Version)
Taylor Swift (feat. Bon Iver) – exile
Taylor Swift – Sad Beautiful Tragic (Taylor's Version)
Taylor Swift - This Love (Taylor's Version)
Taylor Swift – I Wish You Would (Taylor's Version)
Taylor Swift – How You Get The Girl (Taylor's Version)
Taylor Swift – This Love (Taylor's Version)
Taylor Swift – You Are In Love (Taylor's Version)
Taylor Swift – Say Don't Go (Taylor's Version)
Taylor Swift (feat. Ed Sheeran) – Everything Has Changed
Matt Hansen – something to remember

BOOKS BY
ANNA B. DOE

Bluebonnet Creek

Small town sports romance

It Should Have Been Us

Need You To Choose Me

Blairwood University

College sports romance

Kiss Me First

Kiss To Conquer

Kiss To Forget

Kiss To Defy

Kiss Before Midnight

Kiss To Remember

Kiss To Belong

Kiss Me Forever

Kiss To Shatter

Kiss To Salvage

Kiss Me Tenderly

Greyford Wolves

YA/NA hockey romance

Lines

Habits

Rules

Greyford High

Sweet YA sports romance novellas

The Penalty Box

The Stand-In Boyfriend

New York Knights

NA/adult sports romance

Lost & Found

Until

Forever

Standalone

YA modern fairytale retelling

Underwater

ABOUT THE AUTHOR

Anna B. Doe is a *USA Today* and international bestselling author of young adult and new adult sports romance. She writes real-life romance that is equal parts sweet and sexy. She's a coffee and chocolate addict. Like her characters, she loves those two things dark, sweet and with little extra spice.

When she's not working for a living or writing her newest book you can find her reading books or binge-watching TV shows. Originally from Croatia, she is always planning her next trip because wanderlust is in her blood.

She is currently working on various projects. Some more secret than others.

Find more about Anna on her website: www.annabdoe.com

Join Anna's Reader's Group Anna's Bookmantics on Facebook.

47267998R00292